MOONLIT DESIRE

"Mariah?" Whit called, uneasy. He shouldn't have let her go out by herself! "Mariah!"

Twenty feet away, she stepped from behind a wide pecan tree, a hairbrush in her hand. The moon lit her with a beautiful glow. "No need to shout. I'm right here."

She glided toward him. She wore a shawl around her shoulders and a white flannel nightgown buttoned up to her chin. The scantest of women's undergarments had never aroused Whit the way this sturdy nightgown did now.

The full moon behind her, she tilted her head to one side and brushed her hair. Long hair. Red. Thick and flowing. Silken hair invited his touch. He ached to wrap a curl around his finger and bring it to his lips.

"To hell with right and wrong," he whispered. "Let me show you how good it can be between a man and a woman. Mariah, come here. Let me be your man . . ."

HEARTFIRE ROMANCES

SWEET TEXAS NIGHTS (2610, $3.75)
by Vivian Vaughan

Meg Britton grew up on the railroads, working proudly at her father's side. Nothing was going to stop them from setting the rails clear to Silver Creek, Texas—certainly not some crazy prospector. As Meg set out to confront the old coot, she planned her strategy with cool precision. But soon she was speechless with shock. For instead of a harmless geezer, she found a boldly handsome stranger whose determination matched her own.

CAPTIVE DESIRE (2612, $3.75)
by Jane Archer

Victoria Malone fancied herself a great adventuress, but being kidnapped was too much excitement for even Victoria! Especially when her arrogant kidnapper thought she was part of Red Duke's outlaw gang. Trying to convince the overbearing, handsome stranger that she had been an innocent bystander when the stagecoach was robbed, proved futile. But when he thought he could maker her confess by crushing her to his warm, broad chest, by caressing her with his strong, capable hands, Victoria was willing to admit to anything. . . .

LAWLESS ECSTASY (2613, $3.75)
by Susan Sackett

Abra Beaumont could spot a thief a mile away. After all, her father was once one of the best. But he'd been on the right side of the law for years now, and she wasn't about to let a man like Dash Thorne lead him astray with some wild plan for stealing the Tear of Allah, the world's most fabulous ruby. Dash was just the sort of man she most distrusted—sophisticated, handsome, and altogether too sure of his considerable charm. Abra shivered at the devilish gleam in his blue eyes and swore he would need more than smooth kisses and skilled caresses to rob her of her virtue . . . and much more than sweet promises to steal her heart!

Available wherever paperbacks are sold, or order direct from the Publisher. Send cover price plus 50¢ per copy for mailing and handling to Zebra Books, Dept. 2882, 475 Park Avenue South, New York, N.Y. 10016. Residents of New York, New Jersey and Pennsylvania must include sales tax. DO NOT SEND CASH.

ZEBRA BOOKS
KENSINGTON PUBLISHING CORP.

Special thanks to my dear and true friend, BARBARA CATLIN

ZEBRA BOOKS

are published by

Kensington Publishing Corp.
475 Park Avenue South
New York, NY 10016

First printing: January, 1990

Printed in the United States of America

With Love to the Atherton women—
Lois, Gail & Jenny

Prologue

Whit Reagor thought he had seen it all in his thirty-six years. Astride his stallion, the owner of the vast Crosswind Ranch disregarded the rolls of damnable barbed wire lining a rickety wagon. Keeping his blue eyes on the farmer, he pulled his John B. Stetson lower on his dark brow. It was a common occurrence to see his young neighbor stringing fence along the border of his poor excuse for a farm, but this was the first time Whit Reagor had seen him tote side-arms.

A six-shooter was part of the everyday outfit around this valley, but two pearl-handled dueling pistols looked downright foolish tucked behind the belt of the bony, sawed-off greenhorn wearing a crumpled derby, black sack coat, checked trousers, and laced shoes, all of which were covered with half an inch of west central

Texas dust.

Whit was amused, but he tried not to show it. He was the only person in the vicinity of Trick'em, Texas, who didn't make light of the disinherited son of the Earl of Desmont.

But no one had dared to use Joseph Jaye for sport in Whit's presence, not since he had cleaned the floor of Maudie's Saloon with the hide of rancher Charlie Tullos. Though Whit didn't enjoy resorting to fisticuffs, he damned sure wasn't shy about taking up for an underdog.

Whit felt sorry for Joseph, and he admired him for not giving up, for trying to turn a bad deal to good. He had seen others tuck their tails between their legs and head back East under less trying circumstances. Joe Jaye's circumstance was trying. Very trying.

The saddle creaked as Whit swung from his sorrel stallion on this hot September afternoon in 1882. "Say, neighbor," he said, "those pistols looked better on your mantel shelf."

Joseph Jaye, born titled twenty-four years earlier in Sussex, England, gave no reply, only hitched the belt higher on his spindly frame and picked up a cedar post to hammer it into the rocky, hostile soil.

"Meant no offense," Whit said sincerely as he led Bay Fire around a cactus bush's spiny needles.

"My weapons serve me no good on the mantel." Huffing and puffing, Joseph stopped working. "I came to Texas expecting to be a gentleman farmer, not a gunslinger or post-hole digger. But my expectations and the reality here are two different things." He turned to Whit and raised his eyes to make up for the disparity in their heights. "Raiders snipped my fence last night. I must protect my property."

Whit identified with the problem. During his fourteen years of being a land baron, he had struggled to keep his range free of rustlers and sodbusters. But he was a Texan accustomed to the hard life of making a living from desolate land, which wasn't the case with this tenderfoot. If Joseph didn't learn to live by the ways of the West, he might as well start picking out his tombstone.

The erstwhile viscount should have been Whit's enemy. Rancher versus nester. Open range opposed to barbed wire. But despite their differences and their diverse heritages, they shared common interests. In the six months of their acquaintance Whit had grown to appreciate those similarities. Both had an appetite for aged whiskey, good smokes . . . and books, but Whit Reagor would be damned before he'd allow anyone to know the last part. A cattleman had to save face.

He motioned toward the twisted coils of red-painted Glidden wire. "Way I see it, you'll be doing a helluva lot of protecting. Folks around here don't cotton to devil's rope."

"I appreciate your concern, Whitman, but

I—"

"Your property cuts across the Western Trail," Whit interrupted, turning his line of sight to the grove of pear saplings hugging Mukewater Pond. "Come next spring, your fence will keep thirsty cattle from their watering hole."

"I need no reminders." Joseph lifted his derby to push a loose strand of flax-colored hair to the crown of his sweat-dampened head. "But there'll come a day when the whole of Texas will be fenced. It's already begun to the east. Why, even Captain King down south is doing it!" He picked up one cedar post and began to center it in a hole. "Cattlemen will be forced to change their methods."

Whit's back stiffened at the reference to change. His world had been torn apart by the changes brought by the Civil War. During Reconstruction, and in his youthful inexperience with money, Whit had lost the family plantation in Jefferson. The morning the carpetbaggers took Wildwood, Whit had vowed never to be broke or humiliated again.

He had worked hard to become wealthy and to take care of his kin. Cattle drives had lined his pockets, and would continue to. Nothing was going to change. "You're wrong."

"Am I?" Joseph asked. "You wait and see."

Four feet from the fenceline, Whit looped the stallion's reins around a chaparral. "You keep up this fence-stringing, and you'll find I'm not the only one who doesn't hold with change.

Folks like Charlie Tullos don't take kindly to cow-gouging wire."

He wondered if Joseph, who gave no comeback to the advice, was capable of protecting himself. His eyes on the pistols again, Whit said in the neighborly spirit, "If you're gonna pack sidearms, learn to wear them right. The butts should be right round elbow level. An hombre needs his weapon, er, weapons in easy reach."

"They are rather cumbersome. Impedes my post digging, if you will." Joseph shifted the dueling pistols against his scrawny legs and looked defiantly up at Whit. "But I shan't be without them."

Giving thought to Tullos and his ilk, Whit figured there was a grain of smarts to the farmer's determination. However, a dollar to Crosswind's title, Joseph was as useful with guns as Whit was with a skillet. No use at all.

He doffed the Stetson from his black hair and rubbed sweat from his brow. "A pistol has many uses, Joe. If you're lucky, one of those pearlies might protect you from harm. If you're not, well, it's liable to blow a hole in your foot."

Joseph squared his thin shoulders. "If you're implying that I'm not handy with firearms, you're mistaken. I've spent many a morning riding to hounds."

"Used pistols on the foxes, did you?"

"Whitman, you're being facetious. As usual." Joseph pulled his lips into a straight line. "And contrary to what you may believe, I have a duel in my past."

Must've gotten lucky, Whit surmised. Or he was spinning a yarn? False pride had a tendency to stretch Joseph's truths occasionally. "You're not in dueling country. But if you're looking to settle a score, you ought to track down the swindler who sold you this prop—"

A rattle from the patchy grass interrupted his advice. Turning to jerk iron, he eared the hammer. His shot echoing in the hot still air, the single bullet tore the rattlesnake in half. The rattler hissed on for several seconds after its death.

"Texas isn't the land of crumpets and tea, Joe." He glanced at the wide-eyed onlooker. "You're in hell's backyard. Few things, be they snakes or men, survive here. Much less thrive." Whit replaced the Colt in its holster, and decided the fellow still wasn't scared off. "How 'bout I teach you to use a gun?"

"Apparently you weren't listening to me." The white face belied indignation. "I know how to shoot."

"Don't be so touchy."

The Englishman braced his palms on top of a secured fence post, and leaned forward before going back to the former subject. "I know I'm a fool. But I refuse to go gunning, as you westerners put it, for the man who promised me a grove of pears when he should've said prickly pears." He proceeded down the fenceline and started his digging anew. "I'm going to make the best of this land, and I will grow succulent fruit!"

Arguing pears was another exercise in futility. Whit sighed in frustration. He had two options: hightail it back to Crosswind, or again try to bore some sense into Joseph's thick skull. Quitter not being a part of his name, Whit decided on the latter.

He might as well lend a hand, too. Poor Joe had nary a soul to help with the chores. And standing around while others worked went against Whit's sense of right and wrong. Of course it rubbed him wrong, this devil's rope, but wasn't offering one's services part of being neighborly? Wasn't the West being pieced together on that philosophy?

The cattlemen around these parts, including Whit's own men, probably wouldn't agree, but that was their problem. He grabbed a pair of leather gloves from a pocket and pulled them over his work-worn hands. Bending, he picked up a crowbar and plunged it into the ungiving ground. A whip of dust whirled to cover the toes of his boots.

"Joe, give up this fencing business," he advised. "You've got the stockraisers around here riled, especially Tullos. And you know it."

"This is a matter of principle. If I bow to pressure, Tullos and his ruffians will think me weak."

A frown pulled at Whit's angular face. Charlie Tullos headed the Painted Rock Ranch lying east of the pear grove, and he was seeing red over this fencing business. Without much provocation, he'd order Joseph strung from an oak tree.

No longer could Whit tiptoe around the farmer's fragile ego. "Tullos already thinks you're weak. And if you're smart, you'll be careful. He's after your neck, Joe."

"I . . . I—Well, I know he isn't pleased." His voice rattled like a Mexican tambourine as he peered toward the drooping leaves of his sickly orchard. "But I won't have cattle trampling my saplings."

Whit went back to the crowbar. Any fool ought to know fruit trees wouldn't grow in the arid land west and south of Fort Worth. Successful fruit growing in this area stood the same chance as Whit Reagor giving up women and whiskey and wild times.

Females brought another point to mind, and he said, "Might not be a good idea to send for that gal of yours."

Whit watched for a changed expression. There was none; the farmer merely continued his digging. He rarely discussed his future wife, and Whit had an inkling why. Any woman marrying a man who had a fancy title in front of his name would be expecting a lot more than Joe Jaye was offering. That had to weigh on the poor fellow's conscience.

"Mariah and I have been apart for over a

year," the Englishman replied finally. "And I miss her every hour of the day, but our separation won't be forever. Her ship will sail from the Isles right after Christmas. She'll be here in Trick'em next spring."

"Reckon she'll get here in time to see you wearing a rope necktie?"

"It won't come to that."

His statement had the hollow ring of bravado, and Whit snapped, "You're living in a dream world."

He grabbed a handful of caliche from the hole he had dug, throwing the earth aside. Joe ought to be pistol-whipped for bringing a greenhorn woman to his dried-up eighty acres.

And what about this Mariah? Whit wondered and conjured up images of voluptuous beauty, tempestuous winds, and hot wild sex. He cast sharp eyes at the diminutive Englishman, and concluded that he couldn't attract such a hot-blooded beauty, though he had seen Charlie Tullos's wife, Temperence, casting overt eyes at Joseph.

Well, Temperence was peculiar.

No doubt Joseph's limey lady wouldn't fit the description of beauty. More than likely she was a prune-faced shrew of an old maid desperately seeking a husband. After all, she was a schoolmarm.

Defiance faded from Joseph's eyes. "I've a favor to ask. If bad luck should befall me, could you find it in your heart to see after my

Mariah?"

"Whoa!" Whit set the crowbar aside to pat the air. "What you're asking is akin to marrying me off to your bride. Another marriage isn't for me."

"Mariah isn't like your . . . you know, your . . ."

Joseph's pussyfooting opened an old emotional wound, provoking Whit to growl, "Dammit to hell, I was drunk when I told you about her. And if you know what's good for you, you sawed-off pipsqueak, you'll never mention Jenny again."

"Please pardon my blunder, Whitman. What I meant to say was, my Mariah would never do you an injustice."

"Like hell."

"Believe me," Joseph went on, "I don't think anything drastic will happen over my fences, but if you're right, I shudder to think of her alone in Texas."

"Ships sail back to merry ole England just the same as they sail over."

"I'm not asking you to marry her," Joseph pleaded. "But I would appreciate your . . . Just see that she's all right." He stepped closer. "Will you do that for me?"

Whit started. Back in '64, at the Battle of Mansfield, he had been the one to make such a request. A soldier of eighteen at the time, he had been scared to death of dying from his wounds; and with blood pouring from the flesh between his heart and collarbone, he had begged his captain to see after his future wife's welfare, in case he didn't pull through. Well, he hadn't died. But a week later Captain John Coke took a killing minié ball in the gut. Nonetheless, Whit knew the comfort of an oath of honor.

An invisible noose tightening on his neck now, he gave in. "I'll do it. Hope I don't end up regretting it."

"You won't, and I thank you." Joseph heaved a sigh. "I needn't remind you Mariah Rose is the light of my life."

"Reckon you don't." Half a minute later, Whit prompted, "Tell me more about her. Is she nobility like you?"

"Her maternal forebears were of fair breeding, but her father is a mere *connétable*—lawman, in your vernacular—on Guernsey, which is part of the British Empire."

Geography not being a topic of interest, Whit got back to the subject of Joe's woman. "She's a gal after a title."

"Not at all. She's unique, you understand." The former Viscount Desmont lifted a shoulder. "Be that as it may, Mariah's mother and grandmother were quite thrilled she was to become a member of the ruling class. Of course, the old girls are dead now."

As near as Whit could ascertain, after digesting all of this, there could be only one motive for her immigration to Texas. "Your English

Miss Rose must love you a lot."

"Would that she could," Joseph admitted dryly.

"What the hell do you mean?"

"I fear she doesn't love me as much as . . ."

Whit shook his head in bemusement. "As much as what? Or should I ask as much as *whom?*"

"I'm not her first love."

Joseph turned his back, but Whit caught the flush rising in his face.

"I . . . I shouldn't have . . . Ungallant of me to say that. Oh, my, Whitman, it wasn't for me to . . ."

The more Joseph tried to amend his admission, the worse it sounded to Whit, and the pieces were beginning to fit together. Apparently the young man had gotten himself a piece of damaged goods, and Miss Rose was looking to take advantage of a naive fool. She was just like Jenny.

Having experienced heartache in his own past, Whit felt sympathy for the lovestruck Joseph. Evidently his woman bounced from one man to the next, looking for the best deal of hand.

"Tell me something." With the inside edge of his boot Whit brushed a scoop of dirt around a fence post. "Did your Miss Rose have anything to do with your landing here?"

Joseph hesitated. "No. I wasn't in my father's good graces to begin with. My engagement to a commoner was but the *coup de grâce.* So, I decided to make a place for the two of us in a new land. America seemed the ideal spot, then fate brought me to Texas."

"Fate, hell. You got swindled into coming to Texas."

Joseph chuckled, a mirthless little sound. "Well, that's in the past."

"So you say. Seems strange to me, though, renouncing family, title, and homeland in order to marry a woman"—Whit lifted a knowing brow—"who loves another man."

The farmer's face turned crimson. "I don't find it strange. Whatever the sacrifice, she's worth it."

"No woman's that wonderful, even your Miss Rose," Whit replied, a steel edge to his tone. "Look, it's getting late. I'd better head back to Crosswind."

Joseph watched the rancher ride away. As usual, he hadn't bothered to correct Whitman about Mariah Rose McGuire's last name. Though Whitman Reagor was the only person in Trick'em who had shown cordiality toward him, Joseph rather enjoyed keeping something to himself, especially after his blunder.

After asking for Whitman's pledge of honor, he should have kept his lips sealed about her heart once belonging to another. Perhaps here in Texas, though, Joseph surmised, men were more accustomed to young ladies changing their minds about such things.

Of course, Mariah had had change forced

upon her . . .

He had met her in the Channel Islands in her hometown of St. Peter Port, where Joseph had settled to make a name for himself in the Bailiff of Guernsey's retinue. He adored the beautiful redhead at first sight, even when her head was turned by the dashing Lieutenant Lawrence Rogers of the India Corps. For the thousandth time, Joseph gave thanks that Rogers had succumbed to malaria.

Once the competition had been laid to rest, Joseph had been free to court her. Naturally she had been vulnerable and she had, on the rebound, accepted his proposal.

Though he realized her feelings weren't nearly as deep as his own, she *had* agreed to follow him to Texas. They would be together soon, only six months from then, in March.

"So little time, so much to do," he muttered. Somehow he'd make up for the treacherous deed done on the island of Guernsey, the memory of which shamed him. On the eve of his leaving and filled with too much champagne, he had fallen victim to the fiend of lust and forced himself on sweet, innocent Mariah.

The ungentlemanly deed hadn't been completed, but Mariah wasn't so informed. Though she was quick-minded, she led a sheltered life in the Iles d'Normandie. To confess his lack of prowess would have been demeaning, and in the aftermath, he had used her naiveté to his own advantage.

Her supposed tarnished honor wasn't his only hold on Mariah, however. Joseph's sins were many. After he had found his land in such a sorry state, and because of his fear of losing Mariah, he couldn't confess that he, too, had been a gudgeon, though not in the same way. So, his letters to her had been bald lies.

She was expecting fine China, servants, and the genteel life. Furthermore, he had promised her the freedom to pursue her schoolteaching. Once she learned that his money had been spent first on pear saplings, then on barbed wire, and that he could offer no more than a log cabin, hard work, and menacing cutthroats, how would she react? Would she ever trust him again?

If only he had something to give to make up for the lies. Sweat rolled down his quivering backbone. If only he had Whitman's fine dark looks and charm with the ladies, he'd feel more confident. If only he had wealth, a comfortable rock home, and a prosperous ranch like Crosswind, all the material goods Whitman Reagor possessed. If only he hadn't lied.

Joseph glanced at the dusty wake of the man who had so much. There wasn't a lying bone in his friend's body. At that moment he almost hated Whitman Reagor.

Chapter One

March 1883

Naked as the day he was born, a tall lean man barreled out of a modest house, into the crisp dawn and onto the dirt street—deserted except for one spectator.

Mariah McGuire, a birdcage clutched in her gloved hand, averted her farsighted brown eyes, but found herself staring once more. Standing lcss than a quarter block away, she was taken aback by thc fracas, even more so when a wild-haired blonde, wearing a wrapper and wielding a skillet, darted out of the same door in pursuit of the man. Obviously all hell had broken loose on a back street in Dublin, Texas.

Mariah halted. Never in her twenty-three years had she witnessed a domestic squabble as improper as this, though she had been around more than her share of her parents' arguments.

"Dammit, woman." The man's voice was strangely calm as he quizzed the shapely woman gripping the cast-iron weapon. "What the hell's the matter with you?"

"You, that's what. You're just like all the rest. You ain't interested in nothin' but gettin' between my legs!"

Mariah rolled her eyes. Texas was a wild and woolly place, and Texans were a breed all their own. That she had learned from her travels across the state, first by train from Galveston to Lampasas, then by stagecoach from there.

"I've heard enough of your empty promises, Whit Reagor," she heard the brassy blonde screech.

"Promises? I never make promises I don't intend to keep."

"Shut up!" The blonde hurled the skillet at the man. "You never had no intention of marrying me, so get gone and stay gone!"

The missile thwacked against his broad right shoulder, and Mariah flinched. The indecent Mr. Reagor didn't move a muscle. His wildcat assailant dusted her palms and pranced back into the house, the door banging behind her.

He whipped around, charged toward the domicile, and pounded the heel of a fist against the barrier. "At least give me my clothes."

"Your behind's been nekkid all night, so why get stove up about it now?" the woman yelled from inside the house.

"Heavens," Mariah uttered, trying to disregard the loud voices and continued thumping on the door.

She started walking again. How nice it would be to reach the gentility of her new home in Trick'em. Though the town was only four days' travel from here, the connecting stagecoach wouldn't depart for three more days.

"Barbara," Whit Reagor said sternly, "if you think I'm going to prance round in the altogether, you've got another think coming. Open the door before I break it down."

Though she was embarrassed for the two combatants as well as for herself, Mariah felt strangely compelled to halt again. She watched the blonde hoist a window sash, then toss a petticoat at the man's face. The garment was as stark-purple as the hair on Whit Reagor's head and chest was starkly black.

"Try that on for size, you snake in the grass!" the angered female demanded, her challenge punctuated by the window slamming shut.

"Women," the man muttered, shaking his head.

He shrugged one wide shoulder, held the shiny undergarment aloft momentarily before casually covering his lower midsection. As if he had nary a problem, he turned toward the street—and Mariah Rose McGuire.

From the distance of no more than fifteen feet, she caught the lift of an ebony brow. A smirk stretched his mouth. Why, he didn't even appear humiliated.

Even though her parrot issued trilling protests to the approaching stranger, Mariah held her ground. No brazen Texan, even one as fine-looking as this man, was going to send her scurrying for cover.

"How doin', ma'am?"

No reply passed her grim lips. She was headed for Widow Atherton's boarding establishment, even if it meant passing the crudest, most disreputable man she had ever encountered. Mariah lifted her nose as well as the birdcage clutched in her gloved hand, and started again on her intended path.

"Hey, lady, don't be hasty. Wait up," the man called from behind her. "You there with the auburn hair and the parrot. Wait up, pretty lady."

Mariah ignored the pleas, and took ten more steps.

"Lady?"

Seemingly pleased with himself, her parrot mocked over and over, "Lady, lady!"

Gritting her teeth, she admonished, "Hush, Gus."

She glanced over her shoulder and detected that the man was not more than five feet away. Blessed with a head for sums, she calculated him to be a half foot taller than herself, which would make him at least six two. Handsome described him in a word, ruggedly handsome in two. His bright blue eyes contrasted with his olive complexion and dark hair, hair that was curly and short-cropped above clipped sideburns. Whereas Joseph was thin, short, and pale, this man was anything but.

She shook off the comparisons, turned her head, and kept walking. Joseph deserved more than unfair comparisons. He was her savior. Aggrieved over losing so many of her loved ones—first Lawrence, then her mother and grandmother—she had been without hope for the future. At twenty-three, she was too old to make a suitable marriage and too repressed by her father to follow her dreams. But the Viscount Desmont had changed all that.

He offered his love, and in exchange asked for nothing more than her hand. Quite unlike her father, who had hectored in his mélange of English and French, "No *femme* in her right mind wants anything beyond *mariage* and, as long as I draw a breath, I won't have ye wasting yer life with schoolteaching," Joseph understood her aspirations.

And he, a member of one of England's oldest and most noble families, had renounced every birthright privilege to offer his name to a *connetable's* spinster daughter from a lesser part of the British Empire—a spinster who had allowed him liberties with her body. She was fortunate he hadn't cast her aside in favor of a more virtuous woman.

It was her duty to repay Joseph for his sacrifices. But didn't he deserve something better than a wife who felt nothing beyond obligation?

She wished Joseph hadn't made so many sacrifices. When her grief over her losses had started to heal, she had been wracked with doubts about the future. Yet what could she do? There was nothing left for her in Guernsey—nothing but a father who thwarted her ambitions.

No longer was she under Logan McGuire's thumb, but she'd solved one problem to take on another. After leaving the isolated island home that was nearer to France than to England, Mariah had had her first taste of freedom, and it had gone down smooth as thick Guernsey cream. If not for her approaching marriage, she'd have been free to do as she pleased here in Texas. Dash it, she was enjoying her independence!

"For Pete's sake, lady! Wait up. You don't have to be afraid. I'm not out to rob you of anything!"

Whit Reagor's shouted words brought Mariah back to the present. Strange, she thought, that he hadn't raised his voice to the blonde. "Sir, are you addressing me?"

"You're the only person on this street except for me," he replied in a deep baritone, a grin dimpling the right side of his tanned, stubble-shadowed face, "so I reckon I am."

While a gust of wind tugged at her hatpins, she took a hesitant look at him. He was covering himself—partially—with the petticoat. Mariah noted his blue lips, then her line of sight lowered, and she scrutinized his narrow hips, his long hairy—shivering—legs. My, those legs were nicely formed. The sight of them played havoc with her senses.

"Like what you see?"

Ignoring his question and marshaling her wits, she lifted her gaze. "What do you want?"

"Help."

Should she get involved? The blonde might have right on her side, Mariah thought, but she was protected by wrapper and roof, while Whit Reagor was bare to the frigid elements. Putting herself in any charitable person's place, she said, "Let's find some privacy. I'm sure your lady friend is watching us."

The man at her heel, she aimed for a grove of live oak trees a half block away. Privacy assured, she whipped around and nearly collided with his towering frame. "Be kind enough to say your piece."

His indigo-blue eyes twinkled as he apparently ignored her request. "Say, Red, bet you're not from round these parts. Your accent is different, mainly English, but sorta . . . hmm . . . French?"

"I am not addressed as 'Red.' " Having no intention of explaining her Norman French and Scots Irish heritage, she gave him a haughty onceover, which she regretted immediately. One shouldn't do that sort of thing in front of a nude man.

"Many pardons, ma'am." A tease in his tone, he changed the subject again. "My money says you've never got a gander at a naked man before."

Mariah placed the parrot cage on the ground, and stepped to the oak tree. How true. Though she had four brothers, they had kept themselves covered in her presence. And that night with Joseph . . . he hadn't uncovered himself, as near as she could remember.

She shuddered. There were, her now departed mother had told her, certain things a woman was forced to endure. "When you go to the marriage bed, Daughter, close your eyes and think of England," Anne du Moulin McGuire had advised. This one and only piece of advice concerning the union between men and women had proved to be prudent. On the night Mariah and Joseph had toasted their future and had drunk too much champagne to his bon voyage, she had closed her eyes, both in distaste and boredom. And when she awoke, turning back had been impossible.

Whatever spark there might have been for Joseph had fizzled that night, and she dreaded the marriage bed. After all, a woman couldn't drink herself into oblivion every night of her wedded life.

The Texan broke into her brown study by saying, "I shouldn't have mentioned nudity to a lady. Forgive me."

Mariah pulled herself together. "It's not the

state of your undress that's disturbing, sir. It's the state of your affairs. That poor woman is quite distressed. Shouldn't you try to make amends?"

He shrugged. Clutching the purple petticoat even closer to his private parts, he shortened the distance between them. "Barbara's a little hot-tempered. She'll get over it."

Now that Whit Reagor was close by, she got an eyeful of his scarred, hair-whorled chest. How did he get those scars? This thought was replaced by another one. It was an odd yet nice feeling to be eye-to-chest level with a man.

Mariah gathered her wits and responded to his statement. "My sympathies are with your lady."

"She needs condolences like a boar needs teats."

A flush rising in her cheeks, Mariah curled her lip. "Your crudity is only outweighed by your gall."

"Been known to happen." He glanced down, then up. The dimple in his right cheek deepened. "But can't you see I'm in a fix? Can't go sashayin' round in the altogether, Mrs. . . . um . . . you're Mrs. . . . ?"

"Miss," she amended. "And it would serve you right, sashaying round in the—" She laughed at the ludicrous situation. "Oh, heavens, take this."

Mariah whipped the knee-length cloak from her shoulders. "This will cover you much better than"—her finger pointed to the petticoat, her eyes traveling to his wickedly handsome face—"that garment."

"Petticoat," he corrected, his grin widening. Clumsily he maneuvered his left hand to fit her gray woolen cloak around his shoulders. "It's a purple petticoat."

She imagined herself wearing such a damson-plum-colored undergarment. *My, it's lovely, isn't it?* she thought, but realized she'd voiced the question when he said, "Depends on who's wearing it." He winked boldly, dropped the blonde's highly personal wear to the street, and took two steps closer. "I'd bet my spread out west of here that you've never seen a purple petticoat before."

On guard again, perhaps because he was correct, she snapped, "What gives you the audacity to say that?"

"My crudity is only outweighed by my gall." His retort mocked her earlier words. "That aside, the way I see it, there are two kinds of women—ladies and lovers. From the scowl on that pretty face of yours and the blush in your cheeks, I'll bet you're the former."

She grabbed her reticule and parrot. "I've tarried too long. Leave the cloak at the Double Inn."

She grimaced, remembering the previous sleepless night. Her stay at Dublin's stagecoach stop had been less than pleasant, thus forcing her to find quieter accommodations. Nevertheless, she had no desire to acquaint Whit Reagor with her prospective temporary residence, the Atherton home. She had seen more than enough of Mr. Whit Reagor.

"Leave it for Miss McGuire, please. Good day, sir."

"Sir, sir!" Gus squawked.

"Whoa there, Miss McGuire. Don't leave just yet." Whit cocked his head. "If you wouldn't mind, ma'am, could I trouble you some more?"

"What now?" she asked in exasperation.

"If I'm seen like this," he said, in a first show of humility, "I'll be the laughingstock of four counties."

A measure of her instinctive humor returned, and she chuckled. His very human reaction to possible ridicule was strangely endearing. "Actually, not the laughingstock you would've been if I hadn't passed by."

"Got me on that one," he conceded, leaning a shoulder against a tree trunk. "Well, what's it gonna be? Will you or will you not take a message across town?"

She shifted her weight to the other foot. "I will."

"Good girl, sweet angel of mercy. And I thank you."

For the first time she heard, really heard, the vibrating quality to his tone. Nice, so nice. Before she could settle her confusion, he leaned forward to brush the side of his roughened forefinger against her cheek, eliciting an involuntary quiver from Mariah.

Startled, she gazed into the ink-blue of his eyes. Gone was the arrogance, the impertinence. There was a look of undeniable interest.

Was his expression reflected in her brown eyes? Fearing so, and confused by her emotions, she stepped back. "You'd best give me directions."

"I'd love to," he murmured. "Ah . . . um . . . my sister lives on Comanche Street. Tell her I need help. Clothes, and quick." He went on to explain, "She runs a boardinghouse, only one in town. You can't miss the sign. Lois Atherton is her name."

Oh, no! They were certain to meet again, and Mariah, as a consequence of being too sheltered in spite of her advanced years, felt awkward. How would she handle the situation?

"One more thing," he said. "What's your given name?"

Allowing familiarity was neither proper nor prudent. "Miss McGuire is all you need."

All he needed? She might be right. Heart hammering, Whit watched her go. The elegantly beautiful Miss McGuire could fill a blatant desire, no doubt about that. Her shapely body, her burnt-auburn hair, her milk-chocolate-colored eyes got to him.

It hadn't taken him long to figure out she wasn't wearing a corset, and didn't need one.

She was by no means petite, but that type never appealed to him, anyway. He liked his women on the tall side.

Beyond that, he was fascinated by her frosty airs which had rivaled the blue norther whipping across his cloak-clad body. When her ice had defrosted a bit, though, he had liked her even better. He got the idea there was one helluva warm woman beneath that glacial exterior. His kind of woman.

Damn. What was the matter with him? Miss McGuire was a lady, not a trollop. And ladies meant trouble. Parsons and babies' breath and wedding rings.

Whit didn't believe in marriage. Not since his wife had wound up dead in the burned-out ruins of their home. Dead, naked, and in the arms of another man, the man he had thought to be his best friend.

His top teeth ground against the bottom ones. He had learned his lesson about women on the quick side, and it stayed with him. Sixteen years had passed since Jenny had made him a cuckold, but no woman had played him for a besotted fool since then or would in the future.

Whit glanced at the cloudless sky, the sight shifting his thoughts to a more immediate problem. His hundred-section spread hadn't had a drop of rain in months. The creeks were drying up. Of course, it was early in what should have been the rainy season, so the situation might right itself, but Whit was concerned; concerned enough that he intended, as soon as he got back to the ranch, to dam the spring-fed creek along the south pasture.

Whit had another worry. Joe Jaye. The stubborn farmer had continued his fence-stringing. So far, Whit had kept angry cattlemen from the tenderfoot's fences, but how much longer would that hold?

These things preying on his mind, Whit shouldn't be daydreaming about women. Correction. Woman. His mind's eye kept drawing pictures of womanly allure. Miss McGuire. *Will you ever see her again?* a voice echoed within him. Well, he did have her cloak . . .

He decided to make a point of looking her up.

"Well, I'm not surprised." Lois Atherton, whom Mariah guessed to be about forty, shook her head of dark curls. "But I never figured it would take this long for Barbara to toss him on his hind end."

Lois stopped hoeing the newly planted vegetable garden behind her clapboard boardinghouse. "Women are always gettin' riled at my brother."

Mariah wasn't astounded at these frank words. During her travels from the Gulf Coast to west central Texas, she had experienced a great deal of Texas-style candor. In fact, she was beginning to believe nothing further could shock her anymore.

"They fall for Whit . . ." Lois clapped her hands to scare away a huge tabby cat that was eyeing Gus as if he were a joint of Sunday beef. "Scat, Fancy!"

While moving the parrot cage closer to her side, Mariah cast a menacing glare at the sharp-eyed feline.

"As I was saying," Lois admitted, "Whit never sees fit to call a preacher and buy the ring."

"Maybe he hasn't met the right woman."

"Hmmph."

"Perhaps luck just hasn't been with him."

"You may be right." Lois lifted a palm. "But I doubt it. You've heard the expression 'once bitten, twice shy'? Well, that about sums up Whit's problem."

She assumed his sister would admit more about Whit Reagor, but Mariah didn't press the subject, even though she was curious. For some odd reason, he hadn't left her thoughts since their inauspicious meeting. Hair as black as a dark night, blue eyes tinged with dark gray, height tall enough to make her feel short . . . He was like no man she had ever met before, not even Lawrence, but . . .

Why couldn't she be practical? Despite the memories of that wretched night in the shadows of Castle Cornet, where her virginity had been claimed, Joseph was the man for her.

Lois brushed her palms down the front of her gingham apron. "The 'right' women don't perch in saloons. 'Course, if he'd tie up with ladies instead of strumpets, the story might be different."

"He p-pays ladies to . . ." Had it been only minutes earlier when she'd thought nothing further could shock her?

"Whit? Ha! He doesn't have to pay. Not to say he isn't generous." Lois yanked a weed from a mounded row. "Buys his gals trunkful after trunkful of fancy duds just for the pleasure of strippin' those duds off their backs."

Mariah blushed again, something she seemed to do often where Whit Reagor was concerned. Though she had tried her best to adjust to life in this often bewildering land, she was a product of her Calvinistic background. The females of Guernsey didn't discuss men they barely knew, much less bedroom intimacies.

As for the man in question, here she was chattering with his sister while he waited to be rescued. "Mrs. Atherton, your brother *is* waiting for your help."

Lois lifted a palm in an air of dismissal. "Aw, it'll do him good to cool his heels awhile."

A gust of air blew.

"Oh, all right. I'll rescue the jackanapes. Come on in the house. Gotta fetch his clothes. Better bring that bird of yours. No tellin' what Fancy might do." The proprietress took off for the house. "I keep a room just off the kitchen for Whit, not that he uses it for much." Short of the back porch, she said, "Too bad he's too old to turn across my checkered apron. I'd teach him a lesson or two."

Mariah grinned. Imagining that rough-and-tumble Texan—a man probably in his late thirties!—turned over an aproned lap was rather humorous to imagine.

Cage in hand, she followed Lois inside. The kitchen was toast-warm from the iron Chandler stove, and the scent of bacon and the soda bread Texans called biscuits filled her nostrils to remind her of the breakfast skipped at the Double Inn.

As if she sensed Mariah's hunger, Lois offered, "There's a plate under that cloth. Grab yourself a bite."

"Oh, I can't take someone's food."

"I was saving it for Whit. Always do when he's in town." The words had a wistful quality to them, but they were replaced with her former tone. "Usually feed it to the chickens, though. Go on, girl, eat up! If he's hungry after I fetch him, I'll fry up a half-dozen eggs." Lois winked. "No matter how mad I get at Whit, I wouldn't let the baby of the family go hungry."

Underneath the brusque attitude toward her brother, Mariah believed Lois loved him very much. He did, she realized, have a way with women. Without a doubt, the man was spoiled rotten.

As the older woman disappeared into the room adjoining the cooking room, Mariah set her reticule on the table, lifted the cloth, and reached for one of the salty-pork, butter-dripping biscuits. Heaven's! The staple diet for this frontier state, beans and fried-to-shoe-leather beef, had begun to get tiresome. But, she reminded herself, everyday life would be rosy after reaching Joseph's estate.

She dabbed the linen cloth to her lips and fed crumbs to Gus. "Thank you," she called to the adjoining room.

"Come on in here where I can hear you proper."

Mariah found Lois Atherton folding a chambray shirt into a valise. The room smelled of leather and tobacco. Trousers, shirts, and a buckskin jacket hung from hooks in the wall. A cartridge belt lay on the oak bureau. Though she remembered Whit Reagor saying he had a "spread out west," she wondered if he was a gunslinger. After all, there were those translucent-white scars on his upper body. She knew what they looked like, but how would it feel to touch them . . . ?

Ashamed of her caprice, Mariah considered the gunbelt. Surely he wasn't a gunslinger; her imagining him so had been the result of too many traveling hours spent reading too many dime novels. After all, her own reticule held a revolver, which didn't make *her* an outlaw.

"My purpose for being here is twofold," Mariah said, determined to get down to business. "I'm waiting for the Yuma stage, so I'll be needing accommodations. Mrs. Watson at the inn said you might rent me a room."

"I don't board nobody lest I know somethin' about them. Said you're headin' for Yuma, right?" Not waiting for an answer, she continued. "That's a long ways for a woman alone to travel. Tell me about yourself."

Mariah made explanations of her island homeland.

"So what is a lady from Guernsey doin' in Dublin, Texas?"

"I'm on my way to a calling. Schoolteaching."

Lois's look was wary as she grabbed a pair of worn yet shiny boots. "I never figured you for a schoolmarm."

"Well, I am, and I'm proud of it."

"How'd you come to be a schoolmarm?"

Running her palm across a polished oak bureau, Mariah thought about an answer, and decided on the truth. "Actually, I'm not a full-fledged teacher as yet."

"I see. But you still haven't told me *why.*"

"I traveled to London when I was seventeen, and my heart went out to the street urchins. They seemed so hopeless."

Mariah wouldn't admit feeling a kinship toward those children. The hurt was too deep. If she lived to be a hundred, she'd never forget the long years of her miserable childhood yearning for her father's affection.

Hopelessness she was well acquainted with. And she needed to be needed.

Though she had long given up on Logan McGuire, she had left him a letter on the day of leaving St. Peter Port. She'd spelled out her frustrations and anger. But she'd signed it with love. Did one ever *not* love a father, no matter how difficult he might be?

Lois asked, "Don't they need teachers in Guernsey?"

"Of course, but—"

"You'd have to be ugly, which you're not, if you've crossed the Atlantic just to force the three Rs down younguns' throats. Must be another reason."

Her mind not on Joseph, Mariah could have told her about Lawrence, but didn't. With unseeing eyes, she pretended to study a paperweight. For years she had loved the dashing lieutenant. At eighteen, she had met him and her head was never turned by any other Guernseyman from then on. Her feelings for him had been so strong that she'd pushed aside her teaching aspirations, for all she'd needed to make her life complete was Lawrence Rogers, and their dreams—marrying, living in India, rearing a dozen children. Then the subcontinent's killing climate foiled those plans.

Why, oh why, did it still hurt this deeply?

"Gone dumb on me?" Lois asked, interrupting her thoughts.

At long last, Mariah answered the woman's question. "I'm engaged to a fine gentleman in Trick'em. It's west of here."

"Oh, I know where Trick'em is, all right," Lois said with a chuckle. "The Crosswind

Ranch—"

A petite young woman with brown hair popped her head through the doorway. "Did I hear you say Trick'em?" Catching sight of the stranger, she said, "Oh, hello there!"

"My daughter Kimble," Lois explained. "She's gettin' hitched tonight. Kim, this is Miss McGuire."

After introductions were complete and Mariah's best wishes extended to the bride, Kimble inquired, "Okay, now what was all that about Trick'em? Has Uncle Whit arrived?"

"Of a sort." Her mother turned to Mariah. "My baby brother owns a ranch in your intended's neck of the woods. Looks like you've gotten a jump on meeting your neighbors."

Mariah's heart slammed against her chest as she inhaled sharply.

Chapter Two

Joseph Jaye felt like bawling into his morning tea. His sleep had been disturbed by a nightmare in which his saplings were trampled by pounding hooves. Yet he wasn't concerned so much about nightmares as he was about Mariah. She'd arrive in a week, the next Saturday, and her arrival should be made special.

But at the rate things were going, the welcome would be grim. The one-room log house's roof, if one could call it that, was beginning to fall in, and now dirt was filtering into his teacup and onto the wobbly table.

"Won't Mariah be pleased to see this hovel?" he asked aloud. Talking to himself was a frontier-acquired habit. "Yes, just as delighted as when you first laid eyes on it."

He hadn't been pleased. Nothing had turned out as planned since he had become engaged to

Mariah.

Lapsing into memories, he recalled the nightmare of confronting his father. Joseph, full of wedding plans and high hopes, had arrived in Sussex on an autumn day in 1881. The Earl of Desmont had received him in his study.

Skilled in the art of intimidation, Damien Jaye was seated at the raised dais of his massive desk. Without rising to offer his youngest son a welcome, he had deigned him to the small chair.

Joseph explained his intentions, and the Earl of Desmont bellowed, "You'll not marry that woman."

"If you'll agree to meet Mariah Rose," Joseph said, forcing courage, "I'm certain you will change your mind."

"Never!" His father's voice boomed. "I won't allow you to bring one of your strumpets into the family."

"Mariah is different."

The earl picked at a fingernail. "Haven't I heard this before? About a milch maid at your grandmother's estate in Hesse-Nassau. Karla Strack, wasn't she called?"

The fragile chair squeaked under Joseph's light weight as he fidgeted. Yes, he had been smitten with Karla, but his feelings for her had nothing to do with his love for Mariah. Besides, he'd been but seventeen at the time. "Karla was a nice girl," he said meekly.

Damien Jaye threw back his head, laughing, jeering. "What a chump you made of yourself, sonny boy, challenging your elder brother to a duel over her charms."

"I did nick Reginald's ear," Joseph said in defense.

"His pistol wasn't loaded, fool! He let you shoot him!"

This humiliation hurt. He idolized his half brother, and couldn't have loved him more if they were full siblings. He'd never thought Reginald wouldn't respect his dignity. But Joseph wouldn't delve on the duel's shame. Reginald approved of Mariah and for that Joseph would forgive him anything.

Light reflected off the good earl's quizzing glass, lancing into his scapegrace son's eye. "You'll not marry a common piece of baggage. She's after title and money. Give up that Island hussy or be turned out."

The study grew deathly silent, save for the ticking of a clock. Joseph knew his choice would be a final one, as lasting as his love. The small chair tipped backward. "Papa, you have forced my hand. I will marry Miss McGuire."

The Viscount Desmont departed Sussex as plain Joseph Jaye. Disinherited, a return to the Norman archipelago was out of the question, for his father had tarnished his name with the elderly bailiff. Joseph had set out to establish himself, and America beckoned as the best place for a young man to start afresh and make a home for his bride. New Orleans, a favorite of Reginald's, was the area he first decided on.

In the Crescent City, a gentleman, or so he seemed at the onset, offered title to his farm. The St. Charles Hotel's bar was the setting for the conversation.

Leroy Smith's meaty hand made a grand sweep. "Pears grow in abundance in Coleman County. Step right outside the door, Lord Desmont, and pick 'em by the bushel!"

"Mr. Smith, I've read that Texas is a barren state."

"Not all of it." His booted foot resting on the brass bar rail, Smith winked conspiratorially and shoved a drink at Joseph. "I'd surely hate to part with such a gem of agriculture, but I could make you a special price."

"If your pear plantation is so prosperous, why do you wish to sell it?"

"I'm getting on, you understand. Why, I'll be fifty next month! So I'm off to make my fortune in the oil fields of Pennsylvania. Have to think of my old age, you see."

This made sense. "Does the farm havc a home?"

"Why, my esteemed fellow, you wound me! Of course it comes with improvements. Never would I offer a nobleman such as yourself anything but the finest."

Now a year older and many thousands of dollars poorer, Joseph took a good look at the "improvements." Smith had played him for a fool. The sparsely furnished log house could only be categorized as a shack with its earthen floors, a sod-patched roof, and cracks between the logs. As if on cue, a gust of biting air ate into Joseph.

He grasped the lapels of his threadbare coat. If he hadn't spent two hundred dollars for every mile of barbed wire, he could have afforded to build Mariah a good solid home.

Pulling himself together was the only answer. The house situation would rectify itself. Recently he had written Reginald, instructing him to sell the London townhouse, which was Joseph's only property save for this Texas land. In the past he'd wanted to keep a tie to England, but no more.

But he should've written to Reginald as soon as he had seen the horrid state of this farm. What a bloody idiot he was. Soon he'd be answering for his lies!

On the other side of the coin, what could Mariah do to him? Leave for home? She had little beyond the modest dowry bequeathed by her du Moulin grandmother. She would be forced to make the best of the situation, same as he had.

Joseph sympathized with himself as he considered the swindler Leroy Smith. Should he be thankful there was any kind of house at all he wondered, but gratitude did not swell his chest. Until his money arrived, he was possessed of nothing beyond a bad investment and a body racked with unfulfilled lust. Too long he had been denied comforts, be they material or female.

A rat scurried across the floor, halted in the middle to peer with beady red eyes at him. Tail twitching, the rodent ran for cover. It bumped into Joseph's watering pail.

The bucket was a reminder of chores to be done. Since no rain had fallen in months, he'd been forced to carry water from the pond to each and every one of his saplings. Peasant work. It was beneath his dignity, but he had to tend the orchard. Then he'd fix the roof.

Roof repair wasn't in his repertoire of skills. But then, what was? His upbringing had prepared him neither for life on the range nor for the grip of a handle or a hammer.

He pitched his tea—dirt, leaves, and all—to the earth floor and made for the hide cover that served as a door. The air outside the cabin was bracing, and he inhaled a deep draft while walking the quarter mile to his pear trees.

Nearing the orchard, Joseph picked up his pace. His heart raced. "Oh my God!" he yelled. A long section of the fence was cut into small pieces! His saplings were trampled! He looked to the ground. The soil had been packed by horses' hooves.

The nightmare hadn't been a dream. It was reality.

His eyes burned with tears, tears quickly blinked away and forgotten when heavy footsteps approached from behind and a forearm whipped around his neck, jerking him backward.

"Last night was just a warning from Mr. Tullos, Jaye. You string your fences agin and we're gonna kill ya."

Joseph was scared witless. Texas law didn't protect him against fence cutting, yet through his fright he made a frantic oath to himself that he'd extract his vengeance. Someway, somehow, the lowlife Charlie Tullos was going to pay for sicking his pack of brigands on him!

He needed help and where was Whitman when he needed him?

Whit approached Miss McGuire. She was sitting pencil-straight on a bench in front of the Double Inn, the rectangular log building that served as the small town's stagecoach stop. Gnawing at the underside of a wing, the caged parrot sat next to her.

Lois had given Whit a blow-by-blow account of the redhead's visit, including her change of heart over accommodations and her hasty departure from the boardinghouse.

Damned if she wasn't avoiding his eyes. Damned if he didn't guess why. He had been a little slow earlier this morning, what with dodging Barbara's skillet and his parading naked in front of Miss McGuire, but now Whit suspected she was in fact Joe Jaye's Mariah Rose.

Trick'em was a dot on the map, a typical small town. Word got around on who was marrying whom, and only one man expected a foreign bride, though no one had known the particulars of her arrival.

"You left something at my sister's place," Whit informed her. Now fully clothed, hatless, with his hair slicked back by pomade and his clean-shaven cheeks reeking of bay rum, he tucked her cape and needlepoint handbag under his arm. "Thought you might be needing your reticule."

"I . . . I was"—she moistened her lips, an obvious gesture of agitation—"was planning to fetch it in a few minutes." She didn't reach for the handbag. "Thank you."

Whit swung around to seat himself on the bench with the bird between them. Except for the occasional buggy passing by on this quiet Saturday morning, they were alone on the tree-lined street. While eyeing the parched cottonwoods across the gritty road, he extended his long legs, leaned back, and settled his elbows on the bench top.

Joe Jaye must be an idiot to let this high-toned beauty out of his sight, he decided. A man, Whit being no exception if he weren't the careful type, would be perfectly willing to make a fool of himself over her.

So what was her story? he wondered. What about that first lover of hers? The fellow must have been daft to let her go. But maybe he was akin to Whit, only interested in women on a temporary basis.

And who said she was pure as the driven snow before meeting the fellow? Certainly not Joe. Whit knew, real well, that women couldn't be trusted.

Distrust pushed aside for the moment, he stole a glance across the wicker cage's top, taking in her perfect profile, her pinned-up auburn hair. Just looking at the enticing Miss McGuire warmed places inside him that ought not to be warmed by someone else's woman. Joe's woman.

Whit couldn't imagine her in that runt's arms. Somehow neither could he imagine her living in the shack her future husband called home, nor picture her holed up in some musty schoolhouse. There were a lot of things beyond Whit's ken.

Funny, though. Joe had failed to mention either her last name or her beauty. What else had he kept to himself? For the first time Whit questioned the dandy's honesty.

On top of these suspicions, aggravation set in. That title-born farmer had left his future wife to her own devices in a state chock full of horny cowboys on the lookout for females of the available, or at least persuadable, variety. If a man—even one from the lowest rung on society's ladder, much less from Joe's former station—offered for a lady's hand, he ought to take proper care of her.

Was she a lady? No highfalutin woman with the sense God gave a buffalo would consent to what Joe offered, unless she lacked looks or character. And this one surely didn't lack for looks!

At a loss for words, Whit settled on a compliment. "This reticule of yours is pretty."

"Thank you. I stitched it myself," she offered. "On the journey across the Atlantic."

Her reply was issued in a soft tone, like the tinkling of water in a calm brook, and he appreciated the sweet sound.

"Must be good with your hands." What would it be like to have those fine-boned fingers caress him, to have them prove their dexterity? A horny cowpoke himself and making no inward apology for the fact, he fidgeted on the bench and gained a splinter in the posterior, which pride forced him to ignore.

Thinking back on his concerns for her welfare, he said, "You needed a room. Why didn't you take one at Lois's?"

"I decided . . ." Her nervous fingers laced together. "To tell the truth, I was a bit unsettled."

That made two of them. He took a slow gander at the woman he had wrongly conjured up to be a soap-ugly, shrill-voiced schoolmarm. "Mariah, you're not what I expected."

"How did you know my name!" She slumped back in the seat. "Never mind. Being from Trick'em, I imagine you know."

"Yeah, reckon I do."

"I'm Miss Mariah McGuire. Lord Desmont's

intended. I assume you're acquainted with him."

"I know Joe all right. We're neighbors. My main ranch lies north and west of his farm," he said. "I knew he was expecting a bride, but I never thought he wouldn't meet your boat in Galveston."

"If that's an insult to Lord Desmont, I'll thank you to keep your opinions to yourself. And furthermore"—she shot him a withering glare—"if you're implying I can't take care of myself, you're mistaken."

"Oh, I'll bet you can." He chuckled. The bulging reticule under his arm drew his next comment. "Any woman known to tote a gun is the take-care-of-herself kind."

Her arms crossed over her full bosom, Mariah twisted around to face him. Indignation was written on each of her pretty features.

"You . . . you snooped in my reticule!"

"Don't jump to conclusions, Red. I didn't mill through your belongings. That satchel of yours is as heavy as a chunk of lead, and I couldn't help but feel the outline. That's all." He paused. "Know how to use firearms?"

Her arms lowered. With a wide swipe she brushed a piece of lint from her gray skirts. "Don't tempt me to demonstrate my prowess. That is, if you're partial to your toes."

Whit laughed. Well, at least she was better prepared than her bull-headed future husband for life on the range. "Joe teach you?" Whit asked, knowing that wasn't the case.

"He didn't."

"Well, who?"

"You're nosy, Mr. Reagor."

"Right," he said. "But don't call me mister. Whit'll do. That's my name, and I make it my business to know what's going on."

"I'll just bet you do."

He ignored her sarcasm but responded to the subject. "Granted. And I know something about you. I know Joe loves you. A lot."

She looked away. "Yes."

Whit noted her lack of "And I love him, too."

She was trying to hide it, but Whit now felt certain she was smitten with him. Since the moment in the trees when their eyes had locked and he'd detected interest in her gaze, he'd known there was potential for something more than casual friendship between the two of them.

Poor Joe. Whit felt sorry for him, but more for himself. Whit Reagor might be many things, but woman-stealer wasn't among them.

"Mariah, um, do you mind if I call you Mariah?" When she shook her head, he pulled the reticule from beneath his arm and reached around the cage to hand it over. "Mariah, you'd better hold on to this."

A sudden jolt shot through Whit as their fingers met to exchange the small yet heavy bag. As if in shock, she lifted her soft doe eyes to his face, then dropped lashes that were thick and gold-tipped. The charge he'd felt, the same one she had apparently experienced, could be attributed to the dry air, but Whit pegged it on his earlier conclusion.

He wanted her; she wanted him. Getting to know her in the most satisfying way was impossible. What was he to do? The answer, unfortunately, was simple. Common sense urged a quick retreat, but he couldn't ignore Mariah Rose McGuire, soon to be Mrs. Joe Jaye. After giving the Englishman his oath to see after her welfare, Whit figured it was his duty to escort her to Trick'em safe and sound; and during the trip and afterward, he vowed he'd ignore and deny his hot-blooded desires.

But dammit, he reasoned with himself, that didn't mean he couldn't at least enjoy the pleasure of her company. And if her "company" included a few harmless flirtations, he'd simply enjoy them. For a while.

How far would she go? Plenty far, he'd gamble. Whit frowned. If she went beyond proper, he intended, for poor ole Joe's sake, to show her the wrong of her ways. He decided to test her right then.

"It's gonna be nice having you round Trick'em. You'll pretty up the area. Good thing for me, too, 'cause we'll be seeing a lot of each other."

"I've seen more of Joseph's neighbor than would be considered proper."

Whit would be drawn and quartered before backing down. "Yeah, you saw a lot of me." He glanced down at his spread legs. "Don't let the size of me scare you, Red."

"Why, you crude, rude, conceited scoundrel!"

Not denying her accuracy, he set the cage to the ground and, splinter ignored, inched closer to Mariah. The bird—Gus, wasn't it?—protested the move. Ignoring squawks and ruffled feathers, Whit eyed her reticule. "You didn't answer my question a minute ago," he goaded. "Who taught you to handle a gun? I'll bet such a pretty gal like you had a score of admirers willing to show you."

She shot to her feet and drilled a look of loathing into him. "You despicable snake, I oughtn't to answer your question, but I will to shut you up. My brothers taught me to shoot." She grabbed her reticule and cage. "This conversation has gone far enough. Thank you for bringing my belongings. Now we're even for favors. Good day."

Whit watched her stomp toward the Double Inn's rough-hewn door, her derriere twitching. Funny how a lady's rear end could look indignant. He grinned. The smile turned sour as a young cowboy rode into view.

"Whee doggies." The cowman hauled his black gelding to a dust-stirring halt in front of Mariah, blocking her path. He whipped a battered hat from his wheat-colored hair. "Howdy there, lady. My, my, you sure are a purty filly."

She whirled around and, with one arm akimbo, glared at the interloper. "I'll thank you to—"

"Make tracks," Whit interrupted, rising to his feet. "And I do mean now, Culpepper."

Slim Culpepper patted the air. "Sorry, Reagor. Didn't know she was your woman."

"Well, she is. And keep that in mind."

The man headed his mount away.

Mariah rounded on Whit. Her eyes shooting dark sparks, she pointed a shaking finger in his direction. "I'll have you know that I answer to no man—not until I reach my future husband. Furthermore, I am *not* your woman. And I feel certain Joseph wouldn't appreciate your calling me such!"

"Probably wouldn't." Whit ran his fingers across his lips. He admired her spirit, but . . .

"A man's gotta do what a man's gotta do to keep a lady out of trouble."

"I've stayed 'out of trouble' all the way from Guernsey, and I don't need a strapping brute to help me now!"

"Is that so?"

"Yes, that's so," she spat, pulling herself upright.

Now it was her bosom's turn to look indignant, Whit thought as she shouted, "You're no better than that odious Culpepper person! And I won't put up with it! Understand? *Now leave me alone, Mr. Reagor!*"

Her obvious agitation roused Whit's gentler side, and he regretted his actions and words. She'd been right; he had acted as reprehensibly as Culpepper. But, Whit was pleased, for Mariah McGuire had passed the first test. Despite her questionable background, she wasn't an out-and-out floozy.

If there was ever a time to act the gentleman, now was it. "Mariah, I'm sorry. Could we call a truce?"

"Never!"

"Please."

"No!"

He gave up gentlemanly behavior. "Have it your way. But you're not getting rid of me." He strode forward and, trying to ignore the sweet scent of roses, took her elbows. "It's my duty to escort you to Trick'em. You see, I promised your man I'd look out for you in case something ever happened to him. He's okay as far as I know, but—"

She wrenched away and stepped back. "Joseph would never ask the likes of *you* to see after me!"

"He did. And you're going to accompany me to my sister's boardinghouse, where you'll take a room until tomorrow. My niece is getting hitched tonight, and you're invited to the wedding. We'll strike out for Trick'em in the morning."

She retreated two steps. "I unequivocably refuse."

"Don't be too sure of yourself. I intend to see you get to Joe Jaye in one piece." Determined to use whatever force necessary, Whit *would* accompany her to Trick'em. "If I have to hogtie you and throw your pretty little butt over my saddle, I *will* see that Joe gets his woman. Unharmed."

"Why, you overbearing—!"

For the second time in one day, Whit Reagor got something thrown at him. This time it was Mariah McGuire's reticule, and damned if the weight of it didn't smart his chest.

Chapter Three

The tapestry reticule bounced off the wall of Whit's chest, then thunked to the brown earth. His eyes turned to blue ice, and Mariah stepped back as he advanced toward her.

Fright tensed her muscles, sent her heart thumping. Would Whit Reagor strike her in retaliation for her actions? Well, if he did, she'd give as good as she took.

She stood her ground in front of the Double Inn. "How dare you order me about as if I'm yours to obey?"

"*Order* you?" His voice held an even tone. "I prefer to call it strong suggestion."

"Order isn't even a strong enough word, Mr. Reagor. You threatened to bind me and throw my person over your saddle. No woman in her right mind would respond to that."

Contrary to what she had imagined he'd do,

Whit took her hand between his callused palms, and after all that had been said between them during the past few minutes, she was astounded at his gentle touch.

"Mariah, you're absolutely right."

Giving up an argument wasn't her nature. "Of course I'm right. And I won't stand for any more threats. If you—"

"What's the use of fighting?" One roughened hand exerted a slight pressure. "We're adults, not children. Surely we can come to an agreement that'll appeal to your sensitivity."

Still wary of his motives, she said, "You confuse me." In more ways than one! "I've traveled a long, long way on my own, and I'm no worse for the wear. Now that I'm within a few days of reaching my destination, I see absolutely no reason to change my travel plans. Yet you're bound and determined to take me under your wing. Or should I say throw me over your saddle? Why are you doing this? For my safety?"

"Exactly." Whit gave a lopsided grin. "I've told you why this is important to me. I made Joe a promise. Out here in the West, we all depend on our neighbors." He dropped one hand, rearranging the placement of his fingers so his grip was now a handshake. "I couldn't sleep at night if I thought I hadn't done all I could for Joe. And for you, as well, since you belong to him."

On a less solemn note, he added, "Besides,

you can cut three days off your travel time by not waiting for the stage."

His statement penetrated her misgivings somewhat. Her hand was still held by his, and despite the honor his words implied, Mariah couldn't help but notice the tightness pressing against her breast and settling below her midriff. She made up her mind to ignore it, however, and to ask the question that had nagged her for the past half hour. "What caused you and Joseph to become friends?"

Whit shrugged. "We're neighbors, that's all . . . but I do respect his determination."

"I'd like to hear more."

"For Pete's sake, I don't know how to word it."

"Try."

He gave the indications of discomfort—shuffled feet, cleared throat, restless eyes. "We share common interests."

Baffled by her feelings as well as by the unlikely situation between this rough-and-tumble Texan and the soft-palmed nobleman, Mariah shook her head. "But you and Joseph seem to be opposites."

"Right." He offered no further explanation. "Now, what's your answer?"

She was beginning to weaken. "It wouldn't be proper, my accompanying you without a chaperone."

"No problem, if that's all the bother. There's a gal in town for my niece's wedding. Lives close to Trick'em, you see. I'm sure Gail Strickland can be persuaded to act as your chaperone."

If Gail was anything akin to the boisterous blonde, Mariah was leery of such a companion. "I've seen one of your gals, and she isn't my cup of tea."

"Gail is a relative, not just any woman." A muscle tightened in his cheek. "Furthermore, there's nothing wrong with Barbara Catley. Granted, she's no grand lady marrying a viscount, but she's a hardworking woman who's making the best of what life has to offer."

"I meant no offense." Mariah's words were sincere; she hadn't wished to sound snobbish. "Maybe you could tell me more about Gail?"

"She's married to a Coleman County rancher. You might find her a tad sharp-tongued. Sort of vinegar and sugar, if you will. Anyway, I think the world of her. Gail Strickland is . . . uh . . . rather like the daughter I never had."

Ignoring an elderly woman with her ear trumpet trained on their conversation as she hobbled by them, Mariah glanced at the ground. She had seen Whit in action with Barbara, had heard tales from his sister, yet his feelings were tender for a sharp-tongued relative. And apparently he was just as loyal to Joseph. Whit Reagor was a more complex man than she had first imagined.

While the issue of propriety was out of the way, what about her improper excitement that wouldn't settle down?

"Will you allow me to escort you to Joe?" he asked.

Wordlessly, she took three steps to the Double Inn's log outer wall. Using it for back support, she leaned against the wood, oblivious to the rough texture and to the slight scent of pine emanating from the building. The road fronting the stagestop that led to the center of town was now alive with wagons and horsemen, yet she took no special note of those activities, either.

She was appraising Whit Reagor. He knew it, and she didn't try to deny it. Nor was a word spoken to ask for her denial or comment.

He strode over to the hitching rail, rested one palm on the cedar post, and hitched a thumb through his belt loop. Less than ten feet separated them. He was studying her but she wouldn't let that get in her way.

Her attention centered on his hands. She knew how they felt, callused and rough and filled with strength, yet with fingers that knew how to be gentle. Her gaze moved. She was well aware of the muscles and sinew that roped his long, long bones. Physical exertion had developed that brawn, and she knew he was proud of his hirsute body, for not once during their first meeting had he displayed modesty. But why should he be anything but proud of his physique? Such a gift, from God and from the toils of labor, was made for appreciation.

But none of that had anything to do with

whether she should trust him.

"You can trust me," he said, as if reading her mind. "I promise."

Her head cocked to the side, she absorbed the sincerity in his drawling timbre. He continued to look her straight in the eye and she admired that character trait of his.

At that moment he neither laughed nor frowned. Honesty and sincerity lived in his expression. She analyzed the total picture. His was a bony face. All angles and sharp edges sometimes softened by dimples. Though his thick black lashes were long and his eyes matched a moonlit midnight sky, there was raw masculinity to his features. His face was young though old, as if he had lived a thousand years during his short days on earth and had experienced heartbreak and sorrow.

She recalled his smile. When he had grinned at her, there was a boyish charm to his juts and edges, as if he knew happiness and all the good things that could happen to the blessed. Enigmatic. That was Whit Reagor.

She laced her fingers. "I think you're sincere."

"I am. My word is my bond," he affirmed.

What should she answer? She had to deal with the situation, but was sooner better than later? Within days they would be neighbors, and Mariah could neither deny nor ignore this fact. As for her unexplainable fits of inner wantonness surely those feelings would pass.

If that didn't happen, however; could she

trust herself? the voice of her conscience questioned, but she refused to listen. "I'll go with you, Whit."

"Thatta girl." A grin, big and wide, split his face as his hand left the hitching post. "Guess I'd better collect your things and make a few arrangements."

Making a few arrangements turned out to be a bigger chore than Whit had anticipated. He had heard of wedding trousseaux, but Mariah's ten heavy cases and eight heavier boxes beat all, he groused inwardly while arranging to leave the majority of her luggage at the Double Inn until he could beg, borrow, or buy a wagon.

With Mariah beside him, he headed Lois's buggy toward Comanche Street. He didn't ask about the contents of all those cases and boxes, and she offered no explanations. He figured that whatever she'd brought to her penniless groom, she was going to need . . . and need bad!

Whit cast a covert eye at Mariah. She seemed to be studying her hands.

"Thank you," she whispered, taking him by surprise. "Joseph will be grateful for your kindness." She tilted her chin Whit's way, and her expression was soft. "We must have you to dinner one night soon. As soon as I can get the staff organized. Is that agreeable?"

Whit offered no reply. It was obvious she didn't know about Joe's circumstances.

Why was honesty so difficult? With one big

exception he refused to dwell on, he'd never had this problem before; his honest streak was a source of pride. Yet to hurt Mariah with the truth . . . Who could be proud of causing pain? No way would he tell her that Joe's "staff" was Joe.

The red cobbles of O'Neil Street resounded with the click of horses' hooves and wagon wheels, seeming to point out the silence between him and Mariah.

Her arched brows quirked. "Well?"

"Yeah. Okay. Dinner sounds fine." Why had Joe led her to believe she was arriving to comforts? There was no excuse for it. But he must have his reasons, Whit decided and it wasn't his place to butt in.

Whit pulled the buggy to a halt beside Lois's barn, which had been cleared for the wedding dance. Keeping out of Joe and Mariah's business meant he'd better pull Gail aside, posthaste, and order her to keep mum.

Mariah's mind was put to further ease when Whit introduced her to Gail Strickland. The heart-faced, black-haired young woman of nineteen in no way resembled Barbara Catley; she was effervescent, warm and lovely with no signs of vinegar.

Almost immediately, though, he took her into a back room, clearly for a private chat. Mariah found this peculiar indeed, but wouldn't borrow trouble. A few minutes later, Gail returned to the parlor, saying, "I'm pleased to be a third on your trip to Trick'em, Miss McGuire."

"Thank you," she replied. "And I'd be pleased if you'll call me Mariah."

Whit broke into their friendly chatter. "Excuse me. I've gotta find a wagon for your trousseau."

Thankfully he didn't question Mariah about the contents of her voluminous stores. All the way from St. Peter Port, she'd offered explanations and paid extra fares for her dowry of farm and home goods. Extra weight had been added in Galveston: schoolbooks and supplies. She was relieved not to be now interrogated further.

Her belongings brought another thought to mind. Mariah had been reared on the fertile loam of an island known for its gardens. Texas, even the lush parts near the Gulf of Mexico, wasn't so blessed by nature. Unless the arid terrain improved, she doubted it could support a grove of pear trees. Yet Joseph had mentioned black land and a ready water source. She had to trust his integrity, just as she trusted Whit Reagor to escort her to Trick'em in all safety.

That afternoon, Gus's cage was sitting on a table beside Mariah. While he frolicked in a dish of water, she relaxed in her bedchamber's oak rocker. Lois had suggested her boarder nap before the wedding, which was to commence at five sharp, but Mariah was not good at being idle, nor at whiling away afternoons.

Her fingers, holding a crochet hook and

thread with the proper amount of tension, were making swift movements around a pristine-white antimassacar. Though she had begun the project some days earlier with the intent of using it in her new home, she'd decided to make it a wedding gift for Kimble Atherton, the future Mrs. Clutch Magee.

From the kitchen Mariah heard the stir of activity, the sound of two female voices chattering and laughing. She felt the urge to join them, but no invitation had been issued.

All of a sudden, a falsetto "Here, kitty, kitty, kitty" filtered around Mariah's closed door.

Gus stopped his bathing. His round eyes blinked twice, then he turned his head from side to side. "Here, ki—"

"Hush up, you crazed bird," she ordered. "The last thing you need is to summon that cat."

The last single crochet finished in an edge's shell pattern, Mariah snipped the cotton thread and pulled the loose end through the finished product.

Now what was she going to do? The bureau clock read three P.M., and two hours needed to be killed before the nuptials. Her clothes were unpacked and smoothed of wrinkles; she had freshened up; Gus was fed. An hour ago she'd finished the last page of *Les Travailleurs de la Mer,* Victor Hugo's exciting novel of love, betrayal, and adventure in Guernsey.

Again she heard laughter from the kitchen.

So what if she hadn't been asked to join the kitchen crew? Perhaps Lois Atherton had been reluctant to ask her, Mariah being a guest.

She walked to the kitchen, which smelled of just-fried chicken, nut pies, and the piquant aroma of pickles. A kettle whistled on the wood-fed Chandler stove. Fancy, the overweight feline, perched as still as a statue beneath the round table centering the kitchen. No doubt the sharp-eyed tabby was hoping for something edible to drop.

"Hello, there," Gail said, and Lois echoed the salutation.

"Yes. Hello."

The room was warm and homey, and though the smells were different from those in Anne du Moulin McGuire's Norman-style *cuisine,* these things still reminded Mariah of home. Guernsey. And of her brothers. And of her mother and grandmother, both now resting in the St. Martin's churchyard, alongside the stone menhir, La Gran'mère de Chimquière. Homesickness and sorrow squeezed her chest. Don't be silly, she warned herself against the inappropriate sentiment. What remained of her family was only a father who offered no sweetness or understanding.

"I'd like to help." She indicated the baskets of food being prepared for the wedding feast. "What may I do?"

Both Lois and Gail peered at Mariah as if she had suggested they step on a puppy.

"You're a guest," Gail reminded as she poked through a gunnysack of potatoes. "Guests don't work."

"You're a guest, too. I don't see that stopping you."

Lois spooned beets into a bowl. "She's kin. She's expected to lend a hand."

"I see. But I'm not about to sit around that room all afternoon twiddling my thumbs. I'm used to work, and I like pulling my own weight."

"Well, gal, you've come to the right neck of the woods." Lois hitched a thumb toward a wreck-pan of dirty dishes. "I was just fixin' to tackle those beauties, but if you're serious about that offer, make yourself at home."

"I am serious." Mariah grabbed an apron and a quilted hotpad, then went for the kettle of boiling water. "I don't feel right unless I'm up to my elbows in suds."

"Well, thanks. I'm beholden for the offer, seeing's how my help's out back settin' up the hoedown."

"I'd better see if Kimble can use some help gettin' dolled up," Lois added, and stopped short of the door leading into the hallway. "You know, Mariah, I like you. You're the kinda gal I'd love to see my brother hitched to."

Gail rolled her big blue eyes.

"I'm promised to another," Mariah reminded.

"Too bad." Lois waved a goodbye.

Mariah blushed and turned to the dishes.

From behind, she heard the peeling and dicing of potatoes. She turned her thoughts to the positive aspects of the future. Within a matter of days she'd be working in her own kitchen, or at least supervising Joseph's cooking staff. And soon, she'd be busy with Trick'em's youngsters, teaching them the rudiments of education. Though she had many reservations about becoming Joseph's wife, Mariah was certain her tomorrows held promise.

She began to hum a tune, an ageless folk song from her homeland. While drying a plate, she put words to the music.

"Is that French?" Gail asked.

"Yes. Mostly we speak Norman French in Guernsey.

"McGuire isn't a Gallic name."

"My father hails from the north of Ireland," Mariah explained, swallowing the bad taste in her mouth.

"You don't speak English like the Irish I've met. You sound more like Big Dan Dodson. Well, sorta like his accent, anyway, but yours is kind of Frenchified. He's a Texas Ranger now but was originally from England."

"The Guernesiais accent resembles our Anglo cousins." Mariah stopped her explanations to furrow her brows. Since Gail Strickland lived in Trick'em, why didn't she mention Joseph's accent? Surely she was acquainted with him. "Do you know my fiancé?" she asked.

"Oh, no."

"How strange. I know everyone in my hometown."

Gail dimpled. "Listen, Coleman County isn't Guernsey. I've seen your country in an atlas—geography's always interested me. I know that island of yours isn't big enough to swing a cat in." She picked up another potato. "Mr. Jaye lives on the opposite side of Trick'em from my place."

"But don't the people get together on market days?"

"Yeah."

"And you've never seen Joseph Jaye?" Mariah asked.

"No."

"But you've heard of him. You know where he lives."

Gail grabbed a chicken gizzard, then bent at the waist. "Looky, Fancy. Look what Auntie Gillie has for you."

"Meooow . . . !" The cat swiped the morsel, taking a clawful of her benefactress's finger and drawing a yelp.

"Damn cat!" The annoyed woman flapped her injured hand and shoved Fancy aside with the toe of her slipper. "Whit should've put you out of your misery months ago!"

Mariah laughed as the cat hissed and batted a paw at Gail's hem. "Fancy does seem a bit forceful of spirit, but doesn't she belong to Lois?"

"Nope. She's Whit's. He adopted her as a

kitten, but never had a way to carry her over to Crosswind."

Thinking of Gus, Mariah cringed. "You don't suppose he'll take her with us, do you?"

"I wouldn't put it past him."

"Sacrebleu."

"What does that mean?" Gail asked.

"It's . . . uh . . . not very nice for a lady to utter."

"A cuss word, huh?"

"Yes."

The lovely brunette cackled. "You're all right, Mariah McGuire. I think you and I will get along just fine."

"That would be nice, especially if you'll be honest with me. I think you're holding something back."

Gail laid the knife aside and straightened. "All right. You want the truth, I'll give it to you. Yes, I know Joe Jaye. He's a troublemaking cuss who's stringing barbed wire across the Western Trail. None of us approve. Coleman County is cattle country, not farmland."

"Guernsey has cattle and farmland. The two are harmonious."

"Don't be naive, Mariah. We don't graze dairy cows. Our beeves feed the East, as well as provide tallow and hides for the nation. I'm talking thousands upon thousands of beeves, and they've got to be driven to the railhead . . . a thousand miles north in Kansas." Gail took a breath before starting again. "Devil's rope keeps our cattle from grasslands and from water. We ranchers won't stand for it. We'll do whatever it takes to protect our interests."

Mariah's hackles raised. "This country was based on individual freedoms, am I right?" Not giving Gail a chance to answer, she went on. "Farmers, Joseph included, have a right to protect *their* property."

"Everyone's entitled to his own opinion, but if I were you, I'd keep those sympathies to myself. You're outnumbered around here."

"Does Whit share your beliefs?"

"You'll have to ask him."

Bracing her palms against the drainboard, Mariah said, "He told me they're close—he and Joseph."

Gail picked up the knife again. "Mr. Jaye has taken advantage of his good nature. Whit's stood up for him on this fencing thing. If push comes to shove, though, things could get nasty, and I'd hate to see Whit on the wrong side of it."

Busying herself, Mariah ruminated over this statement. Poor Joseph! Whatever possessed him to settle in such a godforsaken place? "I think Whit is to be admired for being a good neighbor."

"Yes, I can tell you admire him, but not particularly for helping Joe Jaye." The brunette pointed a potato at Mariah. "Be careful. I saw the way you and Whit were gawking at each other, and—"

"That's not true." A fruit jar nearly dropped from Mariah's paralyzed grip.

"Okay. But let's take a 'for instance.' Whit is the best man I've ever known, but he does have his faults. If a woman sets her cap for him, she's liable to get hurt." Gail tossed a spud into the bowl. "He's after the conquest. Nothing more."

"You don't have much respect for him."

"Yes, I do. Loads of it. I adore him. Always have. We're related, you know. When I was a child, he was the one I ran to when my knees were skinned or my feelings were hurt. He's got a big heart, but it doesn't extend to his lady friends. He got trampled on one time, and that one ruined him for other women."

Mariah did not utter a word. Her heart went out to Whit; she understood how deeply lost love could tear at one's emotions. Of course their situations were different. She had lost out to the grim reaper, while Whit had apparently been cast off by a very alive female.

"I've been around him and his ladies," Gail continued. "Someone always gets hurt. And it isn't Whit."

"You may profess to love him, but your harshness speaks another language."

"I didn't set out to give that impression. I was merely trying to warn you."

"What Whit Reagor does or doesn't do is none of my concern." Mariah placed a dish on the table. "I'm in Texas to be with Joseph Jaye, and he's everything I've ever wanted in a husband," she prevaricated.

Silence stretched before Gail said, "I . . . uh . . . I'd better get back to these potatoes."

As the sun settled to resemble a half wheel of yellow cheese on the horizon, church bells chimed at the appointed hour. Mariah followed what seemed to be the whole of Dublin into the little box church. Greenery and beeswax candles decked the altar. An elderly woman wearing a lace cap over white ringlets played wedding music on the tinny piano. Guests crammed into ten rows of pews, Mariah at the end of one. What had started as a chilly morning had turned into a warm afternoon; Texas weather was strange that way.

The minister took his place, followed by Clutch Magee and his best man. The music picked up in tempo, then the maid of honor began her march. Kimble Atherton, dressed in white satin and radiance, started down the aisle on the arm of her uncle Whit, who was frowning. His scowl didn't stop Mariah's heart from taking an extra beat nonetheless. He wore a black wool suit well fitted to his frame, a white shirt, and a string tie. His pitch-black curly hair had lost its slicked-down look of earlier that day. She liked it better this way. And the sheer bigness of him made an overwhelming impression as he filled the church with his presence.

As they approached Mariah, Whit turned his head to her. A smile softened his stern expression. *My,* she thought *he's handsome.*

If only Joseph were more pleasing to the eye . . . Mariah gave herself a mental shake. Looks meant nothing. Joseph loved her, and he was going to allow her to practice her schoolteaching. What more could she ask out of marriage?

"Dearly beloved, we are gathered . . ."

Mariah merely half listened. She kept trying to picture herself in Kimble's place, all breathless with love and affection but no matter how hard she tried, the image didn't fit. Nor could she superimpose Joseph's image on Clutch's face. She was quite often able to focus, however, her recalcitrant attention, however on the man who offered his niece in marriage.

Why did he look as if he were ready to flee?

"Do you take this man to be your lawfully wedded husband?"

She watched the bride, her eyes glistening, smile up at her groom. Her breathy "I do" wrenched Mariah. Such a promise lasted a lifetime, and a lifetime lasted the rest of one's life!

"Will you love, honor, and obey him for as long as ye both shall live?"

"I will. Oh, yes, I will!"

Mariah grabbed her hankie. There was nothing unusual about crying at weddings, but the abject seriousness of marriage weighed like a hair shirt upon her shoulders.

Marriage is forever. Forever! She could expect, if she lived to an old age, to be married at least forty years. Four decades. She gulped. No matter how much she respected and appreciated Joseph, she couldn't imagine spending all those hours, days, years with him.

"I now pronounce you man and wife. What God has joined together, let no man put asunder."

Her mind raced at the gravity of that pronouncement. The walls seemed to close in on Mariah. Breathing was difficult, for the air had left her lungs. Would it be fair, either to Joseph or to herself, if she promised these vows before God? She didn't love her betrothed, had never loved him—not in the way a wife should adore her mate. It wasn't in her heart to love him, ever. Her head had been turned by grief, not by devotion, understanding, and love.

Her motives, she realized for the first time, were purely selfish. He had offered her a chance to escape from her father's home, the freedom to be a teacher, and he would protect her good name . . . but what could she give him in return? Nothing!

She was vaguely aware of the bride and groom as they passed her, but she couldn't bring herself either to stand or to follow the guests from the church.

Mariah kept remembering . . . Joseph's kisses had elicited no response within her. From the beginning she had regarded him as a companion, a dependable friend.

He deserved more than she could offer.

She wouldn't marry him—couldn't! She had the uncontrollable urge to run, to get away, to get as far from Trick'em as possible. She rose to her feet, but it wasn't to follow the path the wedding guests had taken up the aisle.

Chapter Four

"I'll be damned if she's not running away," Whit muttered as he stood on the lawn with the rest of the wedding party and watched Mariah McGuire, cloak on her arm, charge out of the church. She didn't stop to greet the newlyweds, didn't even turn their way. She was walking, fast and with her head down, toward the business section of town.

Had Gail spilled the beans about Joe?

Whit didn't know Mariah's behavior patterns, not to speak of anyway, but he read people's actions well enough to understand something was wrong. Something bad.

He whispered an excuse into Kimble's ear and hot-footed toward Joe's woman. Half a block from the church he caught up with her, falling in step beside the redhead, whose pinned-up hair was a veritable halo in the fading sunlight.

"A lot of us are parched for a snort of Lois's rum punch," he said, making light and wishing to touch her splendid hair, "but there's no need to rush. She's made enough to drunk-up every cowpoke and cowgal in Texas."

Increasing her pace, Mariah directed her sight straight ahead. "I . . . uh . . . need to take care of something."

"Whoa now, Red." Whit grabbed her elbow, threw back his head, and chuckled. "There's a privy behind the church. No need to get your drawers in a wad."

She stopped so fast that dirt stirred around her skirts. "That isn't what I meant." Her strapped reticule swinging from a forearm, she crossed both arms and twisted around to face Whit. Her eyes speared him, as she suppressed a grin. "And if you're trying to be funny with your uncouth phraseology, you've failed miserably."

"Then why are you chewing the inside of your cheek?"

She glanced down while drawing in a breath. "To keep from crying," she whispered, finally, brokenly.

"I didn't mean to insult you."

"My feelings have nothing to do with you. I—I . . . well, I need to be alone. That's all."

"The wedding got to you," he surmised.

"Yes."

"Thinking of *your* upcoming wedding, Mariah?"

She nodded. "I'd like to be alone right now."

He stepped in front of her, taking her chin within his palm. Her skin was soft as a rose petal and he stroked its bud-smooth texture, knowing that each time he smelled roses he'd always think of Mariah Rose.

"If you've got second thoughts about becoming a missus," he said hoarsely, "don't marry Joe."

"Maybe you're—" She moved backward. "Wait a minute. Why are you trying to talk me out of it?"

"Hey." He waved a hand. "Don't turn the emphasis to me. You're the one who's having second thoughts."

"I never said that."

"You didn't have to."

Neither spoke. Mariah shuffled her feet. No more than three arms' lengths from her, Whit crouched back on his heels, picked up a pebble, then tossed it down Main Street.

An elbow on his knee, he fell to deep thought. Joe Jaye was hardworking, determined, and in love. The last part of Whit's thought jarred his senses. To this point, he had been a little slow on the uptake. Not now. Apparently Joe hadn't been frank in his letters for fear of losing his precious Mariah.

Once Whit had been desperately in love. Love's a funny thing, he thought, feeling more than his years. In most relationships, one person's love was deeper than the other's. Such had been the case with him and Jenny. Back then, he'd been a moonstruck, gullible wet-ears who wouldn't listen to the naysayers' warnings that he was too young and randy to know his mind. Or Jenny's. His wife had married him to get away from her parents; he'd married her because he couldn't live without her. Two years later, she was dead. Time had proved he could live without her . . . and live a damned fine life.

He correlated his past troubles to Joe's. Though the Englishman was twenty-four, a couple of years older than Whit had been at the time of Jenny's death, Joe still had a lot to learn from the academy of hard knocks called life.

Glancing up at Mariah, Whit admitted, "Joe reminds me of myself when I was young. So much in love that it overpowers everything and anything, beyond rhyme or reason."

She gasped. "Don't say that. Please don't."

"You don't love him, do you?"

She took several pacing steps, then whipped around and squared her shoulders. "Define love."

He was nonplussed. Whit Reagor was the last person on earth to be asked for such a definition, but Mariah didn't know that. Could he even remember how love felt?

"Can you define true love?" she pressed.

"Love." His fingers tugged at his suddenly tight shirt collar and he rose to his feet. "Well, I'd say it's desire, passion, probably obsession.

Wanting to share your life with another. Needing to be together all your born days . . . having the urge to procreate." He gave a half grin. "Guess the best way to describe it is . . . say you haven't eaten in two days, and you're extra sweet on pecan pie. You get a big piece of it, all fresh from the oven and smelling like heaven. Rather than gobble it down yourself, you'd give it to the one you love."

"I've had those feelings."

She didn't qualify that statement, Whit noted. Without a doubt, her feelings had been for that other man, not for Joe. But she *had* loved and lost, that was certain, and in the aftermath was bound by the strictures of society to make an honest woman of herself.

Whit suffered under no illusions; it was different for men. He had gotten over Jenny by hellin' and whorin', but respectable women weren't allowed those freedoms.

If he were a woman, he'd damned sure hate having marriage pushed on him. Nonetheless, Mariah *was* bound by society if she wanted a home and a respectable sex life, which his instincts told him appealed to her for sure.

And thinking of sex, Whit stared at the doe-eyed beauty. He imagined what her shapely body must look like in the flesh, yet he couldn't picture her and the sawed-off farmer in a carnal act. For Pete's sake, she was a good two inches taller than Joe, and probably had ten pounds on him. But then again what the hell did that have to do with anything? What he couldn't see was her hair in wild disarray and flowing over Joe's chest as she rode him hard and fast, her face flushed with excitement, her husky voice moaning his name.

Whit had no trouble putting himself in the picture.

What the hell's the matter with you, Reagor? he asked himself. Snap out of it. Mariah Rose McGuire was Joe's woman. Period. And at this point, she needed something different from Whit's sexual musings.

"Look, you've got a case of bridal jitters, that's all. You shouldn't be alone. Come on, Mariah, let's go to the wedding hoedown." He offered an arm. "If you need a shoulder to cry on, mine's available for you. Okay?"

After a moment she agreed. She slipped her arm through the crook of his and started back toward the churchyard.

She wanted to confide in Whit but wouldn't dare. She couldn't open a vein to this man, who was Joseph's confidant and . . . the object of her fascination.

Furthermore, it wouldn't be right and proper not to explain her decision to Joseph in person. The broken engagement would injure his pride and, with those problems Gail had spoken of involving the barbed wire, Mariah was determined to cushion the blow as best she could. She had to finish her journey.

In the meantime, she'd wrestle with her conscience and prepare for the confrontation. But tonight she simply wanted to blank out thoughts of the heartbreak she would cause in Trick'em. She prayed Whit wouldn't bring up the subject of Joseph again, and her prayers were answered. Wordlessly they rode to the Atherton residence, this time in a sky-blue covered wagon with red spoke wheels.

Buggies and wagons littered the grounds surrounding the Atherton property. Horses were tethered to hitching posts and trees. The barn was freshly mucked out, clean-smelling, and streamers hung from the loft and eaves. A half dozen pot-bellied stoves toasted the air. The sun had set, leaving the barn bathed in the glow of a wealth of hurricane lamps.

Scores of people gathered around the blushing bride and proud groom. A troupe of ladies set food, plus a white, iced cake, on long tables. Cups of pink-tinted rum punch were passed around. Two fiddlers resined their bows, Whit explained to Mariah, and music, helped along by a paunchy dance caller, filled the tall building.

Lois pulled Whit aside, and while he was gone, Mariah's toe tapped to the music. She missed his attention. Her thoughts turned to something he had said outside the church. Joseph reminded him of himself when he was young. "So much in love that it overpowers everything and anything, beyond rhyme or reason." Who was the woman he'd loved with such abandon? Even Gail had mentioned her, but with no specifics. Was she a blonde, a brunette, or a redhead? Where was she now? Mariah was curious why she had turned her back on such a man. Why hadn't she wanted his love? From all Mariah had gathered, he was a good man, decent and honorable.

"May I have this dance?"

She turned to the deep sound from behind her, turned to Whit Reagor. Again that strange, magical, unexplainable feeling assailed her. Was it his golden voice? Though his inflections were indicative of Texas, she noted—and not for the first time—the special richness imbuing his tone. It should be a sin to be so handsome, she thought while drinking in the sight of his black hair and tanned, olive-toned face, the coloring that complemented and contrasted to his blue eyes. But, it was not those things that were the most appealing aspects of Whit Reagor, but rather the tenderness he tried so hard to hide.

Hitching a thumb at the dance floor, he dimpled a grin. "Well?"

Though the tune held a waltz's tempo and a line about "pretty new shoes" went along with the rhythm, she was unfamiliar with the dance steps. "I'm sorry, Whit, I can't dance to that."

"I'd be honored to teach you."

He aligned his right side with her left, then instructed her to bend her elbows up. He grasped her fingers, and she caught the clove scent of bay rum and warm, clean man. Whit's scent.

"Point your left toe," he instructed, deep and sweet. "Now cross it over your right ankle. That's it, darlin'. Now step forward with your left foot, then your right."

Mariah tried. Her heel encountered her petticoat and the sound of ripping material caused her to freeze. "I'm no good at this."

"Just relax. Let yourself go with the feeling."

That was exactly what she did and within moments she was caught up in the music . . . and the grace in which Whit executed the dance. He exuded power and confidence, attributes much admired by his partner.

Whit angled his chin to whisper in her ear, "Farthing for your thoughts."

"Farthing?" She giggled as the wind of his breath wound down from her earlobe. "How British."

"Just wanted you to feel at home." The piece ended, and Whit whirled around to grasp both sides of her waist. They were standing under the loft in a shadowy area well away from the crowd gathered around the bride and groom. "You're wonderful, Mariah."

"You're pretty nice yourself."

"I'll bet you're good at everything you do." His eyes held hers, and his mouth dipped low.

Heart racing, she parted her lips. She welcomed his kiss, had yearned all day for it, even though she hadn't made that inward admission. His warm, punch-scented breath tickled her lips, and the ability to breathe deserted her. Oddly, he changed course, the kiss landing on her cheek. Disappointment grabbed her heart.

"Hullo, you two. Issa beautiful wedding, izshn't it?"

They broke apart at Gail's inebriated words.

"Are you all right?" Whit asked the teetering woman.

"Yeah."

Despite her embarrassment at being caught by the very person who had accused her of being interested in Whit, Mariah was surprised at the brunette's state. Obviously Gail had consumed a great deal of alcohol in a short period of time, and Mariah wondered what had caused her to do so.

"Say, Whit, how's about getting us two little ladies some more hootch. I mean"—she hiccuped—"I mean punch."

"You're drunk already," Whit observed.

"So? Go 'way. I wanna tawk to Mariah!"

"Gail Ann Sutherland," he said sternly, taking her arm, "I'm going to walk you back to the house."

Yanking away, she demanded, "Lemme tawk to Mariah!"

"You won't have much privacy with the crowd you're gathering." He gestured to curious the eyes of several onlookers.

Lois stepped through the crowd. "Behave yourself," she hissed to Gail before turning to the observers. "Haven't you got anything better to do than gawk? There's a bride and groom waitin' to cut the cake. Get goin'!"

The bystanders receded, and Mariah watched Whit take the young woman's arm once more. "Ready to go, honey?"

"Not yet. I said I wanna tawk to Mariah."

"Leave her be," Mariah said.

Whit and Lois looked at her, making certain she was sincere, and, satisfied, they retreated. Mariah watched Whit stride through the barn, watched first one guest, then others, stop him to offer back slaps and cups of punch.

"Let's siddown." Gail plopped down on two bales of hay that were stacked atop each other. She patted the adjacent makeshift chair. "Come on. I won't bite."

Mariah smoothed her skirts, then eased onto the bale.

"Didn't I warn you today about Wh-Whit?" Gail covered her lips as she hiccupped again. "Better watch out."

"We were dancing, that's all."

"He was gonna ki-kiss you."

"Gail, that's really, truly none of your business."

"Didn't mean to be a busybody." Her unfocused eyes blinked. "I'm just . . . You gotta understand."

"Understand what?"

"Nothing. I'm just crazy t'night." Gail shook her head. "Would you fetch me a cuppa coffee? Please."

Mariah scrutinized the young woman who was too young to be so troubled. Such a shame. She rose to her feet and started across the straw floor . . . but then stopped in her tracks.

Whit had his arm around Barbara Catley! A burst of jealousy flashed behind Mariah's eyes. This morning the blonde had been wild-haired, crude, and devoid of lip rouge. Tonight, wearing a pale-blue gown of crossbar lawn and with her blond hair upswept, she was a vision of loveliness. Mariah glanced down at her own frock, wishing she had made a better effort at choosing her attire.

Brown bombazine that had seen three years of wear could hardly compare with pastel lawn! Perhaps it was self-centered to wish herself the belle of Whit's eye, but Mariah wished it nonetheless.

Insanity! For crying out loud, she admonished herself, why shouldn't he hold his lover close? Evidently they had settled their differences, and she ought to be happy for the spurned woman, the object of her pity just that morning. She *should* be pleased . . . but wasn't.

Remembering her mission and the young woman whose problems were evidently much greater than clothes and male attention, Mariah sallied forth to the coffeepot.

The steaming cup in her hand, she made a point not to look at the happy couple as she returned to the tipsy woman.

"See." Gail pointed toward Whit and Barbara,

who were stepping to a reel. Her voice had lost much of its slur. "He forgot our drinks. He's too busy with that one. Don't expect him back at the house tonight."

"I don't."

"You were."

"Drink your coffee," Mariah said.

Staring at Whit, Gail took the cup to her lips.

Does he have anything to do with her drunken state? Mariah wondered. Though Gail was a married woman and related to Whit, did she have feelings for him that transcended familial ties?

"You love that fickle-hearted man, don't you, Gail?"

"Sometimes."

"Do you love your husband?"

"Oh, yes." Gail cupped her hands around the steaming mug. "It's a different kind of love, though. Whit, I want to see happy. Ed, I try to make happy. Love of family, and romantic love. Understand?"

"Yes," she replied, remembering the feelings for her brothers as opposed to those for Lawrence.

A young sandy-haired man strolled up who was vaguely familiar to Mariah. Then she remembered. Slim Culpepper. The odious cowboy who had called her "purty" in front of the Double Inn.

"Can I have this dance, ma' am?" he asked, but she declined his offer.

Gail set her cup aside. "Slim, I'll dance with you."

The two whirled onto the sawdust, and Mariah tried not to glance at Whit and his lady friend . . . but her eyes moved as if they had minds of their own. He was bending down to listen to something Barbara had to say. Mariah could take no more.

Quick as her feet could carry her, she departed the barn. She took a shuddering breath of bracing air. How was she going to get through the next few days, being in such close proximity to Reagor, who had no problem turning from one woman to the next in the blink of an cyc?

"Have you no shame?" she asked herself aloud while ascending the porch steps. "Within minutes of deciding to break Joseph's heart, you're all over Whit, like butter on bread."

Trying to get a grip on herself, she glanced from side to side. The covered veranda ran the length of the two-story boardinghouse's front porch. A porch swing hung from the ceiling and two rockers faced the road. Climbing roses grew up thc rails and amazingly to a woman from the cold climes of the English Channel, the scarlet roses were blooming. She walked over to pull a stem gingerly toward her nose.

"Smell sweet, don't they?"

Whit. Whit! Gail had been wrong. He was here. But maybe he's made a detour to pick up a smoking jacket, Mariah thought facetiously.

Or maybe he's after an extra set of clothes in case Barbara tosses him on his behind again.

"I love roses," Mariah said, her tone benign.

"Better enjoy 'em while you can. There aren't any roses in Trick'em. 'Course, once you get there, the story'll be different."

"That's the kind of thing a man says when he's courting a woman."

"Is it?"

"Yes— Ow!" Mariah slapped her wrist. Beneath her fingers she felt a small insect. "Something bit me!"

"Probably a red ant. Let's get into the light and I'll look at it."

"That won't be necessary," she replied, remembering his arm around Barbara. "Don't you have somewhere to go?"

"Not tonight. And I said I'm going to look at your wrist." His voice brooked no argument.

A calm satisfaction settled in Mariah's veins. He wasn't sleeping with that blonde, at least not tonight, and she couldn't help but be pleased. His big hand settled against the small of her back, and Whit led her into the kitchen, where a hurricane lamp glowed on the round center table. Music from the barn filtered through the room, a soft and romantic melody.

Dance music swimming in his head and a grin spreading his face, Slim Culpepper strode toward Lois Atherton's house. He had seen Whit headed this way, and Slim needed to talk with him. Earlier this evening Reagor had offered him the job of top hand, and he was ready to accept the rancher's offer.

He stepped onto Lois's back porch, the one leading to the kitchen. His fist poised to knock on the door, Slim peeked through the window-pane. "Would ya look at that?" he whispered to himself.

There wouldn't be any job talk tonight; Reagor there had his hands full with that purty Brit gal, and from the plumb daffy look in the lucky devil's eyes, Slim reckoned he had better get gone.

As Reagor took her wrist in his palm, Slim left.

Gently, Whit turned Mariah's wrist first one way, then the other. The scent of roses, sweet roses, drifted to him. "Looks like an ant did get you," he commented huskily. "It's gonna burn like hell for a few hours."

"Isn't there something I can put on it?"

"My mama used to say a kiss can make anything all better."

"Did she?" Mariah laughed, a nervous little sound. "I'm sure she's a resourceful woman, but I had something more medicinal in mind."

"Let's give it a try anyway." He brought her reddened flesh to his lips, and—damn!—she tasted delicious.

"You're not very subtle," she murmured shakily.

Trying to control himself, Whit stepped back. "Lois has some salve she made up. We can give it a whirl." He reached into the bottom of a pie safe. Taking a healthy glob of the yellow goo onto the tip of his forefinger, he smoothed it over Mariah's left wrist. "Feel better?"

"I . . . I think I'll live."

He grinned, wrapping his fingers around her slender forearm. "Yeah, I think you will."

She felt so good to him. He had been going crazy all day, all night, over her. He'd tried to ignore her charms, had tried to be a gentleman monk. He'd even tried to get interested in Barbara again, but nothing had worked.

Whit Reagor would have to be deaf, dumb, blind—and dead below the waist!—not to notice the beautiful Mariah and the signals she'd been throwing him all day. He had set out to test her, but realized *he* was tested past the limit.

His cravings superceded honor, integrity, and reservations. His free hand touched her waist. Ignoring the goo on her injured wrist, he brought her hand to his chest. Did she feel the hammering of his heart?

Gazing into the softness of her eyes, he was lost. "You're so lovely." He murmured, "What would you do, if I were to kiss you?"

Chapter Five

"What're you waiting for? Do it now! Ooooh. Mmm."

The former Viscount Desmont bestowed the buxom woman a smile of superiority as he shoved his member into her. Fast and furious, Joseph pumped as her heavy legs folded around his skinny back. Temperence Tullos, Mrs. Charlie Tullos, was his sweet revenge for the humiliation he'd suffered at the hands of her husband's thugs only this morning; and now, at ninc o'clock in the evening, Joseph's self-esteem was once more intact. He was a man in control.

He didn't speak, but his log cabin was alive with the woman's groaning vulgarities. His eyes closed while he playacted Temperence was his Mariah. Yet he knew she wasn't, not really. Mariah wasn't a cow of a woman, nor did she bathe herself in cloying perfumes, nor did she shout obscenities worthy of the lowest of classes—which he was loath to admit, even to himself, he enjoyed, though he did regret not saving himself for his bride.

The woman-cow screamed in ecstasy, and Joseph tumbled over the brink, his climax swift. He rolled to his side, and did up the buttons of his red long-handles.

"You know, for a skinny runt, you're not half bad-looking."

"Thank you, madam." His chest puffed from the left-handed compliment, and, Mariah forgotten, he swept his eyes across the pendulous breasts that looked as if they were ready to burst through Temperence's thin, vein-shot skin.

His feelings turned gleeful. What a day this had been, going from the horror of land-plunder to the pleasure of making love to this older woman of thirty, who had given him a windfall in more ways than one. Her husband and his gang had trampled his saplings and threatened his life before riding away, leaving him face-down in the orchard. That afternoon, while Joseph had raged at his predicament and searched for a method of revenge, Temperence had arrived by horseback at his door. She had not been empty-handed.

On the floor beside him lay a bag of Charlie Tullos's gold coins. Joseph had thought it strange, Temperence giving him money, but with some unspoken misgivings about the decency of accepting her offer, he had taken it.

"Pay some attention to me, m'lord."

Temperence, a veritable Angus heifer though her face was rather comely and her ankles trim, ran her hand up his thigh to cup his manhood and fiddle with his fly.

"Stop that! I'm too tender for more antics."

"It has been rather tiring . . ." Lying on her side, she glanced at the moonlit, grease-paper window as Joseph perused the roof's crack.

"How long have we been at this, honey?" she asked.

"Quite a while. Since midafternoon, actually."

"Mmm." She lifted a brow. "Aren't you going to ask me why I gave you all that money?"

Feeling guilty for accepting the five hundred dollars, he slammed his eyes shut. What would his father say if he knew about his ungallant deed? What would Whitman think?

"What's the matter, m'lord?"

"Nothing." Determined not to show his inner turmoil, Joseph pulled himself up and complied with her previous request. "Why, my dear Mrs. Tullos, did you see fit to give me money?"

"Charlie told me what he and his men did to your property, so I figured a peace offering would be nice." The nail of her forefinger made a circle on his upper leg. "To get the, um, *powwow* going."

"You've lusted for me in the past?" he asked, pleased she would go to such strides.

"You'd better believe it. Ever since you took up this land, I've been wondering what it'd be like to hump royalty."

"I'm not royal."

"You're the closest I'll get to the crowned heads of Europe." She fluttered a hand. "I hate being stuck out here in the middle of nowhere. I'm a Virginian, you know. Oh, to see my dear ole mammy once more . . ."

He didn't give a care about her dreams or wants. "Well, how was it? Humping royalty."

"Need you ask?" She rolled over, covering him with her body as she worked his buttons. "It's never been this good before," she lied.

"Not even with Charlie?" Joseph prompted, oblivious to her untruth.

"Ha! Don't make me laugh." She leaned to nuzzle his neck. "He'll have us killed, you know. That is, if he finds out about this."

"His brigands are already out for me." Joseph shivered. "You're not going to tell him, are you?"

"No way would I ruin what we've got going, your lordship. I want lots more of this." Her hand scooted inside his flap. "Ah, what a man you are."

Joseph enjoyed having his ego stroked. Oh, what pleasure! He had Tullos's money *and* his wife; and the indignities he'd suffered from the hook-nosed rancher were somewhat negated by the knowledge that he, now a common farmer, could rouse the lust of the rich cattleman's wife.

And Temperence Tullos was filled with loathing, both for her husband and for the man beneath her. She wanted to hurt Charles for running off her lover, Leroy Smith. Leroy, who was the only match in the world for her, sexually! What better way to spite her husband than to fornicate with the bane of his ranching empire?

Men! With the exception of Leroy, she hated them all, and perhaps she hated Leroy, too. All her life, starting with her foul-breathed, rutting father, she had been treated as if she were no more than a receptacle. But never again. She was the head hoss now.

She impaled herself on Lord Joseph Jaye, and swallowed back the bile in her throat. She had this vain pipsqueak wrapped around her proverbial little finger, and that's just where she wanted him. When the time was right, she'd use the simple-minded nester even further to extract her vengeance against Charles Vernon Tullos. Through Lord Joe she'd scheme to get Leroy back in Trick'em.

"Lovely, simply lovely," Joseph moaned.

Little did this man know that the alms she had tossed him were nothing more than an investment in her future.

"What would you do," Whit repeated more urgently, "if I were to kiss you?"

Mariah's lips parted in invitation as she curled her fingers into his lapel. "What would you do if *I* kissed *you?*"

"You'll not have the upper hand in this, sweet witch."

His free hand yanked her closer, his hard mouth bearing down to meet the softness of her lips. She tasted as sweet as nectar, and he had to sip his fill. He heard a sigh as his tongue found hers, and his insistence became tenderness as heightened passion coursed through him. No woman had ever tempted him so!

The hand holding her insect-bitten wrist moved to the swell of a firm breast, and as he caressed the side of it he felt the shiver of delight running through her. Their bodies swayed to the faint sound of music filtering into the kitchen from the barn, and Whit was dying of need . . . a longing that could only be assuaged by Mariah.

After his lips canvassed her smooth cheek, the side of her nose, and her closed lids, he buried his face in the auburn locks that had worked free of their pins. "Feels so good," he murmured, and heard her sigh of acknowledgment.

Suddenly, strangely, unbelievably, an urge filled him. He yearned to hold her close and protect her against Joe's cruel world.

He hugged her in the cocoon of his arms. "Ah, Mariah, my sweet. You've known all day, all night, I've wanted you here in my arms."

"Yes," she whispered. "Whatever shall we do?"

The sound that escaped his lips was half

groan, half chuckle. "I shall take you to my bed and make love to you until you're too weak to tempt me again."

She worked free of his embrace, her chin dropping. She was confused. Before Joseph had taken her virginity, she had been partial to caresses. In the aftershock, she felt nothing. Now, the emotions Whit evoked within her were too frustrating to confront.

Whipping around, she made for the door leading to her room. "Good night."

"What's wrong?" He caught her before she could turn the doorknob. His fingers wrapped around her shoulders. "Why call it a night? It's just getting interesting."

"The interesting part is over."

"Beg to differ, darlin'." His tensed fingers squeezed into her tender flesh. "Tell me why you had a change of heart."

"You move too fast. It seems as though I'm caught up in a whirlwind and can't get my footing. All day long I've tried to keep my wits about me, but every time you're near, I . . . I lose control."

If he hadn't known about her past, Whit would have fallen for her routine of frightened innocence. Recalling her hasty departure from the church, he decided Gail had mentioned Joe's sorry circumstances, and Mariah was now out for bigger game than an indigent farmer.

"Answer me something," he implored. "Did Gail say anything to you about Joe?"

"Yes . . . but what's he got to do with this?"

His suspicions confirmed, Whit grimaced with bitter memories. Without a doubt, Jenny Reagor had pulled the same thing with her lover. Colin Pierce had been a wealthy planter, and Jenny had wanted more money than her impoverished husband had provided.

Mariah was after Whit's riches, though he had no problem with that. He *did* have a problem with her switching loyalties!

"So," he said, responding to her confession, "you can't keep your wits. Sure had me fooled, I'll admit. I thought you knew exactly what you were doing when you . . . Woman, you've teased me since the moment we met, with your twitching rear and hungry-eyed gazes."

"Me flirt with *you?* Ha! You've been flirting with me since the instant I saved your bare posterior from ridicule!"

"You got that right. We've both been sniffing and cooing and sidling up to each other." His lips dropped to her clean-smelling hair. "Don't you know you can only push a man so far?"

"Your escort to Trick'em doesn't mean I owe you my body in return," she replied in a schoolmarm's sharp pitch.

"You owe me nothing, that's true." Wrapping his arms around her waist, he pulled her back against his hard desire. "But let me tell you something. I don't know how women act where you come from, but here in Texas, if a woman throws herself at a man, she damned sure knows what to expect."

Only moments ago she had been confused by her emotions, but her head never had been clearer than at this instant. Whit Reagor was not going to chop her into mincemeat! "Well, where I come from, if a man forces his attentions on a woman, she has the right to plead before witnesses, *'A l'aide, mon prince! On me fait tort'*, and she receives an immediate injunction against the culprit."

"What the hell does that mean?"

"Help, my prince! I am being wronged." Throwing off his hands, she rounded on him. "You, sir, are wronging me."

Damn, he almost believed her. "And you, ma'am, are wronging Joe Jaye."

"Why, Mr. Reagor, are you a man of the cloth?"

He would have gladly wrung her neck. "Let me warn you, Mariah Rose McGuire. I'm not a young fool, and I'm on to your two-timing tricks. You've gotten wind of Joe's problems, and you're out to trap me in your plans."

"Plans? I have no *plans* for you! Why would I have plans for a scoundrel who can't even keep his word?"

She did bring out the worst in him, but he'd be gored by a raging bull before admitting anything. "And what about you? Just how trustworthy are you? You've crossed an ocean to marry Joe Jaye. Yet here you are, standing in this kitchen with me, my kiss fresh on your lips.

How many other men have kissed the blushing bride since you've last seen your husband-to-be? One? Two? A dozen?"

Her face went white. "None. I've kissed no one."

"Until me, eh? Well, how is it, having two men on the string at once?"

"Not bad, actually," she volleyed. "How was it, embracing your neighbor's fiancée? And speaking of behavior, don't you Texans have a code of honor about such things?"

Her questions ripped into him. "Kissing you was no more right than your wanting to kiss me."

"Seems we both carry a bit of blame, wouldn't you agree?"

She flounced away to slam her chamber door. He started after her, but forced himself to a different direction . . . into the darkness of his own room.

His boots, suit, and shirt thrown off, he yanked back the bedclothes and fell into bed. Sleep eluded him. He grabbed a cigar from the bedside case and lit up. Smoking did nothing to ease his fires. What was wrong with him that twice in his life he had found two-timing females attractive?

The cigar ground out in a battered tin cup, Whit tossed to one side, then the other. The sheet twisted around his leg, and he kicked the covers away. Curling his hand into a fist, he punched the pillow, then raked shaking fingers through his hair. If only he could forget her . . . Impossible. Even though he knew the dangers of her kind of woman, Whit still yearned for Mariah with a ferocity he'd never known existed within him. He ached for her more mightily than he had ever ached for Jenny. Or any woman before or after his marriage. How could this be happening?

Lunging to his feet, he stalked, naked, up and down the hooked rug. Loss of control wasn't the only thing that ate at him, like a vulture tearing at a carcass. How would Joe feel if he knew Whit was stalking a lonely bedroom, pining for his bride-to-be?

Whit groaned and clenched his teeth. Joe. The gullible young fool who wanted Mariah for the rest of his life, whereas Whit only needed his fill of her.

This disconcerting fascination with the auburn-haired witch had to cease and Whit was determined it would.

The next morning as she tried to eat the morning meal at Lois's big round table, Gail was nursing the worst hangover of her life. She yearned for a hair of the dog that bit her last night.

She eyed the only other occupant of the dining room. After asking about her health, which she had glossed over, Whit hadn't said a word all morning. He was devouring a huge plate of steak and eggs. What was wrong with him? Usually he had a disgustingly cheerful morning demeanor.

"Whit, have you got a bottle in your room? I could sure use a drink."

"No." He downed a cup of steaming coffee. "And even if I did, I wouldn't give it to you. Your drinking's getting out of hand, Gail Ann."

When he called her by her full name, she knew he meant business, but she seethed nonetheless. How dare he! Forcing nonchalance, she said, "You're making too much of it."

"Am I? Ed says you're in the corn every night."

"If my husband . . ." She clammed up. Her problems with Edward were too painful to admit, especially to Whit.

"If Ed would do what?"

"Nothing."

"Has he mistreated you?" Worry in his eyes, Whit studied her. "You don't have to put up with any sort of cruelty."

"Sure am glad that norther's blown over."

"I get the picture." He picked up his fork, but set it down again. His worried eyes scrutinized her before he offered, "Gail, remember, you always have a home at Crosswind."

"Yes, Papa," she teased. Determined to change the subject, she asked, "Have you seen Mariah this morning?"

"No." He scowled. "That McGuire woman told me you flapped your mouth about Joe."

She flushed. "She kept pressing me, and I . . . I—"

"What exactly did you say?"

Ashamed of herself for reneging on her promise, she replied, "I mentioned his trouble-making. About the fences, you know. That sort of thing."

His blue eyes turned to chipped ice while the muscles of his jaw tightened. He muttered a foul oath.

Her mettle once more intact, she shot back, "Aren't we in a pleasant mood this morning?"

"Drink your coffee."

She spooned generous portions of raw brown sugar into her cup, adding a goodly amount of milk thereafter, and downed the revolting contents.

"Good morning" came a cheerful, lilting greeting that beat against Gail's head. Mariah McGuire had made her entrance.

Whit didn't say a word to her, and their observer caught the undercurrent of tension flowing between them. " 'Morning," Gail replied, watching Whit's jaw work. "Sleep well?"

"Tight as a tick. And you?"

"Fine."

Mariah turned to Whit. "Good morning."

He growled something unintelligible to the woman he had gone to such pains to impress yesterday, Gail noted. How could he be unaware of her Wedgwood-green frock or of her thick wavy hair that was pulled to her nape in a loose bun? Okay, some men weren't aware of fashion or hairstyles, but Whit wasn't among them. How could he not notice a creamy complexion or a cameo-lovely face? And where were his manners?

Gail put two and two together. He wasn't oblivious to anything; he was trying to ignore Mariah. They'd had a tiff.

After a moment, Mariah apparently gave up on Whit's manners and seated herself on one of the high-backed oak chairs . . . well away from him.

A serving girl brought forth a platter of fried eggs and burnt-edged sirloin to serve Mariah and to replenish Whit's plate. The smell roiled Gail's stomach. Pouring herself another cup of coffee, she noticed Mariah had barely touched her food. Gail felt sorry for the woman who kept taking covert, though haughty, glances at Ole Tight Jaws.

Join a long line of the brokenhearted, Gail wanted to say.

She watched the redhead dab her lips with a napkin, then take a dainty sip of coffee. Gail's sympathies deepened. The lady was class. Joe Jaye had been some sort of prince or something in England, but he was nothing in Coleman County. Since he'd squandered his money on devil's rope, everyone knew he was as penniless as Pablo Martinez, the poorest Mexican in five counties. Poor Mariah was in for a shock.

Gail laid her spoon on the saucer. "Mariah, I

apologize for last night."

"Think nothing of it. Many people were enjoying Lois's fine punch."

"I didn't mean that. I meant for what I said." Doggone it! Why had she alluded to Whit? The subject of her warnings was women-talk and shouldn't be spoken around Ole Tight Jaws. "We can talk about it later, if you'd like."

"There's no need for further discussion," Mariah replied, her eyes warm as she smiled at the younger woman. "Think nothing of it. Really."

Gail's estimation of the redhead rose to an even higher plane. Her curiosity was piqued, though. Why would such a fine lady marry that snoot Joe Jaye? She decided to ease into finding out the answer. "Lois told me you're a schoolteacher . . ."

"Oh, yes." Her voice was warm and tender. "I love children."

"Is Mr. Jaye going to allow you to teach after—" Gail saw the prudence of switching the topic again, seeing as how Whit had warned her against mentioning the farmer's dire straits, and he was turning his head slightly to drill a warning look her way.

On top of that, why point out Coleman County had more than its share of schoolteachers?

Her next question was addressed to Whit. "Ready for the cattle drive up to Dodge City?"

"Just about." He turned back to his plate.

"When will you leave?" she asked while observing Mariah's closed lips.

"The herd's leaving after roundup. I'm not going."

"What!" Gail couldn't believe her ears. "You've never missed a trail drive."

"I am this time."

"Why?"

"If it's any of your concern, Gail Ann, I've got other things to do. We've got a drought, remember?"

"Well, excuse me, Sour Puss." She eyed the other woman. "Do you know anything about Longhorns, Mariah?"

"Nothing. But I *am* familiar with Guernseys."

"Milch cows." Whit curled his lip. "Sissy cows."

"I beg your pardon," Mariah said hotly.

He speared a piece of meat. "You heard me."

Gail had had enough of his behavior. "I think you owe Mariah an apology!"

He downed another cup of coffee and continued to avert his eyes. "Tell you what, Gail Ann Strickland. I'm gonna put you in charge of heaven and music. When I want your goddamn opinion, I'll whistle."

"Kiss the south end of a north-bound horse, Whitman Reagor." She noticed Mariah was chewing her bottom lip to keep from laughing. Gail loved an audience. Her hangover ceased to bother her. Dramatically she brought her hand to her chest. "My, my. Hasn't the conversation deteriorated?"

"Actually," Mariah replied, "I'm enjoying it. And I'm in total agreement with you."

"Thank you. And pay no attention to Mr. Reagor. He really can be a bear at times. Let's hope his attitude improves, though, before we have to spend four whole days riding with him in his gaudy new covered wagon!"

She watched Mariah glance at Whit. Neither of them commented. Well, Gail thought, so much for that. She turned serious. "Mariah, are you packed for our journey?"

"All set. Whenever you and Mr. Reagor are ready, so am I."

The dark head that had been bent over his plate jerked upward. "You're still going?"

"I most certainly am. We made *plans*." Mariah added emphasis to her last word. "And I'm not one to break *plans*. Are *you* wanting to welsh on them?"

"Damn." Holding his arms over his chest, he glowered. "You've got it all *planned* out, don't you?"

Mariah lifted a shoulder while closing her mouth around a bite of egg.

His jaw was rock hard with anger. "Just remember what I said last night. I'm on to your tricks. And if you don't behave yourself, Joe will be the first to find out."

"My, my, Mr. Reagor. Are you a tale-carrier?"

"I, um, think I'll get packed," the third party to the argument announced, but no one was listening.

Leaving the dining room, Gail furrowed her brows. She knew Whit and his behavior. Nonchalant detachment was his usual treatment of his ladies. No woman raised his ire, much less got her hook in him—even Gail's mother had tried that. Now Mariah had him on a line, Gail was certain, and all she had to do was reel him in.

"I guess it's about time," she murmured, and decided to do her part in furthering the match.

Chapter Six

A half hour after the dining-room fiasco, the wagon pulled out of Dublin. Gail led the team, Mariah rode at her side, and Whit was astride Bay Fire. Mariah spent the rest of the day, plus the next two, wondering about her sanity. Why had she insisted on his escort? He alternately ignored or snapped at her, the knave.

The proper course would have been to follow her original plans—Lord, how she hated that word!—and continue on to Trick'em by stagecoach. Of course she had done no such thing. This was a matter of pride.

Though the memory of Whit Reagor's kiss was a force to be reckoned with, her anger boiled each time she remembered his accusations. Apparently he had thought she wouldn't fight for her good name. Ha! No one could tag " 'Fraidy Cat" behind her name, either. And no arrogant, conceited . . . handsome Texan could run her up a tree . . .

Which was where Fancy could be found this Wednesday morning. Covers pulled to her chin, Mariah lay on her pallet in the wagon, listening to Whit as he tried to coax his cheeky feline down from a tree adjacent to their campsite.

Naturally he'd brought the cat along, probably to annoy Mariah. And so it had! Fancy had been caged when the Conestoga had rolled, but Whit had insisted on her freedom while they were camped. The feline had made the most of those hours, keeping her fangs trained on Gus, and Mariah had spent a good bit of her time keeping feathers and fur apart.

Her female companion had been helpful in her quest. Initially Mariah had had her doubts about Gail, but she now considered her a friend. On the trail extending westward from Dublin, there had been plenty of opportunity for the two women to begin to understand each other, for Whit, opting to ride his sorrel stallion, had refused to join them in conversation.

"Well, Mariah, reckon we ought to help rescue Fancy?"

She turned to the yawning Gail, who, with sleep filming her dark-blue eyes, stretched her arms above her head.

Propping herself up on an elbow, Mariah frowned. "You can. As far as I'm concerned that cat can stay up a tree."

"My sentiments exactly."

"Damn you to hell." Whit's bellows filled the covered wagon even though he was yards away. "Stay up there. Stay up there all day. Do whatever you please, you wench you, but I'm not gonna stand here, hollering and begging you to get off your high horse." He shouted a further invective to the cat, then ordered: "Ladies, get your backsides outta that wagon, and get the fire started. I'm going after breakfast."

Neither woman moved a muscle beyond those utilized to curl their lips. Mariah heard the crackle of twigs and limbs as he stomped away from the campsite. She cupped a hand to the side of her lips, and said in a tone barely above a whisper, "Doesn't he know the first thing about females? Hollering ne'er won the fair kitty. Nor do orders a friendship make."

Giving Whit a half minute to get out of earshot, Gail spoke. "He knows. There's no excuse for the way he's been acting the last couple of days. But he certainly has it in him to be cordial. Really, he does."

"You can't prove that by me."

"You're under his skin, that's why he's short-tempered."

Mariah threw back the covers and got to her feet. The wagon swayed. Gus squawked. She gathered her clothes.

"He's under your skin, too," Gail stated, sitting up.

"No, he isn't."

She lifted Mariah's petticoat a half inch.

"Then why are you putting this on inside out?"

The interrogated's shoulders wilted. "I hate him."

"No, you don't."

Mariah shot back, "I do."

"No, you don't."

"Yes, I do."

"Lord," the younger woman said, glancing up and back again, "we sound like a couple of six-year-olds."

"I agree." Sitting down on top of a wooden crate, Mariah laced her fingers and squeezed them tight. "I don't hate him. I don't like him, but I don't hate him."

A knowing expression crossed the brunette's features. "I know it's been rough, his temper and all, but I'll bet you've found a few things to like about Whit."

Perhaps if she weren't furious with his behavior since the night of Kimble's wedding, Mariah might have remembered a few charming qualities. As it was, she couldn't recall anything remotely nice about him. "Nothing."

"Try harder."

"You really can be a pain at times."

Gail pursed her lips. "That's why you think I'm wonderful."

"Probably. Okay, yes. I like you for yourself. Vinegar and sugar," Mariah said, an odd feeling assailing her as she repeated Whit's analogy of the previous Saturday. It was as if there were a bond between herself and Whit. Well, Gail *was* their mutual interest.

"Since you've mentioned those wonderful particulars about yours truly, humor me," her companion cajoled. "Tell me three things you admire about Whit."

Mariah turned away, but her defenses weakened and several pleasant points came to mind. She felt dainty against his height. His dark good looks affected her in a way she didn't care to be affected. His arms were strong, and before he'd become insulting, she had enjoyed his kiss. And his kindness . . . Kindness! What made her think that?

Being honest with herself, Mariah realized her self-appointed guardian angel did possess a streak of kindness. How many men would have gone to this much trouble for a neighbor's fiancée? Very few. And Whit *could* be charming, ever so charming. Plus, he had the love and respect of two good women—Lois and Gail. He wasn't all bad.

It was prudent, nonetheless, not to put words to those thoughts. Gail would get the wrong impression.

"He's light on his feet while dancing," Mariah replied, not as coolly as she intended, "and he chews with his mouth closed."

"A real swain, hmm?"

"Not hardly." She wrinkled her nose when Gail reminded her to name a third. "He's got a lot of stamina" was Mariah's response.

Gail winked a sapphire eye. "That's what I've

heard."

"Pardon? What do you mean?"

"Stamina in bed."

Mariah flushed. "I meant he never seems to tire."

"Sorry. I forgot you're a maiden."

Only in name. Peering shyly at her married friend, Mariah had a wealth of unanswered questions. Back home, she'd never found the gumption to ask a contemporary about intimacy, what with the other girls' prim behavior. This, however, was a different time, a different place, and she needed to understand what had happened between herself and Joseph.

"Have you . . . Do you en-enjoy . . ." This was hard to put into words! "Do you l-like being married?"

"I think you're asking me if the sex is good."

Mariah's face went hot; her cheeks flamed. "Yes."

"I love it. Can never get enough. Unfortunately, the only time Ed and I aren't at each other's throats is in bed."

"Why don't you get along?" Mariah asked, her own problems pushed aside.

"It's a problem that's gone back a long time." Gail covered her eyes with a forearm. "A few skeletons rattling in the family closet, you see. Please don't ask me to explain, because I won't! Anyway, I expect Ed to show a little sympathy, and he doesn't. Nor does he have any patience with my, quote, attitude, so he's not above withholding his 'favors'. He knows that's the best way to aggravate me."

"Perhaps you should work on your attitude."

"I've tried, but . . . well, it's a complicated situation. Ed doesn't respond to my efforts. He's not perfect, either, I want you to know. Far from it. All he seems to care about is his damned cattle." Gail took her arm from her eyes. "But I'm handling it in the only way I know how. I've got a whiskey jug to toast my toes."

If there was one thing troubling Mariah about her newfound friend, it was Gail's drinking. She drank in the evening, when she thought her companions weren't watching, and this indicated real trouble. Mariah had suspected a man was at the bottom of it.

"Do you think spirits might be part of the problem?" Mariah asked hesitantly.

"One part." Shrugging, Gail went on. "But I'll be fine, once I have kids to keep me occupied. 'Course, at the rate I'm going, I may never have younguns. Well, anyway, I hope you don't ever know how it feels to be rejected."

"There's not much chance of that." Shamed at her arrogant-sounding statement, Mariah pulled a copper-hued dress over her head. "I mean, I don't long for the marriage bed."

"How do you know if you haven't tried it?"

"Believe me, I do not long for the marriage bed!"

"Sounds as if you *have* tried it." Gail's face

displayed an uncanny awareness, her former doldrums gone. "I don't think you love Joseph Jaye. You haven't mentioned his name, not even once, on this trip."

Mariah grabbed a hairbrush and began to yank it through her tangled hair. "You're entirely too observant."

"Are you doing the right thing, marrying Mr. Jaye?"

The tip of her tongue held a lie, but Mariah clamped her teeth around it. Suddenly she felt compelled to confess her soul. "I'm not going to marry him."

Gail beamed. "That'll leave the field open for Whit!"

"Please get it out of your head I've set my sights on that man."

"I won't. I think you're just right for each other. He needs someone who'll keep him on his toes, and what woman wouldn't want an attractive man who chewed with his mouth closed? Especially when he's wealthy and generous. Did you know he gave me and Ed our ranch?"

"How nice for you. But, Gail, I'm through chatting about the god of good deeds. You told me you're having personal problems, and I'm concerned about you," she said. "I'd like to make a suggestion. When you get home, why don't you put away the whiskey jug? Make your husband sit down and listen to you. Make the biggest effort of your life to work through your problems."

"I've tried all that."

"Give it one more try."

"Rowww!" Fancy hissed, interrupting the conversation as she jumped into the wagon. Tail as straight as a dorsal fin, she licked her chops and pranced over to Gus's cage. Eyes dilating, she batted her paw at the hasp.

"Don't you dare!" Mariah grabbed the gray scruff, and the cat went on the defensive. "Ouch!" Pain stabbed through her forearm as she banished the predator outdoors.

Gail sat stock-still. A few seconds later, she raised her eyes. "Listen."

"To what?"

"Listen. Cattle!"

Whit heard hooves, thousands of hooves, probably no more than a quarter mile away and to the south, but moving west . . . no doubt to the Western Trail. His line of sight turning in that direction, he spied a cloud of dust above the trees. He smiled. A moving herd was manna to a cattleman.

And here he was, crouching on his heels beside the drying-up Pecan Bayou, cleaning a slimy crappie for breakfast. Aggravation gnawed at his gut. He set the fish and his Bowie knife aside, and wiped his hands on a bandanna. His place was with the Crosswind herd.

Whit's ears detected a faint "Hee-yah," probably from the cowpunch riding drag, and he exhaled. It didn't seem right, him not keeping an eye on his fortune or not being with the Crosswind Cattle Company's men when they and their lifeblood headed into Dodge. He had made the trip seventeen times, each spring since losing Wildwood Plantation to the carpetbaggers. He was acquainted with every turn, every stream, every Indian, along the way to Kansas.

And he knew, really knew, a lot of the women between Trick'em and there. Women! Thankfully, he was free of Barbara, but he'd gotten rid of one problem to take on another. Mariah McGuire. He had made up his mind to ignore the opposite sex for the next few days, thanks to her, and he was proud of himself.

Grimacing and eyeing the cerulean sky, he turned his thoughts back to business. Another damned beautiful day, he thought facetiously.

The ground was so dry he could smell it. The air snapped with static electricity. The sun baked down. Despite the occasional blue norther, March wasn't overly cold in Texas, not like the chill he had felt while fighting for the Confederate cause in Louisiana, but Whit couldn't remember a spring this hot in west central Texas. Or this dry. He hated being a prisoner to forces beyond his control.

Twenty minutes later, Whit approached the clearing that separated him from the wagon. Raising his gaze from the ground, he rounded a wide pecan tree . . . And his heart jumped into his throat. Fifty feet in the distance, a huge Longhorn bull was cutting a jagged track back and forth *in front of Mariah!*

Like a statue with its fists clenched at the sides, she stood at the clearing's edge, a good distance in front of the wagon.

Whit eyed the dunnish brown, white, and rust-colored bull, assessing the wide length of horns, the bulging shoulder muscles, the massive back thews. At least a ton of power, thirsting for blood!

Anger at Mariah forgotten, Whit dropped the crappie and started to run forward to take aim with his rifle, but reason replaced instinct. The trajectory on his brand-new rifle—bought in Dublin for this trip—wasn't up to par, and he couldn't chance a missed shot. Furthermore, if he made his presence known, she might make a quick move, which would provoke the bull to charge her.

At that moment the enraged animal threw back his head, bellowing forth a potent warning, "uh-uh-uh-uh." Whit didn't stop to wonder what an uncastrated bull was doing with a herd of steers, or how it got away from the drovers. Nor did he ruminate over why Mariah was in the clearing, or about Gail's whereabouts. He took action.

Quiet as an Indian, Whit stole around the clearing's perimeter, shucking his shirt and pushing the collar into the waistband of his breeches, and made for the distressed woman. Soon he was behind Mariah, though partially hidden by a low-growing oak branch.

The Longhorn stopped his pacing to paw and gore the earth, sending up a cloud of dust. His tongue lolled out of his slobbering mouth.

"Mariah," Whit called in a monotone, hoping she could hear him, "don't move."

Her shoulders stiffened, but she didn't budge.

He exhaled with relief. "Listen to me. Stay calm. I'm going to move away from you, and get his attention. When the bull turns toward me, you back away. Slowly. As soon as you clear the tree behind us, turn and run for the wagon. Understand?"

Mechanically, her head ratcheted, left and right.

"Don't argue with me," he ordered.

His eyes pinned on the animal, Whit cut twenty feet to the side, to the safety of a low-growing, sturdy live oak branch, which he intended to climb in case his shot missed the bull. He started away from the tree's cover.

"Hey, boy! Lookie here!" Winchester under one arm, he waved his shirt, making taunting passes back and forth a few steps in front of the tree. "Come get me, ole boy!"

Dropping the shirt, he raised the gun and took aim. His trigger finger in place, his right thumb cocked the hammer. "Come on, *toro!*"

The bull froze for a moment, then hoisted his front haunches in Whit's direction.

"Go, Mariah! Go now!"

She didn't budge.

His mighty head raised, the bull emitted a succession of excited bellowing cries, alternately sinking into hoarse grunts, then rising to a primitive scream. A huge hoof pawed the ground. The Longhorn jerked and twisted his head, lowering his horns to drop one pointed weapon down for a side entrance. Belying his size, he leaped toward Whit.

"Get gone, Mariah!" Whit shouted as the animal advanced on him. With the rifle's trajectory off, he had to wait until he could feel the heat of fury before firing his one shot. "Go, dammit!"

For the first time, Mariah moved. She whipped the pistol from her skirt pocket. Steadying her right hand with the fingers of her left, she aimed and fired.

Gunfire rent the air, then another, one of the bullets taking its intended mark on the bull, not five feet in front of Whit. One far-carrying bawl shattered the sudden quiet. The animal teetered for an instant caught in time. Bloodshot eyes popped before gushing blood covered its head.

A harsh boom sounded as the mammoth bull plummeted to the ground. His death knell was hoarse and deep, akin to thunder on the prairie.

Mariah squeezed her burning eyes shut. Strong arms wound around her shoulders, pulling her against a wall of hairy, sweat-drenched muscle. A wide hand splayed at her nape, and tender lips touched her forehead.

"Now, now," Whit whispered, "everything's okay."

Her nails dug into his upper arms, and she drank in the comfort of his presence. "I know. But I was scared."

"Believe me, I was scared, too. Scared I couldn't get to ole Toro in time. That was a lotta beef steak after your pretty little hide."

Mariah tensed. The big man thought he had saved the helpless little woman, and he was crowing about it! She was touchy about these things. Her father had belittled her capabilities, calling her a "typical female". But her shooting abilities had impressed him. Something deep within her wouldn't allow Whit Reagor, or anyone else, to malign her marksmanship.

She drew back, lifting her narrowed eyes. "I wasn't scared for myself. I've been around cattle all my life, and I knew to stay still until something else got his attention." She stepped back and parked a fist on her hip. "For heaven's sake, I was scared the bull would gore you."

Whit's expression turned from protective to pleased. "You were thinking of me? Ah, Red, you're a wonderful gal."

Before the compliment sank in, she demanded, "If you were so concerned about saving my 'pretty little hide', what took you so long to fire a shot?"

Whit dropped his arms and stepped back. His eyes turned to the blue steel of a rapier's edge.

"Beg to pardon, ma'am. I didn't want to take a chance of missing."

"Well, you can thank me for taking a chance. I hit him first."

"That's doubtful. You were a good twenty feet away."

"What makes you think I can't hit a moving target at twenty measly feet?" she asked, the corner of her eye spying Gail bent over the carcass.

"What makes you think you can?"

"In case you've forgotten, I told you the day we met that I know how to handle firearms. Furthermore, Mr. Whit Reagor, I am an excellent shot."

"And you're saying I'm not?"

"For all I know"—she flipped a hand in the air—"you couldn't hit the side of a barn."

His lips curled back over his incredibly white teeth, but Gail spoke up. "Mariah, you killed him."

She smiled triumphantly as Whit strode to the bull.

"What do you mean, she killed him?" he asked.

Gail dodged the pool of blood as she slid a forefinger across a nick in the horn's hole. "You got his horn, Whit. Wow, Mariah, you're a great shot. You got him square between the ear and the eye."

"I beg to differ." Whit rubbed his boot heel across the bull's temple to uncover the wound.

"He turned his head just the moment I shot him, undoubtedly from the shock of Mariah's bullet hitting his horn."

"Not possible," Mariah protested after walking up to the others. Why didn't Whit put his shirt on? She assembled her wits and, remembering her annoyance, ignored his masculine appeal. "Look at the hole in his horn. His head would've had to turn to the left, turn my way, in order for my bullet to hit at that angle."

Whit didn't utter a word. Dammit, she was right. He had known it, probably from the moment the bull had fallen. His male pride hadn't wanted him to believe he had been bested, though.

He retreated, but not before placing a gold piece on the bull's rump to placate the drovers who were sure to look for the stray. Stepping over the rifle he'd dropped when flying to Mariah, Whit stomped away. "I'm not going to argue with the two of you," he threw over his shoulder. "We need to get going. The whole herd will be here before long. They can smell water a mile away, which no doubt is why that poor bastard was headed this way. Thirst got him killed."

He stopped in his tracks, swinging around. "Why, Miss Crack Shot McGuire, were you in the clearing when any thinking woman would've stayed in the wagon?"

"I was trying to save your cat from certain death!"

"And you think Fancy doesn't have enough sense to climb a tree to get away from danger?"

He had a point, but no admission was going to pass Mariah's lips. She flounced over to face Whit. "I don't know Fancy's capabilities, but I can tell you one thing. This whole situation could've been avoided if you'd caged her!"

"Cat hater."

"I love cats. Nice cats that curl in my lap when they aren't earning their keep by catching mice. Fancy fits neither bill. Your cat is not nice!"

"Maybe she's a good judge of character. Who'd want to curl in a shrew's lap?" His upper lip quivered. "And—who knows?—maybe she prefers . . . parrots!"

"Oh, my God!" Mariah ran toward the wagon. "Gus!"

Chapter Seven

Whit was now contrite for participating in a ridiculous argument. Ready not only to admit Mariah's shot had felled the bull but also to apologize for his remarks, he hot-footed toward her swaying derriere. "Mariah!" he called, but she continued toward the wagon.

She couldn't have been more than ten feet from her destination, Whit about five from his, when a series of sounds emitted from the Conestoga's interior. Bass squawks. High-pitched yowls. Damn! Fancy had hold of Gus.

"No-o-o-o!" Mariah screamed, jumping up and diving inside the covered wagon. "Let go of him!"

Whit leaped in. In the center of the narrow aisle, Mariah had Fancy by the scruff; Fancy had Gus by the neck. Green feathers and gray cat hair were flying. Whit took a giant step in the narrow confines, going for the feline's mouth. Prying it open, he pulled the parrot free.

In midair the fat tabby, a feather dangling from her mouth, her claws unsheathed, flipped sideways and raked a paw across Mariah's face, drawing a pain-filled cry. Blood rose from the wound and Mariah's palm went to her cheek.

Wings flapped against Whit's arm. He placed Gus gently in his cage and fastened the hasp that the cat had pawed open. None too gently he then grabbed a hissing Fancy, thrust her hackled body into her wooden box, and secured the clasp.

Wiping a feather from his chin, Whit said, "I was wrong. Your shot got the bull."

Mariah's tear-glistening eyes focused on a spot to his right before she turned her back and bent down to push her finger through the birdcage. Stroking the distressed parrot, who appeared to be in one piece except for a slew of missing feathers, she cooed, "Poor Gussie, are you all right? Don't worry. I'll make certain you're protected." She took a small wafer from a nearby tin and offered the treat. "Biscuit?"

" 'Scuit, 'scuit?" The bird turned his head to the side, one round brown eye surveying the wafer. A ragged wing flapped before his three-toed claws edged to the far side of his perch.

"Everything will be okay." Once more Mariah guided the morsel to a spot beneath his beak. "Gussie want a biscuit?"

Gus blinked twice, pulled himself up as if he were the proudest of fowl, and responded to her tender loving care by devouring the palliative and trilling a two-note song.

"Looks like he's all right," Whit commented, and edged between Mariah and a wooden crate to seat himself. Lifting her chin with the crook of a finger, he asked, "Will you listen to me? We need to talk."

"I don't see the point."

"I do. I want to apologize for being hard-headed about that bull . . . and for making those remarks about you."

"We were both being a bit stubborn, I suppose." She glanced at the bald-spotted Gus.

"Believe me," he said, "I didn't want anything to happen to your parrot."

"I never thought you did, not really . . . Whit, I realize this is your wagon, but it would make the trip more pleasant for all of us if you would keep Fancy caged."

"All right. Except for her necessary times."

"Thank you." She handed her pet another wafer. "And he thanks you, too."

Curiosity got to Whit. "You're sure attached to ole Gus there. Any particular reason?"

"He was a gift from my brother," she answered hesitantly, and wiped her scratched face with the back of her hand. "Dirk's a sailor. He brought Gus from South America."

"So when you're around the parrot"—Whit stood, and took a clean handkerchief from his pocket—"you feel you have a small part of your brother?"

She nodded at his wisdom, and Whit wiped the blood from her cheek. "I guess it's hard, leaving your family in a faraway place."

"Life's challenges don't frighten me."

"Brave lady." For some odd reason he couldn't remove his hand from the smooth skin of her jaw, nor could he stop his little finger from sliding beneath her earlobe. He heard her sudden intake of breath, and saw her dark eyes widen. Whit's heart hammered against his chest. *Back off, Reagor.*

"We'd . . . uh . . . better hit the trail," he said, yanking his hand to his side and doing an about-face to alight the wagon.

Ten minutes later they were headed westward again. For two hours they traveled, bypassing the herd from which the bull had strayed. Neither of the women spoke a word in all that time.

Finally Gail broke the silence. "I hope you noticed I kept my distance when you and Whit went after Gus and Fancy. I take it, though, you two didn't get anything worked out."

"He did admit my shot was the fatal one."

Gail nearly dropped the reins. "He did?"

"You seem astounded."

"I am. Whit isn't one to apologize."

"But he has," Mariah said. "More than once."

"Well, I'll be dipped in bat guano." The heart-faced Gail tilted her bonneted head.

"Since you're not going to marry Mr. Jaye, why don't you set your cap for Whit?"

Not really seeing, Mariah studied the scruffy low hills, the parched terrain they were rolling past. "Don't start that again."

The wagon lurched to the side as a wheel hit one of the many ruts, but neither Mariah's request nor the jolt hindered Gail from pursuing the topic dear to her heart. "You can't keep your eyes off him, and he has to sit on his hands to keep 'em off you. If you'd give each other a chance, I'd bet money, marbles, or salt that you'd find a lot of things to cherish in each other. For a long time."

Mariah wasn't ready to acknowledge her fascination with Whit, but she had, days before, realized the emotions he roused in her. Nonetheless, she was free for the first time in her life to do as she pleased—or would be as soon as she disentangled herself from Joseph. Why would she want to muddy up the future with another romantic involvement?

"I don't mean to sound cruel," she said, confused by her own emotions as well as by Gail's ardent campaign, "but I find it strange, your promoting a match between me and Whit. With your own words you've said your marriage isn't happy. It seems to me you'd be reluctant where romance is concerned."

"I'm not soured on men. I'm sure my problems with Ed are my fault. Furthermore, I want to see Whit happy."

"If you feel so strongly about him, why didn't you set your own sights on him? Before you married, of course."

"Me and Whit? Goodness, no." The young woman blushed. "He's family!"

"Cousins have been known to wed."

"I assure you my love for Whit is entirely platonic." Whit's champion finished her matchmaking a few minutes later with, ". . . and he's quite well fixed, too. His ranch is the biggest one in west central Texas, and his home is the most luxurious I've ever seen."

"How nice for him. But I think you're prejudiced where Whit is concerned. He's not the gallant you believe him to be. He accused me of being after him, Gail. So he did a quick retreat."

"He doesn't scare easily. He may have backed off, but you're not out of his mind. And he's not out of yours." A finger pointed at Mariah. "Now patch up your differences."

"Why start something just to end it?"

"All romances start at the beginning."

"Truth be known, Gail, he doesn't fit into my plans." Mariah studied the sky. "I can't live in Trick'em. Not with Joseph there."

"Hogwash. All's fair in love and war . . . So says the Bard. Mr. Jaye will recover."

Shaking her head with vehemence, Mariah crossed her arms. "I wouldn't do that to Joseph. I don't love him, but *do* respect him and his feelings."

"Give the girl a crown of thorns."

"I'm not a martyr!"

"Okay, Mariah, what are you, then?"

"Confused. Unsettled. Scared."

"I think I understand. You've come a helluva long way just to break an engagement." Gail looked down at the reins in her hands. "Will you sail back to Guernsey?"

"No. There's nothing for me there."

"No family?" Gail asked.

"Only a father who hates me." Mariah recalled the night she found out why. His tongue loosened by apple brandy after an evening of dancing and merrymaking, he had pounded on his wife's locked bedchamber door, his shouts filling the loft where his only daughter had been sleeping. At ten, she had been too young to understand the meaning of his anger, but now she understood his words.

"My mother never slept with him after I was born," she explained quietly. "She refused to bear more children and he blames me for it. He made my life miserable."

"I can see why you don't want to go back."

"Exactly. That's why I must make a new start, and find a teaching position." Mariah paused. "Somewhere."

"Teaching will take care of your days," the brunette said. "But what about your nights?"

"I'll sleep."

Gail's face pulled into a mask of disgust. "You'll moulder away to a shriveled old schoolteacher who raps younguns' knuckles because she's sour at the world for not taking opportunities when they came along. Do those poor children a favor, give yourself a chance."

The discourse on what her future might hold took Mariah aback. Would she become old and bitter and alone? Though her dreams for a career had been paramount in her plannings, she also yearned for a home and children.

"Since you haven't answered me, I take it you're weakening," Gail said. "Listen, I've got something brewing in my ole noggin. My older brother and his family live a few miles from here. I'm overdue for a visit. Sharon's with child, you see, and Raymond left with his herd for Dodge last month. I'm going to tell Whit to leave me at their ranch. You two need some time alone."

Mariah considered her offer. "You, my dear Gail, are a real friend."

Whit knew it was a mistake leaving Gail behind at the Chapman Ranch this afternoon, but he hadn't voiced an objection. Right now, as the sun began to sink over the horizon and as the land grew progressively more desolate, he wished he had protested.

Mariah was driving him insane.

He had little control over his wits, with her sitting close to him as he led the team of grays along the rutted trail to Trick'em. She hadn't been invited to ride shotgun. Gus, whose cage was shoved behind her feet to protect him from the now caged Fancy, had been the excuse she'd used to park her delectable rear next to Whit—so near he could feel the warmth of her body, could smell the rose perfume that drove him wild, could hear the sweet tones of her soprano as she sang a French melody. It was all her fault, his tangled temper . . . his taut nerves . . . his obsession.

Would he make it to Trick'em without losing all control? Get a grip on your reins! He told himself.

The left front wheel hit a rut, throwing her against his shoulder. Instantly he took both reins in one hand and steadied her with the other.

"Thank you," she murmured.

As he'd done since they had left Gail with Sharon Chapman, Whit didn't look at Mariah. Through clouds of dust, they had traveled miles and miles without a word passing his thinned lips.

"You're welcome, Mariah," she said, obviously mocking his inattention.

He clicked his tongue, snapped the reins, and relented. "You're welcome, Mariah."

Taking a sidelong look her way, he sucked in his breath. Her chocolate-brown eyes were troubled, and when she caught his stare, she averted those big beautiful mirrors of unhappiness. Making certain the wagon was still on course, he prolonged studying her profile. Freckles had popped out on her blistered and scratched cheek.

When she brought her hand to her face, he eyed the little felt hat she wore. "Haven't you got a bonnet to wear?"

"It's packed."

"You'd better fetch it. Your skin . . . well, that hat you're wearing was made for beauty, not practicality. The Texas sun's brutal, you know."

"My bonnet case is surrounded by boxes."

"Now that you mention it, what is in all those boxes and crates?" Whit voiced the question that had come to mind on several occasions. "They're mighty heavy for a trousseau."

Her thumbs sliding beneath her chin, she steepled her fingers across her nose. "Household goods. School supplies. But for the most part, they're packed with seeds. Guernsey seeds are nonpareil, you see, and Joseph requested them for the vegetable garden."

Pity came over Whit, and he couldn't help think that when she married the farmer, it wouldn't be long before her sensitive skin would be blackened by the sun. How long would it take for work to melt the softness from her curves, drawing her into gauntness? Such a shame. A woman of her beauty ought to have a man to provide, and provide well, for her. A man who would clothe her in silks and velvets and soft satins, and protect her from the rough frontier.

Joseph could offer no such luxuries. *But you could, Reagor.* His home was a haven from the wilds of west central Texas, and money was no problem. Whit warned himself against his thoughts of setting up Joe's woman.

He had to get away from her, and quick. "There's a creek over there." He steered the heavily weighted wagon to the right. "Night's on its way. Might as well make camp."

She smiled. "Wonderful!"

The minute he brought the team to a halt, she grabbed the wicker cage and jumped down. "Oh, it's lovely to have our feet on the ground, isn't it?"

She made for the gurgling stream and bent over the water's edge. Untying Bay Fire from the wagon's rear and unharnessing the horses to allow them to crop the meager grass, Whit watched as she bathed her face, then opened the cage to offer a palmful of water to that blasted parrot. Exasperated, Whit wished she'd offer him a sip of water.

He grimaced and set to finishing the chores. If he could just get through this night . . . Come hell or high water, they were going to make Joe's farm tomorrow. Then *he* could deal with her twitching behind and bewitching presence.

If Whit could make it through the night.

But that was not to be. When she returned from the stream, he saw how raw her face was from the blisters. Finding an aloe vera plant, he sliced one of the spicate leaves lengthwise and brushed the medicinal juice on her reddened face. His hand shook and he took his leave. Fast. Using his Colt, he bagged dinner. She prepared the rabbit, plus a salad of wild greens and a pot of delicious coffee. In addition to her intriguing physical attributes, Mariah was a helluva good cook.

Darkness fell. He tried to bank his fires with a plunge in the cold stream. Beside the campfire, he crouched back on his heels, and she sat on the ground, hugging her knees and staring into the orange glow. Theirs was an uneasy silence.

"Any coffee left?" she asked.

"Yeah." He reached for the pot to refill her cup. Their fingers brushed as he handed it over. A jolt shot up his arm, passed by his heart, and landed in his groin. He jerked away.

"No matter what you think of me, you don't have to treat me as if I'm belladonna." Hurt was in her voice. "You were wrong the other night. I never set out to entice you."

"You did a pretty damned good job of it though."

Her eyes leveled with his. "So did you."

Nipping the end off a cigar, he struck an acrid-smelling sulphur match to the tip. The cigar glowed orange as he ruminated over the situation. A puff of smoke rose in front of his face as he rested an elbow on his knee. "Before

I knew who you were, I decided to go after you."

"Then your conscience took over?"

"Right." He pitched the cigar into the fire. "I don't believe in stealing another man's woman." His gaze settling on Mariah, he said, "You're Joe's fiancée."

Truth was on the tip of her tongue, but before she could utter a word, Whit said, "You're more than his intended. You're a two-man woman, and that gets me in the craw."

"Dash it, I don't know where you get your ideas!" She wanted to continue of her tirade, but on second thought, she cooled her temper. It did appear she was playing Joseph false. Beyond that, his were the words of a jaded man hurt by love. She yearned to know about the woman in his past. "Who made you lose your faith in women?"

"My dead wife." He drained his tin coffee cup, and with measured words Whit told her about the ending of his marriage. "Now you know why I don't trust unfaithful women."

Astounded at his admission, and her heart going out to his suffering, she said, "I'm not like Jenny."

"Think Joe would agree?"

Mariah stretched her legs before drawing them to her chin once more. "Probably not."

"I respect your honesty."

"Thank you for that." Her voice was devoid of self-pity. "I was beginning to think you couldn't find anything to respect about me."

Whit stared at her. Rising to his feet, he rounded the campfire and squatted down beside her. He wrapped his fingers around her cold hand. "I admire a lot of things about you. You're a fine shot; kept me from getting killed this morning. You're a good cook, and a fine hand to have along on a campout." On a lighter note, he added, "Except when it comes to Fancy, you've got a tender heart."

Her free hand playfully thumped his rock-hard shoulder. "Leave that cat out of this," she warned, grinning.

"Fine with me. As I was saying, it takes guts to leave your home and family to follow a man to the wilds of Texas. Who wouldn't admire your spirit?"

When she glanced away, as if uncomfortable with his statement, Whit went on. "I understand why Joe loves you. I . . . I . . . oh, God!"

Suddenly he was holding her. Burying his face in her hair, he groaned. "Too bad we had to meet. Too bad for all of us. You, me, Joe. Oh, Mariah, beautiful lady, the temptations . . . temptations that can only bring heartbreak to your man."

These words, a mirror into Whit's soul, brought Mariah to her senses. Though it was unfair to Joseph, she needed to tell him about her decision, but first she must be honest about herself.

Pulling free from his warmth, she began the

truth. "The other night when you kissed me, I wanted that kiss. And I've thought of it since. You are a temptation the likes of which I never dreamed possible. I don't know what's wrong with me. My mother taught me to be a lady, but I seem to be a prisoner of my . . . of my . . ."

"Needs of the body," he finished for her.

"Yes."

"Marriage ought to fix that."

She picked up a twig to break it in two. Aligning her gaze with his, she admitted, "Marriage won't fix what's wrong with me. I don't want the marriage bed."

He drew back. "Why not?"

"I . . . I d-don't like it."

"Maybe you didn't pick the right partners."

"Partners! There haven't been *partners.*"

Was she telling the truth? Somehow Whit believed her. "Okay. Partner."

Whit tensed, thinking of Joe. Had he been gentle with her? Whatever the Englishman had done, it hadn't satisfied her needs. Beyond that, why had he lied about her past? "You've never been with anyone but Joe?"

"Never. What makes you think I have?"

"Ah . . . um . . . he mentioned someone else."

"How dare he gossip and imply that I—!"

"Great Scott, Mariah, I probably made too much of it."

"Maybe." With the remaining piece of twig

she drew small circles in the dirt. "There was a man in my life. I loved Lawrence Rogers with all my heart, you see. We were engaged to be married, but he d-died."

Near tears at those remembrances, she could speak no more of dear Lawrence—of anything! "Excuse me," she said. "I'm going to turn in." She jumped to her feet, took a lantern, and stepped toward the wagon. "Good night."

"Good night," Whit echoed, issuing no protest and allowing her to cut the evening short. Her admissions had been difficult, and she needed time to collect herself. Whit realized Mariah had turned to Joe in grief, and he understood the pain of loss.

He unrolled his bedding, drew off his boots, and stretched out, using his saddle for a pillow. Her silhouette against the wagon's canvas cover drew his attention. He prayed she wouldn't undress within his sight, for how much tantalization could he endure? Her vulnerability made her no less desirable.

She didn't doff her clothes in the wagon. He watched her alight from the Conestoga and disappear into the darkness. Her ablutions, he figured. Closing his eyes, he tried to sleep. Impossible. He craved what the scrawny Englishman had had a taste of.

"Damn you, Joe." Whit yanked his Indian blanket over his legs to ward off the night's biting air.

Ever since he had discovered Mariah's identity, he'd been eaten up with doing right by the erstwhile viscount. Why should he feel honor-bound to a liar? What kind of man gave the impression his intended had known more than one man?

A sidewinder undeserving of either loyalty or a beautiful intriguing woman like Mariah, that was who.

Should he go after her? Some measure of sanity warned him against such a move. Your justifications don't mean a damn, Reagor, he told himself. She's still Joe's woman.

His ears trained on the night sounds, he listened to crickets, cicadas, a wolf's bayings. Where was she? A panther screamed its woman-like cry. Or *was* it a panther?

"Mariah?" he called, uneasy. No answer. Damn, he shouldn't have let her go out by herself! Whit jackknifed to his feet. "Mariah!"

Twenty feet away, she stepped from behind a wide pecan tree, a hairbrush in her hand. The moon lit her in beautiful relief. "No need to shout. I'm right here."

"Don't scare me like that." He forced those words past his frozen throat. "Didn't you hear that panther?"

She glided toward him, but halted. A wool shawl around her shoulders, she wore a white flannel nightgown that was buttoned up to her chin. The scantest of women's undergarments had never aroused Whit the way this sturdy nightgown did now.

Whit took ten steps toward her. Five feet separated them. He swallowed hard. The full moon behind her, she tilted her head to one side and brushed her hair. Long hair. Red. Thick and flowing. Beautiful hair that invited his fingers. He yearned to take the hairbrush from her hand and pull it gently through those dark-russet tresses. He ached to wrap a curl around his finger and bring it to his lips.

"To hell with right and wrong," he whispered. "Let me show you how good it can be between a man and a woman." Whit offered his hand. His voice was hoarse with desire as he murmured, "Mariah, come here. Let me be your man."

Chapter Eight

"Come here," Whit repeated above the surrounding night sounds. In the light of the full moon, he held his arms out to Mariah. "Let me hold you."

Her pulse quickened, yet she didn't comply. Her heart filled with doubt, she glanced at his tousled curly hair, then lowered her gaze to the dark tufts of hair on his chest revealed by the unsnapped shirt, which was pulled free of his close-fitting dungarees. Sensuality emanated from him.

They would make love. It was inevitable, she realized. Since their first meeting she had refused to admit the force majeure of it, but no more.

Would lovemaking be different with Whit, different from Joseph's fumblings?

"You don't have to be frightened, sweetheart," Whit said huskily. "I just want to show you how good it can be."

"I might not think it's good."

"Don't bet on that." Whit rubbed his chin. "But if you don't want me, say the word and I'll back off."

"No. Please don't." She shortened the gap between them, but her muscles were stiff with uncertainty.

"Relax, sweetheart." He combed his fingers through her hair. "Let yourself go with the feeling."

How was she supposed to do that? With Joseph she'd been asleep. With Whit she knew there would be no sleeping.

"Go with your instincts, sweet baby."

She did. He drew her close, the heat of his body blanking out the chill brought by evening, bringing ease. Now pliant, she murmured his name. Her arms lifted to his shoulders. Leather and tobacco and wood smoke mingled with the warm clean scent of him. Lowering and tilting his head, he covered her lips with a kiss of fire and tenderness.

Feeling the tip of his coffee-tinged tongue touching her teeth, sliding into the interior, she was surprised, and delighted, by this new experience. She welcomed his deepening kiss. Her fingers slipped through the curls at the back of his head; his hair was soft, though coarse, and the feel of it tingled the nerve endings in her fingers. His lips moved to her neck, his hands to the curve of her waist, and he caressed her midriff with his thumbs. The tender ministrations aroused her senses. Overwhelmed by the sensations coursing through her body, she gave up her dread.

"Put your arms around my neck," he requested, then swept her from the ground to carry her to his bedroll and there to lay her across the thick cushion.

Her arms reached for him as he stripped his shirt from his sinewed torso. "It's cold without you," she whispered.

"We can't let that happen."

He descended to their lair, bringing her gowned body against the warmth of his flesh. Anew he kissed her, his big hands caressing her cheekbones and earlobes. Instinctively she thrust her pelvis against his, receiving an answering movement in kind, and felt the hard bulge in his britches. She was aflame.

With fluid grace he removed the barrier to his manhood by sweeping the denim trousers from his long, long legs. Fascinated, she stared at his naked splendor.

"You're more magnificent than I remembered," she admitted, yet a fleeting moment of uncertainty wrought from innocence plagued her. "But must you take your clothes off?"

He smiled. "It's better this way, darlin'." Levering above her, he touched the hair that enticed him so, spreading those locks across the rust-colored Indian blanket. "Am I going too fast for you, my sweet?"

"Yes, but maybe not. I . . . I don't know, really."

"Hey, now. You're not an innocent," he replied, his thumb and forefinger working the buttons of her nightgown. "Don't be shy." His callused palm slid over a firm, rounded breast. "Tell me when it feels good."

"Th-that feels good," she murmured as he tweaked her nipple.

Brushing the nightgown bodice to the side, he placed his lips where his fingers had been. "I could do this for hours," he murmured, drawing her nipple into his mouth.

Trembling at his magic, she held him to her breast. And when his palm traveled along the inside of her thigh, she was caught in a wondrous vortex, swirling and spinning. Her legs refused to be still, those movements causing her nightgown to ride up her thighs. Her hands wandered over the taut muscles of his back. Scars and all, he was male perfection.

Whit's talented fingers and lips found other sensitive places—the inside of her elbows and wrists, the hollow of her collarbone, the center of her ear. Something within her begged for him to possess every inch of her body. And she wanted all of him, too.

"Still like it, sweetheart?" he taunted in a silky tone.

"Oh, yes." Having no wish to be coy about her desires, she was totally abandoned to the wonder of discovery.

"You'll like this even more." Whit's hand caressed her shapely body, making its way slowly, provocatively, between her thighs. "I haven't been able to keep my wits," he murmured huskily, "thinking of doing this to you."

Ever so gently and carefully, he slid the tip of his finger rhythmically across the bud of her desire. She moaned with pleasure. Never, never had she imagined lovemaking could be anywhere near this rapturous!

At the point when she believed nothing could be more fulfilling, Whit positioned himself between her spread legs. The tip of his manhood touched her portal, and he leaned forward to take her lips in a kiss of wild, unbridled desire.

"Why must sin be so sweet?" he asked, his voice a mixture of agony and bliss.

An answer eluded her, for she was beyond reason and clear thought. Instinctively, her thighs tightened around his hips, for something within her now sensed there was something more . . . more exciting and fulfilling to be discovered.

And he had to have more. He thrust into her, but was stopped by her virginal barrier. "Oh, my God," he groaned in agony, his teeth clenching. "Why didn't you tell me?"

"T-tell you wh-what?"

"No man's had you before, Mariah. No man."

All she knew with any certainty was that her

primitive needs were unsatisfied. "D-don't understand. J-Joseph—"

"Goddamn Joe Jaye." Whit tunneled his fingers through her hair, his thumbs pressing her jaw. "And goddamn me, too, because I can't stop, and it's going to hurt you."

"D-don't want you to stop."

"Sweet mercies." With one powerful lunge he claimed her, and she cried out. Once more, Whit stilled his movements. "I'm sorry," he whispered after inhaling several times. "Please don't cry. The pain will pass, I promise."

"I'm not crying. I feel better already. But . . . are we finished?"

He chuckled. "Not hardly, sweet witch."

At first gently, then with surer rhythm, he moved within her. Within seconds she was on fire again, aflame with passion, thrashing with ecstasy. Deeper and deeper he lunged to draw heightened awareness from both of them. Over and over he groaned her name in rhapsody's litany, and her fire—their fire!—turned to a conflagration of passion. Barely able to breathe, she reached the pinnacle of ecstasy. Raising her hips to receive his final thrust, she realized for the first time in her life what she'd been created for. To be a woman to this man.

Breathing fast, he rolled to the side, bringing Mariah with him. Her head nestled against his shoulder, he pulled his Indian blanket over their bodies. "You okay?" he whispered, wiping the beads of perspiration from her brow.

"Whit, you talk too much," she teased, then she drifted into contented, sated sleep.

Whit, however, could not sleep. With quite an effort, he managed to fish a cigar from his saddlebag. Striking a match on a rock, he drew smoke into his mouth. Now that his breathing and wits were halfway back to normal, he wondered why Mariah had lied to him about her virginity.

"You've just deflowered Joe's woman," he muttered, snuffing out his smoke. Guilt plagued him, but there was no turning back now.

He didn't know what the hell he had gotten into, but the trouble was, he wasn't sure he wanted to get out of it. He'd made love to more women than he could ever remember, but none of them, not even Jenny, had aroused him this mightily. With only tonight to love Mariah, how could he get his fill of her?

His hand cupped her elbow, his mouth touched her temple. Only tonight . . . Tonight was theirs, and he was determined to make the most of it. Which he did.

By morning, however, Whit Reagor knew if he lived to be a hundred, he could never get his fill of Mariah McGuire. But that took him back to his problem. He hadn't been able to get his fill of Jenny, either.

Whit didn't speak of his thoughts as they readied the wagon to begin the last leg of their journey, and he sensed Mariah, too, had something on her mind. Both delayed the inevitable, for to voice their questions and statements would burst the moment's bubble. They were enjoying those final hours together—before the time came to confront Joe Jaye.

At noon, they stopped the wagon to make love again, this time in one of Crosswind's line shacks, which Whit had made a slight detour to reach. In the aftermath, they rested amid the rumpled sheets of a narrow bed, Whit leaning against the wall with Mariah settled between his spread knees as he gently drew a hairbrush down the curled length of her hair.

"Mmm, that feels marvelous," she said, then teased, "and you have exactly two weeks to stop."

"Glad you like it, darlin'."

"Your gentleness amazes me. How can a rough-and tumble rancher . . . ? Tell me about your ranch."

"It's just a li'l ole place," he replied modestly.

"Whit, don't kid with me that way. Tell me."

"All right, it's a hundred sections of cattle land. Not all in one piece, but scattered around west central Texas—my headquarters ranch, and home, three miles southwest of Trick'em. Now, enough about me. Tell me about Guernsey."

She did, and he tried to imagine being cooped up on an isolated island in the English Channel. He was glad for the wide-open spaces of Texas.

The brush encountered a tangle, and Whit tried to be easy in the untangling, but she jumped forward. "Ow!"

"Didn't mean to hurt you."

"You didn't. I hurt myself scooting on my bottom." Pivoting her face toward him, she blushed. "I'm a bit sore."

His question could wait no longer. "Mariah, why didn't you tell me you were a virgin?"

"I thought I wasn't."

"Care to explain?"

Shame-faced, she summarized the events of that night with Joseph, finishing with ". . . I had no idea, and he never told me any different."

"Oh, my poor innocent baby. He duped you." Wrapping his arms around her, Whit guided her to a prone position and rested the side of his head against her breasts. "Sweetheart, what did he write you about . . . uh, about his farm?"

"That pears grow in abundance and that he's doing quite well."

Whit put his legs over the bed's edge. "He lied."

"How so?" Mariah's eyes rounded before she shuttered them. "Don't answer that. I think I know. Since leaving the port of Galveston, I've seen this big state grow more and more desolate. How can pears thrive here?"

"They can't. Joe's broke."

"Poor Joseph." Rising to a seated position, she pulled the sheet up, tucking it under her arms. Her hair cascaded forward as she dropped her head. "Whatever will he do?"

"Whatever will the *two of you* do, don't you

mean? Soon you'll be his wife."

She shook her head slowly, and her eyes were veiled as she admitted, "I'm not going to marry him."

"Why not?" Whit asked suspiciously, his face turning to stone. "Because he can't provide for you in the manner befitting a nobleman's lady? Or because . . ." He lunged to his feet and yanked on his breeches. "Or because of what we've been doing since last night?"

"My decision had nothing to do with you," she replied quietly. "I decided days ago that I couldn't go through with the marriage."

"Why didn't you tell me?"

"Was it any of your business?"

A few seconds later, Whit nodded. "You've got a point."

She rose from the bed, wrapped the sheet around herself, and made for the pitcher of water sitting on a crude table of unvarnished wood. Studying her movements as she bathed her perfect body, Whit reached for a cigar and lit up. Should he believe her words about him having nothing to do with her decision? He wanted to . . . or did he? Last night he had realized he wanted her within his reach, and now she'd told him of her impending freedom. She'd be free, he *was* free, and they could continue what they had started.

So what if history repeated itself? So what if she, like Jenny, found another man and took off? Well, this time in his life there would be no binding ties to make his suffering all the more difficult.

"You're my woman now," he stated.

The plain white chemise she was slipping over her head stopped moving halfway to its destination. "I beg your pardon?"

"You heard me. Your place is with me."

Her brown eyes trained on Whit, she fitted the undergarment around her hips. "What do you mean?"

"Yeowwww!" Fancy screeched from her cage, interrupting their discussion. She began to twist and writhe in the small confines. Again, she howled.

"What's the matter with her?" Mariah crossed the room.

"Beats me."

Together they observed the fat cat's strange behavior. Fancy continued to display distress. "She's in pain," Whit said. "We'd better get her out of there."

Mariah eyed Gus to assure herself his cage was out of harm's way. "Yes."

Whit unfastened the hasp and took the tabby into his arms with extra care, but she would have none of it. Hair on end and still yowling, she took flight. But just as suddenly, her distress eased and she collapsed in a corner to lick her rump.

Whit strode to her, sat back on his heels, and ran his palm down her coat. He chuckled. "She'll be all right."

Mariah stepped over to the cat. "How can you say that? Something must be wrong with her."

"Only the thing that has plagued females since the beginning of time." He winked up at Mariah. "Labor."

"Oh, for heaven's sake." Instantly she felt terrible for all the rough treatment she'd given an expectant mother. "What can I do to help?"

"Look over there in the cupboard and gather some rags and bring them here," he said when Fancy's contractions started anew. "A soft bed will make her more comfortable."

"Do you think she'll be in pain for very long?"

"This isn't her first litter. She'll deliver soon."

"Thank goodness."

Mariah fetched an old linen sheet, Whit folded it, then moved the cat to the soft pallet. Comforted, she looked up at him and purred.

Although Mariah was on pins and needles to press Whit about his vague words of only minutes earlier, she knew now was not the time for such a discussion. Instead, she boiled a pot of coffee.

He said I'm his woman, and my place is with him. That can only mean he wants us to marry.

She felt confident. Gail was right, she thought. We did find something to cherish.

By the time the second pot of coffee was consumed, Fancy was in the final stage of birth. "You're doing just fine, girl," Whit murmured, stroking her forehead. "That's right. Give it a good hard push."

Fancy's body stiffened. A glistening golden head appeared, and a few seconds later, the kitten was born.

The tabby bit through the birthing sack and licked her tiny yellow kitten. Within seconds it began to mewl, and the mother nudged it to a nipple. Minuscule paws began to knead Fancy's tummy.

"Let's leave little mommy be." Whit got to his feet, and put his arm around Mariah's shoulder.

She nodded as he tightened his grip. In unison, they retreated four steps. "Isn't the kitten precious?" she asked softly. "Oh, I can't wait to hold it. I wonder if it's a boy or a girl."

"Do I detect a bit of the cat lover in you?"

"Nothing is cuter than a kitten."

"Not even me?" he teased.

"Well," she said, pulling out the word, "now that you mention it . . ."

He laughed and kissed her neck, his touch raising goosebumps on her flesh. "You're cuter than a kitten, too," he said.

At that moment Fancy gave birth to her second offspring, this time a pitch-black one, and Mariah smiled.

"Beautiful thing, birth," Whit said, squeezing her shoulder. "No matter how many times I've been around animals bearing their young, I never cease to be awed."

She was viewing a whole new side of Whit

Reagor—the sentimental man—and it was touching. "You'll make a fine father, Whit."

He dropped his arm, and she realized something was wrong—even before he said, "Never in a million years."

"You don't want children?"

"Fancy needs a bowl of water."

In a quandary, Mariah watched him act on his words. "Why didn't you answer my question?"

"After what I told you last night, I'm surprised you'd ask." He stomped to the bed they had abandoned, sat down, and rubbed his eyes with the heel of one hand. "Raising children takes a wife. And a wife means marriage. I'm a ribbon-wearing veteran of that war."

"You weren't proposing before Fancy interrupted us! Then what *did* you mean?" she asked woodenly.

Her stricken countenance shamed Whit. He wished he could grant her heart's desire, but he couldn't. "I'm sorry you took my meaning the wrong way, but I've told you how I feel. I won't make the same mistake twice."

"Don't talk in circles. What are you getting at?"

"I want you for my mistress."

If it had been humanly possible for Mariah's blood to rush out of her body, she couldn't have felt more drained. "I won't be Barbara Catley's Trick'em counterpart."

"Why not? You know you and I are compatible in bed." Not feeling as flippant as he sounded, Whit lit a cigar and tossed the match into an ashtray. "You have a lot to gain. I can take care of you in the manner you were expecting from Joe. You'll have a fine house in town, and all the things that go along with being my woman."

"I'm not for sale."

Blowing a slow stream of smoke toward the ceiling, Whit leaned back and balanced on his elbows. "Who said anything about buying you? I want to provide for you."

"I can provide for myself, thank you ever so much."

"If you're going to be a schoolteacher, I realize you've gotta think of your reputation. But we can be discreet."

"How kind of you to consider me," she bit out, and shot him a withering glare. "Your confidence amazes me."

"I didn't get where I am by being meek," he said, and got back to the subject. "I'll give you everything you need—and save you from yourself."

"Save me from myself? You're mad, Whit, stark raving mad."

"Probably." He took another puff from the cigar. "Let's look at this from a practical standpoint. Whether or not he was impotent, you did spread your legs for ole Joe."

Whit despised himself for these cruelties, but he was powerless to stop himself from comparing Mariah to Jenny who had also played the innocent. "You've proved you can be had," he said, "by more than one man."

"You rotten scoundrel! How dare you speak to me as if I'm a trollop!"

She grabbed the empty water pitcher used for her morning toilette and hurled it at Whit. But her aim was poor, and the vessel crashed against the wall, missing Whit by a foot. Shards of crockery went flying.

He jackknifed from the bed, stomping to her, and whipped her into his arms. "Better you should've gotten your gun if you're wanting to hurt me."

"Despicable, callous scoundrel!" As she tried to free herself, her fingernails raked his face, drawing blood. Satisfaction surged within her maligned heart.

"Right." He lifted her from her feet, carrying her to the rumpled bed and throwing both of them down.

"You blackguard, take your hands off me."

"Not for a long, long time."

Once more he branded her with the mark of his possession . . . and roused the passions she couldn't deny.

Hot, wild, and angry was their loving, for he was trapped by his wretched past and she was prisoner to her body and soul, an entirety of spirit that desired—and yes loved—a man too bitter for love.

Chapter Nine

In the aftermath of what had happened in the line shack Mariah was thoroughly disgusted with herself for allowing Whit to show his physical superiority. Why, oh why, had she been so weak? Why had she responded to him with such ardency? Because she loved him, she realized. That emotion was beyond her control, but she would be tarred and feathered before *again* allowing him to know how deeply he had hurt her.

The covered wagon was rolling along the path that led from Crosswind's outlying reaches to the Jaye property. Since they had left the line shack, Whit had been trying to cajole Mariah into changing her mind about his proposition.

She'd have no part of it. To be an old-maid schoolteacher had to be better than being just another notch on Whit Reagor's bedpost. She had a right to be angry. He was callous, heartless. He had, it seemed to her, delighted in his hateful words, even though he hadn't mentioned her tarnished character since she'd hurled that water pitcher at him.

Mariah faced reality. Once more she had lost, and this was the most wrenching loss of her life. But she couldn't take to some lonely bed and hide her grief. She'd deal with her hurt as she had done with her past disappointments. She'd throw herself into the challenges of getting on. That was the only way she could survive emotionally. "We'll be at Joe's farm in a few minutes," Whit said, continuing his crusade and snapping the reins. "Sure you won't change your mind?"

"I won't."

"I don't like the idea of leaving you there with him."

"Aren't you gallant?" she asked snidely. "Never fear, my knight, your presence isn't needed."

"It could get ugly."

"Really? My dear Mr. Reagor, how could anything get uglier than the last couple of hours with you?"

"I'll forget you said that." He grimaced. "Will you leave as soon as you tell him?"

"That's my plan."

"Shall I wait around, say down by Mukewater Pond, and pick you up later?"

"Absolutely not. I never want to see you

again."

"Don't make declarative statements you don't mean." His big wide hand moved to her knee. "Think about all I've offered, and get over your snit. I'll be waiting for you at Crosswind."

She swatted his touch away. "How many times do I have to tell you I won't be your mistress."

"You're already my lover. What's the difference?"

"Little things like principles, scruples, reputation."

"Cut it out, Mariah. You won't shame me into marrying you, if that's what you're about."

"Maybe I had fleeting thoughts of being your wife, but believe me, that's the furthest thought from my mind now. As soon as I break my engagement, I'll be free to do whatever I please. And what I please doesn't include you."

"I wish it did."

"Too bad." She disregarded his intense blue stare. "You and I are finished."

Not for a moment did Whit believe her statement, but he now realized he hadn't counted on her pride. Why not give her a bit of a victory? "Okay, you're through with Joe. And you're through with me. You have to take a step in some direction. Which one will it be?"

"I'll teach school."

She'd had her victory, and he wanted his. "What a waste . . . You could have anything you want." His brow hiked. "You know you want the same thing I want."

For a moment he thought she'd weaken, but she imparted an arch look and said, "You can get that from your blond floozy in Dublin."

"Barbara is past history."

"Oh? Did she turn you down at the wedding fete? Is that why you came running after me?"

"We came to a final parting of the ways. To answer your second question, I wanted to see you because I wanted to see you. Barbara had nothing to do with it."

"I wouldn't stake my soul on that."

"Aw, now, Mariah, settle down. You'll see things differently once you're over your pique."

"Don't underestimate me. When I make up my mind to do something, I do it."

"That so? Seems to me you'd made up your mind for babies'-breath and white lace. Sure did change your tune quick."

"I know when to quit, and this war of words has gone far enough," she said as a rider and calico mule topped a hill.

"Fine with me to stop arguing. It's just in time, too." He motioned toward the man who was approaching them. "Want to meet one of Joe's neighbors?"

Being neighborly was the last thing on her mind.

Whit brought the wagon to a halt, and the stranger came abreast of them, reining in his mount. "How doin', Lamkin?"

The open-faced man took a battered hat from his shiny pate. "Fair to middling. Hello, ma'am."

In the course of the men's chat she overheard several things about the farmer. A.W. Lamkin was not a well man. Malaria had driven him to the healthy, arid climate of Coleman County. The most astounding part was he and his family were farming a tract of land *on Joseph's property!*

"Yep, Mr. Jaye's been good to us," A.W. commented.

"Yep," Whit mocked in good nature, "and it's a good thing you didn't try to homestead on Crosswind."

"I know you're agin us grangers, Reagor, but I'll say this fer you. You been right neighborly. The missus shore did appreciate those canned goods you had sent over."

"Now, don't be spreading that around."

"I wouldn't dream of it, Reagor. But I jist wanted to offer my appreciation. Molly and Aggie gobbled up those peaches like nobody's business. You ought to've seen the grin on those younguns' faces."

This testimony to the sterling characters of both Whit Reagor and Joseph Jaye did little to allay Mariah's aggravation. "It's been nice to meet you, Mr. Lamkin. Whit, shouldn't we be going?"

"Yeah," he replied. "See you later, Lamkin."

The wagon moved on. Mariah had no wish to converse with Whit, so she said, "I'm going to check on the kittens."

She heard his intake of breath as she climbed across the seat, her thigh touching his shoulder. The urge to scream, to pummel him, to laugh in hysteria, raged within her . . . but why give him the satisfaction?

Sitting down at the back of the wagon, she unfastened the cat's wooden quarters and stroked Fancy's head. Being away from Whit gave Mariah a certain peace.

"Look at all you sweeties," she said, giving full attention to the feline family.

The mama cat, her foreleg around the two kittens, a satisfied smirk on her whiskered mouth, moved against the pressure of Mariah's hand. Fancy glanced at her babies, then up at Mariah, as if to say, "Didn't I do good?"

"You did good." Mariah took a bite-size piece of jerky from her pocket and offered it to the mother cat, who worked it between her teeth. "You know, Fancy, I never thought I'd say this, but I'm going to miss you."

"Meow?"

Scratching the now-purring cat's ear, she said, "Around you, there's never a dull moment."

At long last Mariah and the feline were friends. No longer would Mariah and Whit be friends. She closed her eyes, lost in thoughts of the past, of the present, and of her fuzzy future . . .

"Mariah, we're here."

Whit's voice from the wagon front jarred her. A tear rolled down her cheek, her voice catching as she whispered, "Goodbye, Fancy. Take care of your sweet little kits."

Goodbye. She brought her trembling fingers to her lips. Within a matter of minutes she'd be saying farewell to Whit and she knew it would be the hardest thing she had ever done in her life.

"Mariah? Did you hear me? We're at Joe's farm."

The wagon halted. Forcing herself to face the conflict with Joseph, she descended out the back. Her mouth dropped open, and she stared in disbelief. Whit had warned her that Joseph was broke, but when she laid her eyes on his homestead, she was speechless.

Joseph bounded out of the log cabin and crushed her into his bony arms, but realizing his breach of propriety, he stepped back and began his many questions.

Unable to speak, unable to look him in the eye, she depended on Whit to make explanations of their meeting and decision to travel together. Numb, both from the wrenching time with Whit and from shock wrought from the present situation, she leaned against the blue-painted wagon and took in the scene before her.

A small log cabin, a plume of smoke rising from the cracked chimney, stood twenty feet away, its exterior glinting gray in the sunlight. One rickety cart filled with rolls of red-painted barbed wire stood next to the lone mesquite tree. Three scrawny white chickens tripped around a bleached cow skull scratching for a handful of corn kernels in the rocky area fronting the cabin. Inside a poorly constructed lean-to stable was a bony horse, obviously of advanced years. Her shock turned to dismay.

Where were the fruits of Joseph's letters? Where were his Spanish-style home of native rock and tiled roof, his new barns, his fat stock, not to mention his pear groves? Oh, there were pears all right. Hundreds of flat-jointed, spiky green cacti dotted the barren landscape. Prickly pears.

Disgusted with Joseph and the bald lies of his correspondence, she was anxious to get away. Should she put aside her misgivings and go with her heart . . . with Whit?

"Shall we unpack the wagon?" she heard Joseph ask.

"Not just yet," she answered, measuring her tone. *Whit, look at me!* she pleaded silently. *Say you want us to be together—legally!*

He didn't.

"Please come in the house," Joseph requested, motioning to Whit and taking Mariah's travel-stiff arm. "I'll fix us a spot of tea."

"None for me." Whit stepped to the wagon, reached beneath the driver's seat, and took the parrot cage in his hand. Setting Gus in front of Mariah, he looked into her eyes. "Better get on to Crosswind. Got a family of cats that need to be settled."

Despite the warm sun and her woolen cape, a

cold chill ran the length of her spine, and she felt empty at the thought of being without Whit. She told herself not to be foolish.

"Please take tea with us," Joseph said. "I want to hear why you two have scratches on your faces. My goodness, you look as if you were in the middle of a cat fight."

"You got that right. I tangled with a wildcat," Whit dimpled a grin at Mariah. "One helluva wildcat."

How can you stand there and flirt with me!

Joseph didn't appear to catch Mariah's tension. "How dreadful for you," he exclaimed. "Well, I am pleased you both arrived relatively safely. I must say, I wasn't expecting you this soon, dearest. You caught me unawares."

"I *am* a couple of days early."

Whit doffed his black Stetson. "Gotta shove off."

Gotta shove off? That was all he had to say to her? She stared at the hard-packed ground. Well, she could be just as offhanded. Raising her hand, she waved her fingers. "Toodle-oo."

Whit caught her coolness and it lanced into him, but he collected his wits. She'd get over her anger. Little wonder she was edgy beneath the indifference. After all that had happened between them, he wasn't himself, either.

She was facing a difficult discussion with Joe, so why add to her problems by making a show of himself? One thing Whit was damned glad of: She wouldn't marry Joe Jaye. He was determined to provide for her in any way she'd accept, and wouldn't leave her stranded at Joe's mercy. "The Conestoga," he thus offered. "Keep it as an engagement gift to the bride."

"I wouldn't think of accepting such a gift," she said, wanting no part of his burnt offering.

Joseph spoke up. "Thank you for the wagon, old chap. I'm sure it will come in handy."

"Joseph!" she protested.

Whit had the impulse to extend his hand to the frosty redhead who had been so hot-blooded in his arms. He itched to cosset her, to keep her imprisoned in his arms for as long as the fire raged between them, but she would have to make the next move. Whit Reagor would not beg. Never again.

She'll be at the Crosswind before dawn, he thought. Without glancing her way, he swung into his hand-tooled saddle and clipped a salute. "Later."

He's gone! Forever! Mariah watched her lover point his sleek sorrel stallion to the west. Emotionally spent, she continued to stare at the muscled back she knew so well.

Then a miracle happened. Bay Fire made a circle, and horse and rider headed back toward Mariah. She was ecstatic realizing Whit hadn't given up on them.

The stallion pranced up to the cabin, and Whit vacated the saddle. Hat in hand, he half grinned. "Couldn't get away without . . . Well, I forgot something."

Her heart hammered against her breast as Mariah took three steps in his direction. Expectation in her tone, she said the simple word "Yes?"

"Forgot my cats."

Cats! It was all Mariah could do not to scratch his eyes out. Blast him. "Heaven forbid you should leave something behind."

Grabbing Gus's cage, she instructed Joseph to lead her inside the cabin. She would proceed with her life, sans Whit Reagor and that was that. Her determination however did little to ease her pain.

In the confines of the one-room log cabin, she eased into a rope-latticed, high-backed straight chair. Joseph took a kettle from the fireplace cleek and poured water into a pot of tea leaves. She sat motionless.

Two steaming cups sat on the rough-hewn table, and he unfastened the lid from a jar of dried apricots. "Have one. They're quite tasty."

"No, thank you."

He sighed. "I've missed you, dearest."

Staring at the earthen floor, she didn't reply.

"I'm pleased you made friends with Whitman. He's a fine chap, has been terribly kind to me this past year. Did I mention him in my letters?"

She shook her head, both in answer to his question and in hopes he would stop discussing that scoundrel Whit Reagor.

"I should have. He's—" Joseph abruptly raised his head, his line of vision stopping on the straw-filled mattress of his bed. Bloody hell! One of Temperence's cotton stockings peeked from the covers. Thanking God the woman had left two hours earlier, Joseph hastened to the offending article, gathered it and a pile of clothes, and shoved the lot into his watering pail. How was he going to rid himself of that baggage Temperence Tullos? A nightly visitor, she had promised to return this evening.

He had to get Mariah away from the farm. Never would he allow his beloved to be hurt by his meaningless indiscretions.

Beyond those anxious thoughts, Joseph had lost the train of his previous chatter. What had he been saying? Empty words mattered not, not really. His problems were far greater than idle talk. He read disenchantment in Mariah's silence, and taking her cold hand into his barbed-wire-scarred one, Joseph knelt in front of her. "You're too quiet, and that's not like you. Please say something."

Her eyes averted, she asked, "Why did you lie?"

Backed into a corner, Joseph had to do something. He would rather die than lose her. Knowing Mariah, he decided to play on her sympathies. "Pride was my undoing. My situation is an embarrassment, and no one feels it more deeply than I. I couldn't tell you, simply couldn't!"

He cleared his throat before continuing. "My heart told me you were a dutiful woman who would accept our fate once you were here. My faith in you is unshakable," he said, heartsick for resorting to manipulation. Despite his tryst with Temperence, he truly loved Mariah.

Joseph squeezed his eyes shut. Charlie Tullos's wife had been nothing more than a release for pent-up lust, and a handy vehicle for revenge against her husband, unsuspecting though Tullos might be.

"I love you with all my heart," he said truthfully. "As a desperate man, I had to make certain we'd be together again. Please tell me my wretched efforts weren't in vain."

For the first time since arriving at his "ranch," Mariah inspected her fiancé. He wore an earth-encrusted lounge suit of blue serge and a polka-dot bow tie stained with heaven-knew-what. His face was tanned to leather, making him appear at least ten years older than his twenty-four years.

In Guernsey, she had seen him wear the lounge suit and tie. Back then the apparel had been as natty as the young nobleman who wore it. But clothing did not a man make, and his present attire said more for him than had his previous dapper appearance. He bore the mark of honest toil.

Joseph hadn't been born to the earth, and certainly not to these dismal surroundings. Mariah cringed as she glanced around the pathetic cabin. Joseph Jaye, the Viscount Desmont, peer of the realm, scion of one of the Empire's most noble families, was living in a serf's circumstance. If not for me, she thought, he'd be enjoying the comforts of his family and title.

Yet he'd tried to make the best of his situation. He was trying to grow fruit. By his generosity, the Lamkins had land. He had tried to protect his property, she recalled, thinking of Gail's words and warnings about his fences.

And she remembered the many kindnesses he had shown her in her island home. Joseph had sacrificed so much, so very, very much for her yet now she must break his heart.

"Joseph, I—"

"Someday we'll be rich," he interrupted. "I'll give you all the luxuries my letters promised. I have a bit of money—five hundred dollars—and I've asked my brother Reginald to sell my London holdings. The funds will be arriving by post any day now."

"It's not the money that matters," she said honestly, realizing she had to be totally frank. "Joseph"—her heart went heavy, like sodden bread—"Joseph, it hurts me to say this, but I don't love you as a wife should love her husband."

"I've always known that. All I ask is for your presence, dearest. I love you enough for both of us."

"That's not fair to you." Why does this have to be so difficult? she asked herself. "It wouldn't be right, our marrying. I can't give you what you deserve in a wife."

He jerked to his feet, crossed to the fireplace, and leaned his arm and head on the mantel. His balled fist made three short taps on the mantelpiece. "Why did you come here then? Why didn't you simply write a kind letter? Why . . . Oh, God!" He swung around, and tears filled his eyes. "How can I lose you now that we're together again?"

She went to him and touched his cheek. "You'll find someone else. I know you will."

He collapsed against her, his arms tightening around her waist as if she were a lifeline. "No one could ever take your place."

"Please, Joseph. Pull yourself together."

"Yes." He hiccuped. "That I must."

He sank down in the chair Mariah had vacated. She prepared him a fresh cup of hot tea, which he downed in one gulp. The tracks of his tears etched his forlorn face. Despite all his lies, she had never felt such sorrow for another human being.

"I've a present for you, Mariah. I meant to give it to you on the occasion of our marriage, but since you're leaving . . ." He directed his eyes at a sidesaddle that was sitting in a corner. "Take it. It's yours."

The gift shamed her. Such a lady's saddle of fine oiled leather was out of place in the humble surroundings. Her voice riddled with remorse, she said, "Oh, Joseph, I never wanted you to make sacrifices for me."

"What's done is done, but I had no regrets

. . . until this day. I regret I've disappointed you."

"I regret disappointing you.

"You won't return to Guernsey, I should imagine, not with your father as he is." His voice gained strength. "I remember how I used to comfort you when he made you sad."

"You were my rock."

"Yes, I was and I was proud to ease your pain when Lieutenant Rogers went to a greater reward."

Oddly, for the first time the mention of Lawrence's death did not give her a stab of grief. Whit had begun to heal her broken heart, before he broke it anew.

"You needed me," Joseph was saying, "and I never disappointed you. Before today. But I pray you can understand why I lied. I love you for an eternity."

"Don't do this to me," she pleaded.

"I don't know what else to do! Mariah, I beg you. Please give the two of us a chance. If you'd like, we needn't marry in the next week as I'd planned. I'd already made arrangements for you to board at Mrs. Birdie Turner's establishment in town until we were wed. But you can stay there for as long as you need to reacquaint yourself with my finer qualities." He steepled his marred hands in front of his old man's face. "Give me one more chance, please. Don't discard me, not after all we've gone through together. Please!"

Guilt consumed her, and his begging was more than she could bear. Her mind in turmoil over the developments with Whit, she was no longer confident of her future. Furthermore, she didn't want to become the shriveled old schoolmarm of Gail's warnings, and Joseph had made promises . . .

"From the beginning," she said, "you promised I could pursue my teaching. Was that another lie?"

"No. Oh, no!" He clasped both of her hands between his palms. "Do whatever you want. Just don't leave me."

What would it hurt to grant his happiness? Honorable in his intentions—whereas Whit was not!—Joseph offered his love and his ability to compromise. She loved him as a friend, and she did owe him for the past.

If she turned her back on Joseph, she, a woman well beyond the prime age for marriage, might never have another chance for a good man's love and the home and family that adoration provided.

But can you live so near Whit? a voice from her heart asked. Are you capable of seeing him without wanting the succor of his arms?

Mariah walked to the hide door, pulling it back to view the pitiful sight before her eyes. After two soul-searching minutes she came to a decision.

Feeling as empty as the land before her dry, scratchy eyes, she dropped the door into place and swung around to face Joseph Jaye, the man who needed and wanted her.

Whit Reagor did not need her—not forever and ever, anyway. Yet she would never forget him nor the passions he had awakened within her—not forever or ever.

"Will you be my wife, Mariah?"

Her voice seemed as if it were far, far away as she gave him the answer that would change her life. Forever and ever. "Yes."

"Thank you, dearest." Expelling the breath he had been holding, his narrow face brightening, he rushed to her side. "I promise you won't regret your choice."

His hand trembling, he grabbed her arms to land a kiss on her cheek. "Now, we must hurry into town and meet Mrs. Turner."

Chapter Ten

The proprietress of Trick'em's only boarding establishment was a kind, silver-haired lady of diminutive stature, and Mariah's spirits were buoyed by the reception. Blanking her mind of Whit and her approaching marriage, she accepted the friendship the Widow Turner extended, and within minutes the two women were on a first-name basis.

Nonetheless, as the hour wore on, she noticed Birdie Turner excluded Joseph from the conversation. How odd. Or was it? Hadn't Gail told Mariah he had problems with the local cattle people? Birdie had been a cattlewoman, but arthritis and advanced years had forced her move into town.

Don't seek trouble, Mariah scolded herself and tried to be reasonable. She herself could be classified as a farmer, and the elderly lady had shown no resentment toward her. Besides, it wasn't unusual, she was well aware, for two women to monopolize a chat, and perhaps she was as guilty as Birdie.

"Would you care for another cup of tea, Mariah?"

She decided to test Birdie, and waved her hand over the cup on the marble-topped parlor table. "No more for me, thank you." Her gaze moved to center on Joseph's empty cup.

"Oh, my goodness, where are my manners?" Birdie obviously caught Mariah's not-so-subtle hint. "Would you like another cup, Mr. Jaye?"

From that point on, Birdie couldn't have been more cordial to Joseph.

After he left, the wrenlike old lady showed her new boarder to her room. "It's not much," she said, her gnarled hand indicating the narrow bed, a lone chair, and one pine bureau, "but maybe you won't be too uncomfortable."

"Everything is fine." Mariah smiled. "I won't be here except to sleep. My fiancé and I have much to accomplish at his farm. It's planting time, and the house has to be put to rights."

Birdie smoothed the front of her gingham dress. "Mariah, I pray you won't take this the wrong way, but do you think it's proper being alone with Mr. Jaye at his farm? If word gets out, people will talk. I'd sure hate for you to get off on the wrong foot."

"My reputation concerns me, too, Birdie. Trouble is, I don't know what else to do. Since

I'm new in town, there's no one I can call on as a chaperone."

"I have an idea. There's a family squatting down by Home Creek, fairly near to Mr. Jaye's farm. And if you can keep their bellies full, the Martinezes need you as badly as you need them." She rushed on, explaining the Mexican family's desperate plight before expounding on their abilities. "They've got a girl, about fourteen she is, and Conchita and her mother would be a big help to you in the house and garden. I can vouch for their work being good. Before they moved out to the Home, I put all three of them to chores around here."

"Why didn't they stay?"

"Pablo wasn't happy in town, and he has ideas to claim his own land and farm it, but he doesn't have the supplies or money to build a cabin, which a party's gotta do if he wants to file a claim in the Land Office." Birdie pursed her wrinkled mouth. "Poor souls, they're living under the stars."

Mariah placed Gus's cage on the bureau top. "I'm afraid Joseph and I couldn't provide any better. There's only his cabin."

"Pablo's a fair hand with a hammer. With the proper tools, he could put a roof over their heads in no time. They'd sure be a help to you and Mr. Jaye. Till you can get your place going good, anyway."

The Martinez family's assistance would be a godsend, and what would it hurt to extend a helping hand their way? "You've convinced me. I'll call on them tomorrow."

With this decided, Mariah could turn to the consolation of teaching sooner than expected, and she began to speak of her plans. ". . . and I'm counting the days until I ring the schoolbell."

"I've got a big piece of buttermilk pie downstairs that's got your name all over it, Mariah. Let's go down and find it."

She was perplexed at the older woman's abrupt change of subject, but, nonetheless, acceded to the suggestion. As Birdie poured tea and sliced the dessert, Mariah recalled Gail's warning that day in Lois Atherton's kitchen . . . and Birdie's initial attitude toward Joseph.

"Birdie, do you mind if I ask you a question?"

"Go right ahead."

"I've heard rumors ranch people are opposed to farmers. Is that true?"

"Yes." Birdie swallowed. "Just like the other ranchers, I don't hold with farming, not here in cattle country noways. But I try to keep an open mind about whatever a party does to make his living."

The contradictory statement puzzled Mariah.

"Maybe I should explain," Birdie said. "I was reared on a plantation, which is just a fancy name for a farm, so cultivating the land is my heritage. My roots are in Alabama, in farming country. But Texas isn't Alabama, and

I've grown to see the Texas side of things. Cultivating the open range upsets the grass-lands, and cows have to eat."

"So do Texas farmers."

"I realize that. I'm not immune to their struggles. That's why it hurts me right in my heart to witness their troubles. Grangers have come here from all over—the South, the North, even from foreign countries. They're in Coleman County out of desperation; they've left worn-out or overcrowded fields, or no fields at all, in hopes of feeding their families. I know what it's like to be desperate. When Mr. Turner brought me and our son to this barren place called Texas, we were hungry and homeless and scared."

"Oh, Birdie . . ."

"Now don't go getting soft, girl. I'm not after pity, I'm just explaining myself. Believe me, I don't have anything against farmers personally. There's a difference, you know, between farmers and farming. One is human, the other a result."

Mariah let those words sink in. Birdie, she decided, was a woman caught in the middle of her way of life and her compassion for others. What a terrible place to be.

She admired Birdie's clemency, and had her own compassion toward her new friend's inner turmoil.

"You're not eating, Mariah. Something wrong with my baking?"

"Oh, no. This custard pie is delicious." And it was. The last crumb of her portion eaten, she brought her teacup to her lips. "Would you share the recipe?"

"My pleasure." Birdie paused. "Mariah, when we were upstairs, you mentioned . . . Well, I've been trying to keep my mouth shut, but I'm not good at that, as you've probably guessed. Anyway, I think you ought to know something." She sighed, her wrinkled throat quivering. "You've come to the wrong place for teaching. If there's anything Trick'em has enough of, it's teachers. We've got a two-story schoolhouse, and two masters to run it."

Disappointment sank through Mariah, but she forced herself to be positive. "That won't stop me. I will find children who need an education. I know I will."

Birdie studied her, and admiration lit the old eyes. "Yes, I believe you will." She smiled. "Keep that faith in yourself. If you do, I'll bet you get everything your heart desires."

No matter her resolves, Mariah's heart desired Whit Reagor.

After a fitful night of sleep, Mariah rode Joseph's decrepit old nag to Home Creek, and prevailed upon Pablo Martinez and his family to accept her offer of employment. After some reluctance, the middle-aged Mexican agreed to pull up the stakes of their tent.

"We will be there tomorrow," he promised.

Relieved, Mariah turned Old Glue toward Joseph's farm. On her arrival, he greeted her with a kiss, then took her on a tour of the pear grove. She was dismayed by the wilted saplings but tried not to show it, especially when he displayed marked enthusiasm for the project. *Well,* she decided, *let him have his pears. I'll plant a market garden.*

Back at the cabin, Mariah made mental notes on all that had to be done in the house. Determined to keep herself busy, and to keep her mind off Whit, she looked forward to the challenge of making something out of nothing.

"Yoo hoo. Mr. Jaye? Are you home?"

The caller wasn't one but two. A.W. Lamkin's wife and youngest daughter. Patsy Lamkin, a sweet woman with light brown hair, had an air of pioneer spirit. Her daughter, Molly, was an adorable five-year-old.

After polite getting-acquainted banter, Patsy said, "Didn't expect you till Saturday. That's why I brought this." She held out a covered bowl. "I wanted dear Mr. Jaye to have some peach cobbler to offer when you arrived."

Peach cobbler made from Whit's canned goods, no doubt, Mariah thought, and sighed at the irony. She accepted the baked treat, then brewed a pot of tea.

"I met your husband yesterday," she said, opening a tin of toffee for the little girl, who beamed and said a "thank you" before squatting down to dig into the sweets.

"That was you?" Patsy's green eyes rounded. "A.W. and I thought . . . Well, it doesn't matter what we thought. Welcome to Trick'em, Mariah. You don't mind if I call you by your given name, I hope?"

"Not at all, Patsy." Sensing that gossip might start over her means of transport to the area, she enlightened her visitor about her "friendship" with Whit. Naturally, she gave only the sketchiest details.

"He's such a nice man, almost as kind as dear Mr. Jaye," the guest said. "Good gracious, Molly, come here and let me wipe your face. You've got candy all over it."

Mariah gave another sigh, this one in gratitude for the change of pace. "Molly, you're a very pretty girl," she said to the strawberry-blond youngster.

Molly craned away from the rag that was being rubbed across her mouth, and said with the lisp of missing baby teeth, "Tho are you."

"Thank you." Mariah sat down in the rocker and patted her lap. "Why don't you come see me, Molly pie?"

A gap-toothed grin widened the girl's round face. "Yeth, ma'am." She crawled into Mariah's lap and snuggled against her. "You thmell nice, Mith Mariah."

Mariah tightened her arms around Molly. *Children are God's most wonderful gift.* Someday she'd be holding her own children, and that was a grand thought; it gave her hope. Maybe once she and Joseph became parents, she'd love him.

Molly's tiny hand curled against her chest. "Do you have any little girlth?"

"Not yet."

"I have a thithter."

"A sister?" Mariah asked with mock astonishment. "What's her name?"

"Aggie. The's nine, but mean and won't let me play with her doll. If you had a little girl, I could play with her."

"Sounds as if you're lonely, Molly. Tell me, don't you go to school?"

"No." A thumb went to her mouth.

"A.W. and I wish our girls could get an education, but I can't read and my husband is too poorly for lessons after a day's work, so we're in a pickle. I'm afraid Trick'em's school isn't for squatters' kids," Patsy said sadly.

An idea germinated in Mariah's mind. Why not form a free academy for farm children? Of course, she wouldn't be able to organize it right away, not with so much to be done at the farm, but . . . "I'm a teacher, and I'd be more than happy to tutor your girls."

"No, thank you."

"If it's a matter of money—"

"Everything is a matter of money, Mariah." She held her chin level. "We're poor folks."

"I wouldn't charge for the tutoring. I need to teach, need it as much as your children need my services."

"But you're not settled in yet."

"The school will have to wait for a while. My calling won't. Let me tutor your girls."

A half minute later, Patsy nodded. "Okay, yes. And I'm much obliged."

"When may I start the lessons? How about tomorrow?"

"That could be a problem. A.W. needs all the hands he can get for the plowing and planting. Both of the girls do their share of the chores. I'm afraid until after the fields are in, we can't accept your offer."

Mariah thought it was a shame, young children laboring at farm work, but she shouldn't be judgmental. No doubt the Lamkins were doing their best and she'd take her victories as she got them.

"All right," she said. "After the planting is over, Molly and Aggie will be my students."

A half hour later, Patsy and Molly took their leave. Mariah was jubilant. Soon she'd be teaching. Singing a merry tune, she set to tidying the cabin. Her mood changed, though, when she put the bowl of peach cobbler aside.

Whit's peaches. Whit. Once he discovered her marriage plans, would he be sending her his canned goods?

For the second time since he and his cats had left her at the farm, Mariah had an awful thought. As Joseph's wife, she and Whit would be neighbors. How could she live in his shadow and ignore him? How would he behave in her presence? Would he remember their hours together?

His eyes red from imbibing more alcohol than was his habit, Whit stared at the nude woman. She reposed on a tufted fainting couch, a thin swatch of material draped across her shapely hips. Her forefinger was touching the nipple of a full yet pert breast. Her hair was a mass of red curls, her big brown eyes half lidded with obvious desire.

The painting that hung on the wall behind the bar of Maudie's saloon reminded Whit of Mariah.

"Damn you to hell," he muttered, tossing down yet another shot of bourbon.

Standing with a boot cocked on the brass rail, Whit was alone at the bar, alone in his disappointment. Behind the far end of the massive walnut bar, the barkeep, Roy Everett, better known as Heavy, polished glasses and held them up to the fading light of dusk that streamed through the windows. Behind Whit, in a corner of the watering hole, a cardsharp was fleecing three locals of their wages. By the swinging doors, the lazy sheriff snoozed over a table laid with dominoes.

Whit was aware of the activities, but he couldn't have cared less.

Again, he eyed the canvas redhead. "I waited

up all night for you."

Yesterday, when he left Mariah at the farm, Whit had been confident he'd hear from her right after she bid Joe her so-long's. He hadn't.

Maybe she hadn't lowered the boom on Joe. Yet.

"Heavy!" he bellowed. "Gimme another drink."

The portly son of a gun who doubled as ticket agent for the stageline shoved the whiskey to Whit and wiped a hand down the front of his white apron. "Two bits."

"Have a shot on me, buddy." Whit tossed a half dollar on the bar. Though he wasn't a man to ask for advice, he felt the loosening effects of the amber spirits. "Say, Heavy, a woman ever been under your skin?"

"I reckon. Slip of a gal named Ernestine be one I'll never forget." The bartender, chuckling and shaking his head, pulled cigarette papers and a pouch of tobacco from his pocket. "A man can't live with 'em, and he can't live without 'em."

"I've done a good job of living without them."

"Oh, yeah?" One of Heavy's bushy gray brows hitched up his forehead. "Whaddya doing holding up this bar, then?"

"Just having a friendly drink."

"Your face is longer than an old horse's teeth, Reagor, so I'd be guessing you're drowning your troubles in rotgut. Ain't nothing wrong with that," he added. "And you ain't alone in your miseries. This place does a right handy business on fellers that be needing a little consoling."

Wordlessly Whit quaffed his drink, and Heavy's speculative eyes watched his every move.

"You never was one to moon over the gals," the bartender commented. "Your lady friend must be real special, 'cause she's plumb got you in the gettin' place."

Mariah was special, and Whit was got in the gettin' place. The hardest thought was if she left town without seeking him out, he'd never see her again!

Had she left?

"Say, Heavy, how's the stage business? Have many customers today?"

"Not a one."

Whit relaxed. She hadn't left Trick'em. "Next stage isn't due for another couple of weeks, right?"

"At least." The barkeep nodded. "Anyone I should be looking for?"

"A redhead. New in town. Tall and good-looking. Mariah McGuire's her name."

Heavy Everett rubbed his stubbled chin. "Redhead, you say?"

"You got it."

"I believe I've seen the lady you be looking for. Staying up to Birdie Turner's she is. Tall gal, no lil 'un for sure, but purty as a speckled pup."

A grin split Whit's face. If she was staying at Birdie's, Mariah had done it, had made her break with Joe. There was nothing to keep him from calling on her.

Hold your horses, Reagor.

What had happened to his determination of yesterday? Then he had told himself she'd have to make the next move.

Besides, he couldn't let her see him in this condition. Whit decided to sober himself up and think on whether he'd be making the right move.

"Brew up a pot of coffee, Heavy."

Chapter Eleven

Sobered, Whit bribed Birdie's kitchen maid out of a tray of foodstuff and drink . . . and the key to Mariah's quarters. As the horse-faced young servant had warned, however, the renter wasn't on the premises.

The second-floor bedroom had a woman's touch, he noted while pacing the confines. Knickknacks, brushes, combs, and the like. He halted to unstopper a glass vial of cologne. *She ought to own crystal and perfume.* Roses wafted to his nostrils, yet the aroma lacked something—the mingling womanly scent of Mariah!

The wardrobe held a collection of frocks, most of them dated and threadbare. The old outfits would have to go. He made up his mind to clothe her in the finery befitting her beauty. That would please her. What woman didn't want the finer things in life? Mariah was surely no exception. After all, she had a few nice ensembles, and had dressed herself in them after Kimble's wedding. The Wedgwood-green gown she had worn on the morning they had left Dublin had held his attention. It was a beautiful dress, sheer and soft. He had been loath to admit how, back on that day he'd seen her wear the batiste, but he'd admired this frock and the beauty of its owner.

So much had transpired since then. Arguments, understanding, plus undeniable and insatiable desires. He regretted their last day together—not the passion, but the difference of opinion that had spoiled their final hours together. But he hadn't changed. Mariah wanted more out of him than he was able to offer.

He closed the wardrobe and brushed his hand down his face. He still couldn't give her his heart. Who'd want the damn battle-scarred thing, anyhow? In light of his bitterness, marriage would be a miserable undertaking.

Perhaps he should leave. No. He wanted one more chance to talk, and caress sense into Mariah.

He strode to the bureau, taking a piece of cold chicken from the tray of food. Again, his eyes swept over the room. An odd feeling ran through his veins. Something was missing, but he scoffed away his uneasiness. Mariah's presence was missing.

For hours he waited in the night's deepening

dark for her return, not bothering to light the lamp. Finally, he shucked his shirt, boots, and socks to stretch out on her bed. The bedclothes held her scent, and he swallowed. Closing his eyes, he silently rehearsed the words he'd say to Mariah, a speech that would, hopefully, keep his ego intact.

But concentration became impossible. Wind gusted through the trees, the howl penetrating the walls. Over and over again, the spring leaves quaked. A flash of lightning opened his eyes, and thunder clapped.

"Please let that rain fall on Crosswind," he said aloud in an invocation to Providence.

No rain fell on Birdie Turner's boardinghouse. Another streak of lightning illuminated the bureau clock, which read ten P.M. Where was Mariah? Another twenty minutes passed before he heard her footsteps in the hall.

The hinges creaked as she opened the door. A shaft of light from the hallway outlined her form, and it was a lovely, lovely shape. He smiled. His memorized speech departed him. She was there, and a fist of emotion seized his chest, a strange mixture of happiness, longing, and pain not often experienced by Whit Reagor.

She turned to fasten the lock and he realized she hadn't seen him. Just laying eyes on the woman who dominated his thoughts, senses, and passions softened his resolve. He was on the verge of throwing himself at her feet to tell her whatever she wanted was fine with him. *Don't be a sap, Reagor. Don't give her any quarter. Make her your mistress, and that's that.*

Reaching back with a fist to plump the pillow, Whit said, "So, how's the world—"

She shrieked, and jumped.

"No need to be scared."

"Whit, what are you doing here!"

"Oh, I don't know. Any takers for a quilting bee?"

"Sarcasm hasn't deserted you," she said, as if gritting her teeth. "Get out before Birdie finds you."

"Birdie went to bed with the chickens."

"Well, I suppose her whereabouts are neither here nor there. You have no business in my room."

She's upset at being startled, he figured. He lit a match and reached to light the kerosene lamp. Now that he could easily see her, he read anger in her milk-chocolate eyes. "Does it rile you, my being here?"

"You could say that."

He pushed himself to a standing position and walked slowly toward her. "I'm a bit riled myself. Why haven't you brought yourself to Crosswind?"

"Why should I?"

"I won't dignify that with an answer."

Hugging her arms, she spun away from him. "Why can't you leave me alone?"

"Is that what you want, Mariah?"

She didn't reply, and kept her back to him.

He took three more steps, lessening the space between them. His fingers wrapped around the angle of her shoulders, and he leaned to kiss her petal-scented neck. Heat leaped into his loins at her nearness. She shivered, and it wasn't from the dislike of him, he figured.

Weakened in resolve not to show any mercy, he said in a low tone, "Let me take you to Crosswind, baby. Now."

"No. And I'm not your baby."

Stung, he asked, "Have you forgotten our trip to Trick'em?" He turned her around and brought her into his arms, lifting her off her feet to the heat of his hips. "Have you forgotten the way you melted into my arms, the way you— Aw, hell, baby, when we're together, we're both hotter than a chili pepper, and you know it."

Swept off her feet, both physically and emotionally, she trembled and swallowed. She wanted him. He had the wicked ability to arouse her with no more than a touch. She couldn't deny it, at least to herself, but what about Joseph?

Not to tell Whit the truth about her marriage plans would be dishonest and it would be disloyal to the man who offered her his name.

"Go away, Whit," she whispered.

He set her down and retreated one step. The

room went aglow with lightning; thunder cracked almost simultaneously. Whit's gaze welded to hers.

Rain pelted the tin roof.

"I won't leave, Mariah, not unless you tell me, straight out, that you don't want any part of me. But be true to yourself and honest with me. Say you don't want me to go."

Her conscience warred with her desires. It was wrong, being affianced to another while wanting Whit so. But she was aching for more of Whit's touch, and no matter how hard she had tried over the past days to convince her heart to the contrary, she had ached for the loss of his presence. She loved him, and to deny that love was impossible.

Suddenly another thought occurred to her. Whit's presence made its own statement. She had made her stand perfectly clear before he'd left her with Joseph. He wanted, she was certain, more than a mistress.

But what about Joseph and his sacrifices? Twice she had promised to be his wife. Twice. Was she strong enough to repay him? If she found this strength, she would lose a second chance at love and happiness. With Lawrence she'd had no choice. With Whit she'd be the one to make the decision.

By going with her principles, her conscience, she would sacrifice everything, but her honor would be intact. All she had to do was turn her back on Whit. That was a simple enough thing to do. Just turn her back . . .

So she moved away in the darkness, away from Whit. There, she'd done it! Her insides contracted in pain. "I . . . I want you to . . ."

Whit stepped to her, his fingers touching her shoulders and his breath caressing her cheek, and she lost all strength of will. Somehow she'd make Joseph understand, somehow she'd reconcile with herself.

She turned into Whit's arms. "I want you to stay."

"Thank God."

His work-roughened hand found the softness of hers, and he carried her palm to his lips. Gentling a kiss to the salt-tinged center, he slid his free arm around her waist. The hand at her back smoothed over the swell of her derriere and, a groan of desire vibrating in his throat, he took her lips with a kiss of passion. Beneath his mouth, hers opened. His tongue slid past her teeth to taste the yielding softness of the candy-flavored interior.

"Candy?" he murmured, pulling away only slightly.

"Toffee."

"Give me another taste."

And she did.

Savoring the sweetness of her lips, he felt her fingers curl into his hair. The ache in his loins cried out for release, but he was determined to take his time, no matter how difficult the effort. His palm canvassed the rise of her breast, and she was shuddering with life beneath his questing fingers.

"I'm going to undress you," he whispered.

"Turn out the light" was her murmured response.

He yearned to see her beauty in the full bloom of lamplight, but the intermittent glow of lightning had its rewards, too. Making love within the sounds and sights of driving, blessed rain . . . ah, the pleasures of it. The wick was extinguished.

Sitting down on the edge of the bed, he spread his knees and extended a hand in the near darkness. "Come here, Mariah. Let me finish what I started."

She bided his words.

"Rest your hands on my shoulders," he urged, and proceeded to fumble with the elastic bands of her gaiter shoes. Mission accomplished, he tugged the footwear from her narrow feet.

The pads of his fingers slid across the incredibly long toes of her right foot, and she giggled a "Stop . . . I'm ticklish."

He'd allow nothing to spoil the mood, and set to a different course. His fingers reached up to work the small mother-of-pearl buttons at her throat. He was engulfed by a tumult of feelings—anticipation and fervor and restraint—as he spread the frock and placed his lips on the swell of her lawn-covered bosom.

With unsteady fingers he slipped the dress to

her feet and helped her step out of it. In an upward motion, he divested her of the thin chemise. Cupping her heavy breasts in his palms, he circled her nipple with his mouth, and the peak hardened under the ardent worship of his tongue. Her hands combed into his hair, and she held him fast. He felt her quivers, and realized his own.

"Oh, darling, please . . . Can't take any more . . ." Her head dropped forward, her lips touching the top of his head. "Whit," she said, his name trembling on her lips.

He was on the verge of giving in. His manhood, swollen painfully in his now tight breeches, needed release, but . . . "I won't stop. Not yet. I want you mindless when I take you."

"I . . . I already am."

Sudden blue light allowed him to gaze upon her desire-ridden features. His hands spanned her narrow waist. "Before this is over, you'll be more mindless."

To the staccato beat of rain on the tin roof, he inched forward, guiding her a step backward, and dropped to his knees. Plucking the drawstring of her pantaloons, he rid her of that barrier and of her stockings. His face went to her tummy. Her scent, so womanly and uniquely Mariah, wreaked havoc with his control.

He laved the skin surrounding her navel, then slipped his tongue into the indentation.

She moaned, and her fingers wrapped into his hair, tugging. His lips moved lower, and he enjoined her to spread her silky thighs. Finding the honeyed center of her passion, he flicked his tongue in a gentle rhythm of arousal. She swayed. He felt her spasms, heard her moans and cries, and his hands tightened on her buttocks. It pleased him to please her.

Then, he stood. "Now you're ready for the next step, my sweet."

He unbuttoned his breeches, his hands moving downward to rid himself of the tight barrier to his own satisfaction. Taking her fingers, he guided her to bed. The mattress sagged under their weights. Mariah took a series of deep, ragged breaths, and he braced himself on a forearm. His eager hands explored her curvaceous form while he delved into her sweet mouth. A primal groan vibrated in his throat as his fingers thrummed her breast once more. Later, his palm moved past her waist, past her hips, charting a rapturous course for the warmth that beckoned him.

"Wet, so wet," he murmured around her cry of rapture, and when her trills subsided to throaty moans, he anchored himself between her spread thighs. The tip of his shaft embedded at the entrance to her womanhood, he cupped the sides of her breasts and leaned forward to kiss her parted lips.

Then, surging hard into her softness, he filled her. Swiftly and fully. Her nails dug into his back. Surrounded by her moist softness as it tightened in ecstasy, he was struck by the force of how well they fit.

Thus began his movements, the cadence of violent rain and sweet, savage lovemaking. Meeting his unbridled rhythm and crying out her pleasure, she wrapped her legs around his hips, and they agonized and rejoiced in the eternal act of mating. He took everything she had to give, and, in return, gave all of himself as she shuddered and reached the pinnacle of pleasure. At the same moment, his strong release yanked through him, pulling downward from each vertebra in his spine as he spent himself inside her.

Their uneven gasps slowed to deep and synchronized breathing. Reveling in the heady scent of two bodies as one, he closed his eyes, his throat constricting. God, he was in thrall with this woman. And she was free of Joe. Free to be Whit's woman, and that's where she belonged.

His arm held them chest to chest, and they remained a part of each other as he brushed her temple with a soft kiss. "You're one helluva woman, Mariah McGuire." Sliding out of her slick cocoon, he palmed her rosy cheek. "Make a damned good pair, don't we?"

"Are you after a compliment?"

"I wouldn't be offended."

"I never dreamed it could be so wonderful between a man and a woman," she admitted.

"Is that good enough for you?"

"It'll do." When she cuddled against him, he playfully tapped her behind. "You don't have to guess how I feel. I want you again."

He caught the wicked gleam in her eyes as she touched his manhood.

"Well, darling, let's do something about it."

They did.

The rains stopped at a quarter past three, and both Mariah and Whit were famished. Besides feeling hungry, she was a mixture of happiness and dread. Whit made her happy, but not once in their hours of lovemaking had he uttered one word about the future. She didn't take this as a good sign, but why ask for problems?

"How 'bout I fetch our victuals?" he asked after relighting the lamp, the side of his knuckle tenderly chucking her jawline.

"I'll help you."

"Stay put." He threw his legs over the edge of the bed and pulled his breeches over his hips. Buttoning up, he said, "No need to get out of the hay."

"You aren't suggesting we eat in bed, are you?"

"I most certainly am." He brought the tray of food and drink to the bed, and she threw the sheet aside, meaning to stand, but he shot her a warning look.

Whit sat down, Indian fashion, and served two plates of food. The cold chicken was delicious, as were the crackers, the quarter wheel of hard cheese, and the bottle of elderberry wine. Pickled eggs weren't high on her list of favorites, but they had a pleasing taste right then.

They both made veritable pigs of themselves. Whit picked up his last cracker to study it, then held it to her lips. She bit into the wafer, and crumbs joined many others on her chest.

"This is positively sinful," she said with a laugh, brushing food particles away. "Positively disgraceful."

"Aw, now, honeybunch, tell me it's not fun to eat crackers in— Crackers. I knew something was missing. Where's Gus?"

Mariah's eyes widened at the seemingly harmless question. She opened her mouth, then immediately clamped it shut.

Suspicion darkened Whit's intent blue gaze. He unfolded his legs and stood at the foot of the bed. His arms crossed, he asked, "Would that bird happen to be at Joe Jaye's farm?"

The food in her stomach knotted into a lump. "Yes."

"What exactly does that mean? Have you, or have you not, broken off with Joe?"

"Why were you waiting for me?" she asked in a non sequitur.

The room grew deathly quiet.

"Have you broken off with him?" Whit repeated finally.

"Are you here to offer something better?"

"I don't offer deals. You know my terms."

Reality dawned on Mariah. Whit hadn't changed. The last hours had been no more than a sham on his part. Pain and fury ripped into her, pride and a broken heart forming her reply.

"I'm not interested in your terms. Joseph has good intentions, and that's fine enough for me."

"Oh, really?" Whit's expression was murderous. "Good intentions, huh? Well, I wonder if you've thought about what you'll be getting into. There won't be any teaching for the fair Mariah, no sir. She'll be shackled to a dried-out piece of land and a lying numskull who can't even see that pears are a fool's idea of making a living in Coleman County."

"Don't you dare patronize me, Whit Reagor. Helping Joseph achieve his potential is a challenge, not a detriment."

"When was the truth ever patronizing?" he questioned, a hard glint in his eyes. "And speaking of the truth, my guileless Mariah, I do believe there's something you haven't thought of. What will you tell your beloved nobleman when he finds out you're already"—he cleared his throat—"broken to a man's saddle?"

Whit's crude question made her realize, suddenly, that in all her decisions and plans of late, she'd never given full thought to sleeping with Joseph. But she'd never make such an admission to Whit Reagor.

"I won't have to tell him anything," she replied at last, raising her chin in the air. "He'll simply assume that Lawrence had his way with me."

"And if that doesn't work?" Whit challenged, a wry smile on his granite-edged, handsome face. "What then, my innocent?"

"Well—" she mustered bravado "—if that doesn't work, I'll tell him the truth. I'll tell him it was you."

"You're bluffing," he said evenly, his eyes piercing hers.

"What makes you so sure of that, Mr. Reagor?"

"Because it won't be necessary. Because you won't marry him."

"I *will* marry him."

"Is that so? Well, I have a question. If you planned to marry him, why did you sleep with me?"

"I thought you wanted more than a mistress," she replied through her agony.

"And now you know I don't."

"Exactly. That's why I'm going to do everything in my power to make Joseph a good wife."

"Oh, you will, will you? Tell me something, Mariah. Not that I believe you'll go through with the marriage—not for one minute do I believe that!—but let's say you do rise to the challenge." Whit's gaze raked her body, those intimate places he'd caressed . . . "Can he give you what we just shared? Or will you fall asleep every night hoping Joe Jaye won't touch you?"

She was further angered by his low blow. "Better I should fall asleep than be bothered by the devil himself."

"Empty words, Mariah. Empty words."

She used no hollow words while demanding, "Get out."

Chapter Twelve

Later in that same day, Mariah avoided Joseph and the farm. She couldn't bring herself to leave her room and spent a lonely, mournful day.

As evening fell, Mariah came to the devastating conclusion that because of his past, Whit would never allow himself to have faith in her.

Not ten minutes after she had made this heart-shattering realization, Joseph appeared at the boardinghouse. Concerned over her absence, he was solicitous and fretful . . . and quite pleased at the previous evening's rains.

"Every little bit helps," he said, sitting in one of the parlor chairs. "But enough about the weather. I've brought you some chicken soup Mrs. Lamkin prepared. Shall I warm it?"

For some reason, her sorrowful mood plummeted even lower under his thoughtful attentions.

"I feared you'd changed your mind about our marriage," Joseph said, his doleful eyes boring into Mariah.

She quit her chair and, turning to the darkened window, tightened the sash of her heavy dressing gown. "Joseph, I . . . I . . ."

"But then I told myself, 'Surely she's indisposed, and you must see after her.' Wait here, my dearest. I'll only be a moment." Before she could protest, he hastened toward the kitchen. "Warm soup will have you feeling better in no time at all. You'll see."

Joseph served the fare, continuing to watch her attentively while she slowly consumed it. His gaze was openly concerned.

She looked down at herself. Although evening had fallen, here she was still in a dressing gown. With sudden clarity, Mariah realized she had done today what she had vowed never to do. She had taken to a lonely bed to hide her grief instead of throwing herself into the challenges of getting on.

Where was her usual sense of practicality? Unlike Whit Reagor, Joseph Jaye had faith in her. He had accepted her, flaws and all, and she understood why he had lied. He had feared losing her, which was no sin.

On top of this, Mariah realized she must use common sense. Whit had said it himself: "A man's gotta do what a man's gotta do to keep a lady out of trouble." And the same statement applied to the lady herself. She was without funds and gainful means of support. If she left Trick'em, she'd be forced to meander around Texas, friendless and bereft of family or family connections while searching for employment.

She crossed to the window and gazed at the darkened street. She was in a strange country populated by even stranger people. One of her reasons for being in Texas had been her lost virtue, which, as it had turned out, hadn't been true at all . . . until Whit Reagor had changed all that.

If she'd had any hopes for her and Whit's future, they had been shattered in the middle of the night, in an angry exchange of words.

She whipped around to face Joseph, renewing the pledge she'd made, the pledge she'd voiced to Whit only moments before he'd stormed from her room in the wee hours of this very morning.

"No, Joseph, I haven't changed my mind." She elevated her chin an extra inch. "I will marry you."

"Bless you." The tension in his face subsided with the swiftness of an ebbing tide. "Shall we set a date?"

Her chin lowered a fraction. She would keep her vow, both to Joseph and to the stubborn, bitter man who had stolen her heart. But she couldn't bring herself to rush into the marriage.

"Joseph," she said, her words measured, "I've barely arrived in Trick'em, and I'd prefer to get organized before having to deal with wedding plans."

"Whatever you wish, dearest."

Yes, Mariah thought, she would marry Joseph . . . But as she watched him, Whit's words echoed in her mind. Her body would never catch fire when Joseph touched her, as it had each time in Whit's presence. Nevertheless . . .

Mariah swallowed the air lodging in her throat. She would simply close her eyes . . . and think of England.

The next morning Mariah felt somewhat better and got on with her business. She and Joseph had a farm to revitalize, and her teaching was ahead of her.

Bathed and dressed, she prepared a basket of sandwiches and a jug of the chilled tea so many Texans enjoyed, and called on the Lamkins. Mud had kept them from the fields, and they were working at their dugout. Three of them enthusiastically greeted their visitor.

Molly had been feeding the chickens. Lisping a mile a minute, she jumped with joy and wound her grubby hands around Mariah's riding skirts. Patsy put down her whetstone, abandoning the plow blade she had been sharpening, and strolled over to chat. A.W., a sickly pallor to his skin, ceased his roof repair. "Soddies leak like a sieve," he explained, offering a handshake.

Aggie, stopping only a moment for an introduction to Mariah, continued to curry the skinny old calico mule of contrary persuasion.

"I've brought lunch." Mariah took her basket from the saddlehorn. "Hope you're hungry, because I've fixed plenty."

"Did you bring candy?" Molly asked, her hazel eyes dancing in expectation.

"Candy? My goodness, no, Molly pie," Mariah teased. "I won't be responsible for rotting your teeth."

The young girl tapped a forefinger at the space in her mouth. "I don't have any teeth."

"Well, in that case, what's the harm?" Adoring this small bundle of strawberry-blond hair and wide, gap-toothed grins, Mariah reached into her pocket. "How about these for dessert?"

Molly squealed in delight over the wrapped hard candies, and Aggie put the currycomb away to take two steps toward Mariah and say thank you. She turned back to the mule.

"Let's go into the house," Patsy suggested.

Mariah made a detour by Old Glue and fetched a wrapped parcel before following the Lamkins into the soddy. After the sandwiches and drinks were consumed, Mariah picked up the parcel that had been sitting beside her chair.

Molly climbed onto Mariah's lap and, with typical childish curiosity, began to fiddle with the package. "For me?" she asked.

"Yes. For you and for Aggie."

The older girl, who had been quiet as a church mouse during the meal and had kept her distance, tangled a finger into her hair and eyed the giver of the package suspiciously.

"Aggie, I've brought you your very own *McGuffey's Reader.*"

Aggie ducked her chin, accepted the book, and shrank back to run her fingers over the bindings.

"Now, Aggie," her mother chided, "don't be that way. What do you say to Miss Mariah?"

"Thank you, ma'am" was the weak reply.

"You're welcome." Obviously, Aggie was shy, but Mariah reasoned that in time she'd bring the girl around.

Her bubbling personality in full display, Molly set to unwrapping the gift. "Oooh, pretty!" She turned the book over and over in her hand, then her big eyes looked up at Mariah. "But I don't know how to read." Those eyes brightened. "But my daddy doeth. He readth the Bible every night," she ended, stretching out the last part.

"Well, Molly, soon you and your sister will be reading. I'm going to teach you. Someday you can read the Bible to your father. Would you like that?"

She nodded and began to flip through the pages. "Thank you, Mith Mariah. Will I learn thums, too?"

"Oh, yes. Sums are on the list."

"Why don't you girls get back to your chores?" A.W. suggested. "Mama and I need to talk with Miss Mariah."

Molly reached up to hug and kiss her benefactress. She scrambled down from Mariah's lap, skipped over to her mother, and entrusted the reader to Patsy's protection.

Trodding slowly to the right, Aggie tucked her copy of *McGuffey's* into a weathered old trunk.

Once both girls were outside, A.W. said, "We sure do appreciate what you're doing for our younguns, but it'll be a few more weeks afore the lessons can start. We've still got a right smart amount of plowin' and plantin' ahead of us."

"I know. Patsy told me as much. But I wanted to visit with the girls and give them the books. I hope you don't mind my doing so."

A.W. and his wife replied in unison, "Of course not!"

"I'm glad. And I must be on my way." Mariah stood. "I've much to do at the farm."

There was a lot to be accomplished, and over the next two weeks she gave all her energies. She settled into a routine of days at the farm, evenings in Trick'em. Gradually, the hovel changed into a cozy home with draperies, a door knocker—admittedly ludicrous, considering the hide door—and cherished belongings. Mariah gained a great deal of satisfaction not only from her efforts in the house but also from the noticeable improvements in the farm.

She had help, of course. Joseph worked day and night. Pablo Martinez and his family, as Birdie had promised, proved to be able helpers.

In addition to assisting Joseph repair the fence line and the cabin's roof, Pablo had built a small shack of canvas and wood, thus easing Mariah's concern about their living quarters.

Conchita, the Martinezes' daughter, had displayed efficiency with the housework and with the newly purchased flock of chickens. As an added bonus, the young Mexican girl was interested in furthering her education. She could read Spanish, but not English. During the hours after supper, Mariah had begun tutoring her in reading. Conchita was a quick learner, and her teacher was pleased at the results.

Pablo's wife, Evita, had worked alongside Mariah planting a market garden of corn, greens, squash, onions, beans both of the green and pinto varieties, and love apples—tomatoes they were called here in Texas. Beyond those, Evita had provided seeds for peppers with the strange name of *jalapeños*.

Mariah prayed for the garden's success. As far as she was concerned, their livelihood depended on it; she didn't share Joseph's enthusiasm for the profitability of growing pears in

Coleman County.

Of course, Mariah had had many thoughts of Gail during those two weeks of activities. She hoped and prayed everything was now fine with the Stricklands.

More often, Mariah had thought of Whit . . .

Even now as she drove the cart toward town to purchase supplies on this warm April afternoon, she recalled the many unforgettable hours in his embrace. Did Whit have these same memories? Surely he hadn't forgotten . . . Cutting across a stretch of the Western Trail that sliced through Crosswind, she yearned to get a glimpse of the ranch's owner.

She saw a few head of cattle, very little grass, a scattering of bluebonnets, and a lot of prickly pears . . . but nothing of Whit.

Maybe it was better this way, his keeping his distance. Why torture herself with what-might-have-beens?

She veered her regard to the present, glancing at the man sitting next to her. Pablo Martinez, whose white hair belied his middle years, was a proud and pious man of aristocratic Spanish stock.

Pablo had suffered from his decision to live in the country of his wife's birth, Mariah knew, yet he was determined to have his own land. "Soon," he'd said many times.

The fine gray horse, one of Whit's gifts, topped a knoll, and an unusual sight came into view. Not ten feet from the roadway and not fifty feet from Mariah and Pablo, a man and two boys were unrolling barbed wire—on Crosswind property!

"Pablo, would you look at that?"

She tapped the whip, meaning to edge the cart nearer for closer scrutiny of the men, but Pablo put a restraining hand across hers. "Keep going, señorita," he said in his perfect, though accented, English. "Do not get involved."

" 'I don't plan to, but I . . . well, I never thought Whit Reagor would build a fence."

"Those are not the men of Señor Reagor."

Bemused, she asked, "You mean they're squatters?"

"Yes." As they passed the fence builders, he eyed the oldest of the three. "That one is Spuds O'Brien; the others are his sons." Pablo turned his head to nod slightly at Mariah. "They will not be squatters on Crosswind for long, not on the property of the rich Señor Reagor."

"What do you mean?" she asked, hurrying the gray toward town. "Mr. Reagor wouldn't do them harm."

"Who is to guess the actions of a man whose possessions are threatened? If I were he, I would guard what is mine with all my resources."

She disregarded Pablo's personal analogy. "He won't resort to violence over the matter," she stated, believing her words to be true.

"Señor Reagor is a very rich and powerful man, and he is protective of his belongings." At her visible distress, Pablo backed down. "The law is on his side, and Señor O'Brien is not very smart. Apparently he doesn't know he can lay no claim to owned lands." He paused. "Did you know the Jaye farm and Crosswind Ranch are the only properties in this county with deeds?"

"No, I wasn't aware of that."

"It is true." Pablo thrummed his fingers on a knee. "I should add the Strickland ranch to the list. But, in essence, it is part of Crosswind. Señor Reagor gave that land to the Stricklands as a wedding gift."

"I've heard that, but I thought most of the land was owned by the various cattlemen."

"This land had no owner but the Indians until the white man triumphed over those savages. Land and cattle were for the taking, and there was no need for deeds. But times are changing, and that is why so many people such as myself have come here to claim land."

Mariah felt a sense of security. Legally, the farm was protected. On second thought, she realized, recalling O'Brien and his sons, that being an owner didn't mean freedom from trouble.

"Pablo, should we tell the sheriff about the O'Briens?" Should she get word to Whit?

"Señor Reagor will know soon enough."

They cleared the edge of Trick'em. She reasoned with herself that Whit's business wasn't her concern. Anyway, she had her own business to tend. As they drew up in front of Dick Cheatham's general store, she said, "Pablo, ask the blacksmith if he can recommend a good riding horse." She handed him a stack of gold coins. "A mare, preferably."

Pablo nodded, obviously pleased she trusted his judgment in horses, and accepted the reins.

She started toward the white clapboard building housing the general store. "Mariah.! " she heard from behind, and turned to Gail Strickland, who wore a smart calico dress of blue and gray, a pert bonnet atop her head of black curls.

Mariah searched for signs of paleness, of unhappiness, and, seeing none, she embraced her friend. "How are you? I've missed you. How long have you been home?"

"So many questions. I'm fine; I've missed you, too; I arrived the day before yesterday." Gail inclined her head toward the brightly painted building that housed Jackie Jo's Café. "Shall we indulge in a cup of tea?"

Arm in arm they strolled to the eating establishment, which was empty of people save for the proprietress—a stylishly plump woman of about forty with green eyes, a head of rich dark hair braided and fashioned in a cornet, and a bubbling personality.

"I've been wanting to meet you, Miss McGuire." Jackie Jo Jamerson clutched a piece of chalk to write their order on her slate. "Have you really visited London?"

"Yes."

"Oh, how nice! What is the latest fashion?"

"Sorry, but I haven't been there in years."

"That's too bad." Jackie Jo pursed her lips. "I'm planning to open a ladies' apparel shop, and I'd hoped you could lend an expert opinion."

"I'm very much a provincial islander, so I'm afraid I would be of no service, but I wish you good luck with your enterprise," Mariah said sincerely. "Please tell me about your shop."

Jackie Jo launched into an animated monologue. She planned to import fine silks and the like, and a seamstress would copy fashions from *Godey's Lady's Book*. Shoes and millinery would be featured, as well as a full line of lingerie. "Anything the fashionable woman needs, I'll carry," Jackie Jo said, winding down. "Stock is arriving already."

"Could we see it?" Gail asked.

"Well, it's a mite picked over. I had a gentleman customer last evening."

"Surely you jest," Gail interjected. "These cowpokes around here don't give a damn what their women wear! Well, except for Whit Reagor, that is."

"Why, that's exactly who it was! And when I pressed Mr. Reagor about his lady's coloring, he said he was looking for something for a blonde. Wonder who she is?"

Mariah caught her breath, rage was chafing at her high collar. He was up to his old tricks of outfitting the ladies! What had his sister said? As near as Mariah could recall, it was, "He buys 'em clothes just to strip those duds off their backs." Blast him!

Jackie Jo tucked her slate under her arm, and slapped her forehead with the heel of a hand. "Why, of course! How could I be so dense? I'll bet she's that blonde from Dublin who was in here the other day. Barbara, she called herself."

Barbara Catley! The blood drained from Mariah's face.

Chapter Thirteen

"Jackie Jo, we sure could use that tea," Gail said into the café's stony silence, and the proprietress set to her duties.

There would be no more wondering about Whit's absence, Mariah seethed. He had been dressing—undressing!—Barbara Catley. His womanizing was all the impetus she needed to go on with her wedding plans without regret. Heck, *sans souci* . . . ! No, she wouldn't go that far.

Jackie Jo returned with their order. Thankfully she offered no more gossip.

Gail stirred sugar into her beverage. "Are you all right? Your face was positively colorless a minute ago."

"My pantaloons were crawling up my backside," she lied.

"I don't think that's the problem at all.

You've been acting funny since Whit's name was mentioned."

Determined to steer the conversation in another direction, Mariah voiced a question that had edged at her thoughts since Gail had confided in her. "Did you have a talk with your husband?"

"You don't want to talk about Whit?"

"Right."

"Something happened between the two of you," Gail concluded.

"Did you have a talk with your husband?"

"All right, have it your way." The heart-faced young woman sighed and placed her spoon on the saucer. "Yes, Ed and I had a talk. A very successful talk. We've both promised to work harder at saying how we feel."

"Oh, Gail, I'm so pleased." She reached to squeeze her friend's hand. "I hope everything works out."

A becoming blush flowered in Gail's cheeks. "I think it will. Oh, Mariah, I'm so happy! The last two nights have been heaven on earth. The days, too, of course. Not once have I had the urge for a drink."

"That's the ticket!"

"Now let's get back to you," Gail said, riding the crest of happiness and wanting to infuse it in Mariah. "How was the wagon trip from my brother's ranch?"

Knowing her friend, Mariah was certain that skirting the subject of Whit would be an impossibility, so she gave in to a small degree.

"We encountered nary a bull."

"Damn, you can be so close-mouthed when you're set on it. Evidently you and Whit didn't work out your differences."

"Exactly."

"You know, Mariah, nothing pleases me more than to find you here in Trick'em," she said over the rim of her cup, "but does this mean you're going through with your wedding?"

"Exactly."

Gail studied her free hand, which rested on the tabletop. "I trust you'll be happy."

"I plan to."

"Have you set a date?"

Up to this point Mariah hadn't agreed to anything definite, but, still angered over Whit's quick turn to Barbara, she now came to a decision. "I think this Saturday at noon would be an ideal time."

"Two days from now."

"That's right. And I want you to attend."

Uncertainty passed over the brunette's face. "I can't promise anything. Ed . . . well, you know how it is around here, ranchers versus farmers."

Mariah tried to disguise her hurt as she said, "Then I won't pit you between us and your husband."

"I appreciate your consideration, and I'm sorry it has to be this way."

"Think nothing of it. You've only just begun to have a real marriage and you shouldn't be asked to jeopardize it."

They lapsed into silence, both upset at this test of their friendship. At long last, Gail spoke. "Does Whit know you're getting married?"

"I haven't the foggiest idea, and I care even less."

"Milady protests too loud." The younger woman toyed with her spoon, then lifted a brow. "If I were you, I wouldn't put too much stock in idle gossip about Barbara Catley. Whit told me he's through with her, and I believe him. He doesn't lie." She placed a silver coin on the table. "You know, I haven't called on my Reagor kinsman since I've been home. Think I'll mosey on out there and find out for myself about . . . Well, I'll see what he's got to say about your wedding."

"I'd rather you didn't discuss me with him." *Let me get through Saturday!*

"Mariah, I can see through your story. I know something happened between you and Whit, because your face can't lie. I *don't* know what happened to cause you that obvious pain, but you're my friend and I don't want you unhappy. Call me a meddler, call me a matchmaker, but I'm going to take the bull by the horns."

"Please don't. Don't interfere."

"That, for your sake, I refuse to do." The chair legs scraped as Gail shot upward. "See you later, Mariah."

Quicker than lightning, the younger woman

departed the café's interior, Mariah on her trail voicing her protests. Gail paid no heed, but in her rush she caught the heel of her boot on the top of the four stairs. Her ankle twisted, and she lost her balance, barreling forward.

Gail sprawled to the dirt street, her screams filling the air as a bone popped. Her bonnet landed a ways from her head. The air whooshed out of her lungs, and her body lay inert—all in the breath of a second!

"Oh, no!" Mariah hurried down the steps and bent to brush her friend's hair away from her dirt-streaked face. Lifting the unmoving head to cradle it in her arms, she spoke to three bystanders who approached the accident. "Someone get a doctor!"

A fresh-faced youth, wearing a large felt hat and suspenders over a crisp white shirt, whipped around and took off in a run. "I'll get 'im!"

Gail stirred. "I'm all right," she said, her voice faint. " 'Cept for my—ooh!—my leg."

"Lie quiet." Mariah's ears detected a rattling sound, and she turned her line of sight to a spot under the open porch. "Uh oh."

A diamond-back viper was coiled not three feet from them. Several bulbous segments grew on the tip of its tail, which was shaking and rattling. Huge fangs glistened in the sunlight as a forked tongue flicked in and out of its mouth.

"Stay back," Mariah cautioned the crowd that had gathered. She eased her arm from

Gail's neck, and with slow motions, picked up her reticule and extracted her six-gun. No more did she tarry. In the blink of an eye, she cocked, aimed, and fired.

The rattlesnake's head blew off, serpent blood flew, and the coiled body collapsed in a heap of scales.

"Did you see that?" a man asked.

"Boy, howdy, that gal's one helluva shot."

"Oughta put her to clearing out squatters."

"Careful now, Jiggs. She might be puttin' a hole in yer ranchin' hide, instead. She's the sodbuster Jaye's gal."

Mariah ignored their comments. Her actions were squarely on helping Gail, who had pulled herself painfully to a seated position.

"This is what I get . . . for trying . . . to mind your business." As the town's lone physician arrived, Gail wiped her shaking hand across a smear of dirt on her face. "I . . . I'm going to talk to Ed about . . . about attending your wedding. Damn you, be easy, Doc!" she demanded, running the last sentence into one word as Dr. John Metcalfe straightened her leg. Gasping, she went on with her halting words to Mariah. "I'll make him understand. Splint or whatever, we'll be at your wedding on Saturday."

"A weddin'? Well, I'll be danged." A grizzled old man, who had just joined the others, leaned on his cane. "Gonna invite the townfolks to the doin's, young woman?"

"Don't bother, Smiley, you don't want to attend," said a large, pale-complected woman with black hair and condescending airs. "The happy couple happens to be of the farming class."

"Ah, thanks fer tellin' me, Miz Tullos." He flipped a hand at Mariah. "Never mind, young lady. Never mind."

Mariah ignored them, and accompanied the doctor and his conscripted assistant when they carried Gail to his office. The lad who had fetched the physician rode the two-mile distance to the Crazy Hoof Ranch and alerted Ed Strickland to his wife's injury. Mariah lent her assistance as Dr. Metcalfe fashioned a cast of bandage and whalebone.

Gail had suffered a broken shinbone, and Mariah castigated herself over the fall. It wouldn't have happened if she hadn't been so sensitive about Whit.

What difference did it make if he knew about the upcoming wedding? No doubt he was too busy with Barbara to care what Mariah McGuire did, or did not, do. Blast him!

On the second morning after Whit had purchased several items of fine clothing as a peace offering to Mariah, he leaned against the corral, put his foot on the rail, and disregarded the Arabian colt being paraded for his benefit. For reasons he didn't wish to examine, he was aching to see Mariah.

While he had been out on the range supervising the roundup and trying to settle his mind, he had, time after time, gone over their last moments together.

Okay, she had sent him packing, but she'd been seeing red at the time. But then, when wasn't she mad? he asked himself. One thing about Mariah McGuire, she gave better than she got. She was no shrinking violet.

He grinned, recalling the way her newly acquired freckles had stood out and her bosom had jiggled when she was riled. Damn, she was a fetching gal. If only he could get her to listen to reason.

Thankfully, she hadn't made a move toward wedding Joe Jaye; the barkeep Heavy Everett had told Whit as much. That tidbit had reinforced his earlier conclusion. When push came to shove, Mariah would keep a "Miss" in front of her name.

Feeling confident after his talk with Heavy, Whit had visited Jackie Jo for those clothes. Jackie Jo had a way with gossip, and to protect Mariah from wagging tongues, he had told a white lie, that he was dressing a blonde.

His arms piled high with boxes, he had aimed for the back door of Birdie Turner's boardinghouse, but a cowpoke from Crosswind had collared him to say squatters were stringing barbed wire across a stretch of Crosswind.

The duds had had to wait.

It had been late afternoon, yesterday, by the time Spuds O'Brien and his boys were convinced to pull up stakes.

When Whit had arrived home, he was met with bad news. Gail's broken leg and romance had been the last thing on his mind as he had rushed to her side. He had tried to tease her about "shooting horses with broken legs," but she was too woozy from laudanum to comprehend. Funny, though, she had kept jabbering about a blonde. Opium did strange things to a person's mind.

Maybe Gail had been referring to Barbara, who had turned up on the range one night, wanting . . . Well, she had gotten his message, and was long gone.

"Whaddya say, Reagor?"

Whit turned to the familiar voice of Charlie Tullos. Tullos, a bow-legged man of forty-three who wore a rolled-brim felt hat along with new dungarees and a leather vest, alit his paint gelding and wound the reins around the corral rail.

A suspicious eye cast at the bully who, it was common knowledge around Trick'em, took his marital frustrations out on others, Whit frowned. "What do you want, Tullos?"

"A minute of your time."

Whit's scowl deepened, and he crossed his arms over his chest. "My time's too valuable to waste on you."

"Is that any way to talk to a neighbor?"

"Get gone, Tullos."

Tullos rubbed his fingers under his hooked nose. "Hold on now, Reagor. I know you and I haven't seen eye to eye in a long while, what with that Jaye business and all, but I think it's time we settled our differences."

Whit had two choices: send Tullos packing or try to be reasonable. He decided on the latter. "What's on your mind?"

"I need your help. I've got squatters on my property, and they're stringing fence. Besides that, those no-good sodbusters have filed a claim in the Land Office."

"Way I see it, you should've bought your land, fair and square. Then you wouldn't be having this trouble."

"Hell's bells, Reagor, you know nobody but you and Leroy Smith bought land outright. All the ranchers around here, myself included, have been here for years; we should have first claim." When this got no response, Tullos said, "I hear tell you had a little trouble yourself. Spuds O'Brien and his boys."

"They're taken care of."

"Oh, yeah? How's that?"

Whit lit a cigar. Squinting at the smoke, he drawled, "I sent 'em over to your place."

"Dammit, Reagor, what did you go and do that for?" Tullos's face was tight with fury, but his tension appeared to ease after a few seconds. "Aw, you're just sporting me."

"Truth be known, I don't know where they've lit, but their hides are long gone from Crosswind."

"Congratulations. Now put yourself in my place. Don't you think I got a right to what's mine?"

In principle, Whit had to agree. "What do you need my help for? If you're wanting to run them off, you've got your own men."

"This is bigger than just me and my boys. A few of the ranchers got together last night. We've decided to form a cattlemen's association to show those farmers who's in power around here."

"And what if you can't get them to leave, peaceful-like?"

"Draw your own conclusions."

"Fire and bullets."

Tullos grinned. "Give the man a cigar."

"Already got one. And you can count me out of killings, Tullos."

The bully's face twisted into an ugly mask. "Your skin's sure turned a peculiar shade of yellow, Reagor, since you tied up with that Jaye bastard."

"You lookin' to take me on, Tullos?" Whit took a giant step toward the man who hired out his dirty work, and grabbed him by the vest. "You're getting mighty brave here lately. What's going on? Is Temperence finally allowin' you to wear your balls?"

"Leave my wife out of this."

"Gladly. Our little chat's over with, anyway." Whit thrust him backward. "Now, get the hell off my property."

Tullos got his balance. "All right, Reagor. I'm leaving. But don't say I never gave you the chance to side with your own kind on this fencing thing."

"I won't lose any sleep over it."

"That so? Well, I reckon you just might." Tullos swung onto his gelding, pulling the reins to the left. "Yeah, reckon you might, 'cause my boys are gonna give your *compadre,* Joe Jaye, a right smart wedding present."

"Wedding present?" Whit echoed, unable to quell his sudden interest. "What do you mean, wedding present?"

"Well, I'll be. You mean Joe Jaye didn't invite you to his wedding? What a shame, you being his pal and all." Tullos shook his head. "Seeing as how he's keeping you in the dark, I guess I ought to tell you. Jaye and that red-head he imported are getting hitched tomorrow at high noon."

Chapter 14

Anger formed behind two narrowed eyes. Waiting for her husband to return from his appointed task, Temperence Tullos paced her bedroom floor while ruminating over the recent foil to her scheme. Lord Joe had dropped her when that big-tits snoot had hit town, and Temperence wasn't going to let him get away with it . . .

Her gashed pride was secondary to her fury. Both wittingly and unwittingly, Joe had thrown a hitch into the mechanism of her plans. To think she had been on the verge of success in getting Leroy Smith back in Coleman County—and keeping him here! Her trembling hand swept across the perfume bottles that graced her rosewood bureau. Crystal shattered on the floor; scented oils mingled noxiously. The temper tantrum gave her a modicum of relief.

Even though her designs had been thwarted, hers had been a crafty scheme of which she still held marked pride: Lure Leroy back with the promise of "riches." Rumors had circulated around Coleman County since before the war. Oil was to be had for the digging. Temperence didn't believe it, but she wasn't above using anything to its best advantage.

Thus, because it bordered on the Tullos's Painted Rock Ranch, the Jaye farm held the key. None other was satisfactory, not with Temperence wanting Leroy close to her side . . .

And in that vein she had promised Lord Joe another five hundred dollars if he'd sign over the mineral rights to his land. To sweeten the pot, she had suggested he dig a water well, at her benevolence of course, to irrigate his ridiculous saplings. The money-grubbing pipsqueak had shown enthusiasm for financial gain, all the while expressing disbelief at her "wasting money".

Little did he know. As soon as the hole hit a respectable depth, she figured to seed it with a barrel or two of oil. The county newspaper was certain to pick up the story.

Leroy knew the value of petroleum; he'd gone to Titusville up in Yankee country to explore for it. Lately, though, he had told her through his letters that the big shots had shut him out of making his fortune, and he was scratching to get out of Pennsylvania.

Her plan had been to mail Leroy a copy of the newspaper clipping along with funds for the trip back to her arms, as well as the deed made out in his favor. She knew Leroy, knew he would have landed on the deal like a fly on a cow patty. Before she'd had enough time to acquire those rights, however, Lord Joe had turned his scrawny back on Temperence.

"Bastard," she uttered through clenched teeth. "You'll pay for doublecrossing me."

Actually, she had already begun her revenge, and when Charlie returned to the Painted Rock, Temperence cornered him. Pushing a forefinger toward his nose, she asked, "Is the Jaye character dead yet?"

"Now, Shugums honey, be patient. That no-good granger will—"

"Don't you 'now, Shugums honey' me."

"These things take time," Charlie said, using the conciliatory tone he always used with his wife, but his nostrils expanded, and he turned his head from left to right. "What stinks?"

"You stink"—her slippered toe kicked his shin—"you lackadaisical buffoon!"

Rubbing his leg, he explained, "I'm trying to get the other ranchers on my side. I built a fire under 'em last night about all these fences that're cropping up."

Temperence was unimpressed. "Why is it, Charles Vernon Tullos, that you can't accomplish the simplest little task without dragging your feet?"

"You know I've gotta work around Whit Reagor."

She was further infuriated at the mention of

the one man who was immune to her charms. "Why should he be a problem? Kill him, too."

"Whoa now." Charlie patted the air. "I can't do that. Reagor's one of us, and I'd be in more trouble than I could ever get out of."

"How about I kill him, then?" she asked, extracting a carved-handle pistol from her armoire. "How about I kill the both of them?"

"No, Temperence." Charlie hated to see his wife all agitated, and he wanted to please her, but he knew she didn't want Reagor dead. Why should she? *He* wasn't the one who was stringing fences. Charlie felt certain that once Jaye was taken care of, Temperence would settle down about this Reagor business.

He cut to her side and took the gun from her hand. "Killing is men's work."

"Then act like a man instead of a spineless jellyfish. How much longer are you going to let Reagor laugh behind your back? He does, you know, after the way you let his sawed-off farmerfriend get the best of you," she lied. "For Christ's sake, Charles, ever'body's laughing at you since you let Reagor beat the hell out of you that night at Maudie's."

Her loathing for Charles had never been as full blown as at this minute. He was such a coward. She was accustomed to this flaw in his character, but what bothered her was, the one time he had shown a little gumption, he'd used it to run off Leroy.

"To think I once thought you had some power around here," she went on. "Power, ha!

You're not worthy to share my bed."

"Now, Shugums, don't get upset. I'm doing my best, but you ask so much. If you'll give me the chance, I can take care of Joe Jaye. If you could be a little patient—"

"I hate it when you whine."

Turning to the window and peering out the pane, she composed herself. Lord Joe would soon be pushing up daisies, provided her husband lived up to his promise, but what would she do after that? Those mineral rights still wouldn't be in her name, and no telling what would become of his land. Unless his lordship was married . . . ! A new plan formed. That McGuire woman would need money after Lord Joe went to his grave. A sweet deal to the bereaved widow would be in order. A real sweet deal.

Temperence decided to bide her time and wait for the right moment.

Charlie walked up behind her and grasped her buttocks. "Don't be angry with me. I'll put that dirt-turner out of his misery . . . tonight."

"Wait till he's married, then do it."

"Why did you change your mind?"

"Don't question me, Charles. Do it because I said so." Her upper lip curled back, and she made for the table beside her bed. Slowly opening the drawer, she extracted a leather whip. "And if you're the least bit squeamish, send to San Antonio for T-Bone Hicks and his partners."

His eyes widened on the whip, and a grin

deepened the furrows of his face. "I'll do anything you say."

"But you're asking me to do something that goes against my principles." Joseph frowned at his intended, then went back to repairing the final cut in his barbed-wire fence. "I'll grow pears, or I'll die trying."

"Giving more of your time to a cash crop was only a suggestion," Mariah replied patiently, though inwardly she was frustrated by Joseph's lack of farming sense.

This was his farm, however, not hers and thus, she would not force the issue. But at the same time, she and Evita would continue to concentrate their energies on the market garden.

"I must say, though, dearest," he admitted, accepting the lunch basket she had brought from the cabin, "with this drought we'll be lucky to keep the pears alive."

Why mention that they appeared dead already? Joseph was too stubborn to accept the truth. If only he wouldn't be so hardheaded about their crop, they might make something of this farm.

And if only she would quit pining for Whit Reagor . . . In her heart of hearts she longed to see him, but she kept envisioning him with his arms wrapped around Barbara Catley. This thought helped her keep her determination to wed Joseph, tomorrow, as scheduled.

Yet . . .

"Did you call on Mrs. Strickland on your way out here this morning?" Joseph asked.

Mariah collected her thoughts. "Yes, I took her some soup and a pudding. She's feeling stronger. Both Stricklands have accepted the invitation to our wedding."

"Splendid." His booted foot touched an empty pail. "While you're out here, would you mind filling that for me?"

Eyeing the pitiful saplings ringed by the expensive fence, Mariah railed at his request. "What will we do when the pond goes dry?" No reply was forthcoming. "Joseph, I've been thinking . . . We'd have plenty of water, for the pears and for a profitable truck garden, if we dug a well."

"A . . . well?" He blanched. Turning his back to bend over a roll of barbed wire, he said shakily, "Don't you have anything to do to prepare for our nuptials?"

Perplexed at both his reaction, and his reluctance to discuss farming alternatives, Mariah frowned. Why did she get the feeling he was keeping something from her? But she told herself not to make too much of his behavior. What could possibly lurk behind a water well?

Joseph snapped his fingers to catch her attention, and again asked, "Mariah, my dear, are you ready for our wedding?"

"Yes."

"Excellent," he said. "And now that we've named a wedding date, I'm going to call on

Whitman Reagor. I want him to join us for our happy occasion."

Her heart raced. How could she get through the wedding with Whit in attendance? "It's your prerogative to invite him."

"You never speak of Whitman, dearest, and I find that peculiar." Suspicion drew Joseph's blond brows together. "Didn't you enjoy those days in his company?"

"We didn't talk much. Mrs. Strickland was my companion and chaperone," she explained for the tenth time since her arrival at the farm.

"Whitman mentioned being fond of you. You must have spent some time chatting."

And a lot of time making love, she thought. "He is your friend, Joseph, not mine."

"I should have known he's not your type of chap. Too rough. Too much the frontier man."

"Exactly," she lied.

The tension in Joseph's face eased. "But I'm puzzled. You did accept his very generous engagement gift . . ."

"For heaven's sake, *you* accepted the wagon, not me!" She hugged her arms. And I don't feel comfortable about your accepting such a gift from him. I think we should give it back. Pablo found us a fine buckskin mare; we don't need the wagon."

"Mariah, I can't believe you're so ungrateful."

"That wagon and team cost a great deal of money. Let's not be beholden, Joseph."

"Whit would be offended if we shunned his

gift."

"He was giving us charity," she prevaricated. "Doesn't that offend you?"

Studying the ground, he rubbed his lips. "Now that you put it that way, yes, it doesn't seem right. I'll return the wagon when I call on him."

"Thank you."

"Well, that settles that." Joseph brushed the front of his new workshirt, which had been stitched by Mariah. "Let's talk more about the arrangements. Are you certain you don't mind being married in the cabin?"

"The arrangements suit me fine."

"How dear you are." Joseph rushed over to land a kiss on her cheek, an embrace that drew no emotional response. She pulled away. "Why do you always recoil from me?" he asked, his gray eyes worried.

Because you're not Whit. "There will be plenty of time for kisses after we're married."

"We'll be doing more than kissing."

A feeling of dread curled the length of her spine. "We both have chores. I must go."

Without waiting for him to object, and with her eyes downcast, she hastened along the quarter-mile trail to the cabin. Though Joseph had put forth a large effort to make her happy, she couldn't help being annoyed at him, at herself, at everything.

Raising her eyes as she neared the cabin, she stopped in her tracks. A huge sorrel stallion was tied to the hitching post.

"Bay Fire." Whit!

She didn't know whether to laugh or to cry, to run or to stay put.

"Señorita" Conchita Martinez, a teenage girl of tiny stature with olive skin and big dark eyes, lifted the door flap and called across the thirty feet separating Mariah from the cabin, "You have a visitor."

"I know." She took a draft of air and forced herself forward. "Leave us, please.

"As you wish," Conchita replied in her usual timid manner and, ducking her chin, did as bidden.

Mariah moistened her now-dry lips and straightened her shoulders. Lifting the cowhide flap, she entered the small abode. The covering slapped into place, leaving the room shadowed and forbidding. Her eyes adjusting to the change of light, her knees shaking, she took two steps forward but halted as the form of a man came into view.

Whit reared back in a straight chair, one booted foot crossed over a knee and his arms folded over his chest. He said not a word; neither did she. Her starved eyes devoured his image. He wore black breeches, a yoked white shirt with the sleeves rolled up to expose the dark tufts of hair and the hard muscles of his arms. Pulled low on his brow, a gray Stetson did not hide the unreadable expression in his blue eyes.

She watched him ease his angled foot to the floor and spread his legs wide, her pulse racing as the material of those dark breeches cupped his manly lines.

"You never could keep your eyes off me, could you?" he drawled.

"You have that effect on women." *Including Barbara.* Mariah gathered her wits. "You must leave. If Joseph—"

"Why should Joe mind my being here? I'm just making a neighborly little call." He lifted a shoulder. "Place looks nice, Red. China, pewter, doodads. Looks like you're planning to stay a spell. That's what I heard, anyhow." He unfolded his arms, his right hand reaching to the floor behind him to pick up a shirt-size white box with a purple ribbon tied around it. "Brought you a wedding present."

The wits she had gathered crumbled. A tear slipped down her cheek.

"Heyyyy, this isn't"—he shook the box, then untied the ribbon—"this isn't a ticket to paradise, it's only a small token of my esteem. It's not worth bawling over."

"I'm not crying. I've got something in my eye."

"Let me help."

The box in one hand, Whit pushed himself out of the chair and headed toward her, but she scooted around him and made for the opposite side of the room. The bed stopped her.

At her back, she felt the heat of his presence before he dropped the box to the bed and looped his arms around her waist. Tilting his head, he touched the lobe of her ear with his tongue, drawing a quiver from her traitorous body.

"Don't you want to see what I bought you?" he asked huskily.

"No."

"Aw, now. Don't be so stubborn, darlin'." He hugged his hard length to her hips. " 'Course I sent for the present with the expectation you'd wear it for me, but shucks, ma'am, I'm not gonna be a hard ass about who you wear it for."

"I don't want your gifts. Some things in life can't be bought."

"Is that so? Well, I beg to differ. Most things in life *can* be bought."

"That's one of the troubles with you, Whit Reagor. You're used to snapping your fingers, then the world falls at your boots." But all the while she was saying this, Mariah was responding to his touch. "I want you to leave and take your wagon and your wedding gift with you." Impulsively, she added, "Give them to Barbara Catley."

"What?" He drew back. A knowing expression crossed his lean features before he chuckled. "You're jealous." His fingernail stroked her jaw. "Is that what's wrong with you, why you're all riled? No need to be, darlin'. She left for Dublin the same day she got here. On my orders."

"That woman has nothing to do with our problems," Mariah shot back, though she was somewhat relieved. "You've got to leave, and I do mean now—before Joseph sees us!"

"Not until I get what I'm here for." He turned her to face him, drawing her to his tensed body. His mouth dipped to nuzzle her neck. "I want to hear it from your lips. Tell me you're going to marry Joe Jaye."

"I am going to marry Joe Jaye," she replied defiantly.

Whit dropped his arms and stepped back. Damn her mulishness. Damn her defiance! Well, he wasn't leaving until she was hurting as bad as he did at this moment . . . Or at least realized what she would be missing.

"Fare-thee-well then, little darlin'. All the best to ya. And keep my present." He got no satisfaction from the pain in her eyes.

Once more he pulled her to him. "You're gonna look gorgeous in it. It'll drive Joe wild, I'll betcha. Think you'll squirm in his arms like you squirm in mine?"

She *was* squirming. "Don't torture me like this, Whit. Please don't torture me."

"What do you think you're doing to me?" he returned, pushing them both to the bed, the box crushed beneath them. His body covering hers, he grasped her face between his palms. "Do you realize what you're doing to *yourself?* You're a fake. You said you wanted to be rid of Joe, wanted your freedom, but what do you do? You stay here with him, and tomorrow you'll—before God!—promise him abiding faith and everlasting love. Will you give Joe Jaye either one?"

Turning cold at Whit's words, Mariah tried to move her head to the side. "Yes," she hissed.

"Liar. You'll be in my bed before the ink is dry on your marriage license."

"Never!"

"Never is a long, long time."

Again, his mouth swooped down to hers, taking her lips in a kiss that punished and tantalized and left both of them yearning for satisfaction.

"I won't beg you again to be my mistress," he said, hugging her to him and wedging his leg between her thighs. "I'll let you marry Joe, and I won't say a damned word. I won't listen to my conscience when you come begging for the relief only I can give you. I'll take you. Then. And now."

She couldn't allow this to go on. "No. I won't let you hurt me and Joseph. Never again!" She pounded her fists against his arms. "Get away from me!"

The doorflap opened, then dropped quickly, but not before Pablo Martinez's hoarse cry of *"Madre de Dios!"* filled the cabin.

"Sacrebleu!" Again, Mariah pounded a fist against Whit's shoulder. "You knew something like this would happen!"

He rolled away from her. His hand reached under her hips for the box, and he tossed a purple petticoat across her stomach. "Wouldn't you agree that some things need to happen?"

Chapter Fifteen

"Madre de Dios." Pablo Martinez paced the earthen floor of his *casa* and continued speaking in Spanish to his wife. "All my life I have revered the virtue of women, and believed I would defend such honor, but now I am shamed at my cowardice. I should have dragged the evil rancher from the señorita's body."

Evita stopped mashing the pinto beans she was preparing for their dinner. "Did he not stop his rape?"

"Yes."

"Then you should feel no guilt."

"But I do," he replied. "And I feel it is my duty to tell *el patrón* he's been betrayed by the man he admires. You know how Señor Jaye feels about that rancher. 'Whitman this' and 'Whitman that' are forever on his tongue. To think what Señor Reagor has done to him! I must tell."

"Say *nada,* Pablo. Nothing! Think of the consequences if you cleanse your own conscience. *El patrón* may blame the sweet señorita for the rancher's actions, and she would be the one to suffer. We cannot take this chance. She has been too dear and good to us."

"Sin should not go unpunished."

"Do not be so stubborn, my husband. It is not our right as mortals to pass judgment on others."

Incredulous, he asked, "Are you condoning such behavior?"

"You know that is not true, but I feel in my heart that all isn't as it seems."

"You feel too much in your heart. You are soft."

Coyly she gazed at him. "Do you not like my softness?"

He touched her cheek. "I do. For all of our twenty years together, since I stole you from the convent, I have loved your softness . . . and everything about you."

"And I love everything about you."

"We have no money, no land—nothing! How can you love such a man as I?" he asked.

"We have a beautiful daughter, and—"

"—and four sons who lie in a potter's field."

"Why allow the sadness of our past to blight our today? We have a roof over our heads, and our bellies are full. Smell those tortillas and *refritos,*" she said, sniffing the fragrant air.

"The señorita has been kind to us. She brought us from Home Creek and gave us shelter. And now Conchita is learning to read English. Are we not lucky?"

"Yes, God is with us, *mi querida esposa,*" he conceded. "If only he would grant me the wisdom . . . What do I do about the evil Whitman Reagor?"

"Pablo, were you not listening to me at all?"

At this moment, Conchita Martinez entered the canvas-and-wood house. Wordlessly the frail girl carried a basket of laundry, which she began to fold.

Evita said to their daughter, "You are very quiet. For two days you have been this way. Are you unwell?"

"I am fine," she replied, unable to tell the truth.

How could she tell her parents the terrible, shameful truth? If her father knew *el patrón* had defiled her, she feared he would demand they leave this farm. Conchita had no wish to stay here; she yearned to leave, in fact. But for so many days they had been hungry and without shelter, and never again did she want to see her father's eyes clouded with the defeat and humiliation of abject poverty. Never again.

But how could she protect herself from *el patrón?*

From a corner of her downcast eyes, Conchita observed her father as he started to leave their house. Her mother's touch stopped him.

"Pablo, promise me you will leave it in

God's hands."

"Dearly beloved, we are gathered together in the presence of God and these witnesses . . ."

At high noon, Mariah stared at the black-robed minister who stood in front of the cabin's fireplace. To her right was Joseph. Gail, in light of her broken leg, lay propped up in the bed; her husband, a stolid and square-jawed man of medium height, stood next to her. Birdie Turner sat in the rocker. The Martinezes were notably absent, and Mariah didn't have to guess why . . . but, thankfully, Pablo hadn't said a word to Joseph about the previous afternoon.

Another guest stood behind the bridal couple. That scoundrel Whit Reagor!

This was the most miserable moment of Mariah's life.

Yesterday, he'd taken the wagon with him upon leaving. The petticoat had gone with him, too. Small comforts to Mariah's broken heart. He was after nothing beyond trouble-making. Since he didn't want to make her his wife, why wouldn't he leave her in peace so she could become Joseph's?

Actually, she wasn't surprised Whit was attending her wedding. The troublemaker's stare, which she detected as surely as if there were eyes behind her head, drilled into her back. If he spoiled the nuptials, she'd strangle him.

The minister said something, then cleared his

throat.

Joseph's elbow nudged her silk-draped arm. "Mariah," he whispered. "Mariiiahhh."

"If any man can show just cause . . ."

Mariah held her breath.

"Ouch!"

All eyes turned to Gail.

"Something stuck my arse, 'scuse me, Reverend, my sit-upon." She fished behind her, and held up a gold hairpin. "Oh, sorry. It was just this. Carry on."

Mariah gasped. She owned no such fastener. Her face pivoted toward Joseph, and his face was as gray as his eyes. *He's had a woman!* Mariah was shocked, dismayed, stymied.

The bridegroom collected himself, raised his aristocratic nose, and ordered the minister to continue. Reverend Pickle began the vows again, but Mariah's bouquet of wildflowers slipped from her paralyzed grasp.

"D-don't. Don't say any more, Reverend," she said in a stammer, her voice sounding as if it were coming from far away. *I have to think, to think straight.*

Two faces—Gail's and Whit's—brightened at her words, but Birdie, Ed, and the preacher showed true shock. Joseph grabbed Mariah's arm and urged her to be sensible.

"Please, please, Joseph, let go." Forcing her wits together, she turned to the assemblage and stared into Whit's amused eyes. "I'd appreciate it if *all* of you will leave. Surely you can understand that Joseph and I must talk."

Whit winked boldly at Mariah, but to her relief he helped Gail to her crutches, then followed the others as they departed the fiasco.

A couple of minutes after the cabin had filled with tomblike silence, the erstwhile bridegroom got the nerve to speak. "Dearest, what is the matter?"

His attempt at innocence roused a small laugh of hysteria in Mariah. Though she didn't love Joseph, she had respected and cared for him, had considered him as her dear and dependable friend. It hurt to know she wasn't the only woman in his life. He'd let her down. He'd lied to her.

But she had her own sins to account for. She and Joseph had both made mistakes, and that was no way to start a marriage. She supposed she should be thankful for the hairpin's omen of doom, but it still hurt. And now she'd even lost the man who had been her friend.

Joseph tugged at his waistcoat's hem. "I can explain that hairpin. I got a bit lonely before you arrived, but she means nothing to me."

"The bed had fresh bedclothes yesterday morning. You had a woman here last night," Mariah said calmly, dully. "I had to stop the wedding before there was no turning back."

"I understand your anger, but I promise I won't see her again if you'll let me call back Reverend Pickle."

She tugged the simple lace veil from her head. "Oh, Joseph, your mistress doesn't matter. Not really. You see, that hairpin was just a catalyst. Our engagement shouldn't have progressed to the wedding stage. There's someone . . . There's something I must tell you."

"Don't. Please don't."

"I must. Our marriage would have been the biggest mistake of our lives, because—"

"About time she got smart."

The male voice came from outside the hide door. Half a second later, Whit entered the cabin. "Hi."

Rolling her eyes, Mariah refused to take more than a glance at the infuriating man. "Get out."

"Not a chance, darlin'."

Realization broke on Joseph's face. His expression hardened. Parking his fists on his hips, he glared at Whit. "I had my suspicions about the two of you, and never more than yesterday when you left without bidding me so much as a fare-thee-well." Joseph's accusation was directed at Mariah as he said, "He's why you've been cold to me."

"You got that right, pahdner."

Joseph's face crumbled. "When I asked for your vow of honor, Whitman, it didn't include stealing her from me."

Mariah studied Whit. He had the grace to look abashed but was fast on the uptake.

"Yeah, well, that was before I figured out the true Joe Jaye. I owe you nothing." He settled his dark blue gaze on Mariah. "Why don't you let her decide which one of us she wants?"

"You're wanting to take her to wife?" Joseph asked, his voice strangled.

"Marry her! Hell, no. But I am willing to give her a better deal than you're offering, Joe Jaye."

"You callous—!" Joseph's ashen face turned livid with rage. "Is this the type of man you want in your life?" he asked Mariah. "Or is this simply a case of birds of a feather flocking together?"

She understood Joseph's anger and realized the truth in his last question, but she could take no more of either man. "I don't want either of you."

Ashamed and hurt, she rushed outside. As soon as the next stage hit Trick'em, Texas, she was leaving this place—for wherever the stage might take her.

Standing under the mesquite tree that grew next to *el patrón*'s cabin, Pablo held his wife and daughter's hands and watched Mariah McGuire burst out of the cabin and away from the male shouts coming from it.

Without so much as one glance backward, she grabbed the buckskin mare's reins from the hitching post, pulled the silk wedding dress's hem between her legs to tuck it into her bodice, and climbed into Joseph Jaye's saddle. The obviously angry woman sitting astride, the mare took off in a gallop, headed in the vicinity of town.

Pablo concluded Mariah McGuire's secret had been discovered and she was suffering the price of Whit Reagor's mortal sin. The poor señorita.

Last evening Pablo had made two decisions. He wouldn't chance turning Joseph Jaye against his bride, who could not be blamed for her heinous treatment. Also, Pablo had made a vow to God. He had promised to protect the virtue of women.

"I must help her."

"She does not need your help," Conchita stated.

"How can you say this?" he chided.

"Padre, many times I have seen her staring across the valley to the land of Crosswind. I believe she loves the man you would harm. She will not welcome your interference."

Shocked, Pablo stared at his daughter. She was too young for such understanding. But he realized, after recalling the actions of Mariah McGuire, his daughter was correct. Pious indignation directed at their protectress stiffened his shoulders.

At that moment, Whit Reagor barged out of the log cabin, Joseph Jaye behind him.

"You turned her against me," the smaller man accused, sneering and balling his hand into a fist. "I'll warrant you slept with her, too."

"Watch what you say, Joe."

"Who are you to tell me what to say? All

the time you were supposedly protecting her during your journey, was she spreading her thighs for you?" He slammed his fist into the bigger man's jaw, but his blow was puny. "Damn you, Whitman!"

"Get ahold of yourself, Joe."

"May your black heart burn in hell." A shaking hand raked through the light-colored hair that had fallen over the maligned man's forehead. "Hers, too. She spread her legs for me, too, didn't you know?"

"Yeah, I know all about it." The rancher grimaced. "But before you say anything more in front of these good people"—he motioned toward the three Martinezes—"maybe you ought to give some thought to yourself. Any fool would have known that hairpin doesn't belong to Mariah."

Joseph Jaye's mien changed to defiant satisfaction. "It doesn't. It belongs to *one* of my mistresses. *Which* one shall remain my secret."

A strangled gasp escaped Conchita's lips, and Evita whispered a prayer, crossing herself.

"There is evil all around us," Pablo uttered in maligned ethos. "And we were wrong to put our faith in Señor Jaye. I will not trust a fornicator in the presence of my innocent women."

"Pablo," Evita asked, "are you suggesting we leave?"

"We *are* leaving," he stated, brooking no argument. "I will not expose my wife and daughter to the lusts of Joseph Jaye nor the lusts of his neighbor, Señor Reagor."

Already Conchita had left for the *casa* when Pablo conducted his wife toward their abode. They hadn't gotten far when he heard Joseph Jaye shout.

"You can have Mariah for all I care. I don't want her! She's trash. She isn't worthy to wipe my feet. She's nothing but a whore!"

"That's enough!"

Pablo turned to glance at the man whose voice was raised for the first time.

Whit Reagor had the smaller man by the lapels. "I'd hate to have to kill you, you son of a bitch, but if you call her one more filthy name, I'll do that very thing!"

Chapter Sixteen

Before the crack of dawn on the morning after the aborted wedding, Mariah dispatched Birdie and her middle-aged cattleman son, George, to pack her belongings at Joseph's farm and bring them into town. The stage was due in Trick'em this afternoon, and she was anxious to be on it.

When Whit had showed up at Birdie's house the previous afternoon and evening, Mariah had refused to see him. With all the happenings of late she had been in no mood to deal with him—or with anyone else except for Birdie, who had provided several hankerchiefs, endless cups of tea, and a friendly ear for Mariah's troubles.

Now, as a rooster crowed at the bright light of day, she paced her boardinghouse room, waiting for the Turners to return. Her eyes were scratchy and dry; a muscle twinged in her neck. Just as she brought her hand up to rub her aches away, she heard Birdie's scullery maid shout up the stairs, "Miss McGuire, come quick. It's bad!"

Within moments, Mariah left the house and ran to the lawn, coming upon Birdie and George, who stood on the other side of the white picket fence, their backs to her. They faced a buckboard that was parked on the quiet street . . . the unusually quiet street.

Hesitantly and with dread she approached the open carriage. It did not hold her belongings, and chilblains overtook her. What was obviously a body covered by a large piece of canvas lay prone on the bed's rough boards.

"Who . . . ?"

"Mr. Jaye."

"I . . ." Her voice choked, and she dropped her chin. "I didn't want him dead."

"I know," Birdie murmured. "But try not to take it too hard. Remember how he hurt you."

The older woman's reminder didn't register in Mariah's shocked brain. Shaking despite the warm morning, she asked, "What happened to him?"

No reply was forthcoming, and Mariah feared they were keeping something from her.

George Turner, a homely fellow with bushy brows, stepped over to pat Mariah's shoulder, and said to his mother, "I'm gonna take him on over to Doc Metcalfe's."

"You mean he's not dead?" Mariah moved

to administer aid, but George's voice stopped her.

"He's dead all right," he said. "Been that way for hours." His hand brushing across his forehead, he spit a wad of tobacco onto the street. "Doc Metcalfe's the coroner, too. He'll wanna look Jaye over."

"So do I." Mariah, saying an inner prayer, pulled away from the older woman and picked up her skirts to crawl into the back of the buckboard.

"Don't!" George and Birdie warned in unison, but she paid them no heed.

The boards creaked under her weight. Her hand shaking, she lifted the shroud. Nausea waved through her. Joseph lay on his side, his wedding suit tainted with blood, his stiff body doubled over. An unseeing eye was rounded as if in horror, and his mouth hung open. Ants, feasting and scurrying, were all over the fingers that had obviously clawed at his neck. The insects were all over . . . Joseph Jaye had been strangled with barbed wire.

Mariah's free hand went to her lips. "Who did this to him?"

"Someone, I reckon, who didn't like that stuff." George pointed to the twist of wire. "It could've been anybody, seeing how nobody around these parts cottons to devil's rope."

"Now, Son! Now's not the time—"

" 'Nobody' being the ranchers?" Mariah interrupted, and George gave a grudging nod in reply.

She had no wish to pursue an argument over the rights of farmers, not now. Instead, she drew the canvas over Joseph's inert body. He had not deserved to die such a horrible death.

She jumped to the ground, and her determined chin lifted. "Whoever is responsible won't get away with it."

George and his mother exchanged glances.

"Let it be," Birdie said.

Mariah was taken aback. "How can you say that? A man has been murdered!"

"Mariah, I'm fond of you. You're a right nice gal, and . . ." Once more Birdie glanced at her stock-raiser son, then back at the young woman. "I wouldn't hurt your feelings for the world, but . . ."

"There's no need to spare me, Birdie. If you've got something to say, say it."

"Something like this was bound to happen."

"I can't believe you're not horrified. You, of all people!" Mariah cut in, unable to quell herself.

George stepped in front of her. "Joe Jaye stirred up a lot of trouble around here. Trick'em is better off without his sort."

Holding on to the belief she was wrong about her elderly friend, Mariah pushed him aside. "Does he speak for you, too, Birdie?"

Her lined old face paled, and she could not meet Mariah's eyes. "Life was tough for me and my husband during and after the war. Everything we owned in Mississippi was lost to our foolhardy cause, or to the Yankees later.

We were hungry when we heard about the cattle in Texas that was to be had for the rounding up. Ranching saved me and my husband."

Though Mariah sympathized with the woman's story, she didn't see how the past had anything to do with the present. "You didn't answer my question. Is Trick'em better off without Joseph Jaye?"

"Yes, I'm sorry to admit." She lifted her hand to let it fall impotently at her side. "We ranching folk . . . If you could only understand—"

"This isn't a matter of farming or ranching. This is a matter of right and wrong."

"Who's to say what is right?" George asked. "This is cow country, Mariah, and our town is thriving from the Western Trail. Farmers and their ways have no place here."

"I don't agree."

"You're new in Trick'em, so you can't know all the facts." George tucked a new wad of tobacco into his left cheek. "Among other things, devil's rope cuts into cattle same as it cut into Jaye there."

"It cuts cattle, not kills them," she corrected.

"Cuts 'em and they get sick. You ever seen a cow eat up with screw worm infection?" He jacked up a brow. "Naw, don't reckon you have. *I* have. We have a right to protect our herds."

"There's no comparison between livestock and human life."

"Mr. Jaye didn't do right by you," Birdie

reiterated. "Why should you care who murdered him?"

"My personal feelings have nothing to do with the issue. This is a matter of justice. My father is a lawman, and he taught his children to respect the law," she said honestly. Despite the problems she'd had with Logan McGuire, she respected many things about him. His nature was to uphold the law. Was there anything more admirable?

Neither George nor his mother responded to her statement, and Mariah flattened her lips. Appalled and disgusted at their stand, as well as being aggrieved over the loss of Birdie's friendship, she climbed onto the buckboard's driver seat.

"Rest assured, I will *not* give up until I see Joseph's murderer swinging from the gallows! I'm going for the sheriff."

Sheriff Wilburn Taft couldn't have cared less about solving Joseph's murder, Mariah discovered. Nor was he interested in the other senseless murders of the previous night. Her former fiancé wasn't the only nester who had lost his life. Five more farmers had breathed their last breaths, but their deaths had been by gunshot rather than by a vicious twist of sharp wire.

There was, nonetheless, a similarity between the six men. The other grangers had followed Joseph's example by stringing barbed wire around the land they were homesteading. No doubt in her mind, Mariah was certain local ranchers were responsible and Sheriff Taft was allied to them.

Spuds O'Brien and his sons were among the dead. And because their bodies were found on Crosswind property, not far from where Mariah had seen them stringing wire, she was forced to wonder if Whit had had a hand in their murders. But she did a quick assessment of the situation and deduced the finger pointed too obviously at him.

Wanting to be absolutely certain of her conclusion, she visited the site; naturally Sheriff Taft was "too busy" to accompany her. No traces of a struggle, not even blood, were on the hard-packed ground. However, there were definite signs the bodies had been dragged to the location. The O'Briens had died elsewhere.

She was relieved, believing in Whit's innocence, though she didn't want to study the reasons why she cared.

By noon of the day Joseph and the others had been found, news spread of the killings, and the remaining farmers retaliated, gunning down five cattlemen known to be opposed to fencing.

Their actions were not taken sitting down by the citizens of Trick'em and vicinity who believed in the open range, in the superiority of ranching over farming, and that "rustlers" no doubt were responsible for the farmers' deaths. The cowmen were augmented in their revenge by a dozen drovers, the latter having been camped at the edge of town when the fencing war broke out. The chaos didn't diminish over the next few days.

Cattle were slaughtered, and the meager creeks flowed red with their blood, but the farmers soon paid for their actions. Wire cutters became de rigueur for cattlemen. The Land Office was burned to the ground, its manager run out of town. Six farm families were burned off their homesteads, and two ranchers lost their lives in gun battles on the streets of Trick'em. Newspaper editors from as far away as Chicago sent reporters to cover the story.

After he refused water rights to Painted Rock cattle, A.W. Lamkin suffered a loss, but a mild one by comparison to the others. His calico mule was butchered and his fields were trampled. Despite ill health, he joined the other squatters in revolt. Beside herself, and with her pioneer spirit broken, Patsy Lamkin told Mariah, "I've had enough. We're leaving as soon as I can get us packed."

She understood Patsy's concerns. As soon as justice was served, Mariah intended to leave, too. This was a hellish place.

Whit had had hell, too. He took losses of cattle and horses, she learned from A.W. She sympathized with Whit, even though he hadn't made his presence known since the night of Joseph's murder. Nor had he attended the funeral.

No matter how many times she tried to tell

herself, "I don't need Whit—not one whit," she still loved him. Always she had considered him a fair man in dealings with others, but her faith was tested when A.W. informed her Whit Reagor rode against the farmers.

Disheartened, she busied herself in finding Joseph's killer. Her inquiries of Sheriff Taft were treated as if they were nothing more than a bother.

A week after the hell had broken loose, she entered the sheriff's office for the tenth time. Dust and stale smells prevailed in the adobe building, which encompassed a square room with iron bars crossing half the area and a room to the side serving as the defender of justice's living quarters.

Sheriff Taft, spare and dissipated, sat whittling at his nicked and battered desk. A near-empty bottle of rye was within his grasp.

"Do you have any clues to Joseph Jaye's murder?" she asked.

Taft yawned. "Wouldn't say that."

"Well?"

"Rustlers."

"I'm not buying that for a moment, Sheriff. He owned nary a cow."

Picking his blackened teeth with the carving knife, Taft lifted a shoulder. "That Mex he had living out there prob'ly killed him.

"Pablo Martinez? I don't think so."

"He runned off. Same night as yar man got his."

Earlier this day, when Mariah had called on

Gail, she'd voiced this same suspicion. But even Gail, who sided with the cattlemen, had mentioned Pablo's nonviolent attitude. Mariah suspected the Martinezes had left the farm to protest of her behavior with Whit.

She refused to think about the day Pablo had caught her in Whit's embrace, and responded to Taft's remarks. "Granted, Pablo had the opportunity and means, but you're forgetting the first element of crime. Motive.

"It wouldn't hurt, of course," she continued, "for you to send someone after the Martinezes. Quite possibly they'll be able to shed light on the case."

"Lordy, Lordy, ain't ya pure Scotland Yard?" Taft placed his wood project down, propped his feet up on the desk, and uncorked his libation. "Ain't ya got nothing better to do, missy, than to try and run this office?"

She propped her fists on her hips. "I'm tired of your attitude. Dashed tired of it. You'd allow every person in this county to be murdered, and what would you be doing? Whittling or drinking!"

He enjoyed a slug of his rye. "It's getting late. What say I take ya over to the café and buy ya a big plate of supper? Jackie Jo's fried chicken be lip-smacking good."

Supper! She whipped around, facing the jail's shamefully empty cell, then confronted the slothful Taft again. "Doesn't your conscience hurt when you accept your salary?"

"Can't say as it does." The crevices of his

face deepened in a frown. "Anyways, this fencing thing's gonna solve itself. Nobody around here wants me to get involved, and I'm not gonna. And if ya don't like it, missy, pack yar bags and get on back to wherever ya came from."

"I'm not budging from this town until justice is served." How she was going to make ends meet was a good question unless she dipped into Joseph's money . . . and that didn't seem right.

"Mighty big talk." He sneered. " 'Course, with all the talk around town about yar gunning abilities, ya think ya're right smart stuff, don't ya?"

"I'm not here for your approval, Sheriff Taft. I'm here to appeal to your sense of decency. You made an oath when you took office. Why don't you live up to it?"

"Ya don't like the way I wear my star, pin it on yarself."

Somebody needed to be sheriff, but a lady peacekeeper? Who'd ever heard of such a thing?

"Whatever I do, Sheriff, I will be doing *something.*" Exactly what, she wasn't sure.

She took her leave and headed for Joseph's farm, where she'd taken up residence. A hot bath did little to ease her aching muscles or to clear her baffled mind. There had to be someone she could turn to as an ally. Who?

Her head ached, as did every bone in her body. She tried to eat a dish of canned beans, but pushed the fare away and perched Gus on her shoulder. "Well, Gussie, what am I going to do?" She ran the pad of a forefinger along his beak. "Who can I turn to?"

"Toooo, toooo."

"No, who. Who?"

Three sharp raps of the knocker she had installed by the makeshift door stopped her questions.

"Miss McGuire? This is Chadwick T. Nussbaumer, and I must speak with you on a matter of the utmost importance."

Both with relief and disappointment, she allowed his entrance. Nussbaumer sported a pencil-thin mustache and a brimmed hat. He was nattily dressed in creased trousers and flannel waistcoat, and carried a thin leather valise.

The local solicitor was also mayor of Trick'em, and Mariah saw an opportunity. As the town's leading official, surely he was aware of the urgent need for law and order. Perhaps he could use his power and civic position to force Sheriff Taft out of his ineptitude.

After she made welcoming banter, deposited Gus in his cage, and prepared a cup of tea for her unexpected visitor, she joined him at the table. "Mr. Nussbaumer, how do you feel about this range war?"

"It will wear itself out."

"But how many people will lose their lives before that happens?" she asked.

"I've no idea. Moreover, I learned a long time ago to stay out of other people's business."

Another brick wall, Mariah thought, trying to school her feeling of disappointment.

"May I get down to business, Miss McGuire?" He extracted a folded piece of parchment from his valise and flourished the document. "Before his unfortunate demise, Mr. Jaye solicited my services, which I was, of course, pleased to provide." He unfolded the parchment. "You, Miss Mariah Rose McGuire, are the sole beneficiary of the late Joseph Arthur Harold Jaye's last will and testament."

"Mr. Nussbaumer, I can't accept Mr. Jaye's legacy. It was I who called the marriage off."

"If you decline the inheritance, his estate will revert by law to his father, the Earl of Desmont. I do not believe that was Mr. Jaye's wish."

Uncertain of the right course, she sat silent.

"I can appreciate your hesitation, but may I be candid with you?" At her nod, he continued. "Mr. Jaye called on me last September, which, I don't have to remind you, was over a half year ago. He had some concerns about his safety, and he wanted you to be provided for. I believe his words were, 'No matter what happens, I want her to have what is mine.' "

If the will had been drawn during the last day of Joseph's life, would the beneficiary have been different? Well, he hadn't changed the will, and he had been determined to marry Mariah, not the gold hairpin's owner, and that stood for something.

Now he rested in a cold grave and, thanks to Sheriff Taft's disinterest, his murderer was walking free. Beyond that, she had to be practical. She was without funds and a legal abode. The farm, where for all intents and purposes she had been squatting, would be hers if she accepted the legacy. Joseph's remaining cash could be used in her quest for justice—for Joseph's death as well as the others. It was only right his estate be used for this purpose.

Nussbaumer leaned forward. "Shall I enter the will for probate?"

"Yes, thank you."

Knowing she now had a certain amount of security, Mariah felt her spirit rising, her body aches lessening. Today, Sheriff Taft had scoffed away her inquiries, but tonight was going to be different. She'd let him know he wasn't dealing with just anybody and now that she was to be a landowner, she would have some clout. She would advise Sheriff Taft that if he didn't start handling his duties in a competent fashion, he'd simply have to step aside for some man who would!

She rose to refill Gus's food and water cups. "Mr. Nussbaumer, would you mind if I accompany you into town?"

"Not at all, ma'am."

Nussbaumer on his swift gelding, Mariah sidesaddle on Susie the buckskin mare, they rode through the moonlit night. He said his goodbyes at the edge of Trick'em and headed for home. Without further ado, Mariah continued on to the sheriff's office and learned he was at Maudie's Saloon, sharing a drink with Whit Reagor.

Never had she entered a public house, but the thought of doing so didn't trouble her. What did trouble her was the thought of facing Whit Reagor. Would she be strong enough to ignore him?

Chapter Seventeen

His back to the wall as he tried to relax in a corner of Maudie's Saloon, Whit took not only a sip of aged bourbon but also a slow look around. A general air of confidence filled the cattlemen's haunt, wrought no doubt from the inroads cowmen were making in the range war.

The tinny piano blared forth; the smoke-clogged air was alive with a fast-tempoed tune. Dancing girls wearing bright satins and plumes sidled up to the scores of rowdy cowpokes, some standing at the long bar, others sitting at the twenty-odd tables.

To Whit's left, five men were engaged in a game of five-card stud. One of the players was Slim Culpepper, who had hit town a couple of hours earlier to take over as Crosswind's top hand. With most of his men on the trail to Dodge, Whit needed all the hands he could get, and Slim had been born to the saddle.

General topics weren't paramount in Whit's thoughts, though. As usual, he was thinking about Mariah. At first he had let her be, figuring she needed to get her mind straight, what with calling off her wedding and being so annoyed with him.

Then Joe had died. Whit had been out on the range trying to get *his* mind straight about Mariah when word reached him about the funeral. By the time he got to town, Joe was six feet under and Mariah was back at the farm . . . or so he had been told. Strange. Why had she gone back to Joe's place?

A woman, a good-looking one, walked toward him. "Are you Sheriff Taft?" she asked.

"Nope." Whit scrutinized her. Young and beautiful, she had snapping dark eyes and a wealth of raven-black hair. Before he had met Mariah, he might have pursued this gal, but now his desires ran only to one woman: Mariah McGuire.

"What makes you think I'm the sheriff?" he asked.

The raven-haired beauty laughed. "Mr. Reagor, I know you're not Wilburn Taft. I was looking for an excuse to introduce myself." She extended her hand. "I'm Lydia Farrell, on assignment with the *Austin Statesman.*"

"You're a reporter?" he asked incredulously. "Didn't think there was such a thing as a newspaperwoman."

"I'm the first." Lydia's hand touched the

empty chair at Whit's right. "Do you mind if I sit down?" she asked.

Unless it was Mariah, company of the female variety was the last thing on Whit's mind. Remembering his manners though, he said, "Please do," and got up to seat her. "Care for a drink?"

She nodded assent. "So tell me, Mr. Reagor," she said as he poured her a shot from his bottle of bourbon, "how have you been affected by the fencing war?"

"I'd rather not discuss it."

"I've been told you lost your finest bull, and a dozen or more cows. Not to mention your stable burning to the ground. Was it six Arabians you lost?"

Basically, she had her facts right, and Whit grimaced. "I lost five horses."

"What a shame." Lydia shook her head. "Are you confident Sheriff Taft will be able to find the perpetrators?"

"That's what he gets paid for." Whit was fed up with the lily-livered Wilburn Taft, but why trust a stranger—especially a reporter—with the truth?

"Yes, but is he earning his salary?" Lydia asked. "I find it hard to believe you're not livid with rage over the sheriff's indifference."

Whit shrugged.

"He's a disgrace to his badge," she said. "He's not a bit interested in keeping the peace. Right now he's sleeping off the effects of alcohol."

"It's nighttime, Miss Farrell. Everyone's got a right to sleep."

"Well, I'm not the only person who thinks he's slacking off in his job. I've yet to meet her, but there's a lady here in Trick'em who has her complaints. Miss Mariah McGuire. Do you know her?"

He took a sip of whiskey, then replaced the glass. "Yeah, I know her."

He heard a commotion near the saloon doors, and his gaze moved in that direction. Those doors slapped shut, and Mariah entered Maudie's Saloon. *Oh, shit. She'll think I'm with this Lydia gal!*

As he unfolded his frame from the chair, Mariah caught sight of him. He tipped his black Stetson. She was a distance away, but not so far he couldn't read the fury on her face as she continued her visual scrutiny.

"Hate to be rude, Miss Farrell, but I've gotta be shoving off."

His spurs clicking, he navigated around the tables and over the sawdust floor. Mariah's hair was swept into curls on the crown of her head, he noted. She wore a simple brown riding habit, its only adornment the beauty of the wearer. She was trying to ignore him and he didn't have to guess why.

Damn, she was beautiful, and he hadn't realized just how very much he'd missed her. While looking down at the brown eyes that refused to rise, he cocked a thumb against his silver gunbelt buckle. What was she doing in a place like Maudie's?

Wanting to whisk her into his arms and out of the saloon that, before tonight, had been frequented only by women of ill repute, he drawled, "Buy you a drink?"

"No. I'm looking for the sheriff."

"You're about an hour too late, Red. He's gone. Will I do?"

"For what? Target practice?"

"I can explain—"

"Say, Reagor," someone at the bar said, "don't be hogging that beauty."

"Yeah, look at that purty red hair!"

"Let her come on in and make her own choice!"

"Let's get out of here." Whit grabbed her arm to direct her out the swinging doors. The night breeze ruffled the hair at his collar as he said, "We need to talk."

"You beast! Didn't anyone ever tell you it isn't polite to abandon a lady friend?"

He wheeled around to look Mariah straight on. Light from a saloon window cast a halo on her thick, wavy hair, and he touched the beautiful locks. "I just met that woman. We were discussing business."

"Isn't the price usually set beforehand?"

"Sheath your claws, Mariah. I told you she's nothing to me and, by damn, I mean it. She's a newspaper reporter."

"And I'm Victoria, Queen of Great Brit—"

"Lydia Farrell was after a story, that's all. And for your information, I don't want any woman but you, and haven't since the day we met."

Mariah's gaze flew to his. She blinked. "For some strange reason, probably daft, I believe you."

He was struck by the realization that, after the many times he had disappointed and hurt her, she was still able to trust him, Whit Reagor, a callous, bitter, conceited scoundrel and beast—all the deserved names she had called him over their acquaintance. This was one helluva woman. And he didn't deserve her, much less another chance, but . . .

"Let's go." He steered her past a watering trough and to the ever-dusty street.

"Aren't you being a bit presumptuous?" she asked.

"Probably. But the outside of a saloon is no place for talking." He smiled. "You got a horse at that hitching post?"

"Yes. The buckskin," she sputtered, "but—"

"Let's go."

His free hand unlooped the mare's reins, and he gave Mariah a small shove. "We're going to my place."

"I'm not going to your ranch."

"My place here in Trick'em," he amended.

Mariah had had no idea that Whit owned a townhouse, but there were a lot of things she neither knew nor understood about him. Unlike his sister's large home in Dublin, Whit's cottage was small. The clapboard dwelling was situated across from the blacksmith's shop, several hundred yards east of the Turner boarding establishment.

As Mariah entered his quarters, her nose picked up mingled scents—leather, tobacco, and a slight hint of bay rum. The front room bore an aura of masculinity: heavy chairs covered in cowhide; tables and cabinets of no-frills lines; a leather sofa long enough for him to stretch out. On the wall hung a gun rack with two rifles and a shotgun, and bull horns measuring at least nine feet across.

Mariah, sitting down on the cool leather sofa, watched Whit fling his hat to one of the horn's pointed ends, then run his hand through his hair and turn to a sideboard. He extracted a bottle of whiskey and poured two squat glasses half full. Save for his spurs and the big silver buckle of his gunbelt, his narrow-hipped frame was clad in black, the shirt and breeches close-fitting. Around his neck was a black bandanna and shadows of a beard darkened his lean cheeks. He looked like an outlaw. A very handsome, intriguing badman.

"You've been retaliating against the farmers," she stated without preamble. "Cutting fences."

He handed her a glass of whiskey. "Who told you that?"

"It matters not who told me. But I firmly believe it's deplorable to—"

"Before you start the schoolteacher lecture, may I say a word? Yeah, I ride with the rest of my kind—cattlemen protecting their property and rights and I make no apology for it."

She couldn't believing her ears and in light of his words she had to pose a question for her own peace of mind. "I didn't think I'd be asking this, Whit, but did you kill the O'Brien men?"

"No."

"Are you responsible for *any* of the recent murders?"

"No. In retribution for my own losses I've scared a few farmers, but that's all."

She believed him. "Does vengeance give you satisfaction?"

"You could say that. I protect what's mine and as I told you, I make no apology."

She understood his motives, though agreeing with them was another matter. Her faith in his innocence was firm nonetheless. He had said he'd had no part in the murder, so he hadn't. Whit Reagor might be many things, but his honesty had always been close to brutal. And after Joseph, she found this character trait especially appealing.

Whit hoisted his drink and took a short draw of the amber liquid before setting his glass on the table. "I hear tell you've been badmouthing the sheriff."

"Sheriff Taft is a blight on the name of law enforcement."

"All these things you mentioned, do they have anything to do with why you're still in town?" he asked. "Or are you here because of us?"

"The last time I saw you I was determined to be on the next stage, and if Joseph hadn't been murdered, I would be gone."

Whit unbuckled his gunbelt and laid it beside his glass. His eyes riveted to hers. "I'm glad you aren't."

She couldn't control the wild beat of her heart, but she would not be deterred from her purpose. "I won't leave until Joseph's killer is found."

"That so?"

"Yes."

"Rustlers did him in." Whit shrugged. "They're long gone by now."

His stock answer was the same as Taft's. "What makes you so certain?" she asked, gritting her teeth.

"I'm not, but it's as good a guess as any."

"You know he didn't have any cattle to steal," she exclaimed. "Someone killed him over his fences.

"What makes you so certain?" Whit asked, repeating her question of a moment earlier.

"It makes more sense than rustlers. Barbed wire was the means of his death, and I take that as an obvious warning sign from ranchers. Besides, Joseph wasn't the only farmer to die. Ranchers started this war, not rustlers or farmers."

"Well, Mariah, if you want the truth, I don't give a damn who killed him."

"Why?"

"You ought to know why. My eyes were opened . . . real wide . . . when I saw what he was trying to pull on you. The last straw— Let's just say that in the end I had no use for him." Whit folded his long frame into a chair. Unfastening one spur, then the other, he let both fall to the floor and lifted his booted feet to the table. Propping an elbow on the chair arm, he rubbed his stubbled jaw. "Seems to me, *you* wouldn't give a damn who killed him."

"Then you don't know me!"

A lopsided chin deepened his right dimple. "You're saying that to me of all people? I know you, all right. I know every hill and valley of your body. I know what it feels like to . . ." His voice grew hoarse, his eyes flicking up and down her form. "I know what it's like to be buried deep within you."

Her rush of excitement at these remembrances did strange things to her wits. She swallowed. She fidgeted. She wanted . . . *Don't let him do this to you!*

Taking a swallow of the fiery whiskey, she thought about the real meaning of his words. "You know what I am, but you have no earthly idea *who* I am."

"I could if you'd give me the chance," he said. "Tell me about the woman inside the beautiful redhead. I want to know what makes her tick, what makes her so damned loyal to the man who mistreated her."

His blue, blue eyes were honest, sincere, and

she was glad for the five feet separating them. Space gave her a certain strength. In halting tones she began to tell Whit about her childhood, her family, her heartaches and hopes. Even about the silly letter she'd left for her father.

Whit showed rapt interest in her background and prompted her with questions whenever she faltered. As the hours wore on, her already weary body became even more tired. The midnight hour approached, and she began to wind down. ". . . and the lawyer told me Joseph willed me his farm."

"Will you take up farming?"

"I don't imagine so. Right now, I must keep trying to make the sheriff do his job. When I'm successful at that I can continue with the rest of my life. Teaching, not tilling," she added on a lighter note. "I'll sell the property and move on."

"You know, Mariah, my offer's still good. You don't have to depend on that sorry excuse for a farm. I can take care of you."

"How many times do I have to tell you? I don't want to be taken care of. God gifted me with the brains to teach, and I—"

"Why is teaching so important to you?"

"I guess I need to be needed," she admitted quietly.

"*I* need you."

"That is a different sort of need," she whispered. "Could we leave our relationship out of this?"

"If that pleases you.

"Yes." Her head nodded in fatigue. "And thanks for listening."

"No problem." He smiled. "But there's one more thing I'd like to—" Whit shut his mouth. There would be no more questions tonight, for Mariah's gold-tipped lashes had dropped to her cheeks, and she curled against the sofa's arm. An angel asleep.

His angel.

Whit thanked his lucky stars she wouldn't be leaving Trick'em any time soon. He wanted Mariah to stay here close to him.

A band squeezed at Whit's chest as he continued to watch her sleep. Life hadn't been easy for Mariah, and he admired her spirit. Closing his eyes, he recalled her words of this evening. She hadn't wanted his pity and he didn't pity her. Matter of fact, he understood a lot of her pains.

Funny how one's past messes up the present, he thought. His actions since Jenny had made him a cuckold were all motivated by the hurt she'd inflicted and he balked at trust and faith and love.

Mariah, on the other hand, was scared to death *not* to love. She needed to love and be loved. He figured something deep within her heart told her that if she gave all of herself, the object of her affection wouldn't turn away from that devotion.

Yet too many people had abandoned her, each in their own way. Her father had been cruel; her mother and grandmother had left her through death; her brothers had lives of their own.

Once, Mariah had had a chance at the love of giving and taking and sharing with that lieutenant fellow, but fate had intervened. After his death, she had tried to transfer that same affection to Joe but he had used her insecurities, guilt, and need to love to his best advantage. Even from the grave he held her within his grasp.

Damn him to hell.

Whit was almost certain that Charlie Tullos was behind Joe's death, though he hadn't mentioned his suspicions to Mariah. He couldn't prove anything. Nonetheless . . .

Threatening Joe had been a passion with Tullos, but bloody his hands? No. That kind of dirty work the hooked-nose bully left to a trio of hired guns, his ranch hands not being loyal enough to kill for him, but Whit had seen or heard nothing of T-Bone Hicks and the two others in quite a while. If Hicks and party weren't responsible, who was? And what difference did it make anyhow? The world wasn't worse off for the loss of Joe Jaye. No one gave a tinker's damn.

Except for Mariah.

Whit's eyes settled on her sleeping form, and he had better things to think about than murder. He was drawn to everything about her—her thick cloud of auburn hair, her oval face, her shapely body . . . the list went on and on.

Yes, he was drawn to *what* she was, but he felt a more powerful emotion: The *who* she was was even more appealing than her breathtaking outer beauty.

She was none of the things he had first imagined. She was honorable and good and true of heart. Could anyone blame her for almost marrying a rascal who had, for the most part, put her on a pedestal?

Whit had never treated her right, except in passion. He could, and would, change . . . given the opportunity. A lump rose in his throat. Was there a chance she could be as devoted to a lanky, bitter cowpoke as she was to the memory of a no-good viscount? Time would tell.

Watching this adored woman, he mouthed the words, "I love you, Mariah."

It shocked him to realize he meant it. Shocked him, and scared him witless. Love made a fool out of a man.

He felt that wouldn't be the case this time, but he was going to make damned sure Mariah returned his love before he made any sort of commitment for the future.

He prayed she would love him, forever and ever and ever, and if she did, Whit Reagor would never, ever, do her wrong. Never would she find a gold hairpin in his bed.

Mariah, wake up and smell the coffee about Joe.

That Englishman had duped everyone he had come into contact with. Whatever the case,

Mariah was stalwart in her belief that Joe's death had been unpardonable, and she was a woman who stood up for her idea of right.

Whit pushed himself up from the chair to reach for the glass of whiskey he'd deserted hours earlier. While quaffing his drink, he heard a feminine sigh. Mariah had turned to her back on the sofa, her forearm covering her eyes. Her breasts thrust against the material of her bodice, and he had the urge to stretch out beside her.

Not tonight, he told himself. She needed her rest. Walking into the bedroom, he pulled back the crazy quilt, smoothed the sheets, and plumped the pillows, just like his mother had taught him as a lad.

Ida Reagor had been calm as a glassy lake, her patient love extending not only to her family but also to anyone who needed a bite to eat, a place to sleep, or a friendly ear. She had adored his father, and Will Reagor had been just as enthralled with her.

Whit started. In all those years of his bitterness toward marriage, why hadn't he thought of the good life his parents had shared?

He turned his thoughts and his feet to the front room, to the present. To Mariah. Would she balk at his insisting she spend the night? Probably. But he wasn't going to take no for an answer.

He didn't have to. She barely moved when he unfastened her buttons and unlaced her ugly brown shoes. His lips touched her long toes, and he warned himself to stop while stopping was possible. The riding habit slipped off with relative ease. And she didn't seem to notice when he carried her to the iron bed. Okay, so his hand lingered too long on her creamy skin. He wasn't a saint.

Dropping a kiss on the top of her head, he retreated to the sofa and stretched out. Tomorrow he wouldn't be such a gentleman.

Chapter Eighteen

The diffused sun lightened the back of Mariah's eyelids, but her half-awake senses paid little heed. She snuggled deeper in the soft covers, but soon the scent of coffee and food tickled her nostrils. Sounds—horses and wagons and people and a rooster's crow—penetrated her hearing, but those things were muffled, as if . . . This wasn't the farm. Where was she?

She yanked up in bed, and almost upset the tray Whit was setting by her side.

"Morning, glory," he said, winking an eye. "Ever had breakfast in bed?"

Still confused, she rattled, " 'Why, what . . . Good heavens. I shouldn't have . . . Why'd you let me spend the night?"

"You fell asleep in the front room, Red. What was I to do? Strap you on your mare and give the ole girl a nudge in her side?"

A short laugh escaped her throat. "No, I guess not."

She settled back against the pillow and tucked the sheet under her arms. Her now-clear eyes assessed the unshaven, half-dressed man who stood beside her and was placing the tray on a bedside table.

Butterflies tickled her midsection at the sight of his tousled jet-black hair. The flutters increased as she gazed at his olive-toned chest, which was bare save for whorled hair and scars. A pair of denim breeches, the top button unfastened, hugged his thighs. She realized her own state of dress. She wore only her thin chemise. Had they . . .?

Surely she would have remembered their sleeping together, but her head turned to the opposite side of the bed for assurance. The other pillow had no indention.

"I slept on the sofa, Red."

" 'What's the matter?" she teased, relieved. "Was I snoring?"

"You got that right. I never heard such a racket. Thought a big black bear was holed up in here."

"Oh, you!" Laughing, she grabbed the unused pillow and threw it at his face. "Big black bear, my eye."

"I'll teach you not to use violence with me, little red bear."

He slung his leg over hers and, with lightning speed, pinned her hips between his knees.

His fingers wiggled and descended on her ribs. Through her giggling beseeches to stop, Whit unmercifully tickled her.

"I'll withhold your honey and water," he warned in feigned menace. "My fingers will continue to draw the bear's misery until repentance against my poor person escapes those snoring lips."

"Never!" she cried.

"You will."

His fingers stilled for a moment, his hands curving around her sides, and she smiled. She needed to be with Whit, and wanted nothing to diminish this wonderful feeling he roused within her. She wouldn't think about the world outside this bedroom.

"Don't look at me that way," he teased. "I won't be taken in by soft eyes."

Once more he set to tickling her ribs, but she was on the offensive. Her pelvis nudged against the juncture of his legs, and she taunted, "Then what are you going to do . . . about your *problem?*"

His fingers stilled, then moved to cover her chemise-draped breasts. "What would you have me do?"

Brazenly, she locked her brown eyes with the blue of his. "Whatever tickles your fancy."

"Tickles *my* fancy, eh?"

"Yes."

His voice was low as he asked, "You promise you'll grant me all my desires?"

"Yes, Whit, I'll grant your fancies."

His Adam's apple moved up and down his throat once as he swallowed. "Kiss me."

Whatever he wanted was fine with Mariah. Absolutely, breathtakingly fine. "Come here."

He lowered his upper body, his face stopping within inches of hers. She caught mingling smells—soap, the spice of bay rum, warm skin—those wonderful scents which were Whit Reagor. Her hands cupped his unshaven cheeks, and she delighted in the rough feel against her sensitive palms. Her lips parted, her head leaving the pillow as she touched her tongue to the chiseled planes of his mouth. But it wasn't she who continued to give the kiss, for they both were willing participants.

"You taste so sweet," he murmured, then trailed his tongue to her ear, eliciting her quivers of delight.

Her hand smoothed to his chest, encountering an indention that evoked a question. "Whit, how did you get these scars?"

"From a war not nearly as troublesome as you.

"Which war?"

"Civil," he answered, his teeth nipping her chin. "Now shut up about such nonsense."

She didn't say another word about wars or scars, but couldn't get either one out of her thoughts. The American Civil War was fought in the early sixties. Whit must have been very young at the time, and her heart went out to him as she ruminated over what must have been.

"Which side did you fight for?" she asked, unable to give up in spite of his request.

"What in the hell kind of question is that? The Confederacy, of course. I'm a Texan, for Pete's sake."

"Well, I read that Texans were divided in their loyalties. Sam Houston—"

"You wanna talk about Sam Houston when we're trying to make love? Damn, woman, have I got body odor or something?"

"No, silly goose." Chuckling, she snuggled against him. "I do believe you had a bath this morning."

"Well, Red, a man's gotta do what a man's gotta do."

" 'Why doesn't the man in question give me a big kiss?"

"I'll have none of that. Did you forget your promise?"

"No." Her tongue dipped into one of the scars on his chest, and she felt him shiver. "I'm at your beck and call."

He tensed, the air leaving his lungs. His eyes riveted to hers. "Make love to me, sweet Mariah," he said, his deep timbre cloaked with desire. "Let me watch you undress. Grant me my pleasure, as you promised, and you'll be amply rewarded."

Excitement surged through her. Even without the wild energy and skilled attention he had shown to her body on former occasions, she was tingling with wanting Whit. So easily he aroused her.

Drawing the hem of her chemise to the start of her thighs, she rose to her knees, facing him. Her fingers pulled at the top ribbon of her garment, then at another ribbon and another with excruciating slowness. She slipped the strap from one shoulder, and Whit groaned as a plump breast and its hardened peak were bared to his sight.

It gave her great pleasure to see him aroused, and she continued her disrobing enticingly. The other strap was slipped to the top of the remaining breast, but she pulled back the material when his nostrils flared with interest.

"Sweet mercies," he murmured as she continued her tantalization by dropping the chemise to the curve of her waist.

"Had enough, cowboy?"

"Not on your life." But then with a sudden oath he pulled the cotton material to the top of her thighs so that he could flatten his palm on her downy, coppery triangle. His lips moved to the valley between her breasts. "You drive me mad with passion."

Her palm rubbed across the back of his huge, tanned hand, pressing him against her. "I think you've had enough," she murmured.

"I reckon."

He took the lead. His face replaced his hand, and he gentled kiss upon kiss to her tummy. The prickles of his cheeks rasped against her, and the feeling was marvelous, glorious, provocative. Her fingers lost power, the chemise slipping to her knees, and she tunneled her fingers through his thick curly hair. She could hold him like this for a long, long time, but she ached for the pleasures yet to unfold.

"Do you have another fancy, my lord?" she asked, meaning the title and drawing back to rid her knees of the accoutrement.

He chuckled. "I do." Smoothly, he eased back on the mattress. "Unbutton my breeches."

"Yes," she teased, running her palm across his heated, manly bulge. "I can see how you might be uncomfortable. But you didn't say please."

"Please."

The toil was difficult, his breeches being so tight, but she worked one button free and then two more. He is glorious, she thought. Her hand slipped between the V of denim, and his manhood was hot against her fingers, hot and smooth and turgid.

"How you arouse me," he said with huskily. "As none other has done before."

Her heart raced at his confession. Her fingers clamped compulsively around him, the pad of her thumb resting on the smooth, moist tip. With his hoarse tutoring she discovered a way to bring him to even further agitation.

A minute later he urged her to refrain, adding, "Baby, baby . . ."

He swept the breeches from his thigh, sending the blue denim flying across the bed as she laid her head against the pillow. Lightly he covered her naked flesh with his own, his tongue flicking against her earlobe, his finger moving to the center of her desire. Deeper she swirled in the glory of passion.

Tenderly, gently, his finger led her on a journey to the heavens. Stars shooting through every vein in her body, she dug her nails into his back. "Oh, Whit . . . please! I need you."

His lips touched a closed eye. "Not yet. I won't let you renege on your promise."

Barely able to think with any clarity, she lifted her lashes. "Your fancy isn't tickled, my lord?"

His fingers weaved around a long auburn lock of her hair, rubbing it across his rock-hard chest. "Oh, it's more than tickled, but . . ."

"What would please you more?"

His eyes were half lidded, and a crooked grin stole across his rugged features. "Ride me as if I were a stallion."

"Whit, we've never . . .!"

"I know," he replied, his thumb trailing to the sensitive, aroused peak of her breast. "Never. But will you do it?"

She grinned. His idea had appeal. A great amount of appeal, even though it held a hint of the wicked and wanton. But in Whit's arms, she *was* wicked and wanton! And with his hands tantalizing her breasts like that . . . "I don't know how."

"My precious innocent, I'll teach you." Again, he rolled to his back. Guiding her leg across his belly, he insinuated his throbbing shaft against her. His hands canvassed her hips, then lifted her to him. "Surround me with you."

She did, and she heard him groan as he plunged upward, "So tight. So sweet. Oh, sweetheart . . ." were his ragged words. Spreading her hair across her breasts, he said, "I've had so many fantasies about this."

And he was so big, so filling, that she thought she had ascended the firmament as she rode him to the point she knew to be heaven. As he filled her with his seed, she collapsed against him, her face burying into the musky wall of his hirsute chest.

"Thank you," he said, holding her close.

"For what?"

"For being you, my love."

My love. He had called her "my love"! How sweet those words . . . even if they had been murmured in the afterglow of their passion. Oh, to be loved by Whit . . .

She recalled the previous evening, and his patience and understanding when she had poured out her heart. He was a good man, a fine man, a man who was kind to others . . . and who loved kittens.

I love him.

"Love me, Whit. Please love me."

He grinned, and began his tender touches again. "I was hoping you'd ask."

That wasn't what she had meant, but she had her prayers. Someday he would love her, not simply make sweet, beautiful love to her.

In her heart, she knew that to be true. In the meantime, she would enjoy what he offered . . . and he was offering something wonderfully enjoyable right then.

Much later she ran the pad of a finger across his flat nipple. "How are the kittens?"

"Great Scott, Mariah, you're thinking about kittens at a moment like this?"

"What are *you* thinking about?" she challenged.

"Your beauty." He nestled her into the crook of his arm. "There's only one thing more beautiful in this world than your face and body. Your heart."

His sincere, tender words wound through Mariah, and she smiled.

He gave her one more kiss, then scooted away to grab his breeches. "I'll bet you're hungry. Time for breakfast."

Warmed by his tenderness, and by her love, she smiled. Her grin broadened while she watched him tug on those breeches. *He* was the beautiful one!

"Hope you're hungry, Red, 'cause I fixed us a whopper of a breakfast."

Her eyes settled on his now-covered private parts. "I am hungry."

He crossed to the bedside table, all the while pointing a finger at her. "Greedy. Disgracefully greedy, that's what you are."

"Absolutely. I'm hungry as a . . . bear."

He threw his head back and laughed. "You'll get plenty of what you're begging for as soon as we have our breakfast. I'm starving. For *food.*"

Obviously proud of his endeavors, he placed the breakfast tray across her lap, but his face fell. "Guess it got cold."

Mariah's stomach turned. Several pieces of unleavened bread—no, they had to be several flat gray biscuits—garnished a large platter holding a burned-to-black steak and a half dozen fried eggs. Fried eggs, each with a brown lace edge and a coating of congealed fat.

A tear formed, though, when she touched a wilted bluebonnet that centered an empty glass. A thousand roses would not have been more touching.

As Whit filled her plate, then handed it to her, she smiled. "The food smells delicious," she lied, for the fare had no smell at all. "Cold doesn't bother me." She crunched into the dry bread. The biscuit seemed to expand in her mouth. Would she ever be able to swallow it? It was all she could do not to choke as she complimented, "Mmm. Delicious."

He expelled his held breath. With gusto, Whit dug into a biscuit. Gulping, he swallowed and pulled a face. "Jeezus." He grabbed the plates and the tray. "You ever lie like that to me again, woman, and I'm gonna tan your behind."

The biscuit grinding its way to her stomach, she returned, "Promises, promises."

He shoved the tray under the bed and shot

her a murderous look. "Brazen tart, get dressed. We'll feast at Jackie Jo's emporium of fine dining."

"It's"—she glanced at the acorn clock—"for heaven's sake, I had no idea. Whit, it's almost noon. I must call on Taft again."

"The sheriff isn't going anywhere. What's a couple of hours?"

"Another couple of hours that Joseph's killer walks free." She reached for the pile of her neatly folded clothes.

But Whit's hand stopped her. "Forget it, Mariah. You won't get any help from Wilburn Taft. You know he doesn't give a damn who killed Joe Jaye."

"Then the good sheriff will have to be unseated."

"Don't get too smug, Red. He's in office by default. Last year, Taft was the sole deputy when Sheriff Eldon stole his wife's gold and ran off with a saloon gal. No one else wanted the star except Taft, and we couldn't find anyone to accept even a deputy's badge. Those sentiments haven't changed. So who'll take the job?"

"Someone who believes in right over wrong and who will fight for peace."

"Yeah, well, dream on. Sir Thomas More and Prester John have been dead a long time."

"How do you know about them?"

"Why shouldn't I?"

"Um, no reason. I meant no offense." She had never taken Whit for a learned man.

Would she never cease to be amazed by this enigmatic cowman? "Whit," she said, back to the subject of Taft, "I won't give up until we have a competent sheriff. And I need help. Will you be my ally?"

"Against who?"

"Against lawbreakers who burn someone else's home. Or commit murder."

"What are you wanting, to find the person responsible for Joe's murder or to start some sort of campaign?"

"Both."

"Count me out. I'm not in the do-gooder business."

Mariah pushed her legs over the side of the bed, wrapping her nude body with the top sheet and knotting the linen above her breasts. Her palms resting on the mattress, she asked, "So you want to keep on the way things are? Having your stable burned, having your livestock slaughtered. I should think you'd have all the more reasons to want peace. Unless avenging the misdeeds against you is all the tranquility you need."

"You're being unfair."

"Then I apologize." She reached for his hand. "Would you have me hold my tongue?"

"No. Speak your mind."

"Whether you're ready to accept it or not, times are changing. More and more settlers are leaving the East, and they want land of their own; they'll claim it, too. And fences. Fences have pluses, even for ranchers. You'd need less help to handle the herd, and you could preserve the grasslands by rotating your pastures. Cattle drives won't last forever, not with the railroads expanding their lines."

"Yes, and next you'd have me sowing *just a few* rows of corn and peas," he said, his lip curling. He took his hand from hers. "No way, Mariah. My livelihood is the open range. I'll fight for my way of life. I won't compromise."

"You've met other challenges successfully. Why couldn't you be as successful with new ways of doing things?"

He frowned. "You're talking about the future. Just exactly what are you asking of me, right now?"

"Help me get Wilburn Taft fired."

His brows furrowed, Whit leaned an elbow against the chest of drawers. A quarter of a minute later, he replied, "You're forgetting something. Taft sides with the cattlemen. Do you realize what you're asking me to do? You're asking me to turn against my brethren."

"I'm asking you to search your conscience, and then do what you feel is right."

Whit walked to the window and drew the curtain aside. Pressing his arm against the upper sash, he stared out. Several minutes later, he closed the curtain and turned to Mariah, who was still sitting on the bed's edge. "I'll be your ally," he said.

"Thank you." She sighed in both relief and gratification. "Will you speak with the mayor about Sheriff Taft?"

"What good would that do? I told you no one wants the job." A moment later, he added, "But there are some men who could help. The Texas Rangers. I know a captain in the Rangers, Big Dan Dodson. Stationed over in Brownwood. He and I are old fishing pals."

"Let's send for him."

"Hold your horses, Mariah. We have to think this thing through. After Dan and his men settled things down, they'd ride on to the next problem, and where would that leave Coleman County? Without a lawman and with a bunch of folks harboring anger. In no time at all trouble would start up again."

"That's why we need a law against fence cutting. And people to enforce it, too. Whit, that woman you met last night. Didn't you say she was a reporter?"

"Yeah, but what does she have to do with this?"

"The printed word is powerful. If we can get her on our side, Whit, she could be of help."

"Lydia Farrell did mention being fed up with Taft."

"Where is she from?" Mariah asked.

"Austin."

"The capital. Perfect. Her articles might catch a lawmaker's eye, and we'd get some legislation."

"You're getting a step ahead of yourself. Laws and Rangers are fine, but you're forgetting something, Red. The folks round here would still be looking for trouble."

Her shoulders wilted. "Oh, this hellish place." She elevated her mulish chin. "There has to be a way to change their way of thinking. Has to be."

Whit stretched out on the bed, and Mariah turned to face him. "Thing about it is," he said, "if you're wanting to change men's hearts, you change their women's. A man listens to his woman." Whit fixed his eyes meaningfully on Mariah's. "Case in point, me and you. I'm on your side."

"I like that about you." She smiled. "I like being your woman."

"And I like being your man." His palm curved over her thigh. "What do you think about—"

"Heavens, let's not get sidetracked."

"What's wrong with sidetracked?"

"Nothing . . . absolutely nothing. But while we're on the subject of how people behave, I'd like to know something about those men you rode with, against the farmers. Tell me about your partners."

Uneasiness niggled at Whit. Here he'd been talking to Mariah as if she were a man, as if the two of them were set to charge off after the enemy. What sort of fellow let his gal do that sort of thing? Oh, she was capable and intelligent and fearless, but she was still a woman. Whit's woman.

"Mariah, I don't want you mixed up in this range war business. I'll take care of it, and Taft, myself."

"I started this fight."

"And I'm taking up where you're leaving off."

She jumped to her feet. The sheet started to slip, and she yanked it back into place. "I want your help, not your protection."

Exasperated, he said, "Look, Mariah . . . I want to show you my ranch. Today. Right now."

"You're trying to change the subject."

"Would be nice. Why yammer about murders or sheriffs or barbed wire? You and I have been too long gettin' to a point of understanding." He moved to cup her chin. "I'd like to have some more of that me-and-you talk. Go with me to Crosswind."

Mariah looked into Whit's intense blue eyes. When it came to a choice between her cause and her man, there was no contest. "I'll go with you."

Chapter Nineteen

Was it wrong to go with her heart and neglect her quest? Mariah wondered a moment after giving Whit her assurance of visiting his ranch. But she'd made her decision and would stick to it.

"Get dressed," he said and retreated to the front room of his town cottage, allowing her privacy for ablutions.

Ten minutes later, Mariah frowned at her undergarments and wished for fresh ones. She shrugged into the black shirt Whit had worn the previous night. Drawing the material to her nose, she inhaled the lingering scent of him, and smiled. So much had happened between them since she'd found Whit at the public house. She had never imagined he could be so understanding.

He tapped on the closed door, then cracked

it. "You decent?"

"And just when did that become a major concern?" she teased.

"Tart." Now fully dressed in denim breeches and chambray shirt, he stepped into the bedroom. The dimple in his right cheek deepened as he assessed her state of dress. He gave a low whistle. "You look good in my shirt."

She rubbed the lapel against her cheek. "Your shirt feels good, too."

"Well, you can't wear it to Crosswind." He strode to her, taking her elbows. "Mariah, there's something I've been meaning to talk to you about. Clothes. Some of those things I bought from Jackie Jo are in the wardrobe. Don't look at me like that. Listen to what I've got to say before you get your back up. I want you to have, and enjoy them."

Mariah recalled the day Jackie Jo had mentioned his purchases, remembered her anger, replayed Gail's terrible accident. More than anything, Lois Atherton's comment about Whit's penchant for clothing his women was fresh in Mariah's mind. What motivated Whit to give gifts rather than himself?

"I don't want *things*, Whit."

"Why not?"

"I'd rather have you." With bated breath she waited for his response.

"You've got me. So take the clothes, too."

"No."

His spurs clicking, he strode to the wardrobe

and began to place frocks on the bed. A kaleidoscope of colors brightened the masculine room: emerald and jade green, turquoise, black, rust, peach, red, peacock blue, yellow . . . purple. After that horrendous day when Whit had tried to foil her wedding plans, Mariah wanted no part of anything purple. But those clothes were so pretty, so pretty.

He held aloft a lacy black camisole and, sighing with regret, tossed it atop the other garments. "Since you don't want them, I guess I'll give the lot to Gail."

"They won't fit her. She's a slip of a woman."

"No problem. Jackie Jo's seamstress can take 'em in."

"Oh."

He studied a pair of dancing slippers. "Guess I'll have to toss these out. They'll be too big for Gail."

Mariah said, "Don't throw them away."

"You've changed your mind?"

"Yes."

A triumphant grin stole across his face. "Good."

How easily Whit had turned the tide against Mariah, and she . . . Heavens, why had she been pigheaded about his gifts? Why should he be faulted for spending his money?

She dressed in a cotton twill riding habit of emerald green and, at his urging, twirled around for an inspection. He voiced approval and gave her a kiss.

"Thank you, Whit."

"I like a gal who's appreciative of my kisses."

"Silly goose, I meant for the clothes." Her nose nuzzled against his broad, chambray-covered chest. "You are a very generous man."

"Let's not go overboard."

"Well, why not? I've heard stories about you. I've been told you even went so far as to give the Stricklands their ranch."

"I take care of my kin," he said evenly. "What's wrong with that?"

"Nothing. Did you buy your sister her boardinghouse?"

"Yes."

"Why didn't you give her a ranch?" Mariah asked impulsively.

Thunder clouded Whit's face, and he stepped back to light a cigar. "She's a widow who's set on making her own way. And she's in her element around other people. Why would I want to saddle her to a ranch?"

"I didn't mean to offend you. It just struck me funny, I guess, the difference between what you'd do for your sister as opposed to a . . . What is Gail to you? A cousin?"

"Yeah."

Whit turned quiet. Too quiet. He seemed troubled as he announced, "I'll saddle the horses. Meet me outside."

Mariah wondered what she'd said wrong.

Well, she had pried. Nonetheless, she had an uneasy feeling. There was something between Whit and Gail, something strange. *Don't be a ninny. Who shouldn't he spend his money, in whatever amounts, on his cousin? He told you a long time ago he views her as the daughter he never had.*

Daughter. Could it be possible . . . ? Now that Mariah thought about it, Gail resembled Whit more closely than his sister or his niece. He loved the dimpled brunette; she loved him. And Gail had been embarrassed when asked, "Why didn't you set your cap for Whit?"

If these suspicions were true, why had the Reagors hidden the truth? "Because if they are fact," Mariah mumbled to herself, "that means Gail is his illegitimate daughter."

An invisible fist clutched at Mariah's stomach. If he *had* denied one child, what would he do if he were faced with another? She realized it had been foolish not to consider the possible consequences of her passions with Whit.

But she had another realization. If their lovemaking resulted in a babe, she would welcome it, even though her life would be radically changed. Why wouldn't she want Whit's child? Furthermore, why borrow trouble right now?

And if Whit was Gail's father, what was the crime in that? Mariah saw one more reason for closeness with her friend.

Mariah was astounded at the sight before her dazed eyes, and halted the buckskin Susie at the foot of the rise leading to Whit's home. A strange feeling assailed her, akin to déjà vu. Never before had she seen this place, but it seemed somehow familiar. Familiar, yet . . .

"Well, Red, that's my home," he said, riding a few feet ahead of her and smiling with pride of ownership. Bay Fire pranced and whinnied, champing at his bit to gallop, but the high-strung stallion's master brought him under control. "What do you think of it?"

Her hand tightened on the saddle horn. "I'm not sure."

Many times she had drawn mental pictures of where Whit lived and in what degree of comfort, yet while she'd figured there would be a certain amount of luxury, none of her imaginings came near the reality.

The one-story house, built of limestone and roofed with red tiles, topped an incline. At least ten mammoth cottonwood trees shaded the lawn, which was green with grass. Shrubs lined the flagstone path leading from two hitching posts to the arched porch that surrounded the spacious residence.

She touched her heel to Susie's flank and began to ascend the slight grade. Off to her right was a carriage house of two stories. How long had it been since she had seen a carriage house? Several outbuildings and bunkhouses, plus a barn, stood at least a hundred yards from the main house, and she observed a crew at work on a new structure.

Her eyes cut back to Whit's home. Why did she continue to feel a sense of familiarity? Though rock houses were common in Guernsey, and somewhat common in Texas, she had never seen one of this rather Moorish style. It came to her. Moorish . . . Spanish! This was the home of Joseph's letters.

"Something wrong?" Whit brought Bay Fire abreast of her mount, and he leaned to pat the buckskin's withers. "You're awful quiet, Mariah."

"Nothing's wrong," she replied, saying no more.

In truth, nothing was wrong, but she was saddened for the departed Joseph. How he must have envied Whit. Joseph had been accustomed to high living, and it must have been difficult for him—more difficult than she'd ever guessed—to adjust to his lot in Texas.

Whit led her to his home, but she could not stop making comparisons between what he possessed and the lives of people like Joseph, the farmers who lived such a miserable existence in Coleman County.

"Buenos tardes, Señor Whit." A Mexican lad of about ten, who wore a loose-fitting outfit of white and a wide hat, waved a brown hand and hurried to gather Bay Fire's reins.

"Good afternoon to you, too, but where are your manners, *muchacho?*" Whit spoke in Spanish, but did a quick translation for Mariah. "Greet the señorita, Carlos. In English."

Tipping his hat, he displayed a toothy smile. "Hello, missus I am pleased very to meet me. Your name is Carlos."

Whit winked at Mariah. "You'll have to excuse my young friend, and include me in the pardon. 'Fraid my coaching leaves something to be desired, but we're working on it."

He was teaching Carlos to speak English? She smiled. The more she knew this man she loved, the more she was pleased at the many facets to his character. She placed her hand in the grubby brown one and said, "I'm pleased to meet you, Carlos. My name is Mariah."

He said to Whit, "She is . . ." Carlos fought for the phrase. "Maria, she is *muy* pretty."

"I agree," Whit said. "But her name is Maria*h*.

"Mari-huh."

Whit patted the lad's shoulder and said something in Spanish, which gained a beaming smile. Carlos started walking the horses away, but turned back to say, "See you later, Maria*h*."

"He's precious," she murmured to Whit.

"I don't know about precious, but he is a good boy."

"It's wonderful you're teaching him English."

"If he's going to survive in Texas," Whit

said, "he needs to learn the language."

Though her mind had been occupied of late with other matters, first and foremost Whit, Mariah hadn't forgotten about her plans to teach. No more did she have any ideas of leaving Trick'em, though, for she couldn't leave Whit. Of course, the school for squatters' children would have to wait. And with Conchita gone and the Lamkin children leaving soon, Mariah had no promises of tutoring.

"Whit, are there others such as Carlos here at Crosswind? Children needing an education, I mean."

"Most of my men are single. Cowpokes aren't a marrying lot, generally."

"None of your employees are family men?"

"I didn't say 'none.' I said 'most.' There are a few families."

"Who teaches the children?"

"Their mothers."

"And if their mothers are illiterate?" When he shot her a warning look, she ignored it. "Why don't you build a schoolhouse? I know where you can find an absolutely wonderful and dedicated teacher."

"Great Scott, Mariah. If it's not one cause with you, it's another." Whit shook his head in exasperation, then he turned serious. "When my men marry they move away from headquarters. In exchange for keeping the outreaches of Crosswind free of . . . of, well—whatever!—I allow them to ranch a patch of their own, and run a few head of cattle. Those families are scattered over a hundred-mile stretch. Surely you can see the impracticality of one schoolhouse."

"What a shame."

"A lot of things are shameful out here in the West, but that's the price one has to pay for settling a new land."

"I suppose." She glanced at the walk, then up at Whit. "I think you're a good boy for helping Carlos."

"Boy?" A black brow climbed upward. "Shall I direct you to the master suite, and prove I'm a man? Again."

"Oh, you. I'm starved, Whit Reagor, simply famished. What about that food you promised me?"

A late luncheon was served in the long, rectangular dining room situated in the house's west wing. Two crystal chandeliers hung from the raised ceiling, though no artificial light was needed; the sun streamed through four tall windows. The table, carved from mahogany in the Directoire style, could have seated twenty, but two place settings of platinum-edged china and ornate silver flatware were set, Whit's at one end of the table, Mariah's at the opposite.

"Life on the frontier," she murmured after taking a sip of the delicate consommé.

"What did you say, darlin'?"

"Nothing," she answered, but wondered why a frontiersman felt the need to surround himself with such luxuries.

Whit picked up his soup bowl and took himself to the chair to her right. Sitting down, he said, "Damn fool idea of mine, buying this table."

"It's lovely."

"I reckon. But impractical when it keeps me away from my woman."

Pleased, she smiled. "How you do go on."

"I want you to—"

The swinging door opened, cutting off Whit's words, and a serving girl brought a covered silver platter. Her homely face registered surprise at Whit's change of seating, but she schooled her expression and placed the main course on the buffet.

She removed the soup bowls, served portions of a joint of beef and its accompaniments of roasted potatoes and boiled carrots, and retreated to the cooking quarters, but not before a small black furry thing stole around her legs. Barely missing the door as it slapped closed, the kitten padded under the table and batted at the hem of Mariah's riding skirts.

Laughing, she reached for the bundle, bringing the mewing feline baby to her arms. Her fingers scratched behind its ear, and an amazingly strong purr filled her ears.

"Oh, Whit, isn't he adorable?"

"She. *She's* adorable." He, too, began to scratch the kitten, his fingers working on the underside of her chin. "I'd better take her back to her mama. Fancy will be looking for her, and you know how that one gets."

Mariah cuddled the half-pint to the cleft between her breasts. "Can't I hold her for just a couple more minutes?"

"Well, all right."

"What's her name?"

"Haven't named her." Whit winked at Mariah and said, "I was waiting for you to do that."

His gently ardent voice caused Mariah's gaze to fly to him. His eyes were unusually soft, and delightful gooseflesh rose on her arms. She adored this sentimental, tender, sweet, hardheaded, obstinate, aggravating, rough-and-tumble man!

"Well, Red, can't you think of an appropriate name?"

"Wonderful," she murmured, caught up in her musings.

"That's a sorry name for a cat. What happened to Puss or Boots or Beelzebub?"

Mariah held the nearing-four-weeks kitty aloft, and wrinkled her nose. "The first two don't strike me right. Of course, she is black as the devil, but she's a female—and she's going to be sweet, I can tell!—so Beelzebub won't do." Again cuddling the black ball of fur, she lifted a brow at Whit. "Any more suggestions?"

He combed his fingers through his midnight-black hair. "What about—"

"I've got it! Midnight. Her name is Midnight."

"Suits her." He winked. "Can I interest you in a kitten?"

"I can't," Mariah replied sadly. "Gus would never—Gus! He hasn't been fed or watered since last evening—the chickens or Old Glue, either. I must take my leave."

"Whoa, now. They're the least of our worries. I'll have someone go over and feed them."

"Thank you."

Whit rang the bell to summon a servant. When the serving girl answered his call to fetch a ranch hand, Fancy leapt into the room and, hissing, rescued her babe from Mariah's arms. Tail straight as a dorsal fin, Fancy hurried to the door, Midnight between her teeth.

Mariah, with Whit behind her, followed the two to the butler's pantry where a wooden box lined with flannel was stowed in a corner. Fancy arranged her family around her tummy, then her tongue snaked out to rid Midnight of the odious human smell that contaminated her fur.

Both Mariah and Whit chuckled, and she bent at the knees to tickle Fancy's whiskers. "Meow." An approving purr rattled the cat's throat.

"Such a sweet kitty."

Whit laughed. "Never thought I'd hear you say something nice about Fancy! Now wash your hands, you ridiculous cat person." He motioned toward a pitcher and bowl. "Our food grows cold."

After they had rinsed their hands, Whit, his palm at the small of her back, led Mariah to the dining room and seated her. He served their plates with the somewhat tepid, yet still delicious, fare.

Taking a sip of red wine, he studied Mariah. "You fit in here at Crosswind."

Her spirits dropped. Was this a prelude to another offer to be his kept woman? Fearing so, she pointed the conversation on a different tack. "Your home is lovely."

"Guess it beats a covered wagon."

"Don't be modest, Whit." She watched him push his glass aside. "You've a right to be proud," she said.

"I am proud. I've worked hard for everything I've got." He rubbed his mouth. "I've had to. 'Course it wasn't always that way. The Reagors used to have money."

"Tell me about your family."

"My folks died before the Reagor fortune was lost. My mother passed away when I was wet behind the ears, and my dad took a bullet at Shiloh." Whit's expression was grim. "By the time General Lee surrendered to the damn yankees at Appomattox Courthouse, we didn't have much money left. I . . . well, I didn't do a good job of putting the homeplace back together after I was mustered out."

"I'm so sorry," she said earnestly.

"Don't be. I've made up for those losses. Now let's change the subject."

She admired Whit's will to succeed, and was saddened for his heartache. She now understood more about Whit and his drive for security and the finer things in life.

Fear of failure motivated him, which was such a human trait. She found it endearing. Morever, she realized the sacrifice he had made by agreeing to help her in the range war situation. He was putting his fortune on the line.

She had never loved him as much as at this moment.

Into the silence that stretched between them, she prompted, "Tell me about your ranch."

He launched into a description of the many acres of what once had been deep grassland. He told her of the dam project and the contrary Longhorns who waited for that water.

Her curiosity about Whit knew no bounds, and Mariah asked, "How long have you owned this ranch?"

"Been ranching the property since '68—but flat out own it?—since '75, near as I can recall."

"I was eight years old in 1868. How young are you?"

He hesitated before answering, "Red, I'm not young. Far from it. I was thirty-seven last autumn." He leaned to rub his thumb slowly down her index finger. "Reckon I'm too old for you?"

He's afraid our age difference makes a difference, she thought. Actually, he was just right for her. Well, she'd tease him out of his silliness. "Yes, you're too aged, you old goat. You're so decrepit that I—"

"Watch out," he warned and his rubbing turned to a soft slap. "Or you're gonna get as good as you give."

"What could you possibly say about me?" she asked with mock hauteur.

"You have funny-looking feet."

"What's wrong with my feet?"

"They're peculiar. Your toes are too long." He winked and clicked his tongue. "Us old goats have gotta take what we can get, I suppose."

She stuck her tongue out. "Well, grin and bear it."

"I'll do my best." His booted foot moved up and down her calf, drawing a sigh of pleasure from Mariah. " 'Cause I aim to please, ma'am."

"Then how about a kiss?"

He was happy to oblige. A couple of minutes later, he suggested hoarsely, "If I'm going to take you on the tour, we'd better stop this stuff."

"You'll deny me my dessert?"

"You're gonna have plenty of opportunities for your just desserts, my sweet. But if you're really wanting a sugary morsel of food, there's *one* piece of pecan pie left in the pantry." His intent blue gaze welded with the brown of hers. "I'll let you have it."

Recalling the day Whit had defined love for her, she was riveted by hope. "Would the big handsome hunk of cowboy be trying to tell me something?"

"Yeah." His fingers settled against the fast pulse of her throat. "I love you, Mariah McGuire."

"Say it again."

"I love you, Mariah McGuire."

The moment she had waited for was here. She couldn't find the words to describe her happiness, but knew she'd never been this happy. Ever.

"I love you, too, Mr. Reagor."

And he carried her to the master suite to seal their avowals with the passions of true love. Hot, wild, tender, gentle, body-and-soul-satisfying love.

The next afternoon, they were still in bed. Cupping her head, he murmured, "Share my home with me, Mariah. I want us to be together."

He hadn't said, "Marry me." Her disappointment was great. She desperately wanted to hear those words. She loved him. He loved her. She wanted to spend the rest of her life at his side. But Whit, she was well aware, wasn't ready to make a lifelong commitment.

"I'm sorry, Whit, but I can't live here. Gus and Fancy are an incompatible pair," she said, making light of the situation.

"This house is big enough for both of them."

"I'm pledged to stay in Trick'em, Whit, and I hope you can understand that I . . . Oh, *sacrebleu!* Why pussyfoot around? I'll tell you why I don't want to be your kept woman." She paused to take a breath and to gaze into his unreadable eyes. "If I move into this house, I'll be nothing but another in your long line of women. I won't settle for that. We're going to get to know each other better, Whitman Reagor, and it's not going to be here. You're going to court me, good and proper, the intentions being marriage."

Nonplussed, he was still as stone.

"Whit, close your mouth before you swallow a fly." She crossed her arms under her naked breasts. "If my terms aren't acceptable to you, then you'd better speak now or forever hold your tongue."

"I . . . I . . . I . . ."

"Well, Mr. Reagor, are you going to keep your promise of yesterday and show me the rest of this ranch, or not? Remember, though, if you do, I'll take it as an agreement to my terms."

Chapter Twenty

As afternoon waned, Whit tied Bay Fire to a mesquite tree and gazed across the south range where, thirty feet away, a crew of ten was in the process of building a dam on the Indian spring. Grass still grew here. The beeves left behind when the herd had hit the trail to Dodge were grazing on the best pasture Crosswind offered. Half thinking of the cattle drive, Whit no longer missed the trip to the railhead. Being with Mariah had that effect on him.

He liked the idea of courting Miss Mariah McGuire and of taking his time in the doing. He moved behind her, pulling her back against him to wind his arms under her breasts. "Wanna go to the dance next Saturday night?" he asked, dropping a kiss on the top of her clean hair.

"Depends on who takes me," she retorted.

"Witch." He bent to nip her rose-scented neck. "I'm taking you."

"Oh, I had no idea you meant yourself," she said with feigned innocence. "I might be free."

Cuddling her closer to him, he chuckled. "You are truly a witch."

"And you are truly a devil, Whit Reagor." She scooted out of his arms, giving him her profile. "And if you don't stop tempting me with all these hugs and kisses, we're going to embarrass ourselves in front of your men."

"Can't have that."

"Really." She looked at the dam. "When will it be finished?"

"A few more days, I'd say."

"Whit, will one dam be enough for all your cattle?"

"Till the drought breaks, it's the best I can do."

"Have you considered digging for water?" she asked.

"Nobody in their right mind would go to the bother."

She rounded on him, "I've considered it."

"You'd be wasting your time. Rumor has it, you dig for water and get oil, I'm not denying that mucky guck has its purposes for doctoring horses and cattle, but I'd hate to see you tie up good money in something that wouldn't serve your needs."

She planted a fist on her hip. "Surely you don't put stock in someone else's tales. Maybe water wasn't found on other property, but I might find it . . . and you might, too. Look at that Indian spring down there! Its water had to come from somewhere," Determination was written in each of her features. Dig a well, What's the harm in giving it a go?"

She had a point, but . . . A thought came to him. "Wait a minute. Didn't you say you aren't going to farm? What do you need a well for?"

Contemplatively she stared at the ground, then met his eyes. "I have to make a living until my school is under way. Anyway, my market garden will be a success, but I . . . I won't be digging a well."

"Why not?"

"My . . . pond still has water. I'm sure there'll be enough for the vegetables."

He read something in her eyes. He'd bet the ranch she didn't have money to hire diggers. "You know, on second thought, what's the harm in trying for water? We could give it a shot at your place. Soon as those fellows—" He motioned toward the workmen. "When they finish here, why don't I send them over to the farm?"

"Thank you, but no thank you." Her cheeks flushed. "I can't pay their wages."

"I didn't ask you to."

"You're kind to offer, Whit, but I won't have you coddling me."

He had to indulge her mule-headed pride,

"You were right a minute ago. The Mukewater ought to hold till you bring in your garden," There was truth to his words, and suddenly Whit had an idea. "It'll take weeks for you to turn a profit in your garden. My cows need water. Will you lease me the rights to your pond?"

Again, she took a contemplative glance at the ground.

"I'm not offering charity or coddling," he said, "This is a business arrangement. You need cash, my herd needs your pond, and we'd be helping each other."

She extended her hand. "You've got a deal."

He shook on the arrangement, all the while thinking how soft her hand felt in his rough one.

A wagon piled high with rocks drew up to the dam site, and the workers who were constructing the stock tank left their labors to unload the stones. Several of the men, however, took a moment to gawk at Mariah.

Whit said, "It's time we moved on."

"But this is interesting."

"What? Having my men ogling you?"

"For heaven's sake, Whit, you needn't be jealous,"

"I am." He took her arm. "Let's take a walk."

They ascended the low hill from which the spring cascaded downward. Making certain Mariah was above his men's easy sight, he led her to a boulder and seated her, hunkering back on his heels at her feet.

His gaze drilled into hers. "You set down some strong terms about the direction you and I are taking. I agreed to your demands. Before we go any further, though, I've got some conditions of my own and I want your undivided attention."

"I was interested in the dam project, not in the workers. I refuse to be kept on a short lead."

"That's exactly where I'd keep you if I had my druthers. You know what I went through with my wife; I can't forget what she did. And, yes, you're the one who has to pay for her sins. That's a crooked deal for you, I don't deny, but I am what I am, and she was what she was, and you've got to be better. If you can't handle it, let me know. Now."

"I can handle it."

He angled forward, cupping her cheeks with his palms. "I love you, Mariah." He kissed away the tear that formed in her eye. "I love you with all my heart, and I think you can be trusted, but I'm still jumpy about trust."

"I know. But I hope, in time, you'll realize you have nothing to be concerned about."

"I hope so, too, because I love you so much I'd kill for you."

"Don't say something like that. You scare me."

"It was just an expression." He wrapped his

arms around her. Her heartbeat thumped against his chest as he said, "I just wanted you to know how much you mean to me."

"Oh, Whit my dear darling, you haven't a thing to fear. I love you. A thousand times over I love you."

Would she love him, he wondered, if she knew the truth? He had asked for her unquestioned loyalty, had asked a helluva lot from her, yet what could he give her in return, beyond the offer of marriage she wanted?

Well, Whit was getting closer to the idea of taking her to wife. When they married, though, she was entitled to honesty. Honesty he wasn't able to give. All because of a promise to a now-dead woman.

He strode away from Mariah. Reaching down for a cactus flower, he tossed the orange bloom away. Twenty years ago he had been in love with Jenny, had been obsessed with marrying her. Of course, he'd never had his way with her while they were courting. But when he'd been on the verge of joining Ochiltree's forces, she'd made a carnal promise: "I won't let you go into battle without the memory of me fresh in your mind. The night before you leave, I'm going to give you my most precious gift."

His youthful excitement had been overshadowed by fear. As a green kid of seventeen, he'd had no experience in the art of lovemaking. Art, hell. He'd been a virgin. And he'd listened to enough man-talk to know a gal needed more than just a tumble in the cotton patch.

In Whit's mind, then and now, he'd never tried to gloss over the truth. He'd done an unpardonable thing. He'd turned to an experienced widow woman. Lilibet Chapman had been a willing teacher. They hadn't loved each other; both had known and accepted that.

Afterward, Jenny had sacrificed her maidenhead, and he'd strutted toward war, never giving Lilibet another thought except in thanks for showing him a woman's sensitive spots. When the Confederate States of America were no more, Whit had returned to Jefferson. Lilibet was married to his cousin, Kelley Reagor, and she had a babe. It hadn't taken much finger-counting on Whit's part to figure out who was the father. He'd confronted Lilibet, and she'd admitted as much. But she had pleaded with him: "Don't ruin things for me with Kelley. If you do, my marriage and my reputation will be in shambles. And you have to think of the child. Will you ruin her life by marking her a bastard? I want your promise, Whitman. Promise me you'll never breathe a word of this. Promise me!"

He'd given Lilibet his vow of silence and had kept it, even though she had been dead for five years now.

To this day, Whit took no pride in his decision. Back then he had wanted Jenny and had taken the easy way out, never realizing how much he would regret his oath of honor, never realizing how much he'd love Gail, nor how much he would regret not being able to face his daughter and say, "I'm proud you're mine."

Now as he turned to stare at Mariah, he had never regretted his decision more strongly. Would she be able to accept him, knowing he was the father of a daughter only four years younger than she?

"Is something wrong, Whit?" Mariah asked, walking up beside him.

"Yes. I've asked a lot of you, but I wonder what I can give in return. I've done a lot of things in my life I'm not proud of, Mariah."

"I'm willing to accept you just the way you are."

"I hope so."

The sound of hooves and a faint male shout drew Whit's attention. A rider, having topped a north rise, rode ninety to nothing toward the workers. Something had to be wrong.

Five minutes later Whit stood with the dam crew, Mariah at his side, and watched Slim Culpepper jump from his mount.

"Reagor, your trail boss sent a messenger." The cowpoke drew off his sweat-rimmed hat, wiping his brow, "The herd's in trouble. North of Vernon, just this side of the Red River. The drought's worse up there. The cows are going blind from thirst."

"Damn," Whit muttered.

"Sumthin's gotta be done," said his construction foreman, his sentiment echoed by the rest of the crew.

"I'm on top of it." He could order Slim to handle the matter, but Whit was edgy, this being the first cattle drive he'd missed. He had to size up the situation, and do his part. Personally. He could provision himself, picking up riders and water wagons, at Crosswind's northernmost line shack. If he rode hard, he could reach the herd in three days. He fired off orders to his men. That left Mariah to be dealt with. He had promised to take care of Taft and the range war business, but those matters would have to wait.

Whit turned to her. "I'm sorry, but you'll have to go it alone for a while."

"Knowing I have your support is enough for me."

"Glad to hear it. Now let's get you home."

"I can make it by myself. I'll be perfectly safe."

"Safety isn't a matter for discussion. Promise me you won't do *anything* till I get back."

"But—"

"No 'buts', Mariah. Just promise me."

Chewing her lip, she glanced at the ground. Finally, she raised her eyes. "I promise."

"Thatta girl." He turned to Culpepper. "Take Miss McGuire home. Keep an eye on her while I'm gone. If she needs anything whatsoever, you make sure she gets it."

"You bet, boss."

Whit placed a too-quick kiss on Mariah's cheek. "I'll be back as soon as possible. Give me a rain check on that dance?" At her nod, he murmured, "I'm gonna miss you, Red."

"Same goes for me. And good luck, cowboy."

He turned to Bay Fire, hefted himself into the high-cantled saddle, and touched his spurs to the sorrel's flanks. Already Whit was missing Mariah . . .

And a fierce sense of loneliness filled Mariah as she watched Whit ride north. Yet that loneliness was superceded by a stronger emotion. Love.

She turned to her mare but caught sight of Culpepper in the process. This young ranch hand had flirted with her on the morning she'd met her beloved, but after all Whit's jealous talk, he'd left her with this cowboy. Maybe *her* cowboy was more trusting than he realized.

She sat her mount. "Shall we go, Mr. Culpepper?"

Headed east, she recalled her promise to Whit. It would be difficult, not doing something about Taft. She was filled with zealous determination to bring law and order to the area. What would she do until Whit returned? Of course she had chores to tend, plus a social obligation. She had promised the Lamkins she'd tell them goodbye before they left Coleman County. Why not do it right now?

"Mr. Culpepper—"

"Call me Slim. When you say mister, I think you're calling my pa."

"We can't have that, can we . . . But, Slim, you needn't see me home. I'm going to call on the Lamkin family."

"The boss told me I'm responsible for you, and that's what I'm gonna be. You wanna make a detour, it's my job to go with you." He reined in his gelding. "But what do you wanna go messin' around with squatters for?"

"Do you make a habit of putting your nose in other people's business?"

"No, ma'am. Leastways, I try not to." He paused, then said, "Come on, Miz McGuire. I'll lead the way."

Silently they rode on. Dusk began to settle an hour later, but Mariah had no problem seeing trouble. A plume of smoke painted the horizon. The faint sounds of gunfire came from the same direction. Someone needed help.

Eschewing sidesaddle and skirts, she gave the mare her head. Topping a hill, Mariah cried "No!" and raced forward.

The roof of the Lamkins' soddy was ablaze! Three riders were circling the dugout, their guns pointed at A.W. Lamkin, who flew backward from a bullet's impact.

"Stay out of it, Miz McGuire!" Slim warned, trying to block her path.

She skirted the buckskin around his gelding. Reins in one hand, she dug into her reticule for her repeater pistol. The tapestry handbag fell to the ground. From a distance of about forty feet, she leveled her weapon at one of the riders and fired. She missed.

Two of the raiders jerked their intentions to Mariah, and bullets whizzed over her head, at her side, beneath her mare. "For God's sake, Slim!" she ordered. "Use your rifle."

He didn't.

Susie charged toward the marauders, Mariah fired again, this time from thirty feet. Her bullet tore into a rider's neck. Screaming, he grabbed for his wound and fell to the ground, his horse galloping away.

The injured man's cohorts, one of them wearing an eye patch, turned cowardly and scudded in opposite directions.

Mariah was torn between following the two and helping the Lamkins. Crumpled over a water barrel, Patsy Lamkin was dead—there was no doubt of this. Aggie's lifeless body was at her mother's feet. A.W., his face on the ground, lifted his hand.

Sliding from the saddle, Mariah ground-tethered the mare and, skirting around the outlaw's stilled body, she ran to the fallen farmer.

"Keep covered," Slim yelled, at last shouldering his rifle. "That one's not dead!"

The whiz of a bullet passed over her head at the same moment Slim's shell exploded into the gunman's face. The raider's pistol fell from his hand.

She rolled A.W. to his back. Blood trickled from the corner of his mouth. "My baby," he choked, "in the—" His eyes moved in the dugout's direction. A shudder lifted his wounded chest, and he went limp in Mariah's arms.

She rushed to the soddy. Smoke belched from the open door. Choking, she tried to fight her way into the flame-filled room, but Slim's fingers dug into her arm, yanking her backward. She lost her footing and fell to the ground.

"There's a little girl in there," she shouted.

"Stay put," he ordered. "I'll get her."

The young cowman covered his face with a bandanna and rushed into the inferno. A half minute later a mighty crash sounded as the roof fell in, but Slim, Molly in his arms, managed to escape the holocaust and gave the limp child into Mariah's waiting arms.

Clutching the soot-covered girl to her chest, she hastened away from the heat, placing Molly on the ground. The girl didn't move. Crouched down, Mariah put her mouth to the young, blue lips.

She had to save her! Mariah tried to breathe life into the young body. Over and again, she pushed the heels of her hands against Molly's diaphragm. "Breathe, sweeting, breathe!"

"Miz McGuire . . ." Slim put his hand on Mariah's shoulder. "It's no use. She's gone to her Maker."

"Not true!" She wouldn't allow the entire family to be lost. "I haven't given up!"

"Look at her, Miz McGuire. You done your best, but she's gone."

"No." Mariah closed her eyes to the little girl's sightless eyes and took her into her arms, rocking her back and forth. "She was too young to die. She wanted to learn sums, and wanted to read the Bible. And Aggie—" Tears poured down Mariah's cheeks. "She was so shy, so shy."

"You've had a shock, ma'am. Let me put the lass with her family."

"Get away! If you'd been quicker to help."

"If you feel the need to blame somebody, it's okay to blame me." He knelt, pulling Mariah's hand from the girl's arm. "She'd want to be with her parents."

Through her tears, Mariah touched Molly's singed hair. "Heavenly Father, take care of this lamb and her family."

Slim patted Mariah's shoulder. "Guess we'd better get word to town," he said.

"Yes." Her thumb closed the five-year-old's scorched eyelids. "If I live to be a hundred, I'll never forget this sight," she said raggedly, honestly. She looked up at the ranch hand. "I hope you never forget it, either. This is how low man can sink in his inhumanity to others."

"I won't be forgettin', ma'am."

Gently, the lanky cowboy carried Molly

away.

Mariah huddled in grief.

Slim gathered some horse blankets from the Lamkins' shed, and came back to cover the dead. He was ashamed of himself for not going to Miz McGuire's aid right away.

A fellow needed to feel and care for others down deep in his heart, and shouldn't hesitate to ride into a band of no-goods when they were after a family. Slim hadn't been frightened to charge into that melee, he just hadn't been of a mind to. But Miz McGuire hadn't let nothing stop her.

For all of his twenty-five years, Slim Culpepper hadn't let nothing get under his skin. He had witnessed killings and hangings and a lot of hell in the middle. He wasn't one to ruminate over life's ups and downs or about people's deeds. To his way of figuring, one accepted others however they were—good, bad, or in between.

During all that, he had fashioned himself among the good. He had kept his nose clean. He'd never shot nobody before today, had never done no woman wrong, and had always ridden hard for the brand.

After this business with the Lamkins, though, and seeing how Miz McGuire had reacted to all of it, David Walter Culpepper would never be smug again. He was going to take action and if he ended up half as courageous as Miz McGuire, he'd consider himself fortunate.

At peace with himself, he loaded the Lamkins into their old wagon for the trip to the undertaker, then walked over to Miz McGuire, who was standing over the dead outlaw.

"Do you recognize this man?" she asked.

Slim scratched his head. "Well, it's kinda hard to figure out, his face being torn up like that, but I don't reckon he's familiar. 'Course I'm new around here."

"He didn't materialize out of nowhere to do all this harm. Maybe someone in town will know who he is."

"It's Zeke. He's dead. Some woman rode up while we was burning out that Lamkin vermin, and she opened fire. Musta gotten lucky, I'll warrant, 'cause she got him from a good distance."

Resting against the pillows of her sickbed, Temperence Tullos grimaced as she listened to T-Bone Hicks's account. "Was she . . ." A fit of coughing racked her weakened chest, and she tried unsuccessfully to expel the congestion.

T-Bone blew his stubbed nose on a soiled handkerchief, then handed her a glass of water. Too sick to protest the lack of hygiene, she downed the liquid. The fluid eased her distress to some degree and she wiped a wet rag across her feverish brow. "Was the woman alone?"

"There was a feller with her," Spider Black, a single-eyed ruffian with a knife scar slicing through his weathered left cheek, supplied. "I didn't get a good look at his face. We was sort of occupied."

Temperence tossed the rag at his sardonic grin. "Of course you couldn't get an eyeful of him, you one-eyed sidewinder. You were too busy making a run for—" Again, painful hacks wracked her. Finally, she was able to wheeze, "Be gone with you. Now."

The hired guns backed out of her chambers, leaving her alone in her miseries and boiling temper.

She was almost as mad as the night Lord Joe had announced that he had called off his wedding. He had been through with Temperence, too. "Remove yourself from my property, you disgusting cow!" he had shouted at her.

Well, he was dead now. Was anyone more deserving?

Temperence blew her nose and continued to pity herself. Nothing had gone right since she took sick with influenza. Her plans for Lord Joe's property were yet to be accomplished, Leroy Smith was no closer to Trick'em than before, and she couldn't even count on the Hicks gang to rid the area of white trash without bringing in witnesses. Nothing got done unless she gave personal supervision along the way.

Was there no justice in this world? Right then, she had never been more furious at Charles. Everything was all his fault. How, she wondered, could she gain vengeance against her husband for banishing Leroy to Pennsylvania?

At this point, she wasn't certain, but, no matter her weakness of body, she did know one thing for certain. She wouldn't be indisposed forever.

Then heads would roll. Whoever got in her way!

The afternoon following their deaths, the Lamkins were buried in the churchyard. Reverend Pickle said a few words. Mariah and Slim, the only mourners, placed bluebonnets on their pine coffins. The preacher took his leave, and Slim shoveled dirt over the Lamkins' graves.

Mariah hammered wooden crosses into the ungiving ground. Since the murders, a maelstrom of emotions had beset her. Grief, anger, frustration. No one in Trick'em had claimed to recognize the dead raider. Beyond herself and Slim, no one seemed to care that a family of four had lost their lives. And naturally, Sheriff Taft had been as apathetic as usual.

She was anxious for Whit's return, not simply for his presence. *Why did I make him a promise not to go forward with my plans?*

Something needed to be done, and now.

Finished with affixing a cross to Molly's grave, Mariah straightened and turned to Slim. "Thank you for everything. Especially for becoming my friend."

He blushed to the roots of his sandy-blond hair. " 'Tweren't nothing. I'll see you home now."

They rode toward her farm. Slim whistled a mournful tune, no doubt in deference to the dead. Deep in her own mournful thoughts, Mariah was quiet, until Mukewater Pond came into view.

"Good gracious!" she said. "Look at that."

About fifty Longhorns were amassed around her water supply. From a distance of a couple of hundred yards, she made out the figures of three drovers and their horses.

"They're stealing your water!" Slim drew his rifle. "I'll get rid of 'em."

"Put that away. There's been enough trouble." She nudged Susie's flank. "Let's see what they have to say." Nearing the skinny herd, she called, "What are you men about?"

"Don't mean no harm, miss." The trail boss rode toward her. He was a scrawny young fellow wearing ragged clothes and a general air of defeat, she observed. He couldn't have been a day over eighteen. His cowboys, along with a scabrous brown-and-black dog, were closing ranks around him. Assessing the pitiable lot, Mariah said, "You're trespassing."

The youngest of the bunch, a lad of about twelve whose big hat rested on his ears, pulled a rusty Colt .45.

"Thom!"

Slim extracted a pouch of smokes from his pocket. "Put that away, son."

"You ain't got no right to keep them cows from water!" Thom shouted. "Our cows has gotta drink. And we gotta make camp fer the night."

"Not here you ain't," Slim said calmly. "This is Miz McGuire's watering hole."

"We ain't scared of you." Thom peppered the air with a round of shot, and the dog jumped.

"Thom, don't," exclaimed the trail boss.

"Yes. That will be enough." Mariah called up her best schoolmarm's voice. "Thom," she said evenly, "I don't approve of violence." Only yesterday she'd shot a man! "You don't appear to be a young man who's been reared to bring harm to others," she commented, playing on male pride, or at least on guilt. "Kindly holster your gun so I might speak with your leader."

Shamefaced, the lad did as suggested. "Sorry, ma'am."

"Thank you." She directed her next words to the trail boss. "Do you have a name?"

"Andy Floyd." He gestured toward his crew. "These be my brothers, Thom and Luther. We're outta Nueces County. These cows be our ma's."

Mariah nodded to the ragged boys, then centered her attention on the oldest one. "Andy Floyd, didn't your mother teach you it's wrong to steal?"

Resting a palm on the saddle horn, he replied, "Meaning no disrespect, miss, but I done thunk the Western Trail was wide open to cows."

"This stretch isn't. Kindly move your cattle on north."

"Yes, miss." Andy Floyd started to rein his horse to the right, but stopped. "Miss, we've been a long ways since water, and our cows be mighty thirsty. Could we buy some of that water from ya, please?"

Her eyes drifted to the cattle who were crushing to the water's edge. In all conscience, she couldn't let them go thirsty, and she'd wager the Floyds hadn't had a decent meal in days. What would it hurt to show a little compassion? After all, somewhere between here and the Indian Territory, Whit's herd was in trouble. She hoped someone would do them a good turn.

Trouble was, how could she give the Floyds that water without injuring their pride? "Your herd may drink their fill, Andy."

Thom heaved a sigh of relief, and he smiled.

"Follow me to the house," Mariah continued to Andy. "I'll fix us all some supper, and we'll speak about how you and your brothers can work off the compensation."

Not ten minutes after the shaggy-haired young trail boss had sat down at the log cabin's table, he mentioned coming across a family of Mexican vagabonds not three days earlier.

"They was doin' real poor-like," Andy said, shaking his head with pity. "Their horse done died, and they's outta food, so me and my brothers decided to butcher one of our steers. Figgered our ma'd approve; she's a Christian lady, you understand."

"That was kind of you," Mariah replied sincerely, then touched a match to the fireplace kindling. "This family you encountered, what was their name?"

"Don't know their proper names, 'but I heard the wife call her man Pablo."

Barely able to keep from jumping with glee, Mariah got an idea. "Andy, can one of your brothers handle your cattle by himself? At graze, of course."

"Yes, miss. Luther's right fair at it."

"Good," She gathered the makings of cornbread, "If I let your cattle graze my pasture for a few days, would you and Thom be willing to bring the Martinezes back to Trick'em?"

"Well, sure, miss," Andy's expression was uncertain. "Iffen they'll come with us."

"They will. Tell them Miss McGuire . . ." She paused, thinking they might well refuse to help her. "Tell them the sheriff wants to talk with them about a murder case," she amended. She glanced at Slim. "Mr. Culpepper, I'd appreciate your accompanying Andy and Thom. If the Martinezes balk, will you make certain they return?"

Surprise widened Slim's eyes. "What am I supposed to do? Hogtie 'em?"

"No. I imagine that wouldn't be workable." Deep in contemplation, she added a pinch of salt to her cornbread mixture.

What would Whit recommend? Whit. Her promise to stay out of trouble nagged at Mariah. No doubt he wouldn't approve of her taking this action, but what was she to do? Trouble had come to her. The Lamkins had died since Whit had left, and here was a chance—a slight one, but a chance nonetheless—to solve Joseph's murder. Surely Whit would understand her reasonings.

Drastic times required drastic actions. "Ride for Brownwood and ask for the Ranger Captain Big Dan Dodson. Get him to accompany you. And if the Martinezes don't cooperate, have Pablo arrested as an accessory to murder."

Slim rubbed his mouth. "Miz Mariah, I'm getting a bad feeling about this. You're stepping into the sheriff's boundaries."

"Yes, I am. But there are times, Slim Culpepper, when one must put one's self on the line."

Chapter Twenty-one

The next morning, Mariah brimmed with the fire of determination. Until peace came to Trick'em, she wouldn't be hampered by feminine trappings, and thus she outfitted herself in Joseph's belongings—breeches, shirt, western saddle, and gunbelt. The rising sun at her right, she rode into town. Although she had to detour around a crowd of townspeople circling a cart loaded with dead men, Mariah found the lady newspaper reporter with relative ease.

Lydia Farrell was eating breakfast at the café when Mariah approached her. "Whit Reagor told me about you, Miss Farrell. I'm Mariah McGuire."

The women had a mutual purpose that didn't include small talk and they got right down to the business of law and order.

After Mariah explained the problems with

Taft, Lydia asked, "May I quote you and Mr. Reagor?"

"By all means. We want the lawmakers in Austin to know what is going on here in Coleman County. Taft has to go. And we need a law against fence-cutting."

"Fair enough." Lydia made copious notes in a small journal, then she lifted her dark eyes to Mariah. "My uncle, Hayes Farrell, is a state senator."

"Is he sympathetic to the issue?"

"I don't know. But I'll find out, and work on him if he isn't." Lydia took a sip of coffee. "What's your next step?"

"I'll be speaking with the local women."

The black-haired reporter nodded in agreement. "Good idea. But, Miss McGuire, keep your back covered. Change doesn't come without sacrifice."

"I know."

Lydia departed for the capital city of Austin to file her story and to speak with her lawmaker uncle. Mariah headed for the Strickland ranch, which was located two miles northeast of Trick'em. She found Gail seated behind a table on the ranch house's wide front porch.

"Hiya." Gail waved a crutch. "Take a load off your feet. How about a cup of coffee?"

Mariah eased into a chair. "This isn't a social call. I need your help."

"Why do I get the feeling this has something

to do with the fence-cutting war?"

"Your intuition is commendable," Mariah replied, then detailed her strategies for the ladies' campaign. "Because of our friendship, I want to give you the opportunity to be the first ranch woman to step . . . in your case, *hobble* across the line to justice."

"You injure me with your pun!" Gail laughed. Her good humor vanished, though, and she grimaced. "I love you to death, Mariah, but my husband is a rancher, and you know it. Ed doesn't . . . We won't go against our own kind."

"I expected you to say that—Lord knows I've heard that expression enough from everyone!—but I want you to know something." She paused for emphasis. "Whit has changed his mind. He's ready for peace."

"Whit? You're sporting me. He's a rancher through and through."

"Don't underestimate him."

"I never did."

Mariah ruminated over Gail's answer. Remembering her suspicions, she said, "I guess being cousins, you have a lot of faith in each other."

"Yes."

"I've never quite figured out the relationship between you two. Are you first cousins?"

"My father was his first cousin." Nervously Gail toyed with her coffee cup. "Why do you ask?"

"Curiosity, that's all."

"Don't get too curious, Mariah, unless it's very important to you."

"It's very important to me."

Startled, Gail said, "Why? Have you two worked out your differences?"

"We're trying. I love him. And he loves me."

"I see." A melancholy smile came over Gail's face. "I'm happy for you."

"You're lacking your usual exuberance. Why? All along, you've tried to promote a match between us. What, Gail, is the problem?"

"He's my father."

Although she had suspected this, Mariah was shocked. "Why has it been kept a secret?"

"Whit's never admitted anything to me. My mother did, though. On her deathbed. It hurts really bad that he won't speak up."

"Is he the skeleton you mentioned when we were traveling to Trick'em?"

"Yeah," the brunette came back with bitterness.

"Gail, don't be harsh toward him. He loves you."

"I know. Ed helped me to see that, finally." Whit's daughter rubbed her eyes. "I don't want to be bitter. All I want is for my father to acknowledge me."

"Maybe you should confront him."

"No. It's his place for that."

"Would you like for me to talk to him about the situation?" Mariah asked.

"No."

"Gail, I'm going to ask you something as one friend to another, and I hope you'll be frank. Will it bother you if he and I marry? I think we're moving in that direction."

"Will it bother you knowing he has a grown daughter?"

"Not in this case."

"Would it bother you . . . How would you feel if he became a grandfather before he even became a father to *your* baby?"

"It wouldn't trouble me." Mariah lifted a brow. "Are you trying to tell me something?"

Gail blushed. "Yes. I'm with child."

"That's wonderful!"

The two friends embraced. Problems were pushed aside as they reveled in the exciting news. Their voices were elevated as Ed bounded from the house.

"What's going on out here?" the rancher asked, jutting his square jaw. "I won't have your kind pestering my wife."

"She isn't bothering me, Ed. And Mariah isn't a 'kind'. She's my friend."

"She's a farmer making trouble for the sheriff."

"I am those things," Mariah admitted. "That is the purpose of my visit. Will you spare me a minute, Ed?"

"No."

"Ed, please," Gail said. "For me and the baby, will you listen to her?"

He gave a grudging nod, and Mariah spent the next half hour going over how much was to be gained through peace.

When she finished, Ed frowned. "That's all well and good, but you're stirring up a hornet's nest, Mariah."

"Peace won't be easy to attain," she admitted.

He frowned. "If things get ugly, none of us will be safe from harm."

"Are you safe now?" Mariah stared at him. "How many people, including ranchers, have died?"

"Me, I don't worry about, but I do worry about Gail and our son."

"Daughter," Gail corrected.

"I don't want anything to jeopardize my wife and son."

"I wouldn't let that happen."

He crossed his arms. "And just how, Mariah McGuire, could you do that?"

"I promise you. I'll keep an eye on your wife." *On Whit's daughter.*

"She doesn't need a woman's protection," he replied.

"Would you two quit arguing?" Gail rapped her crutch on the wooden porch. "For crying out loud, there's enough trouble around here without having to listen to it in my own home. Another thing. I'm getting sick and tired of this fencing war. Something has to be done. And I thank God that Mariah has the gumption to do it."

Astonished, Ed looked at his wife. "You want me to side with the fence-builders?"

"Farmers share the guilt with ranchers," Mariah stated. "I'm working toward justice, nothing else."

"It would be nice, having this range-war mess at an end." Ed bent to wrap his arms around his wife. "All right, Mariah. I'll do what I can to help."

Mariah's audible relief mingled with Gail's.

"Edward, my darling, I've prayed you would come around and not disappoint me." Looking up, she took her husband's hand. "This country is big enough for all of us, farmers and ranchers and even a few no-goods, too. We've got to learn to live in peace and harmony—for ourselves and for our children. And grandchildren. We'll have to make some sacrifices for that peace, though. We must give farmers their rights." Glancing downward, she laced her fingers with his. "Can you make that sacrifice, Ed?"

"I'm willing to do my part," Ed conceded.

Mariah set out for town. She had expected a lot more opposition from the Stricklands and was pleased to have gained their support.

The ride to Trick'em gave Mariah time to think about Gail and Whit. Why hadn't he acknowledged his daughter? Well, if Mariah had any say in it, he would, but she wasn't going to stew over it, not now. Not when she was sailing on the wings of success.

Success had fleeting glory. Mariah got no cooperation from the ten women she called on later in the day. Nor from the twelve she talked to on the subsequent two days. By Wednesday night, though, Gail had spoken with Jackie Jo Jamerson and with Mrs. Chadwick Nussbaumer, and both women agreed to speak with their husbands.

Thursday, while Mariah was on her rounds, horses had trampled her vegetable garden but she was not going to give up.

On Friday afternoon she had a visitor at the farm while she was investigating the horseshoe imprints left by the marauder's steeds.

Dressed in black and with veiled eyes, Birdie Turner said, "It's not easy for me to admit wrong, but I'm here to do it. I've heard about your campaign with the womenfolk, and I want to help you. I want to help us all. We need law and order in Coleman County."

"Then start by having a talk with George. Make him understand."

"It's too late for that." Birdie composed herself. "My son was killed last night."

Mariah stepped over a flattened hillock of

beans. "I'm so sorry, Birdie."

"I don't need condolences. The only way to ease my grief is to turn something bad into good." The wrenlike woman took a breath of air. "I had a long talk with Reverend Pickle this morning and, as we speak, he's prevailing upon the ladies of the church. We're going to do something, whatever it takes, to make Trick'em a decent place to live."

Mariah's relief turned to anxious excitement as the day wore on. The women of Trick'em rallied around her, giving their support. They quarreled with their husbands and sons over the men's unique views of right and wrong, but when the sun set on Monday night, the pews of Trick'em Presbyterian Church were filled to capacity.

Behind the pulpit, Mayor Chadwick T. Nussbaumer was flanked by Reverend Pickle, Ed Strickland, Dr. John Metcalfe, and Birdie Turner. Mariah and Gail sat in the front row. Sheriff Wilburn Taft, was confident nothing would happen to his job, lazed against a back pew. Charlie Tullos stood in the narthex.

"Wilburn Taft," said the mayor, "as of this moment, your tenure as sheriff is terminated."

"Who y'all gonna get to take my place?" Taft stood and arced his hand across the assemblage. "Come on, boys, don't be shy. Which one of ya wants my job? Who'll be the one to protect farming trash?" No one volunteered, and his laugh was guttural. His finger pointed to the civic leaders. "Y'all stand up there behind that pulpit, telling me I ain't done my job, but what're ya gonna do? It be me as sheriff or nobody."

Mariah was at a point of great decision. Being the only person half qualified for the job, she yearned to step forward. But . . .

She realized such a move would mean sacrifice. For years she had wanted to be a schoolteacher. Though that goal had been shelved temporarily, she intended to follow her drcam . . .

And Whit was her dream. She'd made a promise to let him handle Taft, but she'd broken it already. What would he do if he found out she even considered volunteering to act as sheriff to keep the peace? Surely he'd understand, but Mariah herself realized the perils of such an occupation—that she might not live to follow her dreams.

"There are times when one must put one's self on the line."

Slowly, she got to her feet. "I'm willing to take the job until a suitable replacement is found."

Gasps steepled the church. Male voices rang out. A woman for sheriff? Who ever heard of such a thing? That was a man's job! A gal's hand fit a skillet handle, not a six-shooter's grip. Any hombre worth his salt protected a female, not took protection from her. Unthinkable!

"If you'll give me a moment of your time, I'd be much appreciative." Mariah crossed to the pulpit and faced the citizenry. "Yes, I am a woman, and I make no apology for my gender."

She halted her speech when the church door opened. Slim Culpepper, Andy Floyd, and a giant of a man—a stranger—stole quietly inside. Slim gave her a thumbs-up sign. Apparently the Martinezes were in Trick'em.

"Ladies and gentlemen," Mariah continued, "I've been in the company of lawmen all my life. My father is a constable in the island of Guernsey. Two of my brothers hold like positions in France. From these men I gained a wealth of knowledge in law enforcement methods. I—"

"But that be some foreign country," Heavy Everett interrupted. " 'Tis a different story here in Texas."

"I assure you I have the skills to handle the post of sheriff."

"It jist don't seem fittin', having a lady lawman," a consumptive old man wheezed.

Charlie Tullos stepped down the aisle. "The day we let a farm woman run this county is the day we open the gateway to perdition!"

The round-faced stranger who had accompanied Slim and Andy into the church rose to a standing position. He was a good head taller than anyone else in the church. All eyes turned to the brown-haired giant. Someone uttered a "Why, it's Big Dan" and a hush fell over the crowd.

His voice boomed with an English accent as he said, "Fitting or not, the little lady has something the rest of you are lacking: determination. You'd be well served to accept what she has so generously offered. And thank her for it."

People huddled together for private debate, their voices buzzing. Chadwick T. Nussbaumer banged a gavel on the pulpit. "Order, order!"

Mariah squared her shoulders. "Your Honor, America is a democratic society. Do the democratic thing, and put it to a vote."

Nussbaumer nodded. "All in favor of Miss Mariah McGuire for Sheriff of Coleman County, say 'aye.' "

Chapter Twenty-two

To administer the oath of office to Coleman County's sheriff-elect, T. Jeff McCracken, Judge of the District Court, was pulled from his thundering snores and a vivid dream recalling the day in 1836 when he and the others had whipped Ole Santy Annie at San Jacinto.

He was not pleased to be disturbed out of past glories. Upon hearing the interruption's purpose, he changed his mood. He rinsed his mouth with corn liquor, spat into the bedside spittoon, donned his judicial robe over his nightshirt, and strutted into his parlor for the swearing-in. T. Jeff took pride in his responsibilities.

That Goliath Big Dan Dodson was waiting for him, along with the pompous ass Nussbaumer and a couple of whippersnappers T.

Jeff didn't recognize. Taking a gander at the new sheriff, he got the shock of his seventy years. The electorate had chosen a woman, a young pretty one at that.

"I declare," he said, recovering. "Next thing you know, you gals will be asking for the vote."

Ten minutes later, Mariah had a silver star pinned to her shirt. She wasn't going to ruminate over her decision, or the possible repercussions; she was going to act. Accompanied by the Ranger, along with Slim Culpepper and Andy Floyd, she lit out for Birdie's boarding establishment, where her first official duty awaited.

Pablo Martinez and his wife, having been discovered near the town of Brady, were seated at the round kitchen table. One of Dodson's men was standing guard over them. Conchita hadn't been found with her parents, which Mariah viewed as strange.

Birdie flitted around, clucking her tongue and filling cups. Slim and Andy settled into chairs by the pantry. The cooking room held the faint scent of boiled cabbage and the strong aroma of coffee. Four lanterns lighted the large scullery, and not a shadow crossed the cowed expression of Evita nor the brooding eyes of Pablo Martinez.

What do they have to fear or to resent? Mariah wondered. Forced return, for one, she supposed.

"Birdie," she asked, "would you excuse us?"

"Reimschissel, take the men outside for some coffee," the mustachioed Big Dan put in, and the guard followed the proprietress out of the kitchen. By prior agreement with Mariah, the Ranger captain kept mum and allowed the sheriff to question Pablo.

She tried to be cordial but was met with curtness from Pablo, and nothing from his wife. In the past Evita had been friendly to her, but Mariah realized she shouldn't expect too much. They were a very pious family, and Pablo *had* caught her in a compromising situation with Whit.

Standing across from the white-haired man, Mariah asked, "Pablo, where is Conchita?"

"I do not know," he replied raggedly.

A devoted father's only child had disappeared, and Mariah's heart went out to him. "I'm so sorry, Pablo," she said earnestly. "Is there anything any of us can do to help? I'm sure the Rangers will be happy to look for her."

Pablo lifted his nose. "I know where Conchita is located, but I will not tell you, Señorita McGuire."

"Shall I take over?" Big Dan offered.

"No, thank you." She figured Pablo had remembered the time he had caught her in Whit's arms, but her past actions had no bearing on this situation. "Pablo, we know you were inconvenienced by being brought back to Trick'em, but we beg your indulgence. Something terrible has happened." She hesitated. Pablo and his wife had been devoted to Joseph, and Mariah knew they would be crushed by the news of his demise. "Mr. Jaye is dead. Murdered. I'm afraid his death was gruesome."

"I know nothing about it."

Mariah found his answer highly odd. His eyes, not meeting her gaze, showed no shock, and no utterance of remorse passed his lips at the news that his former employer had met a vicious end. She knew for a fact that Pablo had not been told the particulars of *whose* murder he was being questioned.

Evita, a caring woman of high sensitivity, showed no surprise, either.

"His body was found on the morning of April 7, 1883," Mariah stated. "Pablo, when exactly did you leave his employ? It will help us if you can be specific as to the date and time."

Nervously Pablo wiped his forehead. "I don't recall."

Mariah read his mannerisms and knew he was hiding something. "On Saturday, the sixth of April, I had planned to marry Mr. Jaye. Does that refresh your memory?"

"No."

"But I know you were at the farm on that date. The next morning you and your family were gone." She paused. "And Mr. Jaye was dead."

Pablo's left hand started waving. "Leave us alone! We don't want to be involved!"

She created a ruse certain to get information. "You're under arrest for the murder of Joseph Jaye."

"No!" Evita cried burying her face in her hands.

Blanching, Pablo surged upward, the chair toppling behind him. "I did not kill him! Señor Reagor did it!"

An invisible ax chopped into Mariah's chest to drive pain into every cell in her body. As if from far away, she heard Slim's gasp. *I love you enough to kill for you.* Whit's wretched words sliced through her heart. But it was only an expression! Her Whit wasn't physically brutal and wouldn't take another's life.

"Miz Mariah, are you okay?" Slim asked.

"Yes." She eyed Whit's accuser. "Perhaps you'd care to explain," she suggested.

"The two señors were arguing. The rancher

threatened to kill him. My wife and I heard him, didn't we, Evita? They got into a terrible fight. Isn't that so, Evita?"

His wife nodded, keeping her eyes averted.

"Is that how it happened, Evita?"

The small woman chewed her lip before replying. "My husband speaks the truth."

Mariah didn't believe either of them, though she had learned from her father and brothers that in most statements to the authorities, there were grains of truth.

Whatever the case, she took no joy in grilling the man who had been such a help at the farm. But Whit's freedom was at stake, and she had to get to the bottom of the truth.

"You actually saw Mr. Reagor in the act of killing Joseph Jaye?" she asked Pablo.

"I heard them arguing. And I saw Señor Jaye's dead body."

"But you don't know for certain who was responsible."

"There was no one else at the farm except for the rancher."

"Plus you and your family, and you left Mr. Jaye for the ants," she pointed out. Directing her next question to his wife, she asked, "Why did you run, Evita?"

Pablo answered for her. "We didn't run. We left."

"Why didn't you go for the sheriff?" Mariah

queried.

"I told you. We didn't want to get involved."

"No, you told me you didn't want to be involved in tonight's questioning, not in the murder."

"A mere slip of tongue."

"Interesting. Do you make mistakes often?"

"I . . . I . . . I . . ."

She had him pinned down. "Tell me, Pablo, is there any grudge you have against Mr. Reagor?"

His nostrils flared, and he reared his head in righteousness. Pablo's upper lip quivered. "Señor Reagor is an evil man! A rapist. How can you defend him when it was *you* he defiled?"

She should have been embarrassed by this smite on her reputation, but her relief at his bias overshadowed her loss. "Can you prove your *assumption* to be true?"

"Can you deny it?" Pablo returned.

"Mr. Reagor is not a rapist."

Slim coughed behind his hand. Andy Floyd, whose face had turned beet red, made a hasty exit.

Big Dan poured himself a fresh cup of coffee and asked, "May I have a word with you, Sheriff?"

Disregarding the Ranger, she went on, "Pablo, could it be that you might be blind to some of the facts?"

"I am blind to nothing. Señor Jaye called you names, and the rancher Reagor said he would kill him."

"I think you know something that you aren't telling us," she said.

"Let it drop, Sheriff McGuire," Big Dan boomed. He took Mariah's arm and steered her toward the door to the dining room. "Culpepper, keep an eye on these folks until Reimschissel gets back."

The boards under his feet vibrated as the Ranger directed her through the dining room and into the privacy of the parlor.

She yanked her arm from the giant's grip. "That was uncalled for."

"You were harassing Martinez."

"Harassing? I was trying to get at the truth."

"Your haranguing shows only that you defend your lover."

"My relationship with Mr. Reagor has nothing to do with my questioning. I was trying to do my job. I *will* get at the truth."

"You're new, so you're overzealous. As for the Martinezes, a finer couple you'll never meet. And I'm sending them over to Brownwood till the trial, for protection from your brow-beating."

Seething, Mariah jacked up her chin. "You can't do that."

"Yes, ma'am, I can. I'm pulling rank on you."

"If Pablo didn't actually witness the murder, wouldn't you think he's jumping to a conclusion? Answer me that. Another thing, Captain Dodson. If this were indeed a crime of passion, why would Mr. Reagor resort to the cowardly and clumsy use of barbed wire? Why wouldn't he employ fisticuffs or a gun?"

"Perchance he wished it to appear the murder was committed by someone opposed to fencing the range."

"Well, Captain, you don't know Whit Reagor."

"But *I* do. I'll be honest with you, Sheriff. I doubt Whit is guilty, but until we have evidence to the contrary, he needs to be arrested."

"He's no menace to society. We'll leave him be while I investigate Mr. Jaye's murder."

Slim Culpepper presented himself. "That Martinez feller's story . . . Well, I don't like the idea of goin' against Reagor, Miz Mariah, but I have to live with my conscience," Slim said quietly. "I saw Reagor cozin' up to you in Lois Atherton's kitchen. The night of her daughter's weddin'."

"Are you willing to testify to that?" asked

Big Dan.

"Yes, sir."

"Whit Reagor did not kill Joseph Jaye," she exclaimed. "He is not a debaucher of women. Nor is he a murderer."

The Ranger patted the air. "Calm down, Sheriff."

Surely there was a way she could help Whit. If only Conchita were here, she might be able to shed new light on the case. Where was she? Once, Evita had mentioned family in San Antonio. It was highly probable the Martinezes had been on their way to that city when their horse had died. Could Conchita be there? Doubtful, since Brady lay over a hundred miles from San Antonio.

Where would a pious family, in dire straits, leave a daughter? Mariah asked herself. A church!

She stood. "Big Dan, will you send a couple of your men back to Brady?"

"For what reason?"

"To find Conchita Martinez. We'll need her to corroborate her parents' story." Silently, Mariah prayed the girl would *refute* the story.

"Sounds reasonable," the Ranger replied.

"Have them check the Catholic churches between here and there. All of them. And when she's brought back, make certain she doesn't make a detour by Brownwood to speak with her parents."

Big Dan lumbered across the parlor to loom over Mariah. "Fine, we'll do our job, now you do yours. As sheriff of this county, it's your responsibility to arrest Whit Reagor for the murder of the Jaye fellow."

"I . . . I can't do that."

"Then turn in your badge, and I'll do it."

Dismayed at what she must do, Mariah swallowed hard. "I will do my job."

She consoled herself. At least Whit was away from Trick'em. Maybe she'd break the case before he returned.

Over the next two days, though, she found it impossible to devote much time to her investigation. Taft put up a fuss over being evicted from his cozy quarters at the jail, and it took half a day to convince him that another county would need his "services."

On top of this delay, a farmer was found butchering a rancher's cattle and had been incarcerated. Then a nester's dugout was burned. Luckily, the guilty parties in the blaze had left clues. Mariah, along with Dodson and his men, had her hands full rounding up the five troublemakers. One of the culprits made the confessions that Charlie Tullos was the force behind fence-cutting, though he'd had nothing to do with burning out the farmer. She couldn't arrest Tullos, not without a law against wire-snipping.

At the crack of dawn on the third day after she had become sheriff, Slim Culpepper appeared at the sheriff's office, where Mariah and Gus had taken residence. He tapped on the door leading from the jail to the living quarters.

Hat in hand, he entered the room. "I know you're prob'ly riled at me, Miz Mariah."

"When you went against Mr. Reagor, you went against me. A kiss in the kitchen is not grounds for implicating him in murder."

"I hated to do that, but I had to tell what I saw." He turned his hat around in his hand. "I didn't come here to talk about what I done."

"Why are you here?"

"You need a deputy, and I'm wanting the job."

"To say the least, Slim, I'm perplexed by you."

"I know that, but will you listen a minute? The day the Lamkins got killed, I said to myself then and there I wanted to be as courageous as you. I admire you." He flushed. "I ain't very good with words, Miz Mariah."

"Actually, you're doing fine." His words had deeply touched her, in fact.

He shifted his weight from one foot to the other. "I don't know what happened to that

Jaye feller, but I'm sure you'll get to the bottom of it. You got your hands plumb full, though, with the reprobates that's doin' all this trouble-makin', so let me lend a hand. Please."

"What about your job at Crosswind?"

"Well, I told the foreman about Andy. That boy's no lenty. He's a right smart cowhand. Him and his brothers can use a few extra dollars, so he'll take my place till Reagor gets back."

"All right. The job is yours."

Slim set to work, and Mariah spent the remainder of the day trying to clear Whit's name.

In low spirits, tired, and hungry, Whit returned by dark of night to Crosswind. In the muted light of the study, Edward Strickland was waiting for him.

"How's the herd?" Gail's husband asked.

"Lost half of them. But, Ed, it's four A.M., and I doubt you're losing sleep over my cattle. What's going on?"

"I come bearing good news." He beamed. "The Stricklands are expecting an heir."

"You mean Gail . . ." Whit shook his head. "But she's just a baby herself!"

"She hasn't been a baby for a long time."

Whit shuttered his eyes. Damn! He'd be a grandfather before becoming father to Mariah's children. If he got the opportunity to sire her children. Could he, in good conscience, ask for her hand in marriage without being honest about Gail?

Gail . . . She'd be a mother soon. His baby was having a baby. Concern and pride filled Whit as he strode over to slap Ed's back. "Congratulations."

"Thank you. But, Whit, I'm not here just to spread the good news. There's something you need to know. Mariah McGuire got herself elected temporary sheriff." Ed leaned a hip against Whit's desk. "She called in Captain Dodson and his men. Between her and the Rangers and her new deputy, they've filled the jail."

Whit groaned in exasperation and disappointment. Mariah had broken her word. Why, dammit, why!

When they had shared so much at his place in town, then here at Crosswind, Whit had had his first taste of peace and harmony in more years than he cared to remember. Foolish thoughts had wound through his besotted head, dreams about a lifetime of happiness with a woman he could love and trust.

But she'd nailed her true colors to the mast. She hadn't kept her word.

Another emotion surfaced. Fear. "She could get herself killed! I've got to put a stop to her nonsense." He quaffed a stiff shot of whiskey, then stomped toward the door. "Where is she? Is she staying in town?"

"If I were you, Whit, I'd stay put." Ed put a restraining hand on his arm. "I think you'd better sit down. I've got bad news."

As Whit listened to Ed's explanations, he turned from worried to disbelieving, then to defensive. "I'm innocent," he stated. "She ought to know I'm innocent."

"Be that as it may, she's posted a notice for your arrest."

Pacing up and down the study, Whit raked a hand through his hair. "If Sheriff McGuire wants to arrest me, she'll have to come here to do it." He halted. If he were in jail, at least he could keep an eye on her. "I've changed my mind. I'm going to surrender."

"You're crazy!"

"Shut your mouth, T-Bone!" Charlie Tullos slammed his fist on the breakfast table where his two hired guns were swilling down predawn coffee. "My wife said we don't move against the McGuire woman right yet, and that's that."

T-Bone Hicks thrust out his stubbled, underslung jaw. "You ain't the one with a dead partner. That redheaded piece killed Zeke when we was after them Lamkins. And Spider and I ain't gonna sit on our butts much longer."

"That's right," Spider put in, running a blunt finger under his eye patch. "We didn't come up from San Antone to sip coffee."

Tullos poured himself another cup, then tossed the latest Austin newspaper into the trash. Whit Reagor had turned against his own kind. Tullos's skin crawled at being doublecrossed by a member of the association. That turncoat was going to pay for stirring up the Austin lawmakers. And Charlie Tullos knew a way to extract payment. Everybody in Trick'em knew Reagor was sweet on that drunken Strickland woman.

"Well, boys," Tullos said, "If you want to work off some frustrations, I got a job for you. Set fire to Ed Strickland's house tonight and make sure his wife's inside. Matter of fact, I may just go with you to make sure you earn your pay."

The gunmen's three mean eyes glowed.

"Now get the hell outta here," Tullos ordered. "I'm wanting to eat my breakfast."

Chapter Twenty-three

The clang of breakfast dishes rose from the single jail cell occupied by six belching, smacking, and slurping prisoners. Bent over her desk, Mariah signed the paperwork giving Big Dan Dodson and his five Rangers the authority to move the lawbreakers to District Court.

"You're terribly quiet this morning," Big Dan said. "Anything wrong?"

Mariah had disliked the Ranger that night at Birdie's house, but she now realized he was a good and dedicated lawman. And she admired him for being able to separate emotions from his job, something she hadn't been able to do. Nonetheless, Mariah wasn't of a mind to chitchat. Today was the day she had dreaded. Whit had returned to Crosswind. Today she would arrest the man she loved.

Her heart aching for him, she dated the last order and held the stack aloft. "You'll be back when?" she asked Big Dan.

"This afternoon," he replied as his subordinates attached ankle bracelets to the prisoners' legs. Putting his big frame between Mariah and the other men, he asked her, "Are you certain you don't want help with Reagor?"

"Absolutely certain," she replied, trying unsuccessfully to keep her voice strong.

The sheriff's office grew eerily quiet after the Rangers and their detainees had departed. To break the silence, she set to cleaning the cell. When she finished, she rubbed her tired eyes with the heels of her hands, then sank into her desk chair. How was she going to clear Whit's name?

Until lately, she had dismissed a possible link between Joseph's mysterious mistress and his murder, but yesterday Mariah had decided to consider even the slightest of clues, such as a woman scorned or a jealous husband. She had talked with scores of people, asking them if they had ever seen Joseph with a female. None had. Well, that hairpin hadn't materialized out of thin air.

She kept returning to the question: Why had Pablo accused Whit of murder? There had to be a reason, and catching her with Whit wasn't good enough.

One thing she knew for certain. Whit *had* spent a good part of her almost-wedding-day trying to see Mariah. She was beset with recriminations. If she had welcomed Whit, he'd have an alibi. And later, if she hadn't sent for the Martinezes, Whit wouldn't be implicated in murder.

Of course there was no way to prove the time of Joseph's death, but he had been in a state of rigor mortis when George and Birdie had found him, which meant he had been dead for several hours.

Why didn't I take a closer look at the body? she castigated herself. But the coroner had examined Joseph's corpse . . .

"Top o' the morning to ya, darlin'."

The chair crashed backward as she jumped up to face Whit. Her throat was frozen, rendering her unable to speak, but she drank in the adored sight of him. She yearned to run to his arms and cover him with kisses, but the icy glare in his ink-blue eyes stopped her.

He knows. She was dying a thousand deaths.

Dressed in buff-colored trousers and shirt, a black bandanna at his throat, Whit shouldered the door closed. His stance was deceptively relaxed. "So, how's business? Meaning our business deal. Or have you changed your mind about leasing the Mukewater to a murderer?"

"You aren't a murderer, and of course I haven't changed my mind, Whit. I sent word to your foreman, and—"

"You don't want to talk about piddling stuff like that. The lady sheriff has bigger things on her mind."

"That's not true. You know you're important to me."

"Yeah, especially now." His muscles tensed as he took a step toward her. "I believe there's a warrant for my arrest for the murder of the venerable Joseph Jaye. I'm surrendering."

"I'm so sorry, my darling. I—"

"My, my, Sheriff McGuire, you disappoint me. I've brought you a vicious murderer—myself—and do you try to arrest me and keep me locked away from polite society? No, you stand there stuttering." He took two more steps in her direction. "Are you, or are you not, going to do your duty to the citizens of this county by locking me up?"

She knew his anger went beyond the warrant, and needed to make him understand why she'd broken her word. Shaking, she said, "We need to talk about why I took this job, and what I'm trying to do for you. Please sit down."

"I don't want to sit down. But, yes, do tell me what you're doing *for* me."

"I'm trying to clear your name."

"If you want to do something for me, quit your job."

She averted her eyes from the daggers of his glare. "I can't. Not yet. I made a promise to the people of Coleman County, and I won't go back on it."

"Why not? You're pretty damned good at that sort of thing."

Tension arced between them, for both knew this issue was at the root of their problems.

"Whit, I couldn't wait for your return. The Lamkins—even the children!—were killed, then I got a clue to the Martinezes whereabouts. I had to take a chance, and hope'd you would understand."

"Well, I don't. But do tell me why you instigated a warrant for my arrest."

"It was forced on me. Captain Dodson—"

"Isn't that just great. My woman and my old fishing pal didn't even give me the benefit of a doubt."

Aching and hurting for Whit, Mariah squeezed her eyes shut. "I believe in your innocence." In halting tones, she told him about Pablo Martinez and about Slim Culpepper.

Refusing comment, Whit rubbed the back of his neck. "Do your job, Mariah. Unlock that cell door."

She couldn't bring herself to do it, and Whit fished in her pocket and took the big iron key in his hand. With one turn, he unlocked the cell. The toe of his boot widened the door's opening, and he shouldered his way into the confines.

Reaching through the bars, he thrust the key into her hand. "Lock it, Sheriff." At her hesitation, he frowned. "If you aren't up to your duties," he said, "you'd better turn in your badge, 'cause you're not fit for it."

Captain Dodson had accused her of cowardice, but his accusation had none of the sting of Whit's denunciation. Her trembling fingers secured the lock. "I can do my job."

"Give the girl a star. Oops, she's already got one."

She ignored the barb. "Don't you have anything to say about the situation?"

His eyes cruised up and down her form. "You look damn good in breeches."

Her pent-up emotions exploded. "Dash it. How can you stand there behind bars and say something about my appearance? Don't you have anything to say in your own defense?"

Whit turned his back. "Enough's been said for one morning."

She heaved a sigh of exasperation. But maybe Whit was right. Enough had been said for the moment. And if she was going to clear his name, she'd better get to it.

Ten minutes later, she entered the office of

Dr. John Metcalfe. "How closely did you examine Joseph Jaye's body?"

"With a fine-tooth comb. He died of asphyxiation."

"Were there any marks on his body?"

The dark-eyed, dark-haired physician rubbed his slender fingers across his cheek. "He suffered a slight contusion to the left eye. And there was a puncture wound, very narrow and deep, on his neck. It missed the jugular, though. Probably inflicted by a stiletto."

"Why didn't you mention this?"

"I told Sheriff Taft."

"Doctor, why didn't you tell me?"

"You didn't ask."

She gave herself a mental kick for her ineptitude. "In your opinion, which came first: the barbed wire, or the stiletto?" she asked, figuring the last for the case.

"The blade."

Joseph had been stabbed and, in his weakened condition, someone had strangled him. Who? If Texas men were inclined to carry knives, they preferred the Bowie variety, not slim daggers. But she'd heard that some women of ill-repute favored such weapons.

Mariah's eyes widened. Quite possibly such a woman could also favor gold hairpins.

The midday sun cut a swatch through the high window of Whit's cell, landing on his prone form. He was trying to sleep, but rest eluded him, and it wasn't because the infernal parrot was squawking. Fear for his own welfare wasn't the problem, for he figured the truth would bear out. The dangers of Mariah's job scared the hell out of him, which didn't mean he wasn't furious with her. He had trusted her. *Had*. She had let him down.

"Reagor?"

Whit kept his eyes closed. "What do you want, Culpepper?"

"I guess you heard about my . . . about everything."

"Yep."

"I had to tell what I knew, but I didn't want you to think I'm too sissified to face you."

"Deed done." Whit opened one eye, and the deputy's badge winked at him. "Why did you embrace John Law? You sweet on Mariah?"

"No, sir. But I got a lot of respect for Miz Mariah, and she needed my help."

"It's going to take more than one skinny cowpoke to take care of all she's getting into."

"I'll do my best," Slim said in parting.

Whit frowned at those last words. It was doubtful Slim's best was good enough. She did need help, lots of it. Whit knew Mariah wouldn't give up her job, and his hands were bound.

He heard someone enter the jail, but ignored the noises. Hating his helplessness, he covered his eyes with a forearm. He had to do something . . . but what?

"Never thought I'd see the day Whit Reagor was put in a position to be charged with a crime," Big Dan Dodson bellowed.

"Neither did I." Whit eased off the cot and strode over to the bars. "I understand you've been busy."

"Smartly so."

"Dan, you planning to stay in Trick'em a while?"

The lawman set a cloth bag on the floor. "Yes."

"Glad to hear it. Dan, you've done me some good turns, and I've done a few for you. I need another one. Will you help me?"

"Doing what?" the Ranger asked suspiciously.

"Taking care of Mariah. She's my woman, and I'm scared spitless she'll get in over her head with this fool job of hers."

"You're not worried about yourself?"

"I'm worried about Mariah. If something should happen to her, I . . . Dan, don't let her get into trouble."

"I'll do my best." Big Dan lumbered across

the office, fetched two glasses from the windowsill, and blew the dust out of them before making his way back to the cell. Tucking the glasses under an arm, he pulled up a chair and sat down. "May I interest you in a sarsparilla?"

At Whit's agreement, Big Dan picked up the cloth bag and tipped up a gallon jug to pour two frothing glasses of the sweet, soft drink. Whit took a sip of his, but the Texas Ranger downed his refreshment in one swallow.

Wiping the foam from his handlebar mustache, Big Dan eyed Whit. "Did you know I was the one who insisted on your arrest? The sheriff believes in your innocence."

Thank God! Comforted in knowing Mariah hadn't wanted to grab a noose, Whit turned to mocking humor. "Well, isn't this a fine how-d'ya-do from my old friend?"

Big Dan studied the floor. "Did you kill Jaye?"

"No."

"Do you have any ideas on who might be responsible?"

"Ideas, yes. But no facts. Charlie Tullos threatened him. But Tullos would've sent for hired guns, I figure, and I haven't seen any of them around. Of course, I've been away from here for several days."

"Hired guns? Such as?"

"In the past he's used T-Bone Hicks and his two partners. If they are around, they're in some hidey-hole."

"And you saw nothing of the Hicks gang when you were riding with Tullos against the farmers?"

"Clean your ears, Dan. I already answered that."

Big Dan refilled his glass. "The sheriff tells me Jaye had another woman. Do you know anything about her?"

"Just that she left her hairpin in his bed not too long before he was supposed to marry Mariah. Whoever she is, she might be the guilty party."

"What woman would have the strength to strangle a healthy man, especially with wire rope?"

"A woman bigger than Joe, and that wouldn't've taken much. And, Dan, she could've had an accomplice."

"I'll do some ruminating on that." Big Dan got to his feet and scratched his head. "You want me to have Chad Nussbaumer come by and talk with you?"

"A lawyer seems in order."

The Ranger left, and Whit stretched out on his cot, thinking. Who would have been involved with Joe Jaye? Most of the women around these parts wouldn't have given him the time of day. But there was a hefty gal . . . Why hadn't he thought of her?

Temperence Tullos.

"Mrs. Tullos, what a surprise." Mariah wasn't pleased. She was here at the farm to search the log cabin for clues to Joseph's mistress, and this interruption was nothing but a delay.

Temperence Tullos, bejeweled and powdered and plumed, swept into the modest cabin. "Hello, Miss McGuire. I hope you don't mind my intruding . . . I meant to come by several days ago—I've been ill for quite some time, you see. Influenza. But I do want to offer my congratulations on your election as sheriff."

"Congratulations? Mrs. Tullos, your husband has let it be known that he opposes—"

"You're being unfair," Temperence protested. "And I hope you'll be fair enough not to assume my husband does my thinking."

Perhaps she had been too quick to jump to a conclusion, yet there was something odd about this visit, and Mariah wasn't going to put her trust in this woman whose husband was responsible for causing so much unrest in the area of Trick'em.

"Thank you for your good wishes," Mariah said benignly.

"You're welcome." Temperence stepped over to the fireplace. "You've certainly turned this place around. These figurines look nice on the mantel. Are they English? I wouldn't think to peek at the hallmark. That's so ill-mannered, you understand."

Mariah's time was too precious for chitchat. "Is there something I can do for you, Mrs. Tullos?"

"Yes, there is." The dark-haired woman swept over to the rocking chair. "May I? I fear my strength isn't up to snuff." She seated herself in the rocker. The joints groaned under her weight. "I want to make you a very generous business proposition. Will you sell me the mineral rights to this farm?"

Mariah was taken aback by the strange offer. Didn't mineral rights include water? Well, even if she hadn't leased the pond to Whit, she wouldn't give over precious water for Charlie Tullos's benefit. "I don't believe that would be in my best interest."

"Then let me sweeten the proposition. I'll take this farm off your hands. Permanently."

"Why?" Mariah asked suspiciously.

"Your land abuts the Painted Rock, and you have a ready water supply. Our cows are in need of it, and I'm willing to give you two thousand dollars in gold."

All that money would secure Mariah's

schoolhouse, would ease her monetary woes. It was nothing to sneeze at. But she wouldn't take Tullos money. No decent person enjoyed the spoils of dirty money and, furthermore, the too generous offer had all the earmarks of being peculiar.

"This property isn't for sale," Mariah said.

"Three thousand dollars."

"I repeat, this property isn't for sale."

"Why not? You have no crops or livestock. Everyone knows you're not a woman of means. Surely you don't plan to survive on your sheriff's pay."

"How I make my living is a personal matter, Mrs. Tullos. You'd be wise to mind your own affairs."

Temperence's nostrils expanded. "You're mighty high-handed."

"And you're not going to get the pleasure of an argument from me. So nice of you to call, Mrs. Tullos. It's been a rare treat. Let me escort you to the door."

Rising from the rocking chair, Temperence pointed a beringed finger. "You'll regret this!"

Mariah ushered her out the door and returned to her investigation, but snatches of the conversation kept coming back to her . . .

"You've certainly turned this place around."

What an odd thing for Temperence Tullos to have said. To what had she made a comparison? How did she know what the cabin was like in the past? To the best of Mariah's recollections—and why wouldn't she remember Joseph speaking of such a visitor?—Mrs. Tullos had never before visited the cabin. But obviously she *had* been here.

Mariah grabbed a chair arm. Was she . . . was Temperence Tullos the gold hairpin's owner?

Chapter Twenty-four

Livid with rage, Temperence Tullos cracked the whip over the horse's rump as her buggy bounced toward the Painted Rock Ranch. The nerve of that McGuire woman, not selling Lord Joe's farm!

"And just where does this leave you, Tempie?" she threw to the prairie air.

With a husband she despised. In a land she hated. Without Leroy Smith and no chance of luring him back to Trick'em with the oil scheme. Although she was furious, she did have a vent for her frustrations. Violence. Tonight. Charles was fit to be tied over that Benedict Arnold, Whit Reagor, and he had plans for revenge. Plans that Temperence wholeheartedly approved of. Dammit, she might even join the raiding party.

And when they were finished with their

deed, she'd demand one more killing, that of Mariah McGuire!

This would assuage Temperence's blood lust, and she could get on to making new plans for Leroy. She'd never give up. That wasn't her way.

Ten minutes after Chadwick Nussbaumer had spoken with Whit about a defense, and five minutes after a big brown envelope was delivered for Mariah, she returned to the jail.

Cooling his heels in the hoosegaw since daybreak had given Whit thinking time. He wanted to know why she'd broken her word, but that could wait.

With his fingers wrapped around the bars, he said, "I'd like a word with you, Sheriff."

Hesitantly, Mariah approached the cell. Still wearing the breeches, she held a covered bowl in her hand. "I know it's a little late, but I've brought your lunch."

He couldn't have cared less about pinto beans and cornbread. "Bring it right on in . . . Sheriff."

"I don't like the look in your eye. You're not planning something sneaky, are you?"

"Like what?"

"Like breaking jail."

"Don't give me any ideas," he gritted out,

hating not only the fact that he was her captive in the legal sense, but also that he was a prisoner of love. But, by damn, he'd get the upper hand in this situation. "Open the cell, Sheriff."

She did. When Mariah set the bowl on the small table in his cell, Whit moved one hand to a hiding place. Like a flash and before she could escape, he hemmed her in his arms and snapped a manacle around her left wrist.

She started, giving him an advantage in the tussle.

"What are you doing!"

"Shackling you," he replied, and wrestled to affix the other manacle to the cell bar. He turned the key, then tossed it out of her reach.

"Unlock me. Now! This is highly improper."

"Too bad. Because this is the only way I can be assured of your safety. And I want a few questions answered."

She yanked at her bonds, but neither the bar nor the handcuff gave way. "I know you're angry, but you've no right to do this to me. And you'll wait until your dying day for answers unless you free me"—she glared at him—*"right now."*

Whit realized his wrongdoing, realized brute strength would never work with Mariah. He also realized he could never chain her to him.

He stepped back and retrieved the key.

Mariah relocked the door of his cell and tucked the wrist manacles out of his reach, well away from the branch he'd snapped from the tree outside his window and had used to fish for the handcuffs.

Wordlessly, she went to the privacy of her quarters to collect her wits. Nothing was settled between them. She knew he was still angry over her broken promise, but what could she do to heal his hurts and disappointments?

Dressed in clean breeches and shirt, she re-entered the jail.

"What happened to your new clothes?" Whit asked.

She swallowed. "They were cumbersome."

"Yeah. When a gal takes off after outlaws, she needs to be comfortable."

She crossed to the cell. "Whit, I'm sorry for disappointing you."

"Are you now?"

"Yes. For both our sakes, could we call a truce?"

For a moment, he stared at her, then rubbed his chin. "Yeah. A truce'll be fine."

"Thank you."

"Mariah . . . there's something I've been wanting to tell you. I think Temperence Tullos was fooling around with Joe."

"I think so, too." Mariah proceeded to tell

him about the Tullos woman's visit and about the talk with the coroner. "Have you ever heard a rumor of Mrs. Tullos carrying a stiletto?"

"No, never."

Mariah's obstinate look set her features. "I'm going to bring her in for questioning, anyway."

"Let Dan do it."

She moistened her lips, and her eyes met his. "Would that make you happy?"

"Somewhat. The only way I could be truly happy . . . Mariah, I'm worried about you." Whit's hand snaked through the bars, catching her wrist and bringing her palm to his rapidly beating heart. "You could get hurt. Or killed."

"I can take care of myself."

"Not if you're outnumbered."

"Maybe if you knew why this is so important to me, Whit, you'd understand."

"Maybe you ought to tell me."

She explained the events that had happened after he'd left to see after the herd. "I didn't want to go back on my promise to you, but I had to take action. Put yourself in my place, Whit. What would you have done in the same situation?"

"Sent for the Martinezes, and so on," he admitted grudgingly. "But then, I didn't give you my word I wouldn't do anything to stir up trouble."

"I'm sorry, so sorry, at least for letting you down. But my conscience wouldn't allow me to do nothing."

Whit traced the pad of his thumb across the bow of her lips. "I know you're sorry. And I know about your ways. I'm just sorry your ways don't coincide with mine."

A shudder wracked her shoulders, and Whit hated to see her so troubled. "Aw, baby, don't cry."

"Could you just hold me a minute? Just hold me, and let me pretend . . . pretend we're at your cottage again?"

Through the bars, they embraced, though their kiss was not without tension. Whit couldn't quit worrying about her well-being. As he reared his head away, he said, "Take care of yourself, baby. Don't put yourself in peril."

"Peril comes with my job."

Whit decided she was in her element, tempting the cutting edge of danger. How much longer would it be before she faced it? Despite his disappointment and anger at Mariah, he knew that losing her would be a thousand times worse than the pain he had suffered over Jenny. But he wouldn't ask Mariah to make any more empty promises. What was the use?

"I almost forgot to tell you," he said. "There's a package for you on your desk."

She retrieved the brown envelope, extracting a sheaf of paper and a newspaper. She smiled. Her palm went to her mouth and the papers shook. Whit figured the news was good.

"Don't keep me in suspense. What's up?"

She turned to him, and there were tears of joy in her eyes. "We have a message from Lydia Farrell. Texas law has been changed. Fence-cutting is now illegal!"

"Good show, Sheriff McGuire," he said gently, proud for her in spite of himself.

Twirling around, she shook Gus's cage. As he squawked disapproval, she beamed. "Oh, Gussie, isn't this wonderful? Now we can put Charlie Tullos where he belongs. Behind bars!"

"Great. Just the cellmate I've always wanted."

"Oh, silly goose," she admonished, blowing Whit a kiss. "You'll be free in no time."

A man wearing ducking and a striped knit shirt stepped into the office. In her glee, Mariah didn't hear him, but Whit noted the young man's appearance. Tall and burly, he had a thick head of long, fire-red hair tied at his nape, and brown eyes. His regard on Mariah, the stranger's expression showed familiarity and affection.

Jealousy ate at Whit like a hungry lobo.

"Sheriff," he said, "you've got a visitor."

The stranger widened his arms. "Lovey."

Papers fell from her grasp, and she whirled to face him. Her lovely oval face was a wreath of surprise . . . and delight. "Dirk! What are you doing here?"

"I had to find out how you're getting on."

Like jubilant children, Mariah and Big Red clasped each other. He lifted her from her feet, and she covered his face with kisses. What's going on? Whit asked himself.

Feeling completely abandoned, he stuck *his* face between the bars. "Don't mean to intrude, Sheriff, but how 'bout getting the prisoner a drink of water?"

"Put me down, Dirk. There's someone very, very special I want you to meet." Holding his hand, she led him to the cell. "Whit, may I present my sailor brother, Dirk McGuire."

A couple of minutes after introducing her favorite sibling to the man she loved, Mariah got a bigger surprise.

"I'm not alone. I've got traveling companions." Dirk walked to the office window, leaned out, and cupped a hand to the side of his mouth. "Ahoy, mates! Come topside!"

Her surprise and good cheer were palled by apprehension when a flaxen-haired man and a fifty-year-old version of Dirk stepped inside. The Viscount Atterley followed Logan

McGuire. What had brought Joseph's half brother and the father who despised her to Trick'em?

Whatever the case, this was an awkward situation. She realized the sad news that must be conveyed to Reginald; she didn't know how to approach her father.

"Reggie, welcome. Father, how are you?" Next, she addressed her brother, giving him a sisterly look he was certain to comprehend. "I'm afraid I can't offer accommodations, but there's a respectable boardinghouse here in town. Perhaps you and Father should secure the rooms. I'll meet you there."

Logan—who was often called "Mack"—grimaced, but followed his son. Lord Reginald launched into greetings and questions. The last man, her own father, she avoided.

Mariah turned another look on Whit, one akin to the expression she had used with Dirk. Thankfully, he nodded in understanding and retreated to the shadows of his cell.

"Reggie," she said softly, "perhaps we should go for a walk."

"Heavenly days, Mariah. The dust would fairly choke me . . . and the *heat!*" In a gesture of impatience, he touched the nick on his ear. "I must preserve myself for the journey to Joseph's farm. Let's do sit down, though. You must tell me how you came to be sheriff of this wretched town. And about how my brother is faring, naturally."

She sat in her desk chair, Reginald in the one next to it. "Reggie, there's no easy way to say this. Joseph was murdered last month."

His handsome, aristocratic face grew solemn. "The family feared . . ." He took a breath. "I trust the poor soul's end was quick."

She reached for a bottle of rye Taft had forgotten, poured a stiff shot, and handed it to Reginald. In halting words, she told him the truth about Joseph, and about their estrangement.

"May he rest in peace." The nobleman downed the strong spirits in one swallow. A moment later, he patted his lips with a handkerchief. "My condolences to you, too, Mariah, even though you decided not to become my brother's bride. Dear girl, how frightful your situation! You mustn't fret, though. I brought your salvation. As you know, Joseph appointed me to sell the London townhouse, and the proceeds are in my care. I'm sure he'd want you to have the monies. If you're careful with budgeting, your finances are assured."

"I appreciate your understanding and kindness."

"It's the least I can do." He took her hand. "And I trust you'll return with us. You mustn't stay in this horrid place."

She glanced at Whit, who was dealing a deck of cards onto the cot, but had stopped to lift his head and meet her gaze. She realized he was waiting with bated breath for her reply.

"Many things hold me here, Reggie," she answered finally, watching Whit frown and take up his cards again. He's angry because I didn't say he held me here, she thought. "For one special reason, I won't be leaving Trick'em.

Whit avoided her eyes as Reginald exclaimed, "Surely you're joking!"

She hastened to end the conversation. Later she would speak with Whit and try to appease his anger, but right now she had work to do: Charlie Tullos's arrest. And the questioning of his wife. Now, she must face Logan McGuire.

The sun was setting on the dusty streets of Trick'em when, Reggie at her heels, she ascended the steps leading to Birdie's front porch. Dirk lounged against the rail. Logan quit the rocking chair and started toward his daughter.

She detected something in her father's eyes, a softness never before directed at her. Could it be possible he loved her?

"Hello, Daughter," he said in French, his voice rough with emotion. In English, he admitted, "I've missed ye."

Did she dare to hope . . . ?

She barely noticed as Dirk took Reggie's shoulder, steering him from the porch and saying, "Reg, ol' mate, let's go have a pint."

She sat down on the steps, as did her father. For a long moment, neither spoke. Birds flew to the trees, nesting for night. A buckboard rolled down the dirt street. Roasting meat wafted through the air, superceding the smells of horses and cattle that permeated the town of Trick'em.

Mack McGuire took a pipe from his pocket, and she turned slightly to observe him. Sucking on his smoke, he stared straight ahead. The aroma of cherry-wood tobacco brought vivid memories to Mariah, few of them good.

Running a hand through his faded red hair, Mack met his daughter's eyes. "I read your note."

Dropping her chin, she bit her lower lip. It had been days since she'd thought about leaving that letter for him to read after her departure from Guernsey. Surely he wasn't here to chastise her for expressing her feelings! "And what did you think?"

" 'Tis difficult for an old man to admit the error of his ways." He paused, waiting for Mariah to retort, but she didn't. "I realized what a bloody fool I've been all these years," he went on in the Norman French and English mélange of a typical Guernseyman. *"Le Bon Dieu* gave me a sweet daughter, but I was too blind to appreciate ye. I blamed ye for yer *mère*'s indifference, and that is unforgivable, but I do want ye to know I'm sorry for all I've done."

The hostility of twenty-three years formed into one small tear, and it rolled down her cheek. She brushed it away, and her animosity was gone forever.

"I can forgive you. I do forgive you. I . . . *Je t'aime,* Papa. I love you."

"Je t'aime, ma fille." Joyfully he wrapped his beefy arms around his youngest child. For the first time since Anne McGuire had died, he cried.

Mariah's tears of felicity mingled with his, and she gave a prayer of thanksgiving.

"I wish *maman* could know about this," she whispered. "She'd be so happy."

He pulled back to grasp Mariah's shoulders. "I want ye to know, I loved your *mère*. For all our arguments, I did adore her. If I could have her back, I would mend my ways."

Mariah recalled days gone by. Her father was of the rascal sort, and despite the strict Calvinism of his faith, he had always been ready for dancing and merrymaking. And for his wife.

"Papa, you're not old. Why don't you marry again?"

His cheeks turned red. "Well, m'girl," he said, changing the subject, "tell me about yerself."

She gave him a summary, emphasizing her love for Whit and the trouble besieging Trick'em. "I must get back to my duties, Papa."

"Aye. And I want ye to know I'm proud of what ye're doing for this town."

"I never thought I'd hear you say that."

"Ye've heard it." Mack frowned. "But those Tullos people sound dangerous, Daughter. Ye'll need all the men ye can get. Now, 'tisn't my custom as a *connétable* to carry a gun, but ye know I'm a good marksman. Almost as good as ye! Let me go with ye and the Rangers."

"D'accord!" She gave him a smacking kiss on the cheek. "Papa, you're splendid!"

"I'll fetch the lads from the public house, and we'll collect our horses from the livery and meet you back at the sheriff's office."

Back at the jail, Whit reclined on his cot and thought about Mariah and her visitors. He knew she had been happy to see her brother, but what about her father? The old man had given her hell in the past, Whit recalled. Since he had traveled across the Atlantic to see her, though, the elder McGuire must want a reconciliation. *For her sake, I hope so,* he thought.

As for Joe Jaye's brother, Whit had mixed feelings. The fellow, unlike his brother, seemed to be the decent type, but on the snooty side, which was to be expected. Near as Whit could recall from bull sessions with Joe, Reginald was a viscount, too, through some connection with a grandfather.

Personalities aside, Whit was troubled. The nobleman wanted to bundle Mariah across the Atlantic. Although she had declined, Whit wondered if civilization wasn't the best place for her. This thought clawed at his heart. He didn't want to lose her, but if she stayed around Trick'em, she was liable to get into more trouble than she could handle.

Caught between a rock and a hard place, he raked his fingers through his hair. Would he lose her, anyway?

Mariah returned to the jail five minutes later and came to Whit's cell. From the beaming expression on her face, Whit concluded—correctly—that she and her father had patched up their differences.

"All my life I've yearned for his acceptance." She reached through the bars for Whit's hand. "I feel as if a burden has been lifted from my shoulders."

"I'm happy for you," he replied. "Wish I could do something about this weight on my shoulders."

"Trust me, Whit. I'll find Joseph's killer."

"That wasn't what I meant. Mariah . . . go back to Guernsey."

Thc stubborn look he had come to know settled in her features, but this one held hurt, too.

"I'm not going anywhere," she stated flatly.

Whit's speech of persuasion died in his throat, for the McGuire men, Reginald Atterly between them, entered the office. Dirk McGuire ambled over to give his sister a kiss. Logan McGuire, one eye closed, puffed on a pipe and kept his distance while assessing Whit. Joseph's brother poured himself a shot of rye.

"While we were refreshing ourselves, we heard some disturbing news. You're in this jail for the murder of my brother."

All eyes turned to Lord Atterly.

"Reggie . . ." Mariah rushed over to him. "He's innocent."

Suddenly, Slim Culpepper burst through the door. His cheeks were red, and he was breathless. "Miz Mariah," he said, huffing and puffing, "we've got trouble! Dodson and his men are headed for . . ."

Slim paused to suck in a draft of air, and Whit froze. Don't let her get involved! he prayed.

"Dirk and I will help you, Daughter."

Mariah rushed to the gun cabinet, retrieving rifles and ammunition. "Slim, talk! Where are the Rangers?"

The deputy formed words, but no sound left his throat. He reached for a pitcher of water and guzzled a drink, but still couldn't speak. Reaching for a pencil, he scratched something on a scrap of paper, handing it to Mariah.

Her back was to Whit, so he couldn't see her expression. "Mariah, what does it say?" he asked.

She didn't answer.

After taking another swallow of water, Slim croaked, "We'd better hurry."

Dirk took a rifle. "Will you help, Reggie?"

He waved a palm, then dropped into a chair. "I won't follow my brother to be buried in this godforsaken place. I'll stay here." He imparted a look of disdain at Whit. "I'll keep an eye on my brother's killer."

"Mariah," Whit said. "Come here. Please."

"Wait for me outside," she told her posse. A rifle on one arm, she hurried to Whit.

"Don't go," Whit demanded in desperation, ignoring Atterly's arch look. "Let the men handle it."

For a moment he thought she would consent, but she squared her shoulders and said, "I have to do my part."

He grabbed those shoulders, trying to shake sense into her. "No, dammit, no!"

"Whit, listen to me. Tullos and his gang are raiding . . . I'm sorry, but it's Gail."

Gail! Fear gripped Whit with a strangling hold as his hands dropped to the sides. He was torn, ripped to shreds, by conflicting loyalties. Gail needed to be saved. Mariah was an excellent shot, and zeal spurred her toward Tullos. Which one did he sacrifice, the woman he loved or the daughter he had never been able to claim?

"Whit? I know it's an awful shock. To me, too. Gail is my dearest friend, and I promised to look out for her. I won't desert her."

Forcing rational thought, he came to another solution. "Unlock the cell, Mariah. I'm taking your place."

"Heaven forbid," Reginald put in, but was ignored.

Mariah said to Whit, "I won't. You won't. We can't break the law."

He had never been more furious than at this moment. Futilely trying to spread the bars, he raged, "To hell with the law! Open this goddamn door. Now!"

Mariah opened her mouth to speak but thought better of it and whirled away. "We'll discuss this after she's safe. Right now, I'm wasting precious time."

"If you walk out of here, it's over between you and me. Over. And I've never been more serious in my life."

"Fine." Again, Mariah spun around. "You ought to know by now ultimatums don't work with me."

Chapter Twenty-five

The night was moonless, crosswinds were blowing. Mariah, her kinsmen, and the deputy had to advance slowly lest their mounts lose footing in the rocky, cactus-dotted terrain leading to the Crazy Hoof Ranch.

She refused to grant self-pity free rein, for there would be time for heartbreak after Gail was saved and Tullos and his outlaws were brought to heel.

At long last, the journey ended. It seemed as though eons had passed since leaving Whit behind, but in reality the trek had taken no more than an hour.

She ordered her companions to stay back while she found Big Dan Dodson. "You know my whistle, Papa . . . Dirk. Wait for it."

"Aye, Daughter."

Creeping forward, she discovered the Ranger

captain crouched behind a wagon which stood about thirty feet from the two-story rock house. Except for intermittent explosions of gunfire, not a light brightened the palpable blackness.

"It's bad, Miss Mariah," Big Dan said.

"What happened?"

"I was told by the cook . . . she found me and my men, you see. Well, anyway, Mrs. Tullos wormed her way into the house on some sort of pretext. She pulled a gun on Mrs. Strickland, and the poor woman's leg prevented her from fleeing. As near as I can figure, Tullos and two others were lying in the weeds when Ed got home. Strickland is wounded." Big Dan pointed toward the house. "Six of his hands are dead between here and there."

Now wasn't the time for emotions, yet Mariah was gripped by the hand of dread. "Is . . . Gail still in the house?"

"Yes. They're holding her hostage."

Mariah's hand tightened on the Winchester as she agonized over her friend. Whit's daughter. But she couldn't allow agony to last, not now. "What about Tullos?"

"He's in there with the rest of them."

Think. Mariah. Think. "How many men do you have, Captain Dodson?"

"Three, including myself. Reimschissel and

his partner took bullets."

"I've brought three more men, plus myself. We have them outnumbered." She paused. "We'll have to get into the house."

"Too dangerous. Mrs. Strickland's life is at stake."

"I'm aware of the risk." She whistled. Quick as a flash, her posse gathered around. "Here's the plan. Inch closer to the house, all of you, including your men, Captain. Keep me covered while I go in."

"Daughter, you can't do that alone."

"I didn't plan to, Papa. You're light on your feet. I was hoping you'd go with me."

He clasped her shoulder. "I'm with ye," he said.

Pleased, she smiled. "Keep me covered."

To a round of gunfire, she and Mack made an arc, rushing to the side of the house. A sharp sound from the east wing, like a woman's laugh, reached her ears as she came to the rear corner. Temperence Tullos, no doubt.

Mariah and Mack moved carefully, more by feel than by sight, around to the back. They stepped onto the porch, and the boards creaked. She stiffened. Again guns fired, and she took advantage of those sounds to open the door. The acrid smell of gunpowder bit her nose as she entered the kitchen.

"The bastards have reinforcements!"

Mariah recognized Charlie Tullos's voice from the study.

"I told you you wouldn't get away with this," Gail said.

"Shut up!" Temperence Tullos ordered.

A slap resounded, and Gail cried out in pain.

Mariah gritted her teeth. The rifle that had hung at arm's length was at once high against her chest, the thumb of her right hand tightening on the hammer. Slowly, she and her partner made it to the uncarpeted dining room. Keeping tight against the wall so the boards wouldn't creak, they started into the study.

But her elbow encountered an object, and it crashed to the floor.

"They've gotten in," Temperence Tullos cried.

A match flared.

Whit didn't allow the moonless night to slow him. He and Bay Fire knew every rock, every plant, every twist and turn of the trail leading to his daughter. He rode hell for leather.

A half mile from his destination, he caught sight of an orange glow. Fire!

Fear sent arrows through Whit's veins as he rode closer. Gail's house was ablaze! Fed by the wind, tongues of flames licked the windows, the fiery incandescence eclipsing the dark night. Flames popped. The incendiary stench burned his nostrils. Terrified for what lay ahead, Whit charged on.

Please don't let Gail be in there! He made a vow to himself. If she got through this, he'd make her understand why he hadn't been able to claim her, let her know how much he loved her and always had!

His concerns weren't solely for his daughter. Mercilessly, he dug his spurs into Bay Fire's flanks. "Oh, God, don't let Mariah be in that house!"

He was through with Mariah, but never would he cease being concerned about her. He appeased himself with the rationalization that she had no earthly cause to gain entry. But knowing Mariah . . .

Arriving at the house, he yanked in the sorrel's reins, and Bay Fire came to a dirt-grinding halt. Whit jumped from the saddle, drawing the pistol that had been purloined from the sheriff's gun cabinet, and ran forward.

"You won't need a gun," Big Dan Dodson called out in the agony of physical pain. "Tullos . . . They're all dead."

Nonplussed, Whit eyed the Ranger, who was clutching his middle. Around him was a battlefield of felled men. Then Big Dan's body slackened. He was dead.

Saddened for his old friend, Whit grimaced. At the same moment, Gail hobbled over to Whit and tugged on his arm. "Thank God," he uttered raggedly.

"Not yet," she cried, "Mariah and her father went back for Temperence. They're still in there."

A strangled cry vibrated Whit's chest, his worst fear confirmed. Devastated, but not to the extent he couldn't act, he charged into the house. Smoke clogged his lungs, and he whipped a bandanna up over his nose. He had to hope he wasn't too late and could save her.

"Pull harder, Papa! She's still alive."

About ten feet ahead of him, Mariah and her father were tugging on the inert form of Temperence Tullos. A sheet of fire rolled toward them. Right then Whit would have gladly murdered Mariah McGuire for her misplaced priorities.

Instead, he ignored the oven of heat and the asphyxiating smoke to stomp ahead.

"Help us get her out, Whit!" Mariah shouted.

He lunged on the heavy Tullos woman and hauled her over his shoulder. "Make a run for it, dammit!"

For once, Mariah obeyed, and he gained a modicum of satisfaction. Swaying under his burden and sidestepping the flames, he made it outside and placed Temperence on the ground. Then, straightening up, he faced Mariah. For a second captured in time they stared at each other. Her soot-covered features were cast in orange relief, and there was pain in her brown eyes. Well, he thought, she made her decision back at the jail, and I made mine.

"How did you get out of jail?" she asked quietly.

"Ole Reg helped me break through the bars on the windows."

"Sacrebleu."

"Whatever. You know, you're not the only stubborn person in this world, Sheriff. You ought to know that when I make up my mind, nothing stops me. And I've made up my mind . . . about several things."

A boom rent the air as the roof caved in, that sound echoing the end of Whit and Mariah's relationship. He read sorrow in her features, and knew the same was reflected in his.

Mariah bent over the bleeding woman. He started to turn away, but her, "At least hear what Mrs. Tullos has to say," stopped him.

"You're not going to make it, lady," Mariah said. "Save your soul. Did you kill Joseph

Jaye?"

"No."

"The devil will take you for lying," Mariah promised.

"Didn't . . . kill . . . him."

"Do you know who did?"

Temperence Tullos shook her head weakly, and her eyes closed for the last time, the words "Oh, Leroy . . . my Le—" on her dying lips.

His spirit lost, Whit turned on his heels, and went back to Gail.

Loss. It weighed heavy in Mariah's heart throughout the next week. Whit was lost to her forever.

Oh, he had gallantly returned to the wrecked jail, of which he and Reginald had agreed to pay for repairing, but Whit was stalwart in his determination not to reconcile with her.

Mariah now sat, alone, in Jackie Jo's Café. She neglected her dinner. How could she eat?

She agonized over the decisions that had torn Whit away from her. On top of her broken vow, she had denied him his freedom to take her place and save his daughter. At the time, Mariah had decided not to compound an alleged crime with a real one. She had chosen her badge over her man's feelings.

Mariah wasn't sure what was worse, her speculations over what might have been or the agony of knowing she could never undo the past. Her emotions were in wrack and ruin.

Her sole thread of hope for emotional salvation was to free Whit of the charges against him and she was back to the beginning. She had been certain Temperence Tullos would clear Whit, but the woman was dead.

Mariah shuddered, recalling that chaotic night. After she and Mack had been discovered in Gail's house, she'd shouldered her rifle to kill T-Bone Hicks. Mack had felled Hicks's partner. Dropping her match, Temperence Tullos had known it was over, even before flames had leaped from the table skirting. Screams of hatred directed at her husband, she'd turned her pistol on him and then on herself.

If the Tullos woman had been truthful, then who had killed Joseph?

Mariah pushed the plate of food to the center of the table. So many people had lost their lives, and others had suffered and sacrificed.

Only Friederich Reimschissel remained of the Rangers who'd garrisoned the Strickland home, and he carried a wound in the leg. Slim Culpepper had received a flesh wound in the arm. Six of his ranch hands gone, Edward

Strickland was abed at Crosswind, a piece torn from his left hip.

But in all this darkness there was also light. The remainder of the cattlemen's association had disbanded and for this blessing, Mariah was thankful.

The now-tepid tea brought to her lips, she spied Dirk entering the eating establishment. Smiling, he wended his way through the tables.

"Ahoy, lovey. I bring news. That *fille* Conchita Martinez was found in a convent, and she's waiting for you at Judge McCracken's house."

Mariah closed her eyes, both in relief and uncertainty. By the time they reached T. Jeff McCracken's parlor, though, she had collected herself and her strategies.

Deceptively gathered as if for no more than a friendly chat, two Texas Rangers and the judge were seated in the wing chairs. Conchita, wringing her hands, huddled against the Victorian sofa.

"I'd like a moment alone with Conchita," Mariah said, and the men exited.

Already Mariah regretted the things she must say. She had always liked her former student and didn't want to cause her suffering, but this was the crucial matter of Whit's very life.

After several attempts at putting the girl at ease, Mariah asked, "What do you think of Mr. Reagor?"

"I do not know him but to see him."

I believe her, Mariah thought. Why, then, was so much of her father's anger directed against Whit? Or was it? Maybe Pablo had used Whit as an excuse.

Mariah walked to a table, picking up a figurine to study it. "I spoke with your father, and he told me he'd do anything to protect his family."

The girl brought a hand to her mouth and chewed a fingernail.

"He's sorry he bode Mr. Jaye so much hatred," Mariah lied.

Much more pliable than her father, Conchita took the bait. "*Mi padre* had his reasons."

Ah, ha! "Do you think it's right to take another person's life?"

"No, señorita."

Mariah swallowed, then glanced at the pressed-tin ceiling. She hated to ask her next questions, they were so cruel. "Do you resent your father for killing Mr. Jaye? Will you forgive him when he hangs?"

"No! Don't say that!" Conchita jumped to her feet, bumping her shins against the coffee table. "Papa didn't do it. I killed him!"

"Oh, my God," Mariah whispered, moving to comfort the stricken girl. Yet she couldn't help the selfish thought that Whit would be free!

For several minutes Mariah rocked Conchita until the tears subsided to hiccups. She handed the fourteen-year-old a handkerchief and a glass of water, prompting her to drink. The hiccups turned to shuddering wails.

"It's okay, sweeting. I don't want to hurt you. I want to help you," Mariah said truthfully, dabbing the handkerchief under the girl's tear-swollen eyes. "You're a sweet, fine young lady, Conchita, and I know you must've had your reasons for what you did."

"So awful" was her mournful, wrenching reply.

Conchita drew herself into a protective ball, and Mariah's arm went around her shoulders.

"Tell me what happened, sweeting."

"Señor Jaye, he . . . he did awful things to me. It h-hurt so b-bad."

Mariah clenched her teeth. May that rapist's soul burn in hell!

Again, tears washed down Conchita's cheeks. "I was sc-scared he'd do it again, and I put a knife in my p-pocket. I did not think I would have to use it, because we were going to leave the farm. But Señor Jaye c-cornered me that night you were to marry him. After

Señora Tullos had left. He was very angry, and . . . he had some b-barbed wire in his hand. He p-pushed me to the ground. I . . . I stabbed him, but he still . . . *Mi padre* heard my screams, and h-he hit *el patrón* and grabbed the wire."

Conchita lifted her eyes to the sheriff. "I was the one who stabbed Señor Jaye. I am responsible, not *mi padre.* I will not let him hang for me."

"I promise you no one is going to hang. You acted in self-defense, and your father was protecting his child. No one will blame either of you."

The local citizenry, as Mariah had predicted, understood the motives behind Joseph Jaye's death, and they rallied around the pitiable girl. The evening after Conchita's confession, her parents were brought back to Trick'em, and Pablo was formally exonerated of the crime.

Many people stepped forth and donated money to the Martinezes. The fund was augmented by the very generous donation of Reginald, the Viscount Atterley, who was ashamed of his half brother's wickedness.

Rued by her past actions toward Pablo, Mariah apologized to him for her verbal barrage, and he was graceful in the acceptance.

The Mexican family set out for San Antonio to make a new start.

Reginald took guest quarters at the home of his newfound friend, Whit Reagor. Gail Strickland was there, too, nursing her injured husband back to health.

A week later, and after much grousing about his landlocked state, Dirk McGuire left for Galveston, where he planned to secure a job as a boatswain's mate.

Not once since that night of the Strickland's fire had Whit spoken to Mariah, not even when she'd unlocked his cell for the last time. He had simply turned his back and left the jail. Left Mariah alone with her self-recriminations.

She knew her loss was of her own making. And forever would she pay.

Mariah faced the future without Whit. There was nothing left for her in Trick'em. Mariah had no desire to farm Joseph Jaye's land; the fewer reminders she had of that debaucher, the better. She'd refused the proceeds of his London townhouse, and as for schoolteaching, she could do that anywhere. With her heart so empty, though, she did not even have the desire to follow her calling.

And now, on a Saturday night, she sat in the porch swing at Birdie Turner's boarding establishment. She turned to Mack and said dully, "Reggie is leaving tomorrow for England."

Mack stopped cleaning his newly purchased six-shooter. "I'll miss him."

"I was thinking we should go with him."

"What about your job? That Slim *homme* is still recovering from his wound and isn't able to take over for you. And didn't he say he wanted to go back to ranching?"

"He's able to carry out the duties; he had but a minor wound, for heaven's sake. And he did say he'd wear the badge until someone else is hired."

"I wouldn't mind having the job meself. It appeals to this aged lawman's spirit of adventure."

"You want to stay here?" she asked incredulously.

"*Oui*. As Sheriff of Coleman County."

"I'm sorry to hear that," she said. "I was hoping you'd go home with me. To Guernsey."

"Why Guernsey? I thought you hated it there."

"No, I don't," she answered. "It's home."

"Will ye leave without telling yer man 'God be with ye'?"

"He doesn't want my goodbye."

"Do ye have so little faith in him?"

Faith. That ragged word. "I have all the

faith in the world in him. He has none in me. Deservedly so."

"Ye're wallowing in self-pity, girl." Mack arched a russet brow. "And ye're too easily defeated."

She lifted her chin. "I am not."

Whit Reagor should have been happy. He had his freedom, but freedom to do what? Mope around the ranch, shouting at his employees, friends, and family? Although he and Gail had never been closer since their heart-to-heart talk on the night of the fire, Whit was lost without Mariah.

Sitting behind the desk in his book-lined study, he half listened to Gail as she harangued him about his foolishness.

Her injured leg healed, she perched easily on the edge of his desk, her arms crossed. "Well, are you or are you not going to swallowed that damned pride of yours, and apologize to Mariah?"

"I'm not."

"You should see yourself when you tighten your jaw like that. Pigheadedness is written all over your face. So what if she broke her word? You're no paragon of virtue, Whit Reagor. You've broken a few promises along the way."

The truth of her words chafed at his collar. "Don't you have anything better to do than harass me?"

Not to be deterred from her purpose, Gail replied, "Not at the moment. We owe Mariah a debt of gratitude for saving my life. That Hicks character was fixing to kill me, you know."

"I know. You've told me so a thousand times. But I don't want to see her again."

"For crying out loud, Whit Reagor, someone ought to take a peach-tree switch to your ankles."

He forced humor. "Yes, and someone ought to paddle you for lack of respect."

She stuck her tongue out.

"Gail . . . are you sure it doesn't bother you, my taking so long to tell you the truth?" They had had this conversation before, but Whit needed one last reassurance.

Her demeanor turned solemn. "It doesn't trouble me now, but I was . . . Well, after Lilibet told me about you, I was hurt. I was pretty awful about it until lately. Here was this man who gave me attention and affection but never said the words I wanted to hear."

"And you took it out on Ed and on the bottle."

"Right. But that's in the past, where it belongs. My husband opened my eyes to many things that were blinding me." Circling the desk to drop a kiss on the top of Whit's head, she continued. "And speaking of my husband, I'd better check on him."

Whit squeezed her hand. "Thank you."

"For what?"

"For finding the strength I always knew you had. And for being you."

She scoffed at him. "Aw, get outta here with that mush stuff. Use it on someone who'd appreciate it . . . like Mariah."

Gail departed the study.

Alone once more, Whit listened to the grandfather clock strike nine. Over and over, he thought about his foibles. Yes, he'd broken his promise to Lilibet. All these years he'd kept his oath, only to learn she had told Gail the truth. Yes, he'd betrayed Joe by stealing his woman. Whit didn't regret that. Yes, he had done Mariah wrong by demanding she be something she wasn't. She would never be anything but her own woman.

But, down deep, he loved her for what she was. Independent, spirited, practical. Was it too late to swallow his pride? Would she forgive him, and let him make amends for the past?

A knock sounded at his door and Mariah glided in. His heart pounding against his chest, he stood. She had never looked so beautiful . . . nor her eyes so unreadable.

Wearing a peach-hued frock of crossbar lawn, she had styled her rich burnt-auburn hair atop her head in a mass of curls. Roses, soft and sweet, wafted to him as she approached.

"Hello, Mariah."

"Whit," she said with a nod. "I'm here to say goodbye. I'm leaving for Guernsey tomorrow."

No!

"That one time I was here," she said, "we never made it to your study." Her hand swept in the direction of the lined shelves. "Books?"
"Where do you think I learned about Thomas More and Prester John? I like to read."

"Do you still tutor Carlos?"

"Yeah. It's rewarding."

"I'm on to those same rewards. In St. Peter Port, of course."

"Is that all you want out of life, teaching?"

"No. I'm hoping for a husband and children."

"Just any husband and children?"

She moistened her lips. "Of course not."

"How many children?"

"Several." Mariah glanced away, then back at Whit. "Well, I really must be going."

"Before you do . . ." He took a step toward her. "I want to thank you for saving Gail's life."

"I did it as a labor of love. She's my friend. And I know about . . . Whit, why haven't you been honest with her?"

He blanched. "You know?"

"I do. She told me."

"And you're not bothered by it?" he asked.

"Why should I be? I see it as all the more reason to love her."

Mariah's compassion was all the more reason to love *her.* He decided to take the biggest gamble of his life. Now was the moment he'd draw the line . . . and hope she'd step over to his side by refusing his offer.

His thumb at the sensitive point behind her ear, he said, "I owe you a debt of gratitude. If you'll accept it, I'd like very much to give you the money for your own schoolhouse in Guernsey."

She moved away, turning to the bookshelves. "All right. I accept. On two conditions."

His hopes plunged to the soles of his boots. "Which are?"

"One, that you forgive me for being such a terrible thorn in your side."

"You have been, but there's nothing to forgive." Whit took a step toward her. "Unless you can see your way clear to forgive *me* . . . for a lot of things."

"There's nothing to forgive. You expected

something from me I wasn't able to give," she said. "I've never been biddable."

"I know."

"You're hardheaded, too, cowboy."

He touched a lock of the hair that had always fascinated him. "Never said I wasn't."

"You asked me to choose between saving Gail's life and coddling myself, and I still think I made the right decision."

"Well, Red, you've never been biddable."

"And you've always been a bitter, irritating man who can't forget yesterdays and get on with today."

"Hardheaded and irritating, I can't do anything about. But I can work on changing the bitter part. I don't want to live in the past. I'd like to have one more chance for today."

"Would you like to hear my second condition for the schoolhouse?" she asked as she closed the scant distance between them. He reveled in her petal-scented skin, her nearness, her presence.

Her dark eyes locked with the blue of his, and her fingers twined into the black curls at the back of his head. "I'll accept if you'll build it on Crosswind."

By damn, it wasn't too late! He caressed the curve of her slim waist. "Well, there is a small plot of ground I could spare," he teased.

"Whit Reagor, are you going to force me to my knee to ask for your hand in marriage?"

"Absolutely not. Marry me, Red."

"It's about time you asked."

"Shall we seal it with a kiss?"

She cuddled against him. "I have something better in mind."

"Brazen hussy."

"Insatiable beast, lock the door."

Epilogue

Spring 1884

All of Coleman County was green. Rains had healed the wounds caused by the previous year's drought. Bluebonnets blanketed the hills and dales, the stock ponds brimmed with water. Barbed wire cordoned off farm land but now in deference to the Western Trail and to the local ranchers.

No more did raiders set fires. No more were cattle slaughtered or fences snipped. Peace reigned in Trick'em.

On this bright April day, Mariah Reagor gave her students early dismissal. She hurried to her husband. Whit was supposed to be overseeing a well-digging project adjacent to the little red schoolhouse, but he wielded a shovel with the rest of the men.

He stopped his toil when Mariah approached, and climbed out of the hole to try to wrap his arms around her waist, then settled his big hand on her stomach.

"How's he doin'?"

"She's doing fine."

"Glad to hear *she* is doing fine," Whit replied.

"And I'm glad you finally agree with me." Her hands on her hips, Mariah looked down into in the hole being dug. "Darling, with all the rain we've had, you're daft to dig this well."

"I promised you a well, and you're getting it. You know I don't *usually* break my word. Besides, why not dig for water? It won't go to waste."

He started to bend over and nuzzle his wife's neck, but the sheriff's throat-clearing stopped him.

"Are ye trying to embarrass me?" Mack asked, balancing young Edward Strickland on his hip.

The baby reached for his badge and began to gum it.

"Don't let him put that nasty thing in his mouth," Mariah said. "You really should take him back to his mother."

"But I love the wee lad, and I need something to hold till yer babe is born."

"The ladies aren't enough?" Mariah asked, a brow lifted.

Since taking permanent residence in Trick'em and freeing up Slim Culpepper's return to Crosswind, Mack had made a hit with the widow women and not only for his light step on the dance floor, Mariah knew. Birdie Turner was especially fond of . . . dancing.

"Why don't you remarry and have more children?" Mariah asked.

The lawman patted young Edward's behind. "Birdie's a wee bit old for bairns."

"Are you trying to tell us something, Mack?" Whit asked lightly. "Isn't *she* too old for *you?*"

"Aye, and nay. I'm going to marry the Widow Turner. She's a few years my senior, 'tis true, but she's a good cook and likes to dance."

"Congratulations," Mariah said honestly. "She's a dear person."

"Aye, and she's biddable."

"This one"—Whit put his arm around his wife's shoulder—"will never be that."

No, his wife would never be biddable. She was as mulish as ever. Forever she'd be chasing after windmills. Her latest cause was to bring the railroad to Coleman County. Whit accepted the fact that a rail line would mean no more cattle drives, but he wouldn't miss them.

Matter of fact, he had chosen to stay at Crosswind this spring with Mariah.

During all their time together, Whit had never experienced a dull moment. He had managed to survive some few firecracker-hot arguments, too.

"Mack," he said, "you'll be bored to tears with a malleable woman."

The sheriff tickled the baby's chin, drawing a coo and a smile. "Birdie isn't all that docile."

"Mr. Reagor!" a worker shouted from the hole. "We've hit something."

Whit leaned over the water well. Black oil oozed at the bottom. He grimaced. "Damn."

"Such a shame," Mariah said. "What now?"

"Cover up that useless goo."